WARPRIZE

"*Warprize* is possibly the best romantic fantasy I have ever read. I loved the sequel…I can't wait for number three. Continue please to enthrall me with your storytelling."
—Anne McCaffrey, *New York Times* bestselling author

"Vaughan's brawny barbarian romance re-creates the delicious feeling of adventure and the thrill of exploring mysterious cultures created by Robert E. Howard in his Conan books and makes for a satisfying escapist read with its enjoyable romance between a plucky, near-naked heroine and a truly heroic hero."
—*Booklist*

"The most entertaining book I've read all year."
—*All About Romance*

"*Warprize* is simply mesmerizing. The story is told flawlessly…Keir is a breathtaking hero; you will never look at a warlord the same way again."
—*ParaNormal Romance*

"Ms. Vaughan has written a wonderful fantasy…The story is well written and fast paced…Run to the bookstore and pick up this debut novel…You won't be disappointed by the touching relationship that grows between the Warlord and his warprize."
—*A Romance Review*

WARLORD

"A superb climax to an excellent saga…Romance and fantasy readers will appreciate this terrific trio as Elizabeth Vaughan provides a fabulous finish to a superior story."
—*Midwest Book Review*

"An outstanding conclusion to an inventive and riveting trilogy with a passionate, powerful love story at its core."
—*The Romance Reader*

continued…

"A top-notch series, well written and enjoyable."
—*Curled Up With a Good Book*

WARSWORN
"A moving continuation of the wonderful *Warprize*. Bravo."
—*Jo Beverly*

"Readers will be delighted…Unusual and thoroughly enjoyable."
—*Booklist*

DESTINY'S STAR
"Fans will relish this strong romantic quest fantasy."
—*Genre Go Round Reviews*

"Riveting…The plot moves at a nice clip, and the ending is a masterstroke…*Destiny's Star* is a terrific story."
—*The Romance Reader*

"Bethral and Ezren are marvelous characters to spend time with…[Vaughan] has a gift for bringing cultures and dialogue to life, and I very much look forward to more."
—*All About Romance*

"Vaughan's writing is rich and provocative. Her descriptions [are] gorgeous, watching Bethral and Ezren fall in love…was perfect…I didn't want the story to end."
—*Smexy Books*

WHITE STAR
"An engrossing story which will keep readers enthralled. The characters are interesting and appealing…Ms. Vaughan has crafted an interesting world where myths and reality blur. Filled with magic, gods and goddesses, and heroic deeds, the reader will never want to put this book down."
—*Fresh Fiction*

"There's tension, turmoil, and adventure on every page. The characters—main and side alike—are interesting and enjoyable. The sex is fun, and the romance is undeniably sweet."
—*Errant Dreams Reviews*

"Vaughan world-builds with a depth and clarity that allows you to immerse yourself in the world of the hero and heroine...If you are looking for a book with colorful world-building, solid characters, and sound storytelling, this one might be just what you're looking for."
—*All About Romance*

"A riveting and thoroughly enjoyable story."
—*Romance Reviews Today*

"Fans will appreciate the clever twist that Elizabeth Vaughan writes in *White Star*, as the latest return to her Warlands saga is a welcome entry in one of the best romantic fantasies of the last few years."
—*Alternative Worlds*

DAGGER-STAR

"*Dagger-Star* is the perfect blend of fantasy and romance...A really enjoyable read."
—*Fresh Fiction*

"An excellent romantic fantasy...Readers will enjoy Elizabeth Vaughan's superb, clever return to the desolate Warlands."
—*Midwest Book Review*

"Elizabeth Vaughan pens a story of love and adventure...You feel yourself being sucked into the adventure and don't want to put the book down."
—*Manic Readers*

"In a return to the world of the Warlands trilgoy, Elizabeth Vaughan successfully creates a new set of characters and a new story...A very satisfying read."
—*Romance Reviews Today*

WARSONG

ELIZABETH VAUGHAN

WARSONG

Copyright © 2018 by Elizabeth Vaughan. All rights reserved.

The characters and events portrayed in this book are fictitious or fictitious recreations of actual historical persons. Any similarity to real persons, living or dead, is coincidental and not intended by the authors unless otherwise specified. This book or any portion thereof may not be reproduced or used in any manner whatsoever without the express written permission of the publisher except for the use of brief quotations in a book review.

Published by Birch Cove Press

ISBN: 978-0-9984501-2-4
Worldwide Rights
Created in the United States of America

Cover Art by Craig White
Cover Design by STK·Kreations

*This book is dedicated to Stephanie Loree
Friend and confidant, sharing the trials and tribulations
of our writing lives.*

PROLOGUE

"Is this your first birthing since joining my camp?"

Haya looked up at Elder Thea Olana with a nod as she dried her hands. "Yes, Elder." The warmth of the birthing tent surrounded them as the others tended the mother, gathering close to acknowledge the life-bearer's pain.

"Then take this," Olana gestured with the newborn in her arms. "You know the naming ritual. See to it, and take him to the nursing tent."

Haya stepped closer, taking the baby in her arms. The child wriggled, squirming in its blanket, blinking in the light. "My thanks," Haya murmured as she stepped from the tent.

The night air was cooler, and the babe's eyes opened wider as he felt its touch. He waved his small fists seemingly against the air itself.

"You'll be a strong warrior," Haya smiled down at the babe. "We'll seek your name, then find you a teat to suck, yes?"

Behind her, the all too familiar chant rose from the tent. "We are the life-givers. Life-bearers of the Plains. This is our burden. This is our pain."

Haya walked off, bearing the child toward the naming circle. The sounds of the chant and of the camp faded behind her. She smiled down into the newborn's eyes, who was staring at her now.

The naming circle was just on the next rise, the sod cut away to expose the earth. She glanced at the four bowls at the four points, making sure they were full and properly positioned. She took her stance in the middle of the circle, and gently pulled away the blanket, exposing the naked baby to the air.

The child cried out, like a baby gurtle seeking its mother.

"Hush, little one," Haya chided the babe. "How else can I hear your name when the elements speak it?"

The tiny face scrunched tight.

Haya laughed, rocked him, and sang the traditional tune.

"Heyla, tiny warrior,
Heyla, cease your cries
Heyla, the moon is rising
Heyla, close your eyes."

The babe's face cleared, his eyes wide and fascinated.

Haya faced the east and raised the child high to the morning sky. "Elements," she called out. "Behold. The Tribe has grown. The Tribe has flourished. A new warrior comes to us, and we would ask his name."

She lowered the child, pulling the blanket back around him to keep him warm. She knelt to face the small bowl on the ground, filled with black, burning coals. "Fire, behold. This is a child of the Plains. I ask that you warm him through his life, until the snows and beyond."

The child yawned, pushed his fist into his mouth, and started sucking it.

"Patience, little one," Haya whispered, and turned on her knee to face the next bowl on the ground, filled with dirt and stone. "Earth, behold. This is a child of the Plains. I ask that you support him through his life, until the snows and beyond."

Another turn, and they faced the bowl filled with water.

"Water, behold. This is a child of the Plains. I ask that you sustain him through his life, until the snows and beyond."

The babe sneezed.

One final turn, to face the empty bowl. "Air, behold. This is a child of the Plains. I ask that you fill him through his life, until the snows and beyond."

Haya stood, then, and lifted her face to the star-filled sky. "Elements, name this child of the Plains."

And then she listened.

The camp was silent and still, waiting for the dawn. There was bustle about the birthing tent, but even that seemed quiet and hushed.

The hairs on the back of her neck rose; it felt as if all of the Plains was waiting… watching…

The winds blew, rushing through the tents, setting the pennants flapping. They swirled around Haya and the babe. Haya heard…

The winds died down, as quickly as they had come, leaving silence and peace.

Haya looked down, smiling at the tiny sleeping babe. "The Elements have spoken," she said. "You are named Joden. Joden of the Hawk."

With swift steps, she left the circle and strode quickly to the nursing tent. Best to see that the babe was warmed and had a teat in its mouth before it started to fuss.

Seo greeted her as she entered the tent which smelled of melted gurt and dried milk. "Another this night? The Tribe indeed flourishes," he gestured to a young life-bearer, her breasts heavy with milk. "Come, settle by the fire and give this one his first suck. Make sure your teat is clean, and watch that he can hold your nipple."

"His name is Joden of the Hawk." Haya gave up the bundle willingly, looking about the tent. "Two others?"

"Aye," Seo grinned. "Two feisty males for that one to keep with." He pointed his chin at a life-bearer nursing a dark-skinned baby who was clutching at her breast. "That one is named Simus, also of the Hawk" He knelt back by the brazier, and pulled a pitcher from the coals. "Kavage?"

An angry cry rang out from the other, a pale-skinned baby

with a shock of fine black hair.

Haya glanced to make sure the life-bearer had settled down with Joden before she sat next to Seo. "That one will be trouble."

"Probably," Seo grinned as he offered her kavage. "That one is of the Cat."

"His name?"

"The elements named him Keir."

CHAPTER ONE

Joden of the Hawk, Warrior of the Plains, knew that to become a Singer he would have to undergo Trials. He'd assumed that he'd be challenged physically and mentally to prove his worth. He'd have to prove his knowledge of the songs and chants of the Plains, prove his ability to create songs. Prove as well his understanding of the way of the Plains, and his ability to act as a neutral judge in conflicts. That was his goal, to be a Singer, to join with those who held the knowledge of the Plains in their hearts.

He just hadn't thought there would be so much dried dung involved.

He must have spoken out loud, for a voice came from behind him. "What? You thought the fires of a Singer's camp burned on their own accord?"

Joden straightened from his task, and looked over his shoulder. Quartis sat on a gurtle pad, repairing some armor. The young man looked at Joden through the curtain of his long brown hair, decorated with beads and feathers. His bright eyes were piercing, and around his right eye was tattooed the black wing of a bird. The tattoo of a Singer.

All around them spread the Plains, wide, green with the early grasses, and empty of all but horses and themselves.

Joden looked down at the basket of dried dung in his hands. "No, I didn't think they burned of their own accord, but—"

"Dung must be gathered if we're to have a fire this noon," Quartis said, as if talking to a child. "Para and Thron hunt our dinner. I am repairing my leathers. You, the youngest and newest candidate for Singer, are gathering dung. All is as it should be, yes?"

No, Joden thought but didn't say the word aloud.

"Unless you think you are somehow special." Quartis's voice was silky now, raising the hairs on the back of Joden's neck. "That you are above doing this task?"

"No," Joden replied firmly.

"Well, then." Quartis gestured toward the basket. "And while you are working, continue to recite the teaching chants," the Singer ordered.

Joden sucked in a deep breath, let it out slow. Patience, he reminded himself as he bent to his task. "Fear. Fear holds you still when…"

The words came easily as he recited from memory, striving to appear calm and focused without.

Within was a different tale. In truth, his stomach was knotted, and his shoulders tight.

Two days ago, he'd been aiding Simus in his quest to become Warlord, delaying his own Trials to help his friend. That is until Essa, Eldest Elder of the Singers of the Plains had come to Simus's tent and confronted Joden.

Joden paused in his chanting, swallowing hard against the memory of his shame. He'd avoided Essa, avoided making the request to enter the Trials. Essa had rightfully called him to account for his actions. Once Joden confirmed that he did indeed wish to become a Singer, Essa had commanded him to go with Quartis, without so much as a farewell to Simus or any other.

His heart caught in his throat. What was happening, back at the Heart? How was Simus faring, against—

From behind, Quartis cleared his throat.

Joden resumed chanting.

He'd obeyed Essa, gathering his gear, and following Quartis

out into the rain. There he'd found saddled horses waiting, with two other Singers, Para and Thron. He'd been told to mount and ride, and so he had. For two full days they'd ridden with only short stops before making this temporary camp, a small fire and one-man tents, hidden in the grass.

And now here he was, midmorning of the third day, isolated from friends and tent-mates, collecting dried dung and chanting teaching songs so basic he could do it in his sleep.

He looked at the dried patties in his hands, not quite so brown as his own callused skin, and sighed as he put them in the basket.

Two days ago, he'd been in the thick of things, roaming the camp, talking in support of Simus's goal of being Warlord, and Keir's goals of uniting the Tribes.

He glanced north. What was happening at the Heart? Had the trials begun? Had Simus become Warlord? And what of his warrior-priestess Token-bearer? Had she won her position? And how was Keir going to react when he learned of Simus and Snowfall?

Joden bent back to his task, gritting his teeth at the frustration of it all.

For that matter, what was happening in Xy? Lara had given birth, and he felt a smile creep over his face as he thought of that. Twins at that, and blessed by the elements for certain. Joden had no fears for her health or safety, not with Keir to watch over her. But there would be Xyians unhappy with the news that might prove a threat and—

He'd the barest of warnings, the merest whisper of a step behind him. Joden spun, throwing the basket at Quartis's face, drawing his own sword, lunging—

Quartis danced back, laughing and sheathing his blade.

Joden stood amid the pile of spilled dung chips, breathing hard, his sword ready. "Why?" he demanded.

"Who is more likely to offend than a Singer telling truths?" Quartis said, brushing bits of dung from his leather armor. "A Singer must be prepared for defense, even in the midst of a song." Quartis's grin was bright against his tanned face. "You stopped singing, looking north as if it holds all the answers."

"It does," Joden growled, sheathing his blade.

Quartis reached for the basket at his feet. "We will have answers when Essa joins us, not before."

"And when will that be?" Joden asked.

"When it is," Quartis shrugged. "Focus on the task at hand. Sing the berry song. Gather dung." He offered the basket to Joden. "Not the fresh ones, mind you."

Joden puffed out a breath, and took the basket. "Yes, yes, something so obvious that there is not even a song about it."

"Maybe you'll write one," Quartis chuckled, looking up at the sky. "I'm off to fill the waterskins. You might as well start a fire with your dung, the others should be returning soon. Hopefully with fresh meat, or it's gurt and dried meat for the nooning."

Joden grunted, spun and returned to where he and the other Singers had set their tents, hidden in the grass. Their saddles sat in a circle, quivers of lances resting against them. Their horses grazed close by.

Joden cut away the turf, clearing a spot for their fire, and started to work.

Quartis returned, dropping full waterskins at his side. "I think I hear—"

Joden stood. The sound of hoofbeats came over the grasses. "Riding hard," he said.

"Too hard," Quartis drew his sword. "What—"

Two horses burst over a nearby rise, Para and Thron in the saddles. Both riders were bent forward, the horses covered in sweat, foaming at the mouth. "Down, down," the words screamed from Thron's throat.

"What—" Quartis started.

From behind the riders rose a nightmare on the wind.

Winged, black, and huge, it blotted the sky, gaining height and soaring after the riders.

"Arrows are useless," Para cried as they pounded past.

The monster glided past Joden and Quartis, focused on its prey. Joden heard it hissing as it slid overhead, a beat of its wings bringing a foul stench to his nostrils.

Joden leaped for his saddle, and the quiver of lances. He grabbed one, and threw another to Quartis. They both started after the monster.

The creature was beating its wings now, rising like a hawk gaining height on a mouse. Joden's heart raced. There was no way they could give chase.

Para threw a glance over her shoulder. Joden saw her lips move, and then she and Thron parted, each horse veering off at an angle.

The monster followed Para.

Thron was circling back toward them, riding hard. Quartis stopped running, holding up his lance.

Thron grabbed it from his hand as he passed and raced after Para.

Joden kept running, angling to meet Para, who was circling back as well. The monster was over her, the long sharp claws of its feet close to her back, reaching out—

The creature lunged, missed her but scraped the horse's hind end with its claws.

Her horse squealed, and kicked high. The creature swooped to the left, rose again with a beat of its wings, making a seemingly impossible tight turn, wings spread wide.

Para leaned in the saddle, urging her horse away to the right, in the opposite direction, racing past Joden. He caught a whiff of sweat and blood as they ran past, but his focus was on the monster, turning to pursue its prey.

Thron raced past him and threw his lance.

The sharp weapon flew, catching the creature on the downstroke of its wing, tearing the leathery skin. The creature let out a loud screech and floundered, falling into the grass and sliding, its good wing beating against the ground.

Joden hunched down, running in close, waiting for a chance.

The beast raised its head to the skies, trying to lurch to its feet. But Joden was close, close enough to take a risk. He ran in, and with a bellow, rammed his lance into the creature's chest.

The monster went mad, thrashing in its pain, its tail now over its head.

Joden hit the ground, curled in a tight ball, and covered his head. He could hear air whistling from the wound. With any luck—

He heard the cries of the others as they taunted the monster in its death throws, causing it to lurch and move, dragging itself over him. The creature's belly pressed down, cutting off air and light. The skin was leathery, smooth as it grated over Joden. The smell was enough to kill him.

The creature moved then, enough that he could roll free, running away as soon as he was on his feet, to the cheers of the others.

The monster took some time to die, but die it did.

In the end, they all stood there, around the body, breathing hard, looking at one another with hope and relief and terror.

"What the hell is that thing?" Quartis panted, bracing himself on his knees.

"I don't know," Para gasped, trying to catch her breath. "We tried arrows, but nothing hurt it, so we took a chance to lure it back to you. We thought the four of us could kill it, but look." She pointed north.

Joden turned, squinting against the sun. In the far distance there was a disturbance in the air, as if hundreds of the beasts were flying, circling—

"Is that the Heart?" he asked, almost afraid of the answer.

"I think it is," Thron said softly.

"We should return—" Joden took a step forward.

"No," Quartis coughed and spat. "No, we have strict orders. Straight south for two days then wait." His voice strengthened. "Here we stay, candidate."

"I thought that thing had me," Para said. "I must see to my horse."

"I've bloodmoss," Joden said, releasing the urge to get on his horse and go. "It might aid it."

"My thanks," Para said, lifting a trembling hand to her forehead, smoothing back wisps of black hair that had escaped from her braid. "I thought for certain I was headed to the snows."

"Look at the size of that thing," Thron marveled. "It has to be, what, three horses? Four?" He walked over to the head, trying to pull it to its side. "See its horns?"

Joden could take the time now to wonder at its size, and the two curled horns that lay atop its head.

"You should take one for yourself." Thorn grinned at Joden. "Yours was the killing blow. Make a good sounding horn, I should think."

"Only if you take the other," Joden said. "You brought it down."

Quartis had started to walk around. "Mind the tail," he called. "Something drips from that stinger."

Thron nodded, probing the jaw with his dagger. "Look at the teeth," he pried open the jaw. "Whatever it is, it eats meat, to be sure." He looked up at Joden. "Let's see what it tastes like, eh?"

* * * * *

It tasted rank, as foul a meat as they'd ever had.

"Almost like its already spoiled," Para said, grimacing. They all stood around the fire, as the meat sizzled in a spit.

"Might be the ichor in the stinger," Joden said, sniffing at his piece.

"Well, it was worth trying," Quartis said.

"But the skin will make a fine, tough leather." Thron was pleased. "Think there is enough time to skin the beast before Essa arrives?"

Quartis was looking north.

"He is there, isn't he?" Joden asked. "With the others."

Quartis glanced at him, then looked back to the north. "Yes, but we wait. We'll set watch on the skies for another, if one comes this way. Skin the beast, see to Para's horse—"

"That bloodmoss worked," Para said, with a nod of thanks to Joden. "I'd heard the Warprize had brought it to the Plains, but I'd not seen it in action."

"I've extra," Joden said. "And I'm willing to share. You have to be careful though," and explained to all of them the cautions that the Warprize had explained to every member of Keir's army.

They moved the camp then and dug fire pits around the corpse, setting watch to fend off scavengers during the night.

In the morning they set about rendering the carcass, taking skin and bone and sinew. It was a messy, time consuming task, but they each took turns, watching the skies and the grasses for riders as the others toiled away.

When they took a break for a quick nooning, Thron handed one of the curved horns to Joden. "You have to make your own, you know," Thron offered. "Part of the trials. These will be something special. Not sure what kind of sound they will make."

"You boil it first, right?" Joden asked.

Thron nodded, running his hands over the deep black horn. "To remove the cartilage. Takes most of a day. Once it softens you carefully pick the insides clean, dry it, and then measure its depth to carve out a blow hole. Once that's done, you sand it and then polish it with oil. I like to use sweetfat for a deer or ehat horn, but this might need—"

"Riders," Para called.

Five riders, coming fast from the north.

"Is that Essa?" Joden asked quietly.

Quartis shaded his eyes, his beads rattling as he nodded.

Essa was riding hunched over, as if injured, his face a mottle of black and blue bruising on the one side. He pulled his horse to a stop, and he and his escort walked their horses forward. Essa glared at the carcass through swollen eyes. "You killed one?" he asked, clearly surprised.

Quartis walked forward. "We did, Eldest Elder, but it took all four of us. Joden had the honor of the killing blow. You know of these things?"

"Wyvern, the Xyians name them," Essa said. "Something out of legend, or so that healer claimed. They attacked the Heart, destroyed the Council tent, and killed many."

Gasps surrounded him, but Joden spoke, "And Simus?"

"Survives." Essa seemed less than pleased. "And is named Warlord, to stifle your further questions." He looked at Quartis. "Have you tested him?"

"Yes," Quartis said. "He is qualified in the teaching chants, and in his fighting abilities."

"And collecting dung," Joden added dryly.

"Good," Essa ignored him. "We must leave. Now."

"But the carcass," Para gestured toward the hulk, really only half done.

"I will give you an hour to gather what you wish, after that we ride," Essa said. "We will aid you. The more we know about the monsters, the better off we are. Beware the sting in its tail. The poison is dangerous."

His escort dismounted, and made offers to help as Para and

Thron shared out kavage and gurt. Essa dismounted as well, and Joden confronted him. "Why do we ride? What is so urgent?"

"There are those that wait for us," Essa said sharply. "More to the point, they wait for you, Joden of the Hawk."

CHAPTER TWO

Amyu ran up the stairs of the highest tower of the Castle of Water's Fall and burst through the trapdoor at the top into sunlight and clean clear air. She strode to the low wall that surrounded the top of the tower, and with a puff of breath, tried to send her frustrations out into the wind.

The City of Water's Fall, the largest in Xy, stretched out below her. Beyond that the fields and forests went on and on in the valley sprawled below. Some of her fellow Plains warriors swore that they could see the Plains themselves from here, but the Warprize denied the truth of that.

The wind seized her brown hair, whipping it around her head. Amyu caught the long strands in her hands, and bound them up in a quick knot.

"What's got you so het up?" came a familiar voice.

Amyu looked over to find the old Xyian guard named Enright sitting in his usual position, on a bench facing the low wall, working on repairing a bit of armor. His crossbow sat beside him, cocked and ready, and an alarm bell sat on his other side.

"Runnin' up those steps in full armor," Enright snorted. "This some test of the Firelanders?"

She'd found him here when she'd first sought out the highest point of the castle. He was a white haired older man, with pale skin and big, bushy eyebrows. He'd been placed on watch duty after the initial wyvern attack during Atira and Heath's bonding ceremony. Watchers had been placed all around the castle and the city walls, keeping an eye on the skies for the return of the monsters.

Enright had welcomed her with a nod, and hadn't said much that first day. "I knew how your people feel about the crippled and maimed," he'd explained later. "Didn't think it was proper to start talking."

He'd been right. She'd been shocked to the core to see his leg of wood, strapped on tight over his trous. On the Plains, such a warrior would have gone to the snows without a thought. But he… at first, it had left her speechless.

And when she'd found the words to say that to him, he'd fixed her with a glare. "What, you think my worth was in my toes?"

She'd learned then that Heath, the new Seneschal of the Castle of Water's Fall, had made use of older, experienced warriors for guard duty against the monsters that had attacked the castle. Even those wounded in battle. "Nothing wrong with their eyes, ears, or wits," Heath had explained to the Warlord and Warprize, refusing to remove the guards even after the monsters disappeared from the skies.

Still, it had taken Amyu, and all the other Plains warriors, awhile to get used to the idea. It still bothered her as she settled on the bench next to the Xyian warrior. Those of the Plains went to the snows when they were hurt past healing. When they were no longer of use to the Tribe.

Or like her, when they failed to reach adulthood.

"The stairs are no effort," she said as she settled on the bench. "It's leather armor, not like the metal you wear." She took a minute to adjust her sword and dagger.

"Well, come on," Enright said. "Tell us your worries, then,"

Amyu opened her mouth then stopped. "Us?" she asked.

Enright gestured behind him.

Amyu turned on the bench to look back.

The tower was built into the mountain, and its top was a

half-circle, with the low wall running all around. Large baskets stood at intervals along the walls, with bees hovering around them. And over all, the mountain towered above, its craggy walls stark and unforgiving.

Beyond the trapdoor, Prest of the Wolf stood, pressed against the stone, in almost the exact middle of the half-circle, his normally brown skin was sickly pale, with sweat beading on his forehead.

"Prest?" Amyu asked.

"Amyu," Prest said, his eyes firmly on the stone beneath his feet.

Amyu exchanged a glance with Enright, who simply shrugged.

"Prest, what's wrong?" Amyu stood, and approached the big warrior. Prest was a big man, one of the Warprize's personal guards. A handsome one at that, with his dark skin, bright smile and short black hair. She'd heard that he'd had long braids until he'd been soaked in ehat musk during a hunt with the Warlord Keir.

"Fear," Prest said, not looking up.

Amyu paused, puzzled, then worked it out. "You're afraid? Of this?" she gestured with a wide sweep of her arm.

"He thinks he can overcome his fear of heights," Enright spoke up.

Prest closed his eyes, and took a deep breath. "Fear holds you still when you need to move, and moves you when you need to be still."

"Fear makes you silent when you need to be loud, and loud when you need silence." Amyu recited the next part of the teaching chant. "Fear closes your throat, makes it hard to breathe. Fear weakens your hand and blinds your eyes."

Prest opened his eyes, glaring out at the vista as he finished the chant. "Fear is a danger. Know your fear. Face your fear."

"It's a fear," Enright called over. "It's not like fighting, something you can train yourself to. Stand there for days, it ain't gonna help."

"Yes, I can," Prest said through gritted teeth. "All it takes is practice."

"Which you have been at for days," Enright snorted, and patted the bench. "Come, lass, leave him to it and tell me what makes you stomp up all those stairs. We could hear you a mile off."

Leaving Prest to it, Amyu straddled the bench, taking care to adjust her own weapons as she sat. "It's just that the Warlord and the Warprize... I mean..." Amyu stuttered to a stop."

"I knew the lass when she was a young girl, defying her father to become a healer." Enright didn't even look up from his work. "She is a true Daughter of the Blood and a damn good Queen, but that don't mean she is perfect. Go ahead."

Amyu crossed her arms over her chest. "They won't listen," she burst out. "The Warlord is fixated on those weapons called ballista and I know, I know," she added for emphasis. "Airions are out there, they have to be. If wyverns exist, why not airions?"

"Airions?" Prest's voice wobbled, but his interest was clear.

"Horse-eagles," Enright said. "You've seen them on the tapestries hanging in the castle."

"Winged horses?" There was a distinct quaver to Prest's voice.

"Winged horses," Amyu confirmed. "With fierce beaks and sharp claws." She pressed her lips together in frustration, and couldn't sit still another moment. She jumped off the bench to pace. "There are pictures in the oldest scrolls the Archbishop has that show airions and wyverns fighting in mid-air. And there are warriors mounted on those Airions."

Prest had a pained expression. "Could you sit back down?"

Amyu gave him an exasperated look, but settled back onto

the bench. "No one will talk to me, including that old lady cheesemaker, who's told stories of them in the past." She looked out over the distance, and sighed. "How can Xyians forget when they write down their words? We of the Plains do not forget."

"How do you know that?" Prest asked.

"Eh?" Amyu looked at him, shocked. "We of the Plains remember."

"But if we didn't, how would we know we forgot?" Prest pointed out.

Enright snorted. "Don't know nothing about that, but I can tell you that things get forgotten. You're speaking of ancient days," he said. "Folks got enough on their hands with the day to day, much less thinking on the past."

"There are airions," Amyu said. "There have to be."

"If there were," Enright looked at her with his bushy eyebrows raised. "Why didn't they appear with the wyverns?"

"I don't know," Amyu said. She looked at the sheer wall of the mountain towering above them. "And there's no way to go up to find them."

"Eh?" Enright snorted. "Well, not up there, lass. The mountain above us and to the city walls is sheer and treacherous to keep any from trying to attack from above. But the mountains beyond the walls to either side are covered with goat tracks and filled with caves."

"They are?" Amyu stood and went to the low wall to look further out.

"Aye, for any fool-hardy enough to climb them," Enright said. "Those trails are wild and narrow. One foot wrong and you could find your death fast enough."

"Why would any seek those paths?" Amyu asked.

"Mountain goats," Enright said. "Their pelts are prized. There's also a mountain rabbit that lives up there with fur as soft as anything. They're a bugger to catch, though."

"And caves?" Amyu said.

"Aye, but there you have to have a care as well. Bears and collapsing rocks and ice can be a problem," Enright gave her a wide grin. "I used to climb on the rocks with my friends when I was a lad. We'd—"

Horns blew in the distance.

Enright levered himself up from the bench as Amyu stood, and they both went to the wall to look out.

"Wyverns?" Prest called.

"Nah," Enright said. "Messenger, by the look."

Amyu shaded her eyes. "With guards, it looks like. Maybe from the border."

"Word from Liam or Simus then," Prest said. "About time. The Warlord is out of his mind with worry." He dropped to his knees, and started crawling toward the trap door. "Best we get back to our duties."

Amyu gave Enright a shrug, and stepped forward to open the door as Prest slithered over.

"That's an improvement, that is," Enright said. "Last time he was on his belly."

Prest muttered under his breath as he crawled head first through the opening.

Amyu followed behind, shutting the door as she moved down the steps. Prest sat at the bottom, breathing hard, color returning to his skin. "You did not feel the tower move under your feet?" he asked. "As if it shifted in the wind?"

"No," Amyu said.

"Do not mock me," he growled.

"I would not, warrior." Amyu said, moving a few more steps down. "We should find the Warlord."

"Yes," Prest stood and took the lead, heading down quickly.

Amyu saved her smile for his back.

* * * * *

"Simus has betrayed you, Warlord," Yers said.

Amyu watched him from behind the Warprize's throne. Yers's hands were shaking, his eyes not really focused as he held the Warlord's token.

"Give me your truths, Warrior," The Warlord's voice was a deep rumble.

"It started out so well," Yers spoke of a confrontation with a warrior-priest, of Simus's reaction and Joden's intervention. "That night, the pillar of light… did Eloix tell you of it?" Yers asked.

Amyu sucked in a breath. Yers didn't know, couldn't know, that Eloix died bringing her message to Keir.

The Warprize glanced at the Warlord, but the Warlord nodded. "She brought us word," he said firmly.

Yers nodded. "I started to worry when Snowfall appeared. She's a warrior-priestess, who had been Wild Winds's apprentice." Yers shook his head, and rubbed his nose. "Simus took her oath, and allowed her to contest for Token-Bearer."

Keir took a breath. "A warrior-priestess?"

"Yes," Yers said. "Well, she only had partial tattoos. But still… Simus allowed it. I couldn't understand it. He seemed to come under her influence more and more." He drew a deep, shuddering breath. "Then Joden disappeared."

Both the Warprize and Warlord jerked in their seats. Keir leaned forward. "What do you mean, disappeared?"

"Simus said that the Eldest Elder Singer had demanded that Joden go with him to enter the Trials of a Singer," Yers said. "I couldn't find any who had seen him depart, and it felt wrong. Without farewells? Without good wishes?" Yers shook his head, then winced and put a hand to his head.

"You're hurt," Lara said.

"It's nothing," Yers said.

"Did Simus become Warlord?" Keir's impatience was controlled, but it was clear.

"I do not know for certain," Yers said. "On the last day of the Trials, at the last hour, I rescinded my oath and challenged Simus. And lost."

Every Plains warrior in the room went still. Amyu saw Heath give his bonded Atira a glance, but she gave him a quick shake of her head.

"I feared that Simus had been corrupted. Influenced." Yers said flatly. "I feared... I still fear that he will take those warriors loyal to you and turn on you under the influence of that warrior-priestess."

"You lost?" Keir said.

"Yes," Yers swayed slightly. "A head blow."

"Simus pulled it," Keir said and there was no question in his voice.

"I do not know." Now Yers looked away. "As soon as I could stand, I took to horse to bring you word."

"So, we do not know," Keir said. "We do not know if Simus is Warlord. If Joden lives. If this Snowfall is Simus's tokenbearer."

"No," Yers said. "I left, and I rode... things get confused after that." He frowned, blinking at both the Warlord and the Warprize. "I remember riding, and black birds flying over," he said slowly. "Big, black birds..."

The Warprize stood and walked forward. "Yers, come. You're exhausted. Let's have Heath take you to the kitchens and get you kavage and food, and I will send for Master Eln."

"But the Warlord needs—"

"Obey the Warprize," Keir told him. "Not that she will give you any alternative."

Lara threw him a smile, then reached out and lifted Yers's chin. "You may think you have recovered, but your eyes are still not quite right." She took him by the arm and headed toward the main doors, Heath following behind. "Are you seeing double by any chance?"

Their voices faded off as they left the room together.

Marcus appeared from the shadows behind the Warlord's throne. "Yers is a good warrior. His truths have always been strong."

"He is angry," Atira pointed out. "And rage blinds one to truths." She crossed her arms over her chest and glared at the doors. "To rescind on the last day? Challenge at the last hour?"

The doors opened, and Lara came back inside, a worried look on her face. Keir rose as she advanced.

"He clearly took a bad head blow," Lara said. "It's a wonder he could ride at all."

"He is of the Plains," Marcus snorted. "He could ride dead."

"I do not know what to think," Keir said. "Or what to believe. Simus loathes the warrior-priests as much as I do, but—"

"Keir," Lara put a hand to his chest. "I was once told by someone I trusted that I was to be a slave to a vicious Warlord." She looked up into her Warlord's eyes. "Wait for Simus. Hear his truth."

"The plan was that Simus would become Warlord. Guard Xy's border with Liam's help so that I could return next season to try to become WarKing." Keir covered Lara's hand with his own. "If only we knew what was really happening."

"If Joden was here, you know what he would say," Lara said.

"If you wish to hear the winds laugh, tell them your plans." Marcus snorted.

"True enough," Keir said. "I will wait for word. In the meantime, we need to keep working on those potential weapons to use against the wyverns when they return. I'll not leave Water's Fall helpless before them."

Amyu followed behind as they all swept from the room, intent on their tasks. The Warprize was trained as a healer, and she cared deeply for the lives of her people. It was what made her a great Queen and Warprize, for she considered the people of the Plains her people as well.

But Amyu was a warrior of the Plains, and whatever else she might be, child or adult, she could make her own decisions and give her life to the Tribe - both of her tribes - on her terms.

She followed behind, silent and determined.

She was going to find the airions.

She was going to fly.

CHAPTER THREE

Blue sky above. Crows calling in the distance. Flies buzzing nearby. Grass tickling his nose.

Pain.

Splayed out on his back, Cadr blinked through crusty eyes. His throat hurt, hurt bad. He gritted his teeth and managed to drag a hand over to find his neck covered in dried blood and grass. He pulled his hand back and blinked at the pale-yellow leaves of bloodmoss in his hand.

He let them fall from his fingers, and tried to roll over, to shade his eyes from the sun. His head throbbed.

He took a deep breath, and coughed.

Then he couldn't stop coughing, deep, hard hacks, bringing up blood and spit. His vision greyed, then went black as the agony washed over him.

When he came back, he was lying in his own filth, face down in the grass. His ribs ached. Someone was nearby, trying to rouse him. He couldn't see, couldn't really hear, but he felt like it was someone he could trust.

"Did I oversleep?" he asked, groggy and confused. But the words didn't come, only rough, guttural noises.

There was no tent, no bedroll… just the grass and the sun and the stink of clotted blood.

He risked a shallow breath. And then a deeper one. His lungs hurt, his throat hurt, but he could breathe. He rolled over and then paused, breathing through the hurt. He let the pain wash over him.

Someone moved in the distance, near the horses.

He curled in, forced himself to sit, wrapped his arms around his chest and tried to focus.

He was wearing leathers... no weapons, his belt gone, knives gone, boots gone. He frowned as he stared at his feet, toes pale against the green grasses. He closed his eyes, trying to remember. He'd been riding. He saw a sword come at his throat, and then-

His head jerked up, eyes open, muscles screaming in protest. He'd been escorting the Xyian healer Hanstau with Wild Winds, to join the other warrior-priests in hiding with Lightning Strike, one of Wild Winds's apprentices. They'd been attacked—

He staggered to his feet, breathing through the aches and pains, looking around for—

Bodies.

He staggered over to Wild Winds, and dropped to his knees next to the man, struggling to roll him over. But the cold tattooed flesh under his fingers told him the truth before he saw the wounds.

Wild Winds was dead.

Cadr forced himself to his feet. He stumbled around, searching. There'd been others with them, two warriors...

Their bodies were close by, also stripped of weapons and what could be taken fast.

Of Hanstau, there was no sign. Antas and his warriors must have taken him with them, dead or alive.

Alive, Cadr hoped.

He returned to Wild Wind's body and collapsed, uncertain what to do next. His energy was waning, and exhaustion was close. He'd no idea where or...

Someone was standing next to him, oddly colorless boots, blades of grass sticking through them.

He stared at them, then scraped at his eyes, trying to clear his vision.

There was a horse close, nosing him with stiff whiskers and warm breath against his cheek.

Cadr blinked, looked up. "Gils?" he croaked.

His tall, thin, colorless friend stood there, his curls dancing in a breeze that Cadr couldn't feel. His usual bright grin was gone, only worry in his eyes. Gils reached out and put a hand on the horse's shoulder.

The horse snuffled, and slowly went to its knees, easing down next to Cadr, a clear invitation to mount.

Except Gils was dead, wasn't he? Of the sickness that had killed so many... Cadr shook his head, hurting and confused. Gils was dead. He blinked up at his friend, his dead friend, washed of color, cold and—

Gils raised his eyebrows. It was such a familiar gesture that it made Cadr's heart hurt worse than his throat.

One truth was clear through his anguish. His friend had never let him down in life. The snows wouldn't change that.

Cadr staggered to his feet, but Gils was pointing, jabbing his finger.

Pointing at Wild Winds's body.

With the last of his strength Cadr dragged the body over, and draped it on the horse's shoulders. The animal lurched to its feet as Cadr kept the body balanced.

Cadr stood there, breathing hard. Then he put his head against the horse's neck. "I don't think I can mount," he admitted, the shame almost overshadowing the pain.

Gils walked backward a ways, gesturing.

The horse took a step.

Cadr went with it, leaning on the animal, gripping its mane, balancing Wild Winds's body. Half-blind, hurting, every step brought new anguish. He didn't look to see where they were going, just concentrated on taking one more step.

The horse stopped.

Cadr turned his head to see a place where a rise had been partially dug out. An animal, maybe, starting a den.

Gils was there, and the horse stepped forward, sidling close to the rise. Cadr released his grip, and half fell, half climbed the bit of rise, then mounted the horse. The horse shifted under him as Cadr shifted the body so it was balanced over his knees. He leaned forward and buried his hands in the horse's mane.

"Where?" he croaked.

Gils started walking.

The horse followed.

Cadr nodded. So be it. He wasn't even curious. All he had to do was stay on the horse. He was a warrior of the Plains. He would stay on.

Stay on. All he had to do was stay on.

Stay on.

Stay on…

* * * * *

The flap of the tent was pulled back and Hanstau was hustled inside.

He was blinded by the darkness, compared to the sun outside. But he caught the stench of sickness as rough hands on his shoulders forced him down. With his hands tied behind his back, he had no real balance. Hanstau let his legs fold, but then fell to the side to lessen the pain.

His captor, the big blond warrior, had no sympathy with Hanstau's pain. That had been made clear when he had been taken. He scowled, and uttered a command. The two warriors behind Hanstau reached down and grabbed his arms.

Hanstau's vision cleared as they pulled him up to his knees.

Before him, stretched out on a pallet, was a naked man covered in tattoos from the waist up. He must be a warrior-priest. Hanstau had not met one, but they had been described to him.

The man's eyes were bright and feverish, and there was sheen of sweat over his colorful torso. The cause was obvious.

The man's left arm was gone. Hacked off with something sharp would be Hanstau's guess.

The blond warrior was talking, but since Hanstau didn't have the best grasp of the Plains language, he ignored him. Instead, he focused on the wound. It was swollen and red, with clear pus oozing from burn marks.

"Are you people savages?" Hanstau asked. "You cauterized that?"

Silence was his only answer, and Hanstau looked up, realizing he had interrupted his captor. The man's face was red and furious. He pointed at the tattooed man, and used one of the only Xyian words he seemed to know.

"Warprize," he said, and continued on with what seemed to be a demand that Hanstau treat the wound.

Hanstau might not be a warrior, but he could and did glare right back at the man. He'd been dragged away from his escort, watched this man butcher poor Cadr and the others, strip their bodies without a care, and then drag him off on horseback. "I am a Master Healer of Xy," he spat the words, making sure his scowl was as harsh as his captors. "My hands can heal but they cannot be forced."

The confusion in their faces forced him to use one of the few words he knew of their language. "No."

The blond snarled and made as if to strike.

The warrior-priest spoke then, and his voice sent shivers up Hanstau's spine. He didn't understand his words, but he knew that tone, that expression. The warrior-priest thought he had the upper hand.

The blond grunted, and barked a command. Hanstau was forced to his feet, out into the sun and marched to another tent close by. He only had a glimpse of the warriors guarding this tent before he was pushed within.

There was a woman inside.

Much like the warrior-priest, she was naked and ill. But she was staked down, her limbs taut, tied with leathers straps that seemed to bite into her flesh. From the look of her swollen and chaffed wrists, she'd been captive for some time.

She turned to look at him, her eyes dull and uncaring.

Once again Hanstau was forced to his knees, but this time the blond knelt by the woman, pulled a dagger, and put it to her throat. The blond spoke harsh words, his eyes focused on Hanstau's face.

Her face blank, the woman spoke. "Antas of the Boar says heal Hail Storm, or he will kill me."

To Hanstau's shock, the woman spoke in Xyian. "You are of Xy?" he blurted out.

"Refuse him," the woman closed her eyes as if weary. "For I would die."

Hanstau sucked in a breath.

Antas, the blond, narrowed his eyes and pressed the knife deeper into her flesh.

Hanstau bit his lip, staring at Antas in open defiance. But then, as he knew he would, as Antas knew he would, damn him, Hanstau lowered his gaze and bowed his head in submission.

* * * * *

"Why?" the woman asked.

The question came after Hanstau had treated Hail Storm. His hands free, with his satchel nearby, he knelt by her side and ignored the question. "You speak Xyian," he said.

"Some," she said. "If the words are simple. I was taught by the Warprize as we journeyed. Who are you?"

"I am Hanstau of Xy, sent by Queen Xylara to serve as a healer to Simus of the Hawk."

She sighed, and looked away. "I am Reness, Eldest Elder Thea of the Plains. Now prisoner and sick to death of it."

"How did this happen?" Hanstau stared at her leg.

"Word came that I was needed at a thea camp not far from the border," Reness said. "I left the Warlord and Warprize to continue on their journey. I thought to follow later. But the words that were brought to me were false, and Antas took me prisoner." Reness looked bleak. "Do not ask me how long it has been since I have seen the sky."

"I meant, how did this happen?" Hanstau gestured to her leg.

"Ah," Reness grimaced. "Creatures came, huge winged creatures, and attacked the camp. The tent collapsed on top of me. As they pulled me out, one of the poles pierced my leg."

Hanstau nodded, reaching out to turn her calf toward him. "Only a few days, then."

At her questioning look, he continued. "Those creatures, those wyverns, they attacked our camp as well."

"The Heart?" she asked slowly. "They attacked the Heart?"

"Yes," Hanstau said absently. "I must see to this. How do you say, 'I need hot water'?"

She blinked at him. "The wound is deep and it throbs and is full of rot. It will kill me, for which I thank the elements. If my hands were free, I'd go to the snows."

"By the Sun God," Hanstau sat back on his heels and frowned. "What is this fascination that you people have with killing yourselves? I grant you that it's deep and I am sure it hurts. But all it needs is cleaning and stitching. I might be able to use bloodmoss on it if I can clean it well enough." He started to rummage through his satchel. They'd searched it for weapons and left everything a jumble.

He glanced over to find Reness staring at him

Hanstau returned the look calmly. He was no warrior, although he'd lost a bit of his belly since leaving Xy. "I will clean it," he repeated. "Heal it as best I can, as fast as is safe. Then we will find a way to be free. Both of us."

"You are no warrior," Reness said as if convincing herself. "But you have steel in you."

Hanstau got to work. Demanding hot water from the guards, he worked as best he could as Reness grunted in pain.

"I'm sorry," he said. "But if I am to use bloodmoss I can't leave any dirt behind. There are some splinters."

Reness gasped. He could tell that she was forcing herself to breathe.

"That warrior-priest," he started to talk. "Hail Storm—"

"No names," Reness hissed in Xyian. "They listen."

Hanstau nodded. "There is something wrong with that one. He stared at me as I worked on his arm, as if looking into my soul."

"They are said to have powers," she replied.

"Not anymore," Hanstau said. "Supposedly."

"What?" she asked, her eyes wide. "Tell me," she said. "Tell me the news of the Plains."

"I wasn't there for all of it," he told her.

"Tell me your truths," she demanded.

So Hanstau talked as he washed the wound and dug for splinters. He spoke of what he had heard about the warrior-priests losing their tattoos and their powers. He mentioned the warrior-priestess with the partial tattoos that had offered to serve Simus.

He told her of Wild Winds's death.

Finally, he sat back, satisfied. "We will wait until tomorrow, when the swelling has gone down. Then we can decide if we want to risk the bloodmoss. Faster healing, but if there is debris within it will cause greater problems.

But Reness was staring at the ceiling above them, her brows drawn together. "So Antas has a warrior-priest, one that claims to be the Eldest Elder. He has me, the Eldest Elder Thea. And now you, his Warprize."

"Why does he think I am his warprize?" Hanstau said. "From what I understand of the all the requirements, I am not."

"Truth is no obstacle to Antas." Reness shifted her gaze to look at him. "For him, the truth is what he says it is."

There was a spark back in her eyes, and her color was much better. Hanstau felt the deep pleasure that came from aiding another as he reached to start cleaning his mess.

"Antas really only needs one thing," Reness continued.

"What is that?" Hanstau asked.

"All he needs now for his own Council of the Elders?" she said. "Is a Singer."

CHAPTER FOUR

It didn't take long to break camp, but they weren't fast enough for Essa. Joden watched the man pace impatiently around the carcass of the wyvern, studying the animal as if he hadn't seen one before.

"Careful," came a quiet voice. Quartis was standing next to him, offering a full waterskin. "This part of the ritual always irritates him."

"My thanks," Joden wondered and would have asked questions, but Quartis just strode off.

Joden secured the waterskin to his saddle. Well, at least there was some support there. The other Singers seemed to avoid him as they worked around him. He focused on tightening his saddle girth.

It felt like they knew something that he didn't.

And they were all Singers. Joden tried to look around casually, double-checking his first impression. Everyone, Quartis, the others, the warriors that Essa had arrived with, all bore the bird-wing tattoo around their eyes. His heart started beating just a bit faster. The Trials. *His Singer Trials.*

He looked back at Essa, to find the man staring at him.

Joden dropped his eyes and concentrated on his task.

"Gather," Essa barked the command at everyone.

Joden looked up to find Essa striding toward him, to find all the Singers moving into a circle around him, leading their mounts. He drew a breath, let it out slow, trying to be calm.

Essa stood next to him, impressive despite the bruising.

"Joden of the Hawk, Warrior of the Plains," he intoned. "You have served the Tribes in battle and are free to take any path you choose. There are many paths that such of your standing may take. You can continue to serve in the Armies of the Plains. You can return to the thea camps and guard and teach the heart-blood of the Tribes, our children. Or you can enter the Trials to become a Singer, one who keeps the knowledge of the Plains. What is your wish?"

Joden's mouth went dry, for here it was, his goal, his dream. "I wish to become a Singer, Eldest Elder."

Quartis stepped forward. "Eldest Elder, Joden of the Hawk has met the initial requirements of the Singer Trials with his knowledge of the teaching chants and songs. I, Quartis, Singer of the Plains, declare the proof of this."

Essa nodded. "Joden of the Hawk, if you had failed those initial tests, you would have been sent back to the Tribes, to try again another season." Essa drew a deeper breath. "But now you would enter into the true Trials of a Singer. In these Trials you learn truths only held by the Singers. Fail in these Trials, and we will send you to the snows to preserve our secrets."

It was a shock, but the grim faces of those that surrounded him told Joden the truth of those words.

"So." Essa paused before continuing. "I would ask you once more, do you truly wish to enter the Trials of a Singer? Or do you wish to return to the Hear—" Essa caught himself as the others stirred around them. "Return to your fellow warriors, to serve the Plains in other ways? There is no shame in refusing." Essa paused again, staring at Joden. "None can force your decision. Speak, and it will be as you wish."

And the group was silent, except for the jingle of harness and the wind in the grass.

Joden looked down at his feet, thinking. Here it was, his chance, his dream. It came with a price, though. As all dreams do, he thought ruefully.

Essa stood, and the impatience he had displayed before was gone, as if he were willing to wait as long as it took.

Joden raised his eyes then, looking up and out at the wide grass of the Plains, looking north and beyond, to where Xy lay. He took a deep breath, and knew that he would answer this challenge, take this chance, for his people, all the people both of the Plains and of Xy.

But there was something more as well, something he also knew deep in his bones. He wasn't just doing it for those reasons. He wanted this, wanted the bird wing tattoo, wanted the stature and respect it brought with it.

More than his life.

"I wish to enter the Singer Trials," he said.

"HEYLA," the Singers around him exploded in a cry that shook Joden's bones, lifting their arms in celebration. There was only joy in their faces and hope for him that he could see, and he returned their smiles with a grin of his own as the tightness flowed out of his bones.

They moved in, clapping his back, shaking his hands, some dancing a sudden pattern around him, chanting his name.

Essa stood apart and did not smile. He waited for the exuberance to fade, then spoke. "So be it," Essa said. "We ride," he commanded, and everyone turned toward their horses.

"Where are we going?" Joden dared ask.

"We don't know," Essa said. "They will reveal themselves in their own sweet time." He mounted, looking like he had eaten a bad piece of meat. "We will head south, and ride until we see a camp that consists of a single tent. There is no telling how far we will have to ride, or in which direction. They will appear when they see fit, and not before." Essa grimaced, glancing at Joden. "The last time this took weeks."

Essa started off, everyone else falling in behind, Quartis

and Joden in the center.

"My thanks for your truths," Joden said softly to Quartis.

"Do not thank me until you have your tattoo," Quartis said, just as softly. "And heed this, The Eldest Elder hates this part of the ritual. His temper will be foul until we find their camp. And worse after."

Joden looked ahead, but Essa was topping the nearest rise, far enough ahead not to hear their words. "Who do we seek?" Joden asked quietly.

Essa yanked on his reins, stopping his horse so hard the riders behind his had to pull to the side. They all sat, looking down the other side of the hill.

Joden and Quartis, exchanged a glance and then urged their horses, until they too could see a small camp with a single tent at the base of the hill.

"*Bragnects*," Essa swore with venom in his tone. He leaned forward, stroking his horse's neck as if asking forgiveness. "Joden," he growled. "Prepare yourself to meet the Ancients."

* * * * *

There was no one outside the tent as they rode in.

Essa dismounted. "Take the others off, and make another camp," Essa told Quartis. "Back at the top of the rise."

Quartis bowed.

"Come," Essa said, and went into the tent.

Joden followed behind to be met with a wave of heat reeking of old kavage and fermented mare's milk. Braziers burned brightly in each corner. The heat dried his nose and eyes, making him blink.

"Shut the flap, shut the flap," came a quavering voice. "You are letting out the heat."

At the far end of the tent, on the traditional wooden platform, were three bundles of blankets. In each, sat a… Joden had never seen anyone like them.

They were old, ancient, with wrinkled spotty skin and very few wisps of hair on their heads. Their eyes were milky white and rheumy with age. Joden couldn't tell their sex, and their skin seemed so faded it was hard to tell what color it had originally been.

The three of them sat facing them, waiting.

"Ancient Ones," Essa walked forward and bowed as low as Joden had ever seen him bow to anyone. "Greetings. I have brought—"

"Joden of the Hawk," the one on the far left spoke with a soft whisper. "So wise, so knowledgeable, so smart. In his own mind, at least."

"Would-be-Singer," the one on the far right cackled, high-pitched and irritating.

"Just so," Essa said. He glanced back. "Joden, these are the Ancients."

Joden walked forward, but did not bow. "Ancients?"

"Joden is confused," the one in the center spoke with a quaver. "Wondering what we are, perhaps? Or who we are?"

"Ancients," came the cackle. "There are no ancients on the Plains."

"How can this be," continued the whispering one. "The elderly among us, no longer useful to the Tribe, they go to the snows."

All three laughed, and the hairs on the back of Joden's neck rose.

"There are songs that Singers do not sing," Essa ground out the words, his arms folded across his chest. "Tales we do not tell. Songs and stories handed down from Eldest Elder to Eldest Elder."

The Ancients chuckled. The one in the center grinned, bare gums were all that showed. "Stories not told to children."

"If you don't tell me," Essa growled. "The tales will be lost. They will die with you."

"Why should we tell you, child?" one asked in a mocking tone.

Joden was starting to sweat. The air in the tent was thick and oppressive, but this information made him ignore his discomfort. "You haven't passed down your knowledge?" he blurted out.

Essa's face reddened, whether with anger or the heat, Joden wasn't sure.

All three sat wrapped in their blankets, the laughter gone from their suddenly bright eyes.

"You caused this, Joden of the Hawk," came the whisper. "When you saved Simus and did not give him mercy. You started this—"

"—but will you finish it?" the quaver asked.

"How did you know—" Joden demanded.

"The winds bring word of your deeds," said the cackle.

"Joden comes before you as a candidate," Essa spat. "Give him your usual cryptic blessing, and we will be on our way."

"Leave us," came the whisper.

"Joden stays," came the quaver.

Essa drew himself up, clearly angered. "I am the Eldest Elder of the Singers, not to be treated as a child or as an unworthy—"

Snorts, and more chuckles.

"If you don't tell me," Essa said making an obvious effort. "The songs will die with you. The truth will die with you."

"You are so sure," came the whisper.

"Maybe, maybe," said the quaver.

"Maybe not," said the cackle and they all laughed till they wheezed.

"Besides," the cackle added. "Why should we tell you, child?"

"An insult, it's not to be borne," Essa snarled. "I—"

The three started to sing, a weird three-part harmony that sent chills up Joden's spine.

"Fine," Essa barked, turned on his heel, and headed for the tent flap.

Joden followed, but Essa shook his head. "Stay. Skies above, maybe they will share with you what they have denied me for years." Essa grabbed Joden's arm. "I want those songs," he hissed, then stomped out of the tent.

Joden stared at the closing tent flap, and turned to face the Ancients.

"Sit," the one in the center nodded its head. "Sit before us, Singer-to-be."

Joden obeyed, sitting cross-legged before them. The heat grew even more intense.

"So, you think our ways are sacred," the left one said, in a voice as clear as a bell. "Special, traditional, the Way of the Plains."

"Yes," Joden says.

"But in need of change," the right one said, with a sweet innocent tone.

"Yes," Joden said. "The power of the warrior-priests—"

"Has been broken," said the one in the middle, with a deep timber.

"I—" Joden started.

"You honor the way of the Plains, with all its traditions." The bell tone reminded him. "Yet you broke that tradition when you failed to grant Simus of the Hawk mercy on the field of battle."

"I did," Joden said. "But it brought a Warprize to the Plains, one skilled in the ways of healing."

"Yet it was a Warprize that destroyed the Plains," the bell said. "And destroyed that way of life. She and her Warlord, for their love."

"What?" Joden asked.

"For her Warlord was the Chaosreaver," said the deep voice. "Who left only destruction in his path and the cold, and the silence…"

"Stripped us and stripped the land," the innocent voice was sad in its sweetness. "Stripped us of all we were. Made us what we are."

All three pairs of old eyes burned into his.

"You make it sound as if it was yesterday," Joden said.

"It was-" one whispered.

"—but days ago," whispered another.

"Perhaps we'd tell you…" came yet another whisper. "But only if you took the old paths to becoming a Singer."

"Why won't you tell Essa? Joden asked. "He is Eldest Elder, and honored within the Tribes."

"Essa, like the Eldest Elder before him-"

"—and before him—"

"—and before her," and now the cackle was back. "Would not take the old paths. A child, afraid of shadows and death."

"But there are shadows on the old paths," and now the whisper was back.

"And there is death," came the quaver.

"There is always death," Joden said. "It comes in an instant, all know that. Why won't you tell Essa—"

"He will not pay the price," the center one growled. "Will you, Joden of the Hawk?"

"There is always a price-" Joden started, but they cut him off.

"You do not fully understand the cost," the whisper was full of regret.

"And you won't, until you pay it," the cackle was harsher.

"What will you sacrifice, Joden of the Hawk? What price will you pay?" asked the quaver, as if in hope.

"Tell me," Joden demanded. "Tell me the old paths."

From the folds of the center blanket emerged two hands, almost skeletal, reaching out to the right and left. They too raised their hands, and once joined began to chant together.

The fire warmed you; we thank the elements
Offer your mind; sing to the flames

The earth supported you; we thank the elements
Offer your body; be buried in earth

The waters sustained you; we thank the elements
Offer your soul; wander the snows

The air filled you; we thank the elements
Offer your heart; be reborn in the winds

The power surrounds you; we thank the elements
Offer your dreams; seek to prove your worth

Joden sat, spellbound, as they went silent, and their hands pulled back within the blankets. Eyes that had been bright turned back to milky white.

"I'm cold," came the quaver.

"I want kavage," the whisper came.

"What does that mean?" Joden demanded. "That chant?"

"Seek out Essa," came the cackle. "His feathers will be well and truly ruffled by now."

* * * * *

Indeed, Essa was pacing when Joden walked up the rise toward him. He'd worn a path in the grasses.

"What did they say to you?" he demanded. "They have never done this before, never spoken with a candidate without me, never did more than offer a blessing. What did they say?"

Joden drew a deep breath. "Tell me, Eldest Elder. Tell me of the old paths."

CHAPTER FIVE

"Rest days," Amyu said. "This confuses me. There are no days of rest on the Plains," she told the Warprize. "One does one's duties every day."

"Well, you are in Xy," The Warprize gave her one of her gentle smiles as she nursed baby Kayla. "As such, you will take a rest day." She gave Amyu an impish grin. "Marcus had to take one."

Marcus snorted from his place by the fire, where he was keeping baby Keirson busy. "Foolishness," he grumbled.

Amyu returned to folding the clean nappies for the babies. Of all the places in the castle, she felt most comfortable in these rooms. A large bed of gurtle pads, covered in blankets and furs filled one wall. There were wooden chairs before the fireplace, and a warm fire burned in the stone hearth. A chess board was set up to the one side on a table, its pieces carved to look like strong Plains warriors and clever, sharp city-dwellers. The Warprize's satchel slumped over on a wooden chest where she stored clothes. The Warlord's various weapons hung on the walls, and there were thick, colorful rugs on the stone floor. A blending of the traditions of both the Plains and Xy. A blending of the lives of both Warprize and Warlord.

"Give him here," Lara gestured to Marcus, who surrendered Keirson willingly and took Kayla in his arms.

"You're sure you've milk enough?" the disfigured man said, watching critically as the babe latched on to Lara's breast. "We've goat milk, though gurtle milk would be better."

"So far," Lara settled back in her chair, and gave Marcus that gentle smile. "We'll see as they get bigger. We'll put them down for naps after this. You will stay with them?"

"Of course," Marcus said.

Lara adjusted her breast to aid Keirson's sucking. "Rest days actually started as holy days of the Sun God," Lara told Amyu. "Xyians are supposed to use the day of rest to contemplate the blessings that the Sun God and the Lady of the Moon and Stars have given us. Being of the Plains, you should contemplate the blessings of the elements and find something to do other than your regular duties."

Amyu looked at her out of the corner of her eye.

Lara laughed. "Yes, I know that is a contradiction in truths. Marcus and Keir have both pointed it out to me."

Keirson lost the nipple, and let out a sharp cry. Lara helped him back and he settled down, sucking for all he was worth.

"Besides, you shouldn't stay cooped up in the castle all day, every day." Lara said.

"But what should I do?" Amyu frowned at the pile of nappies.

"Spar," Marcus said as he eased Kayla onto his shoulder, and started gently drumming her back. "Sharpen your weapons. Practice with your bow."

Lara rolled her eyes. "You spar every day," she said. "For the love of the Goddess, Amyu, go out and explore the city."

Amyu's hands stilled.

"Wander around and maybe check out the markets. I will give you coin to spend and—" the Warprize continued talking but Amyu's head buzzed with an idea.

A day. She'd have an entire day. She could try again to have Kalisa, the old cheesemaker, tell her stories of airions. Maybe venture outside these stone walls and see the sky and feel the wind on her face.

She could head up into the mountains.

Not that she could get far, but she could take a small pack, with some basic supplies, just in case, she thought. Cache them for the future. A blanket, some dried—

"Amyu?" The Warprize was frowning, trying to get her attention.

Amyu blinked, pulled from her thoughts. "Yes, Warprize?"

"So it's settled then?" Lara asked. "You'll go into the city tomorrow?"

"Aye," she said.

"You could do me a favor, when you go," Lara said. "I've jars of joint cream for my friend Kalisa. You know, the older woman who sells cheese in the market?"

"Yes," Amyu said, trying to keep her excitement out of her voice.

"I haven't had time to visit her," Lara looked resigned. "I will have to make the effort. From your description, it sounds like she is fading. But take her the cream, and who knows? Maybe she will agree to tell you her stories of airions."

* * * * *

She was out of the castle before dawn, her pack on her back and wearing her cloak.

The city was just stirring as Amyu walked the streets, but this time it didn't seem quite so strange as the last. She knew where she was headed, and where the cheesemaker's cart was usually found.

But when she arrived she was dismayed to find Kalisa's son, Anser pushing the cart into place.

Just as dismayed as he was.

"Amyu," Anser was polite, but there was a worry line between his eyes. "Good morning."

"Good morning," Amyu responded. "I've a rest day and I've come—"

"If you've come for Auntie's stories, you have come for nothing," Anser was firm. "She's been in a foul mood since the last time you talked to her." Anser shook his head. "But then, I hear tell that there are no old people on the Plains."

"None so old as she," Amyu confirmed.

"Well, you've no way of knowing that there's no living with her when her temper's up. And she's having one of her bad spells. Her bones have been stiff these past few days."

"The Queen sent these for her," Amyu held out the basket with three jars.

Anser smiled then, relief in his eyes. "Well, that should help. Master Eln keeps her well supplied, but she swears that the cream from the Queen's hands works better." He took the bag. "My thanks," he added.

"I also did come for the stories," Amyu admitted.

"Afraid I can't help you there," Anser said. "I don't know why she refuses to share them with you. Sun God knows, she repeats them to me and my nephews until we could recite them word for word."

Amyu perked up. "You know them?"

"Well, it's been a while since I really listened," Anser chuckled ruefully. "I've forgotten most of the details." He busied his hands with his trade, but his eyes were thoughtful. "The boys, my sons, now, they will remember."

"Do you think they would tell them to me?" Amyu asked.

"Don't see why not," Anser said slowly.

Amyu stood still, held her breath, afraid to hope.

Anser stood for a moment, looking out over the market square. "The wyverns killed two cows before they cleared from the skies." He gave Amyu a thoughtful look, and then huffed. "Tell you what. I need to go out to the cheese house this day and take the boys their nooning. Mya, my wife, is terrified I will be eaten by wyverns even though Auntie has told her that they won't return until late summer. You can come with me, yes? Keep watch, help with the loading and unloading. And you can talk to my sons. Who knows what you might learn?"

"Yes," Amyu said. "Please."

"Mya will be here to take over the trade in another hour or so. Return then, and I will take you with me."

Amyu nodded, then darted off. She'd use her coin for some supplies, dried bread and maybe smoked meat, a cooking pot if she could afford such. She moved off into the crowd, planning.

Just in case.

* * * * *

To Amyu's relief, Anser's sons were more than willing to share their nooning and their stories. Nerith and Usek both shared their father's strong looks.

"No skin off my nose to tell you her tales," Nerith shrugged.

"Auntie won't talk to her," Anser was already seated, digging in the basket, handing out the thick sandwiches of ham and cheese. They settled under the shade of some trees, close to the crick that flowed down out of the mountain. The great doors to what they called the cheese barn were on the other side of the grass, and cows grazed nearby.

"It might anger her further," Amyu settled her pack behind her, and took the cloth-wrapped sandwich Anser thrust at her with a nod of thanks.

"Well, Auntie wasn't here when those things swooped down and killed two of our heifers, now was she?" Nerith's face held a bitter look.

Usek scowled at the sandwich in his hands. "If you're thinking there's something to those tales, well then, I'll tell ya. Gladly."

"Yeah," Nerith nodded. "So, she talks about the brave riders of the airions, defenders of Xy. She's got stories of fighting off wyverns, and acts them out with her hands." Nerith set his sandwich in his lap, and started waving his hands around. "The airions always have it rough, until they managed to come at the wyverns out of the sun, and grab them with their fore-claws, raking them with the hind."

"They have claws on all four legs?" Amyu asked eagerly.

"Aye," Usek reached out with his free hand and hooked his fingers to show her. "Long, and sharp, and deadly. They sink into the thick leathery wyvern skin, and hold tight." He closed his fingers in to show her.

They started telling tales of riders and airions, taking bits of food between using their hands to describe the tales.

"But know you this," Nerith hunched over, making his voice as creaky as Auntie's as he threw his arm out, pointing off toward the beginnings of a path just behind them. "The airions sleep, awaiting the day of Xy's greatest need. Then shall the chosen ones wake them and once again ride the skies," He cackled. Anser and Usek chortled. "And who knows, young ones, but you might be the chosen ones."

"They are sleeping?" Amyu asked, wide-eyed. "Up there?" she asked, looking off to the mountain side, covered in pines and scrub.

"Oh, aye," Anser said. "She'd insist that was the path. I spent hours roaming up there as a kid, climbing the paths until I got called back to chores."

"As did we," Nerith laughed. "Not sure how we didn't manage to kill ourselves on some of those trails."

Usek gave a nod, taking a drink of the clear cold water in his mug before speaking. "Of course, we didn't climb very far or fast. Path gets really risky as you get above the tree line."

"But it's all stories anyway," Nerith said with a shrug. "Airions don't exist, do they?"

"I am not so sure," Usek said. "You know those saddles we used to play on, back of the cheese barn?"

"Aye?" Anser asked. "What about them? They've been there a stone's age; I used to play on them when my Da was turning the cheeses.

"I always wondered about them." Usek tilted his head. "Let me show you."

* * * * *

Amyu's eyes grew wide as Usek slid back the large, thick wooden door. "It's a cave," she said in amazement.

"Aye," Anser was puffed with pride. "Been used by the family for generations."

Just inside were rows and rows of wooden shelving, each holding wheels of cheese. They stretched back as far as the light would let her see, and off to the sides as well. There was a dry, slightly bitter taste in the air.

"This is all cheese?" she asked.

Anser swelled with what had to be pride. "Aye, best in Xy if you are looking for hard, sharp cheese. Soft cheeses, now anyone can do, but our family dries and ages and—"

"Rotates," both Nerith and Usek spoke as one. "To obtain uniform taste and texture that is the envy of all of Xy and beyond these mountains."

Anser snorted as the boys laughed. "Tease all ya want," he said. "It's true enough."

"Aye," Nerith was reaching for metal lanterns, handing one to his father and brother. "But Sun God above us all, the only thing more boring than rotating the cheeses is keeping track of the cheeses that have been rotated!"

"But that attention to details is what—"

Amyu watched and listened as they argued. Usek was ignoring them, lighting the lanterns with a flint and striker. He took two up, and handed one to her.

"It's an old argument," he whispered. "Come with me,"

and he headed off down the narrow path between the shelves.

Amyu followed.

The darkness of the cave soon enveloped them, the shadows of the cheese-lined shelves dancing strange patterns as they moved past. Amyu wrinkled her nose; it wasn't a bad smell, or even musty or stale, but it was a sharper scent as they moved further in. She glanced up, but the light didn't touch the ceiling. "How big is this place?" she asked as they moved on.

"Big," Usek said. "We don't use it all, but Auntie swears that it used to be filled."

"It doesn't smell stale," Amyu said.

"That's because there is a draft that moves from the doorway to the back of the cave." He stopped then, glanced back at the others, and dropped his voice. "You're going up there, aren't you?"

Amyu froze, but his expression was more of caring than forbidding. "I—"

"Aye, your pack told me," Usek said, giving her a frown. "If you explore caves, make sure you check for signs of bears and cats first, and watch the air flow. They don't all have natural chimneys." He glanced back to where Nerith and his father were coming up behind them. "You understand?"

Amyu nodded.

"Take that lantern," he said, nodding at the one in her hand. "They can burn animal fat if need be. Gets damn dark up there." He turned and kept walking.

Amyu followed.

They came to a gap in the shelves, a wide area between. Now there were only empty shelves stretching beyond, but in the open area, there were—

"Saddles," Amyu breathed and held her lantern high.

There were three, off to the side, on wooden frames. The leather was cracked and curled; Amyu suspected that if a child climbed on one now it would fall apart.

"Not just any saddles," Usek said. "Look again."

Amyu narrowed her eyes.

Nerith and Anser came up from behind, and their lanterns added to the light.

"Not so different from what I remember," Asher said. "Just saddles—"

"No," Amyu said, walking over to trace down the saddle line. "Look at the stirrups. They are made of chains." She stepped toward the back. "And there are two belly straps, and here, back here," her fingers traced the leather strap that looped around the back, drooping on the floor. "On a horse, this would run back, behind the tail."

"And here," Usek got closer. "See these rings? The rider was chained in, I think."

Amyu sucked in a breath as she glanced from him back to the saddle. "Chained in for flight?" She stepped forward. "And these are halters, not true bridles. See where the—"

"Get away from those, you Firelander bitch!"

The shriek of pure rage caught them all off guard. Amyu jerked around, reaching for a weapon with her free hand before she could stop herself.

Kalisa stood there, hunched over a cane, one hand grasping a shelf for support, her face twisted in hate.

Mya stood behind her, wringing her hands. "Anser, I am so sorry, but she demanded we follow you. She—"

"By what right," Kalisa snarled. "Do you let this Firelander touch my things?" Spittle flew with her words.

"Now Auntie," Anser said soothingly, stepping forward with his hand raised in peace. "We were just telling Amyu about your stories, about the airions—"

"No," the venom was strong in her voice. Kalisa stepped forward, tottering, shaking her finger at Amyu. "You are not of Xy, or of my blood. You are not the Chosen one."

"Auntie," the shock was clear on Mya's face. "Auntie, please—"

Nerith and Usek had faded back, letting their lanterns dip a bit, trying to stay out of the line of battle.

"You have no right," Kalisa said. "My stories are not for the likes of you."

Amyu took a step back, but then her anger flared. "You lied," she said, glaring at the old woman. "You knew, and you didn't tell. Didn't tell me, didn't tell anyone." She met the old woman glare for glare. "You withheld the truth."

"How dare you," Kalisa screamed. "You and your kind are not of Xy. Not of the Blood. They will only awaken for—" she clutched her chest. "Ah—"

"Auntie," Asker spoke in horror, and reached out to steady the old woman as she sagged against him.

"I will tell her," Kalisa gasped out. "I will tell the Queen, and she will stop you. She will—" She clutched her chest, and choked on her breath.

"Auntie!" Mya moved to her side. "We must get her to a healer."

Kalisa caught Amyu's gaze and held it, the loathing glittering in her eyes. "Xylara will forbid—"

Amyu turned and ran down the aisle toward the sunlight as Kalisa screamed behind her.

She burst out into the day, grabbed up her pack and pelted for the goat path the boys had pointed out.

The path was narrow, and climbed fast. She was soon lost in the pines and scrub, the voices behind her were lost in the wind as it whistled through the needles of the trees. Her pace slowed as the path switched back and up many times, growing narrower and harder. She'd tried to think of nothing but her footing, moving as fast and as far as she could.

It was some time before she remembered the lantern in her

hand. She paused to blow it out, and tie it on the back of her pack.

She could no longer hear Kalisa, but her threat burned in Amyu's heart. The Warprize could stop her. Might forbid her search out of a sense of caution and fear for Amyu's life.

It was madness, after all. To search a mountain for an animal never seen?

Amyu swallowed hard, her breathing still ragged and not just from the climb. She licked her lips and tasted the salt of her tears. She picked up the pack, easing the strap over her shoulders.

She should turn back.

She had left her duties, her tribe, her thea, without permission, without announcing her truths.

She should turn back, return to the city, face the Warprize.

She should turn back, but her feet kept moving forward.

She should turn back, but her hands kept clutching the straps of her pack.

After what seemed an eternity, the path widened a bit. She stood for a moment, letting her breathing slow, scrubbing the tears from her face.

The trees below her blocked the view of the farm and herds. But further out, she could see the curve of the wall of the city. And the green valley stretching out and away, and the blue sky above as the sun sank behind the mountains.

The saddles had been real, proving the truth of the airions. They existed, or had existed. She ached to ride one, drawn by an urge deep in her heart.

Her hands were cold, and she blew into her fingers to warm them. Then she spread her arms out in supplication, and threw her heart out into the wind. "Skies, aid me," she whispered.

She waited, as the sun seemed to stop in the sky, and the trees went silent around her.

A slight breeze moved over her, playing with her hair. Peace filled her soul, and blanketed her heart with warmth.

Amyu took a deep breath, lowered her arms and hugged them to her chest.

She had her truth. She was no longer Amyu of the Boar, having been cast out of her Tribe for barrenness and disobedience.

She was no longer Amyu of Xy, by her own choice.

She would be Amyu of the Skies. Madness it may well be, but her choice was made, even if it cost her life.

She turned back to the mountain and headed further up the path.

CHAPTER SIX

"Let go, Warrior," the words, the tone, were no threat; the woman's voice seemed kind.

Cadr became aware slowly. The sky, the grass. The horse beneath him, and the heavy body hanging over his legs. He had to stay on, stay on, stay—

"You're safe, you're here," A gentle touch on his wrist brought his focus to the warrior standing by his knee. Her fingers stayed there, warm against his skin.

So she, whoever she was, wasn't dead.

That was good. That was important, but Cadr wasn't sure why.

There were other warriors clustered around his horse, which was standing still, its head hanging.

"Let go," she repeated, and now her fingers laced with his, trying to untangle them from the horse's mane. He'd a death grip on the coarse hairs.

Cadr tried to clear his eyes, tried to see.

She was pretty. Brown hair, brown eyes, younger than he but only by a few seasons. Her face though, was worried, frowning, and her eyes… she was crying.

"Who?" he croaked.

"I am Gilla of the Snake," she said.

But that wasn't right. Cadr jerked his head up. His horse reacted, bunching its legs to bolt, but there were too many bodies surrounding them, too many hands reaching out to soothe horse and rider.

"Peace, warrior," came a broken male voice from Cadr's other side. "I am Lightning Strike. I do not know how you found me, but we are grateful."

"The dead," Cadr croaked, but he wasn't sure he was understood.

"Let us take him," Lightning Strike said. He was a tanned man, dreadlocks hanging down his back. He had the partial tattoos of a warrior-priest-in-training.

Cadr swayed in the saddle as willing hands pulled the limp body of Wild Winds off his legs. The death chant rose around them as they carried the body away.

"Come," Gilla tugged his arm. "Night Clouds will see to the horse."

He managed to dismount, but wobbled, and then fell to his knees. Gilla heaved him up, putting his arm over her shoulders. Strong. She was strong and solid and not dead. "It's not far," she said.

"You are not—" Cadr felt the need to explain but his mouth and tongue were rough and dry.

"My tent," Gilla said as she pulled him within. "Questions and talk can wait. How long have you been traveling?" She settled him on her sleeping pallet. It was a big tent, but she seemed alone.

Cadr swiped at his eyes again, feeling the last of his strength leach away. "Don't know," he admitted in a whisper.

"And here I said no questions," she said ruefully. A cool cup pressed to his lips. Cadr took it in his clumsy hands and drank greedily.

She pressed a bit of flat bread into his hands, and he managed to take a few bites before he lost the strength to even chew.

"Sleep." Gilla pressed him down.

Cadr blinked at her as she took a wet cloth to his eyes, face, and hands. He was content to watch, to feel her work. He blinked muzzily, fading, but the tent flap was pushed open and he looked to see who had entered.

A huge creature silently slipped within.

Cadr croaked a warning, trying to point, but Gilla already had a hand on his shoulder keeping him down. "That's a friend," she smiled ruefully.

The animal sat by her side, its head level with Gilla's, its fur a muddled mess of black, brown, yellow and a kind of green. Its bright yellow eyes stared at him unwaveringly. Then it yawned, showing sharp teeth and fangs.

It started to wash its face with its paw.

"They are the reason I am here, in this camp." Gilla said. "They were born the night of the Sacrifice and exposed to the power that was released by that pillar of light." She knelt back on her heels, and scratched the creature's head. "I am not a warrior-priest, but Wild Winds insisted that I travel with him when he saw how fast they were growing."

"They?" Cadr croaked.

"Six altogether," Gilla said, and gave a sharp whistle. "I call them warcats."

Five more large forms slunk into the tent, eyeing him and sniffing the air. And then a last, much smaller version, no bigger than a new-born babe. It had the same color fur, but its eyes were a watery yellow, with a mean look.

"Baby?" he asked.

"Life-bearer," Gilla said. "It came from the land of the Sacrifice and his Token-Bearer. He called it a 'cat'."

"That is not a cat," Cade whispered. "And how did something so small birth those?" He went up on his elbows, but that was too much. His vision grayed out, and he sagged back on the pallet.

"I know, I know," Gilla said, reaching for a blanket and covering him. "No one else understands it either. Sleep. You are safe, warrior."

"Cadr," Cadr closed his eyes. "My name is—"

"Cadr," Gilla said. "Sleep. We will watch and guard."

He gave her a nod, not that he had any choice as his tiredness claimed him.

Movement then, and a long warm body stretched out beside him, making a low grumbling sound with every breath. He shifted, fearing—

"No," Gilla said. "That's good."

Cadr yawned, past the point of caring if the creature ate him or not. He stretched and then let the darkness take him, listening as the rumbling faded into his sleep.

* * * * *

"If she not move, arms die. Legs die." Hanstau stood in the entrance to the tent, determined to make himself understood. He waved his hands and spoke slowly in his broken Plains.

The two guards just looked at him.

Hanstau huffed. Trying to explain the idea of atrophy with simple one syllable words was not the easiest task.

"They will not free me," Reness said from behind him.

Hanstau looked back at her, grimacing in sympathy. Naked, bound hand and foot with leather ties to wooden stakes pressed into the ground, there was no way for her to move or flex. She had to be uncomfortable as all hell, and yet never once had he heard a complaint over the last few days they'd been housed together.

In many ways, she reminded him of his late wife. Stoic, calm, but Fleure had never had such a biting wit, nor would have borne the lack of clothing well.

Modesty was not an issue with Firelanders, but still. And while Hanstau had tried to ease the binds, tried to keep Reness clean, this had gone too far.

"It's been days. This is intolerable," he said, and turned back to the guards. "She must move, and clean, and eat or she will die."

Reness spoke then, hopefully translating to get the idea through their thick heads.

The guards considered for a moment, then one shrugged and trotted off. The other motioned for Hanstau to go back into the tent.

He huffed, and did so, letting the flap fall.

"I explained," Reness said. "Although I doubt it will accomplish much."

"Worth a try," Hanstau frowned at the naked woman, focusing on her wounded leg. He knelt by her side. "If they will let you walk and bathe, we can see about—"

The tent flap was yanked back, and Antas strode in.

Hanstau stiffened.

The blond warrior seemed to fill the tent with his bulk, armor and weapons all gleaming. There might have been a degree of handsomeness about the man, but it was lost on Hanstau. He'd seen Antas cut down others without mercy; those small eyes held only cruelty and viciousness.

He gave Hanstau a crafty smile. "What does my Warprize ask of me?"

Reness sucked in a breath, but Hanstau was past caring. "That she be permitted to walk and bathe and eat," he said as simply as he could. "Or she dies."

Antas lost his smile, and considered Reness with a frown. To Hanstau's surprise, he gave a harsh nod, then started barking out commands.

The two guards entered, and were on Hanstau before he could raise a hand in defense. They forced him to his knees, his hands bound behind him, a blade at his throat.

Antas studied him. Hanstau snapped his mouth closed and glared back.

Antas smiled again, distinctly gloating. He knelt at Reness's side. "If no thea," he said. "Then no need, Warprize." He paused, staring at Reness. "Understand?"

"Yes," Reness said, grim of tone and face.

Antas freed her hand, stood, and left the tent.

Reness groaned, using the free hand to remove the rest of her bonds. She moved stiffly, and slowly, but she hadn't lost any real strength that Hanstau could see. He shifted slightly, and the blade shifted with hm.

"Antas ordered—" Reness started.

"I got the gist of it," Hanstau said drily. "Go, walk and stretch. Bathe, if they will let you, and keep the wound clean."

"I will not linger," Reness said as she stood, took a few tentative, limping steps, and then left through the tent flap.

The guards, and the blade, remained at Hanstau's throat.

Hanstau grimaced, careful not to move. This didn't seem the most practical way to keep him compliant, but given Antas's savageness, it was probably wise on the part of the guards. He resigned himself to a wait, however long.

He could recite prayers to the Sun God, or perhaps that section of the Book of Xyson that listed—

The tent flap opened, and Hail Storm walked in.

A chill lanced up Hanstau's spine. He flinched, and regretted it. He was a Master Healer after all; nothing should faze him. But there was something wrong with this man, something in the depths of his eyes…

Hanstau wasn't alone. His guards felt it, too; they stiffened as the warrior-priest approached and towered over Hanstau.

But Hanstau wasn't going to take that, he glowered at the man, meeting those dark eyes with his own glare.

Hail Storm knelt, held out the stump of his arm, and unwrapped the bandage.

Hanstau stared at it. It looked good, considering that it had been cauterized to stop the bleeding. But he noticed something else.

The grass under Hail Storm was withering.

Hanstau blinked. They'd been in the tent for some time, so the grass wasn't the brightest shade a green to begin with, given the lack of sun. But the grass under this warrior-priest was curling, browning, even as—

Hail Storm said something harsh.

Hanstau jerked his eyes back up. "Yes," he said, not sure of the words, but understanding the tone. "It looks good."

Hail Storm grunted, his eyes narrowed as he began to re-wrap his stump with the dirty bandage.

"No," Hanstau said firmly. He wouldn't let the Dark One himself do that on his watch. "Use a clean one." He jerked his chin toward his satchel.

Hail Storm grunted again, and pulled it close to rummage within. This ordinarily would have upset Hanstau, but he was distracted by the browning grasses, and now that he thought about it… he squinted a bit.

There.

There was the glow he had seen when he'd been with Simus and Snowfall. The power that Wild Winds had warned him of. It too was there, in the ground, and it flowed away from Hail Storm's presence.

Hanstau became aware that Hail Storm was studying him as he tied off the fresh bandage.

Hanstau noted the signs that the fever had broken, and that the infection in the arm had cleared. The man looked healthy overall. Almost too healthy for someone who had lost a limb.

Hail Storm stood, and Hanstau sucked in another breath. The knife at his belt; the blade was glowing with a purplish-black rage.

Hanstau yanked his gaze away, and focused on the foot of one of his guards. That made no sense; daggers had no emotions. But Hanstau could almost feel the anger in the knife throbbing from across the room. It was as if the dagger pulsed with power. Power about to be used.

Hanstau looked up.

Hail Storm was considering him with a slight smile. He placed his stump against the dagger hilt, and with the other he clenched a fist.

Every muscle in Hanstau's body froze. He couldn't move, couldn't breathe, as if he were clenched in the fist, helpless...

The guards each stepped back, removing the blade from Hanstau's throat. He could feel its absence, but for his life he couldn't move, couldn't take his eyes off Hail Storm.

Whose smile was that much more satisfied.

Panic flooded through Hanstau, and he would have thrashed against the restraint. But he'd no control, and no air, and his vision grayed—

Hail Storm eased his fist open the slightest bit.

Hanstau sucked in the air his body craved, his chest heaving. He still couldn't move, but at least—

Hail Storm tilted his head, and made the slightest gesture with his fist.

To Hanstau's horror, his own head moved in a bow of submission.

He knelt there, unable to move. A deep shiver of fear wracked him, and a cold sweat broke out over every inch of his skin. His breath came in desperate pants. He was helpless, no control, no power.

Over him, Hail Storm laughed.

As suddenly as it had happened, it was gone. Hanstau found himself on his side, alone in the tent. Hands still bound, tears drying on his face. They were gone, the guards, Hail Storm. He closed his eyes in thanks for that.

The tent flap stirred, and he lifted his head just enough to see that it was Reness, naked and wet from her bath.

"I got the bandage wet—" a gasp and she was at his side. Hanstau could feel the warmth of her body against his. "What happened?" She asked as she untied his hands. He couldn't seem to get a breath. His entire body felt cold, numb, and lifeless.

Reness gathered him up, held him close. "Hanstau?"

He clung to her, like a babe to his mother, trembling.

"Breathe," Reness said, her voice the barest whisper in his ear. "Listen to my voice, breathe with my words. Fear is your enemy," she chanted.

Hanstau tried to focus.

"Fear holds you still when you need to move," Reness continued, but Hanstau clutched her tighter as the memory replayed.

"Hail Storm," he whispered, and a shudder ran through him again.

Reness hugged him tighter. "Tell me," she said.

"I am a Master Healer," Hanstau hated the cracks in his voice, but he had to force out the words. "He should not be able—"

"I am the Eldest Elder Thea," Reness admitted. "He makes my skin crawl. Tell me."

Hanstau did, managing to calm even as he forced out the words.

Reness's arms tightened around him as he finished speaking, and she took her own shuddering breath. "They always claimed to have strange powers," she said. "They are evil."

"No, not all," Hanstau sat in the circle of her arms, and swallowed hard as he thought his way through his fear. "Snowfall, Wild Winds," he looked to Reness, to see if she remembered them. "They did not have this feel to them. And the glow embraced Snowfall." He shook his head. "There is something very different about Hail Storm."

"We will find a way," Reness said.

"And if we can't?" Hanstau asked softly. "If he takes control of my body?"

Reness released him, settled back, and looked him in the eye. "I will send you to the snows before that happens," she growled.

"Kill me?"

"Kill you." she nodded.

Hanstau choked out a laugh, finding the determination in her eyes oddly reassuring. "It may be the only way to escape him," he said ruefully.

"I would prefer another way," Reness said.

Hanstau looked down at his hands. Snowfall and Wild Winds had said it was dangerous to experiment with the power he could see.

Maybe 'dangerous' was exactly what they needed.

CHAPTER SEVEN

"They spoke to you of the old paths?" Eldest Essa looked at Joden in shock, then his face twisted into anger. "It's madness, is what it is," he growled, staring down the rise behind Joden at the Ancient's tent. "Madness."

"Who are they?" Joden asked, looking over his shoulder at the large tent, standing alone against the Plains.

"Idiots," Essa growled. He spun on his heel, and stomped up the rise.

Joden followed

"That ritual kills," Essa continued. "And now? Wyverns fill the skies, the Council is sundered, and magic has returned to the Plains. They want what they have always demanded. Why not just take a torch to the withered grass in the dry season to see what happens? Pah," Essa stopped at the top of the rise to take a breath.

Joden stopped beside him. In the valley below them were gathered the other warrior-priests, all turning to look, questions in their eyes.

"Those *bracnects* would lure you to your death," Essa said.

Joden glanced back and then sucked in a breath. "The tent. It's gone."

He blinked again, and stared to be sure, but the tent was gone, with nary a trace to show it had ever existed.

"Every time," Essa didn't turn, didn't even seem surprised. "Every stinking time." He took a deep, slow breath. "I need kavage." He strode off, calling to the Singers. "Kavage," he commanded and kept walking, leaving Joden to follow behind.

Quartis appeared by his side. "He's always in a foul temper after he speaks with them," he said softly. "It doesn't help that when he was attacked he lost his tent and gear as well."

"Ah," Joden remembered the Eldest Elder's large tent, overflowing with trunks, clothes and weapons. "All of that lost?"

"He was lucky to escape with his life," Quartis said. "Come. We've work to do. We will put that dung you gathered to good use, yes?"

* * * * *

I call this Council of Singers to senel. Let our truths be known. Let our songs be shared." Essa sat on a gurtle pad, surrounded by sixteen other Singers that fanned out around him.

Joden stood, facing them all. He tried for calm, tried to remain standing straight and confident before them.

His stomach fluttered.

"This is the time when Singers gather," Essa continued. He looked calmer, stronger, every inch the Eldest Elder. "The Trials for Warlord are complete. The various armies move to war. This is our time to exchange news and truths. To sing old songs and new. And to consider new candidates before we too scatter on our chosen paths." Essa's face was unreadable. "As is our tradition, the candidates are presented to the Ancients, who offer blessing and then disappear into the grasses after dispensing their wisdom."

Joden blinked. Essa's face might be blank, but his tone was withering.

"But here, in this Season, with this candidate, the only candidate," Essa's voice grew dryer. "They decided to speak to him. Alone."

Eyes widened, heads turned, but there was only the crackle of the fires to be heard.

"They spoke to him?" Quartis broke the silence.

"Alone," Essa repeated.

Now all eyes were focused on Joden.

"They placed no restrictions on me," Joden offered.

"Tell us, then," Essa commanded. "Tell us what passed between you and the Ancients."

Joden did. He started from the moment Essa left the tent, and didn't soften the words the Ancients had spoken about the Eldest Elder.

He ended with the chant and the reference to Essa's ruffled feathers. His last words floated out into the evening air and were met only with silence.

"That's more than they have ever told me," Essa's voice was rough.

The deeper silence that followed let Joden work up his courage to ask, "Who are they?"

Head shakes all around.

"We do not know," Essa said. "Those old *bracnect* have tortured three Eldest Elders with their silence and killed more than that with their talk of 'old paths'. Denying us the songs only they know, and their knowledge of the past. Perhaps they were Eldest Elders in their time."

"They didn't have…" Joden stopped himself, thinking back. "They didn't have the Singer tattoos. But now that I think on it—"

Quartis nodded. "The tent is shadowed and dark, their skin wrinkled and mottled with age spots."

"Sexless, but not ageless, no, not them." Essa shuddered. "I would fall on my sword before I would let that happen to me."

"What is the 'old path'?" Joden asked.

"None have attempted the old path since I became Eldest Elder," Essa said. "The price is too high. Who can say if their songs are worth the price?"

"Has anyone ever heard the tales of the Chaosreaver and his Warprize?" Joden asked. "Or that they stripped away the magic from the Plains?"

More silence. Essa rubbed his hand over his face.

Para spoke from the back, "Usually when a Singer candidate is presented to them, they mumble something, bless you in the name of the elements, and then they seem to fade off to sleep." She seemed angry. "Why did they speak to you?'

"Why do they do anything," Essa growled. "It matters not. The ritual they speak of kills. And now? With wyverns flying, this odd power returned to the Plains, what will happen to any that walk that path? No one knows." He took a deep breath. "So, Joden of the Hawk. You will begin the Trials of a Singer tomorrow at dawn. You will be tested for four days, one for each of the elements. You will be tested as a warrior, as a judge, and as a Singer.

"You will stand before us all, and show us your skills in combat," Quartis flashed Joden a grin.

"We will present conflicts, and you will show us how you would resolve them in accordance with our ways." Thron spoke up.

"You will dance," Para spoke as well.

"Most of all, you will sing, old songs and songs of your own creation. For four days and four nights." Essa said. "After which, if you are worthy, we will tattoo your eye and you will be a Singer of the Plains."

"But if I fail these Trials—" Joden began.

"You have been told our secrets," Essa said. "And if you were to fail, we would slay you to keep those truths safe."

"Few fail," Quartis said quietly. "We do not share our truths with those that are unworthy."

Essa gave him a glare.

"It is no less than a truth," Quartis shrugged. "We have observed Joden, and know that he has it within him. The debate that rages about him is—"

"Enough," Essa barked.

"And the 'old path'?" Joden asked. "The chant they—"

Essa stood, drew himself up, strong and dignified. "Joden,

before those gathered here, I would offer you this truth. I may not agree with what you and Simus and Keir would do, or how you would bring changes to our ways. But for all that, I would not have you go to your death."

Essa turned then, to face the gathered Singers. "For that would silence his truth and that is not the way of the Plains, nor the way of the Singers of the Plains. If he is worthy, he is entitled to stand in our midst and have his truths considered with ours."

A murmur arose from the group, some in agreement, some clearly not.

Essa turned back and faced Joden. "The Trials of a Singer are exhausting, invigorating and challenging. But the warriors who emerge as Singers serve the Plains with their hearts and souls. As will you."

"And the 'old path'," Joden pressed for an answer one more time.

Essa's eyes narrowed and his mouth grew grim.

Quartis glanced at Essa, then spoke. "The challenges are the same. Except we clear a challenge circle and—"

"You are tethered within," Essa interrupted, clearly furious. "Naked, but for your weapons. Tied by the ankle with a thin strip of leather to a stake in the middle of the circle. The leather is decorated along its length with beads so that we will know it, and know if it is broken. You are tested for four days and four nights, but there is no food, no water, and as little sleep as possible.

"And when you collapse and cannot be roused," Essa spat. "When you do not answer to the death ritual that we conduct, you are wrapped in a cloth shroud and the leather of your tent, and buried within the earth. Buried deep, as the dead are, and left there until the dawn."

"'Offer your body; be buried in earth'," Joden murmured.

Essa glared at Joden. "Do you understand, Joden? We are told that when you emerge from the earth, when we pull you free from the grave, you will emerge as a full Singer, with the beaded leather cord around your ankle and the tattoo of a bird's wing around your eye.

"Except you won't," Essa continued. "We will dig you up, and find you dead. The ritual kills."

"Even now," Joden asked. "With magic returned to the land?"

"I do not know," Essa said simply.

"But the choice is mine," Joden said.

Essa crossed his arms over his chest, and looked out over the Plains. "Yes," he finally said. "The choice is yours."

Joden nodded, crossed his arms over his chest, and rocked on his heels, considering the grass under his feet. To fail was a swift journey to the snows. But to succeed? What songs would he learn, that no other knew? How much stronger would his voice be in the Councils of the Elders? It would benefit all, Singers, the Plains. Simus. Keir. But the risk—

"This choice does not have to be made today," Essa started, but a few others shook their heads.

"The Trials for Warlord started late, thanks to the warrior-priests," Quartis said.

"Even now, the armies move," Thron reminded them. "And there is Antas as well to consider. Sooner is better than later."

Essa sat back down. "They are right, of course. Speak, Joden."

Joden looked at his hands, then raised his head. "Many of you know that I chose to deny mercy to Simus of the Hawk when he lay injured on the field before Xy. I tried to staunch his wound, and as a result we were taken captive by the enemy."

"This is known," Essa acknowledged with a nod of his head.

"Mercy is the way of the Plains, when a warrior falls and cannot rise," Joden said. "But when my friend and tentmate lay bleeding at my feet, I could not bring my knife to bear." He took a breath. "That is not our way, not the way of the Plains, and yet, I could not do it."

"That is known," Para said. "And counted against you."

"As it should," Joden nodded to Para. "Here I am, asking to be admitted to the ranks of those that hold us to our ways, and yet I broke those ways.

"Because of our capture, Keir of the Cat and his Warprize met." Joden spread his hands. "But the Warprize thought herself a slave, a thing to be owned and controlled. Because of her lack of knowledge of our ways, and of our past, she didn't see the honor Keir offered."

"Until you told her," Essa said.

"The Ancients have knowledge of what has been. And that knowledge might aid us to determine what will be," Joden said. "What our future, what the future of the Plains will be.

"How better to silence those that would oppose me as Singer," Joden said. "Then to take the old paths? How better to show my love of our people then to risk death to learn what the Ancients have withheld?"

"How better to show me up as lacking before our people," Essa snarled.

There was pain in Essa's eyes, an old pain borne of rejection. Joden bowed his head in respect. "That would not be my purpose, Eldest Elder."

Quartis spoke up. "Eldest Elder, I know this touches a nerve for you. But I have often heard you say that you wished to know what the Ancients have withheld. It is no reflection on you. How many Eldest Elders have they withheld the information from?"

"And now they offer it to Joden," Essa said, his eyes hooded and dark. "If he takes the old paths."

"Yet why do they speak to him?" Para complained. "I intend no offense, Joden, when I say there have been better candidates."

"To our eyes," Thron noted. "But not, apparently, to theirs."

Quartis shrugged. "Who can say? But they have offered.

It's a chance."

Joden went to one knee before Essa, and bowed his head. "Eldest Elder, I ask to take the old path to Singer. I do this in full knowledge of the risks involved." He lifted his head, and met Essa's gaze. I do this for the Singers, and for the people of the Plains.

For a long moment there was no sound, no breath. Essa just stared into Joden's eyes. The Eldest Elder's face was a mask of stone. But Essa's eyes dropped, and he bowed his head.

"So be it," Essa's voice floated over the entire group. "We will begin at dawn."

* * * * *

Eldest Elder Essa watched as the challenge circle was prepared, cleared of the sod, the dirt packed under the feet of his Singers.

He watched as the stake was planted in the center; as the Singers gathered to add trinkets and beads to the leather thong.

He watched as Joden emerged from the grasses, freshly bathed and naked, to stand in the center of the circle.

He watched as Joden gave away his gear and saddle, all of his possessions. Joden pressed the wyvern horn into Quartis's hands.

He himself knelt to bind Joden's ankle. He would allow no other the honor.

A stool was brought, and Essa sat and watched as Joden faced his challenges, strong and proud, fighting his opponents, resolving mock conflicts, and singing.

He fought to concentrate on Joden's performance. Not on Keir and Simus's reaction when informed of their friend's death. Not on the possible repercussions of the events of this day. He cleared his mind, and focused on the songs.

He fought his own battle as well, with hateful, jealous thoughts. Joden was strong and in his prime. The ache in Essa's chest had nothing to do with the loss of such a warrior and everything to do with his own loss. The pain grew stronger at the idea of Joden gaining the songs he had so long been denied.

Joden sang as he did everything, with an underlying joy. Essa had known from the beginning, from the first time he'd heard the man's voice, that he was a Singer.

And a crafter of songs. Joden sang of the Warprize and her Warlord, and the love between them. He sang of the successful four-ehat hunt, with the disgusting scent of the musk, and the glory of the kill and the celebration after.

And he sang of the ache in his heart over his conflict between the old and the new ways. Of ending traditions. Of seeking new ones.

Essa watched as Joden fought and sang and judged. And when the young man fell asleep on his feet, Essa watched as he was prodded awake and they demanded more songs.

And on the third day Essa watched as Joden staggered, deprived of water, deprived of food, shuffling his feet in a mockery of a dance as he croaked a last song. As dulled eyes and stumbling words spoke of hopes turned to exhaustion.

Watched as Joden collapsed, face down in the earth at last, at dusk on the last day.

Watched as Quartis entered the circle, and grasped Joden's lax right hand. "Joden," he called loudly. "Joden of the Hawk."

The other Singers were gathered at the circle's edge. Essa rose from his chair, and they respectfully cleared a path for him.

"Joden," Quartis held Joden's left hand in his own. Essa saw his knuckles whiten as he squeezed it.

There was silence as all watched and waited.

"Joden of the Hawk," Quartis called as he moved down to his left foot.

There was no response.

Finally, Quartis took Joden's right foot, putting his hand over where the tether was tied. "Joden of the Hawk," he called out again.

Nothing. Joden's face was lax, his body limp. If he breathed, Essa couldn't see it.

"We will see you again, Warrior," Quartis rose. "Beyond the snows."

Essa stepped forward then, pulling the leather thong from the stake, and wrapping it around Joden's ankle. As he gripped the man's ankle, he felt the barest pulse of life. "Bear this as witness," he said. "As you walk the old path." He rose then, gesturing. "Bring him," he said. "We will give him to the earth."

Many hands lifted Joden's body, and they carried him to the grave already waiting.

There were gasps as they drew close. There beside the grave was a folded bundle of light, white cloth, lengths and lengths, enough to wrap a body many times over.

The Ancients. It had to have been. Essa glanced around, but there was no sign of their be-damned-to-the-snows tent.

Essa gestured, and the others spread the cloth and used it to wrap the body over and over. They put the shrouded corpse within one of the small collapsed leather tents. Once done, they lowered the tent and the body it contained into the grave, and gathered at the edges.

Essa drew a breath. "Death of fire, birth of earth," he started.

Four Singers started to fill in the grave.

"The fire warmed you," the Singers chanted, their voices muted in the night air. "We thank the elements."

"Death of earth, birth of water," he chanted.

More earth, pushed in, covering the leather shroud.

"The earth supported you," the Singers chanted. "We thank the elements.

"Death of water, birth of air," Essa poured his grief into his voice, letting it soar out above them.

Still the Singers worked, on their knees. The level of earth rose almost level to the grass. Essa could almost feel the weight of the dirt on his own skin.

"The waters sustained you," the Singers chanted, their voices muted in the night air. "We thank the elements."

"Death of air, birth of fire," he chanted the final verse.

"The air filled you," came the final response. "We thank the elements."

The grave was filled.

They stood silent for long moments.

"Dawn is not far off," Quartis looked up at the stars.

"Far enough," Essa said bitterly. "Bring drums," he told the others. "He may hear, and know that we keep watch."

"He has a chance," Quartis reminded him as the others drifted off.

Essa shrugged, and settled down to keep watch over the mound as the stars danced above. Not-thinking on what would be. Not thinking on what the dawn would bring.

Around him others gathered, drumming a slow and steady beat.

And when the first faint hint of light broke on the horizon, his hands joined the others as they frantically dug into the earth. No chanting now. Just hard breathing as they all worked.

The dirt was cold and heavy. "His head," Essa commanded, and they centered their focus there.

The earth moved slowly, mounding to the side as they finally reached the leather cover. Quartis tugged it back against the heavy, moist dirt.

No white shroud. No Joden.

"He curled up," Essa gasped, and they dug again, clearing and tugging until the entire leather cover was pulled back.

Essa sat back on his heels, and rubbed his eyes.

The grave was empty.

Joden's body was not there.

CHAPTER EIGHT

Impulsive was one thing; stupid was another. Amyu was not stupid.

She climbed the rest of that day, up mountain paths as high as she could before searching for a place to sleep. In the fading light she found a place, protected by pine trees and a slight overhang of rock.

There was a small circle of stones under the overhang. There were cold ashes in the center and it clearly had not been used for some time. She made a very small fire, more for comfort than anything else, and sat to sort her supplies out, and think things through.

The small lantern was clever, just a metal cylinder with a door and holes throughout. The curved metal bowl at the bottom could burn wood or maybe even animal fat. There was a small stub of a fat candle; she'd have to conserve that for as long as possible.

She'd need food as well, and dug through the pack to check what she had. Bread, gurt, dried meat. A jar of sweetfat, a whet stone, and dried bloodmoss. A small sack of kavage beans, thank the elements. She'd hunt when she could, and eat lightly.

She untied the leather that sealed the jar, lifted it and sniffed. The sweet scent of Plains grasses filled her lungs. It eased a tightness in her shoulders that she hadn't been aware of. She tightly sealed it up again, and placed it back in the pack.

Maybe she should establish a base camp? Amyu chewed on her lip, thinking. It would be good to be able to cache food and gear, with a secure place to sleep. But keeping everything with her gave her more freedom to roam further out.

Both ways offered benefits. She'd see what the next day brought, and then decide.

Her sword and dagger were sharp, and the blankets she'd brought would be warm enough. She had a waterskin, and basic cooking gear. Not that hard to spit a small animal over a fire.

She tore off a piece of dried meat, and ate as she packed the rest away. Her small fire flickered as she took a long drink and stared into the flames.

Now, as to her prey. For in truth, that was what she was doing. Stalking prey she had no knowledge of and had never seen.

So she'd treat it as any hunt. Airions were bird and horse in appearance. But all animals leave trails, so there would be droppings, and feathers shed. Claw marks perhaps on trees and stones. Maybe they marked their territory.

And the bird part, it would have to hunt. She closed her eyes and pictured the tapestry in her mind. That beak. As much as it had a horse's head, that beak meant it was a meat eater. Which meant it was a hunter. It probably hunted from the sky, like a hawk.

Amyu pulled at the meat, and popped another piece in her mouth, chewing slowly.

The trees here were smaller, stunted, not as large as the ones in the valley. Unlikely that the creatures lived in trees, but she couldn't ignore the possibility. 'Up' was something she'd have to remember.

Usek had warned of 'bears and cats', so she'd have to watch for predators.

The bigger question? Where to start.

Amyu finished the meat, and took a long drink of water. At least that was no worry; she could hear water running nearby in the quiet of the growing dusk.

A yawn caught her off guard, and a wave of weariness followed. She spread out her blankets, stripped off her leathers and weapons and piled them neatly beside her. Her sword and dagger came into the bedding with her, close at hand.

She settled in, folding her cloak as a pillow. It felt good, the gurtle pads beneath her cushioned the ground and she'd the pleasure of two blankets; the traditional gurtle fur of the Plains, and a warm woolen blanket of Xy. She wiggled about a bit, enjoying the feel of the cloth against her skin as her body heated her bedroll.

The fire flickered down to coals. She watched it with weary eyes.

She probably should do as she was taught, and remain battle ready since she was alone in unknown territory. But she shrugged off the idea. Being as high on the mountain as she was, it was unlikely that an attack would come.

The boys had said that Kalisa always gestured at this path when she told her tales. She would follow it as high as it went, and start there.

It was a hunt, just like any other.

But a wave of joy passed through her, and she grinned at the dying coals. She might be mad, but it was her madness, her truth. She was where she wanted to be.

She drifted off, and dreamed of blue skies and the beating of feathered wings.

* * * * *

Five days later, she'd lost some of that joy.

Amyu sagged down by her small fire, in another cave she'd found fairly early in the afternoon. The storm clouds had appeared over her head with little warning, another aspect of mountains she didn't care for. But she'd enough warning to gather firewood and water, and made her small camp in this cave. She'd checked it thoroughly, but it was dry and empty, thank the elements. With plenty of wood, she set out dry, long sticks that would break if stepped on. If anyone or anything approached, she'd have warning.

The rain started before she had the fire going.

She took out beans from her precious stash and ground them for kavage. She'd earned it this day. She set the small pot in the fire, and then stripped off her leathers. The stones were cold under her rump as she examined her leg.

The gouge ran the length of her calf. Not deep, but painful. Amyu took some water and started to wash it clean.

Mountains weren't flat; no single step was on even ground. Mountains had rocks that moved under your feet, and underbrush that tangled you and blocked your path. Young trees, sticky with sap and rough bark, that you had to make your way around. Old, dead trees with branches that tore through leather and ripped your skin.

And the wind… Amyu lifted her head as the wind picked up outside, moaning and sighing like the dying.

She drew a deep breath, and tried to ignored the sounds. She'd never been this alone before. On the Plains, there were always fellow warriors around, sharing tents and fires. There was little privacy, and one was rarely this alone. This isolated. Even in Xy, in the castle, you might be alone in a room, but there were sounds of others around you.

Here, the silence was what surrounded her. Silence except for the moaning of the wind, which seemed a constant in the mountains.

Amyu shivered, then grimaced as she rinsed her leg. Thanks to the foresight of the Warprize, she had bloodmoss in her pack. It would be a simple thing to heal.

The tear in her leathers was another thing. She'd nothing to repair that with.

Steam rose from the kavage pot. Amyu shifted it a bit deeper into the fire. Kavage would help, with her headache and her mood, and her overall soreness. Everything hurt. Her feet, her ankles, her hands, still sticky with some of that sap, and rough where she'd climbed over rocks.

She'd no luck hunting, and with the rain there'd be no meat for her meal this night. Her supplies were running low. She'd eat the last of the bread and hope for better luck early.

There was game, but the mountain rabbits were fast. The goats she'd seen, balanced on the sheerest of edges, had just looked at her with disdain and climbed impossibly higher.

She'd not thought to bring a bow.

Amyu pulled her leather trous over, and looked at the tear. She could cut strips and rig a sling. Skies knew there were enough rocks around for her to throw. But she didn't want to widen that tear. Maybe she could sacrifice a strap from her pack.

Amyu shoved the pack away, her headache made all the worse for thinking about making a decision. The golden sparkles at the corners of her eyes glittered brightly. She resisted the urge to rub at the itchiness. That only made it worse.

The kavage was at a rolling boil. She used the edge of her blanket to pick it up, blowing at comforting steam as it rose to her face. The warm, bitter scent was a comfort all by itself.

Because, if truth be told, she needed comfort. She'd seen no sign of airions. Not on land, not in caves, not in the sky. She'd seen scat, and tree scrapings, and feathers, and tufts of fur, but nothing that she could justify calling signs of her prey.

She sipped her kavage, and the liquid stung her tongue. No comfort there, then, or in the truth. Amyu felt her confidence wane as surely as the moon.

She heaved a sigh, set the kavage aside, and dug through her pack to pull out the bloodmoss. See to her wounds, drink her kavage, and then sleep.

The sun would bring another day, and she would start again.

* * * * *

The crack of a stick outside.

Terror woke her.

Amyu rolled out of the blankets, crouching, her sword and dagger in hand, before she was even fully awake. She froze then, her heart racing.

There was something outside the cave. Something large.

The darkness within the deep cave was absolute. She couldn't see her hands, her weapons or beyond. She stilled her breathing, straining her senses, listening.

Something shifted, snuffed at the air. Elements, there was more than one.

Her fright got the best of her. She longed to put her back to the cave wall, wherever it was, but she didn't dare move or give away her position. Her heart thumped hard in her chest, and cold sweat rolled down her spine.

Light. She needed light. But to set her weapons down, to fumble with flint and striker was unthinkable.

Another stick cracked, as if the creatures were gathering themselves up to rush her.

Light, her mind screamed, but she crouched low, frozen in fear.

Small golden sparkles started to gather at her feet.

Sweat dripped into her eyes as she watched, seeing a narrow bit of glow that darted out, in a long line. It fled across the floor and encircled the lantern.

Something deep within her cried out in silent relief, as the motes flowed and flowed into the lantern. She could see her hands, see the blades, see—

One of the creatures snorted, drawing her attention back to the entrance. Deep, deep breaths, getting her scent.

Amyu's heart leaped to her throat; she swallowed hard even as she braced herself.

The glow brightened, filling the lantern to overflowing, boiling up and—

With a roar, the animal charged within. Amyu caught a glimpse of small, cruel eyes, and lips pulled back along its long snout, white fangs flashing.

She brought her blade up, screaming her own defiance and anger and rage—

The lantern exploded, hurling her back, the glare blinding her—

When her vision cleared, there was nothing to be seen of the creature. The entire cave seemed to faintly glow gold.

Amyu just lay sprawled on the floor, trying to breathe, trying to understand. It seemed forever before she could get herself to move, before she finally gathered her legs under her and rose, breathing like a spent horse, her heart pounding. Cold sweat dripped down her spine.

The lantern lay on the stone, its sides bulged out, its little metal door broken off one of the hinges. With a trembling hand, she reached out to right it, and it wobbled where it sat.

Her sword was close, and her hand shook as she gripped it.

The glow of the walls started to fade, ebbing slightly and then more as she watched.

She dropped down by her fire pit, and took up the flint and steel, setting the tinder on fire. Just as well. The glow was gone now.

There was no sound of the creature, but for the life of her she couldn't bring herself to go outside.

Still trembling, she wrapped herself in her cloak and blankets, weapons close. She sat and fed the fire until the first faint light of dawn touched the mouth of the cave. The birds started chirping. She could hear the rustling of small animals in the undergrowth.

But it was still a long time before her fear allowed her to move.

* * * * *

On the eve of the tenth day, Amyu stripped down and crawled under her blankets. She was aching and weary, and just wanted the feel of the gurtle blanket against her skin for this night.

She settled in, lying on her stomach, her arms as her pillows.

This cave was different than the others, at the head of a stream, with ledges on either side. She'd placed her bedroll close to the wall, and built her fire close by.

The fire was dying now, the flames fading into glowing coals. She'd built a small one just to warm her kavage, and give light for her meal. She'd learned the hard way to feed the fire all night. There'd been no other attacks, but she'd take no chances.

She put her head down, determined to keep her thoughts at bay, determined not to think about what lay ahead. She was warm, safe, and… she'd failed.

She twisted around then, struggling with the blankets, and finally laid on her back with a huff. 'A warrior faces the truth', she whispered to the rock over her head, barely glimpsed in the dying light.

The rock was silent and still, as if listening.

"I've plenty of water," she said aloud, and her voice echoed back. "I've flint and steel and tinder, enough to search a while longer. My gear is in good shape, and the weather seems to be holding."

The rock expressed no opinion.

"It's food," she admitted, more to herself than the rock. "The hunting here is sparse. I've had no luck, and my supplies are gone."

The rock stayed silent, waiting.

"And here is the truth," she spoke slowly, softly. "I don't think they are here." She swallowed hard, and felt her tears start. "Airions are myths, creatures of dreams. They don't exist."

The rock absorbed her whispered words.

"I've failed," she said, and saying it out loud made the pain of her admission that much worse. "In the morning, I'll break camp and head back down the mountain to Xy. Tell them all my truths. Ask if they will let me return."

She closed her eyes as the knot in her stomach grew. She wrestled back over onto her stomach, tugging the blankets this way and that, thoroughly frustrated, angry, tired, and scared.

She put her head down on her arms, and gave into the fear. Fear that the Warprize would reject her, that she'd be without a Tribe, without a people, without a purpose.

The flickering coals reflected on her dagger's blade, placed by her side with her sword.

There was always the choice of going to the snows.

But even in the instant she had the thought, she rejected it. Her life had meaning, and she'd not spill it here on cold stone to no purpose except to end her pain. Her death could have other uses, and she'd make it a good one.

The coals shifted, and she fed more wood to them. Once the fire was bright, she closed her eyes. She'd head down tomorrow, and face whatever awaited her there.

Warriors did not weep. There was no one to see, no one to comment, but still she resolved not to cry.

Later, much later, while the wind set the trees to swaying and whispering, she eventually not-cried herself to sleep.

In the morning, she used the cold water to bathe and scrub the dried tears from her face.

It had been a foolish dream; a child's dream. She'd no knowledge of the land or how to survive on her own here. She was lucky to have lived this long, and she was fairly certain she'd be reminded of that fact over and over.

At least she had tried. But that was cold comfort at best.

She filled the waterskin, rolled up the blankets, and packed her meager gear. It had taken her some time to come this high, but she'd been searching as she went. Going down would be fast, but she'd have to take care not to fall. She'd hunt as she went, that would help with the growling in her stomach.

She stepped out to find the sky above clear and blue in its beauty. The recent rains had caused the greens to seem greener somehow. She tried to appreciate what the elements had provided, but her failure sat in the hollow of her chest.

Best to be about it.

She stepped out on the path and the wind died down, leaving everything quiet and still. Even the birds seemed to—

A soft sound floated through the air. Someone singing.

Amyu frowned. The wind playing tricks again was her first thought, even as she turned in that direction. It wasn't possible, but—

A flutter of white caught the corner of her eye, and she focused, looking further up on the mountain. There, above her. There was a darkness, clearly the mouth of a cave.

The wind picked up, and there was a brief flutter of white again.

Amyu bit her lip. A bird? Or perhaps... feathers?

She should go down. There were no airions; she was on a fool's quest.

But what harm in one last cave? It wouldn't take more than an hour to climb up, and the delay would only come at the cost of her empty stomach.

She paused, holding her breath, listening hard.

There it was again.

The merest whisper of a song.

CHAPTER NINE

"Cadr," Gilla's voice pulled him from sleep.

Battle tense, Cadr gripped the hilt of his sword even before his eyes opened.

"No threat," Gilla said, although there was still tension in her voice. "Lightning Strike and the others are ready to offer Wild Winds's body to the flames."

The warmth that surrounded Cadr stirred and moved then, and two of the warcats rose to stand over him, stretching. Cadr tossed back the blankets to do the same, only to stifle a groan.

"I have kavage," Gilla offered.

Cadr nodded. He was stiff and sore, but other than that - he touched his throat, feeling the scar, but no discomfort. He swallowed, hard. No pain.

Thanks to the elements. And bloodmoss.

He rose to his knees, then to his feet, and stood for a moment to get his balance. Gilla's warcats head-butted him, rubbing against his bare legs, tails jauntily in the air.

"Not helping," Cadr muttered, as Gilla stifled a nervous laugh.

She offered the mug of kavage. He took it, then arched an eyebrow at her.

She shrugged at his silent question. "The others are upset. Their anger has grown as they have prepared Wild Wind's body for burial. Doesn't help that a storm has brewed up."

Cadr nodded, drinking deeply, then reached for his armor, only to hesitate. The pieces lay where he'd left them, caked with blood and dirt.

"Here." Gilla handed him a tunic and trous. "Use these."

He nodded, and dressed quickly.

Cadr could feel the crackle in the air when they emerged from the tent. It could have been the clouds that seethed above them, but Cadr had seen enough seasons of war to recognize warriors preparing for battle.

All eyes turned to regard him. The hair on Cadr's arms rose as he took in the angry stares.

Gilla stepped up beside him, and the warcats clustered around, stretching and raking at the grass with long claws. The small momma cat plopped down on Cadr's foot, and yawned.

Lightning Strike stepped forward. "Cadr," he stood stiffly, his voice formal. "I would not offer insult, but you were of the warriors of Simus of the Hawk, and have served Keir of the Cat. I know that there is no love of warrior-priests among—"

"Whatever was, was," Cadr interrupted Lightning Strike, looking him in the eye. He fought to keep his own temper in check. "I gave my sword oath to Simus of the Hawk, that is my truth. But then the night lit up with that pillar of light, and warrior-priests died. Simus of the Hawk listened to Wild Winds, and now walks with Snowfall at his side.

"As to what that means for the Plains, I do not know." Cadr continued. "But between you and I and those gathered here, let there be no mistrust. That is also my truth. I would exchange truth for truth, mourn the dead, and—" Cadr frowned, and clenched his fists. "I would have vengeance, for my charge was taken from me."

"On that, we agree." Lightning Strike relaxed, and there were nods from those around him. "I would offer thanks again," he said. "For bringing Wild Wind's body to us. To that end, let us offer you these," he gestured. Another warrior-priest stepped forward with a belt, a sheathed sword and dagger.

"My thanks." A sense of relief swept over him as he belted them on. "You should know that I was in no fit shape to make any decisions after the attack," Cadr said. "I was guided here, by one of the dead. A warrior, and tentmate."

Lightning Strike's eyes widened. "To have the aid of the dead for this. It means much."

Two of the warcats started to tussle in the grass.

"Join us, both of you," Lightning Strike gestured to where a platform had been raised. "We are about to give Wild Winds to the flames."

Cadr glanced over at the pyre below. Impressive it might be, but to burn a body one needed much more fuel. "Will it suffice?"

"It will," Lightning Strike said, and his tone was grim. "We await the return of those that went to gather more stargrass. They should be here shortly." He walked off, helping others to pile more grasses beneath the platform.

Cadr looked down at the small cat at his feet. She was staring up at him with unblinking eyes. She plopped over on her side, and showed her stomach.

"How small, to have borne such children," Cadr mused, and knelt to stroke the soft fur.

"I wouldn't," Gilla warned, but Cadr had already jerked back his fingers as the cat hissed, and lunged with claws extended. Deprived of her target, she leaped up and disappeared into the grass.

The large cats scrambled to their feet and followed. Cadr watched as they disappeared into the waist-high grass. He had the distinct feeling they were all amused.

He glanced up at Gilla. "Small but fierce," he said ruefully as he rose to his feet.

"You should see the large ones hunt," she said. "I swear they could pull down an ehat."

Cadr nodded absently, watching as the last of the warrior-priests-in-training appeared with sheaves of long grasses in their arms. "That isn't enough fuel to burn," he said softly, nodding at the platform where Wild Winds's body lay.

"I don't think—" Gilla stopped as Lightning Strike summoned them to join the circle around the platform. He waited until all were in place before he started to speak.

"May the elements hear my voice. May the people remember."

The response rose. "We will remember."

"Birth of fire," Lightning Strike began. "Death of air."

One of the warrior-priests held out a bowl, and blew on the coals within, feeding a few stems of grass that caused flames to leap up. A shiver of awe ran up Cadr's spine as he joined in the chant. A quick glance at Gilla showed she felt the same. Words and rituals taught by the theas resonated through him as the elements were invoked.

"Birth of water, death of earth."

Another warrior-priest held out a small bowl, dipping her fingers in and let water trickle down.

"Birth of earth, death of fire."

The third warrior-priest knelt, and crumbled a clod of dirt into the bowl in his other hand.

"Birth of air, death of water."

The fourth stepped forward. She too blew on coals, but the fuel she added caused a thin trail of smoke to rise up.

All four then bowed their heads to the platform and placed their bowls at their feet, rising to re-take their places in the circle.

"We gather tonight in remembrance of the dead." Lightning Strike's voice cracked. "All life perishes. This we know. Our bodies arise from the elements, and return to them when we fall. Our dead travel with us, until the snows."

Softly, the others began to chant. Cadr joined in, reciting the dance of the elements, as the theas had taught. "Death of earth, birth of water, death of water, birth of air, death of air, birth of fire, death of fire, birth of earth."

Tears ran down Lightning Strike's face. "We grieve for what we lost. But our loss is as a result of betrayal, by those who themselves are of the Plains.

Cadr hesitated, as the chant became harsher, angrier. He exchanged another glance with Gilla, but she was taken aback as well. This was not the normal.

The warrior-priest with the bowl of flame, took it up again, and set flame to the pile of dried grasses under the platform. He returned to his place as the flames mounted. Cadr frowned. There wasn't enough fuel to—

"We return Wild Winds to the elements." Lightning Strike was screaming now, his voice hard and broken. He lifted his face and voice to the sky, raising his hands. The others did as well. "We grieve, but we will also seek to avenge."

"Death of earth, birth of water," the chant was hard, fierce, and the hairs on the back of Cadr's neck rose. The storm clouds above roiled, as if in response.

Lightning Strike's eyes were closed, all of their eyes were closed, as if they were concentrating, summoning the new powers. But the chant continued, speeding up now, faster and faster.

"—death of water, birth of air, death of air—"

Cadr fought the urge to step back, to flee a danger that was unnamed and unknown. The flicker of fire drew his attention to the mound below the platform. The flames were growing, changing—

"— birth of fire," screamed the voices as one.

White hot fire roared up, blinding with a flash that burned the eyes.

Cadr raised his hand to ward his eyes, blinking as vision returned. The platform was gone, the body, gone. The ground below was bare and scorched, and tiny wisps of smoke rose from the soil.

But the rage still lingered.

"Aid us," Lightning Strike cried out, and his voice echoed oddly against the clouds.

Cadr stepped back now, a wary eye on the clouds, on the warrior-priests. Gilla retreated with him, both of them instinctively moving slowly so as not to attract attention. Cadr had been there when Wild Winds had warned Hanstau of the dangers of this power. If that rage fell on he and Gilla, they had no defenses.

"Aid us," Lightning Strike cried out again. The clouds above him lit up with streaks of light. "By the powers that were released by the Sacrifice, aid us to avenge—"

A yowling sound cut through his words.

"What—?" Lightning Strike looked down.

The mother cat was seated at his feet, her tail wrapped around her feet, her shoulders hunched, her head down. She was yowling, a long low mournful cry.

The cry was echoed as the six warcats rose from the tall grass, all around the circle, as if copying the humans.

The air crackled as the clouds rolled above, and the wind picked up.

Gilla stopped, her eyes wide, reaching out to catch Cadr's arm. "That sound," she gasped. "Like when the Sacrifice fell from—"

The air over the earth swirled and tore, and a circle of white appeared and expanded. The inside glowed, and rippled like the side of a tent in a storm.

With a cry, the small mother cat ran forward, a blur against the grasses. Cadr saw her leap into the white, disappearing into the glow.

Gilla cried out in dismay.

"Take cover," Lightning Strike called out and everyone scattered into the taller grass. Even the warcats, who showed no sign of following their life-bearer.

Gilla took a step toward the portal, but Cadr pulled her flat beside him. "What are you doing?" He hissed.

"I think—"

A man stepped through the portal, carrying a saddle on his back, and packs over both arms.

Cadr's eyes widened. He was big, black-skinned like Simus, but broader. Bald, with bushy white eyebrows like caterpillars. He wore only trous, and his chest was covered with ritual scarring.

"Home!" he boomed in the language of the Plains. He dropped his burdens at his feet and spread his arms wide. "That which was lost is now found. The wanderer has returned."

Behind him stepped another man, younger, tanned with long brown hair. He wore tunic and trous, but carried the same saddle and packs that spoke of someone used to travel. But that quick impression was all that Cadr had time for.

Lightning Strike rose from the grass, lifted a bow, and loosed an arrow at the pair.

The older man jerked his head, but the younger was faster. His burden dropped, he raised a hand—

—and the arrow dropped to the ground.

Others rose, launching their own missiles, all of which bounced off something surrounding the strangers. With a snapping sound the portal closed behind them, but still the young man held out his hand and the shield held.

Lightning Strike raised his hands, and looked up at the clouds. "I call—"

"No," Gilla stood, exposing herself, her hands held out. "The portal, it was like the one the Sacrifice came through." She stared intently at the strangers as she took another step forward.

Lightning Strike lowered his hands slightly. "Who are you, stranger?"

Cadr watched as those thick white eyebrows rose. "Such is

the hospitality of the Plains, now? Strange greetings."

"Strange times," Gilla took another step. "I am Gilla of the Snake."

The man smiled broadly at her, while keeping a careful eye on Lightning Strike. "Well met, Gilla of the Snake. Ezren Silvertongue spoke of you. I am Obsidian Blade and, this," gesturing at his young companion. "This is Rhys of the Black Hills, also known as Mage."

Gilla narrowed her eyes. "How do we know your words are true?"

Obsidian Knife laughed. "Ezren said you would doubt. He said to say that he held Cosana as she breathed her last."

"You are as you say." Gilla relaxed.

Obsidian Blade folded his arms over his chest. "Now it is your turn, Warrior. What did Ezren tell Cosana as she died?"

"A story," Gilla's voice shook. "Of how the Lady of Laughter lured the Lord of Light to her tent."

"You are as you say," Obsidian Blade bowed his head at her. "Ezren said to share this truth, that he and his token-bearer are well and bonded." He flashed a grin. "I doubt that he will be so pleased at the return of that cat."

"One more test," Lightning Strike called out. "If you are as you say, then summon a horse."

"Summon a horse?" Obsidian Blade frowned, but his companion spoke up.

"Drop your trous first," Rhys demanded.

Cadr lifted his head and stared, to see that everyone was as puzzled as he was.

Obsidian Blade rolled his eyes. "I fear Rhys is still learning our tongue," he explained. "Weapon, not trous," he said, looking over his shoulder.

Rhys blushed, but didn't lower his hand.

"We cannot trust," Lightning Strike said grimly. "Call a horse."

Obsidian Blade shrugged, threw back his head and warbled a cry, he then repeated the call, summoning two mounts.

Every warrior-priest-in-training seemed to hold their breaths. Cadr knew his own lungs froze.

From the herd trotted two horses, nickering and eager, tossing their heads as they walked straight up to Obsidian Blade.

Cadr relaxed as Obsidian Blade reached out to pat their manes, and looked over at Lightning Strike.

Lightning Strike lowered his bow. "Welcome to our tents, Obsidian Blade and Rhys."

Obsidian Blade nodded his thanks. "Are you the warrior-priests-in-training that were with Wild Winds?"

"There is much you need to hear, Master," Lightning Strike walked forward. "For indeed, I think you are the last living warrior-priest."

"Well then, let me hear your truths," Obsidian Blade nodded to Rhys, who dropped his hand. "Over kavage?" he smiled. "And gurt, perhaps?"

Later, much, much later, when the cooking fires had dimmed and the stars were bright above them, and the kavage drained to the dregs, they finally reached the end of the tale.

Obsidian Blade insisted that they name him Sidian as they talked. "It has been too long since I have used the other name. I have shed it like a skin," he explained.

Rhys was mostly silent. Cadr suspected that was due in part to his knowledge of the language of the Plains. But his eyes were bright and he seemed to follow the talk. As Lightning Strike finished the tale with the burning of Wild Winds body, Sidian sighed. "I have been too long away."

"Why did you leave?" Gilla asked.

"Many years ago, the Warrior-Priests held a senel," Sidian said. "I vaguely remember that Wild Winds was there, although he was not yet Eldest Elder. The decision was made to send warrior-priests into the lands that circle the Plains, hoping to find some sign of the lost magic, that it could be returned to the land. I was among those chosen to go, and I have wandered long. When Ezren returned, I asked for the aid of High Priestess Evelyn and Rhys to open a portal to the Plains." Sidian grinned at his friend. "It was Rhys's idea to focus on the cat."

"It worked." Rhys seemed smug.

"Truth," Sidian said. "And now the land glows with the magic of the Plains. But this is all that is left of the warrior-priests?" he gestured to the others seated with them, listening in.

"Yes," Lightning Strike sighed, rubbing his eyes. "Except Snowfall, who rides with the Warlord Simus. And Hail Storm, who we think now wields blood magic."

Sidian and Rhys exchanged glances. "We have dealt with that before," Rhys said.

Cadr squinted at the younger man. While he'd no sign of real age, his voice held a weariness of experience.

"This Keir is new to me," Sidian said. "As is Simus. For a Warprize to have appeared," he shook his head. "The Plains are much changed from the ones I knew."

"You must lead us now, Master." Lightning Strike said.

"No," Sidian shook his head, those bushy white eyebrows frowning. "I am too long from the Plains, with no use of my magic for years. Rhys here is more skilled than I."

"But not with this wild magic," Rhys pointed out.

"We need guidance," Lightning Strike sounded tired and defeated.

"When the lesson is needed, a student appears," Sidian smiled. "I will relearn with you. Rhys can aid us. Gilla knows a few words of Palin, that will help him learn our language quicker."

"But what should we do next?" Lightning Strike asked, his plaintive tone clear.

"We sleep," Sidian said firmly. "In the morning, we rise,

we eat—"

"And then?" Lightning Strike demanded.

Sidian raised an eyebrow at his impatience. "And then I think we get out your scrying bowls and talk to this Snowfall of yours."

CHAPTER TEN

Hanstau breathed easier once they gave Reness a tunic and trous to wear.

He may be a widower, may be the father of three grown children, but he wasn't dead, after all. Sharing a tent with a naked woman was all well and good when she was his patient. Quite another thing when she was plotting their escape.

Her wound was healing well, although she feigned a limp when she walked. She wasn't very good at it, in Hanstau's opinion. But every chance she got, Reness worked to regain the strength she had lost while confined.

She was moving about now, quiet on the grass in her bare feet, making little noise as she eased through a series of slow stretches. The tent flap was closed, their guards outside by a fire eating their nooning. Hanstau had tucked himself closer to the back of the tent to give her room, sitting cross-legged against the wall.

He'd thought to keep his eyes tightly shut, to recite prayers to the Sun God, or perhaps a few stanzas of the Epic of Xyson that he had memorized as a child.

But his control was not perfect. His treacherous eyes would not stay closed. He could only hope for forgiveness for the occasional glance, but the mental image was almost worse, brought on by the sounds of the soft movements of cloth over skin and her breathing.

Her back was turned to him, and she was lunging at an unseen enemy, her trous—

Hanstau swallowed hard, and closed his eyes firmly. His late wife had been dear to him. Their marriage had been arranged, as was proper, and they'd been well suited to one another. They'd been comfortable with their duty and taking pleasure with one another, and they'd shared pride in their children. He'd mourned her death.

A whisper of cloth on skin, and his eyes flickered open to see Reness pivot into a slow, steady lunge at an unseen opponent.

She stole his breath away.

Enough. Hanstau closed his eyes tight, settled back into his seat, and reminded himself sternly that while it was perfectly normal to be attracted to a healthy, muscular, lovely woman, it was not proper.

It didn't help that the tent was warm and the air was still thick with Reness's unique scent. Hanstau could let himself breathe deep, drift off, dream of—

He jerked his head up, stiffened his back, and rejected that thought. Time to think on other things. The Epic of Xyson was dull enough to kill any thoughts of—

A flash of light flickered at his closed eyelids.

Hanstau opened his eyes a crack to see gold sparkles gathering by his bare toes. He frowned at them. That was another bone of contention. Walking in grass toughened the feet of those of the Plains. His feet were far more tender, and pale. They'd taken his boots as yet another way of keeping him captive. As a result, his guards, even Reness, had commented on his pale feet and long toes.

If they gave him back his boots, maybe they wouldn't have to see them.

The power also seemed fascinated. The sparkles jumped around his feet, and he could almost feel their giggles.

'Practice as a child does,' Reness had urged him. *'Try, fail, try again.'*

'Wild Winds warned against that,' he'd told her. 'He said he would teach me.'

'That is no longer an option,' she'd pointed out.

Hanstau frowned at his toes, wiggling them the tiniest bit. The sparkles scattered, then danced around them, growing brighter.

He'd seen Snowfall use her powers just the one time, when she had somehow shielded them from the wyverns threatening them. He'd been focused more on his patient at the time, trying to carry the woman to safety with Snowfall's help. But he seemed to remember that she had pulled the glow within as they'd moved, drawing power into herself. After, Snowfall had been tired, she'd said something to Simus about…

"I had to carry, and concentrate, and move," Snowfall shook her head. "Not as easy as I thought."

Concentrate… Hanstau thought about that. Snowfall had been talking about her thoughts, but maybe the sparkles could be brought together. Like boiling willow bark down to a thick paste for fever's foe. Absorbing it through your skin to aid the whole body.

He wiggled his toes again, and the sparkles clung like gold dust in the dim light. Like putting on joint cream to help stiff fingers and toes. He'd often wondered what caused the stiffness to be so bad in some, and not as bad in others. But the joint cream, applied thickly and then covered well with wool socks warmed by the fire, was a remedy that eased the pain of those that suffered.

Hanstau stifled a yawn, and continued to stare at the glow as it grew and then diminished, wrapping in and around and through…

He could see his toes. No. See *through* his toes. He could see the bones, the muscles, the blood rushing through healthy flesh, see the joints in all their complexity. So many bones. He flexed his foot, and then his ankle, watched the interplay of healthy flesh under the skin, watched bone and muscle work together. Entranced, he stared in wonder at—

"Antas wants the male," came a gruff voice from outside.

Hanstau started, disoriented. The vision was gone, and he was left blinking in the light as the tent flap was thrown open. Had it been a dream? He felt odd, tired, drained and yet... elated.

Reness had calmly moved, swift and silent to sit on her pallet. She gave him a puzzled glance as one of the guards stepped within their tent.

"Come," the warrior gestured. He dropped boots and a hooded cloak at Hanstau's feet. "Antas summons you."

Hanstau reached for the boots, and quickly pulled them on. The cloak was for a much bigger man, and he was lost in its folds. The warrior frowned, pulling the hood up to cover Hanstau's head. Satisfied, he grunted, and held the tent flap open.

Hanstau glanced at Reness.

"Be careful," she said in Xyian. "Assume nothing."

Hanstau nodded in the depths of the hood, and followed the warrior out of the tent.

It wasn't far. Hanstau noticed for the first time the size of Antas's tent, nearly as big as Simus's. A warrior waited for him at the flap, she bowed him in, holding out her hands for the cloak.

"Greetings," she said. "I am Catha, Token-bearer to Antas of the Boar.

The tent was warm, lit with braziers. It was set up the same as Simus's had been, with a low wooden platform. A general meeting area, Hanstau remembered. Even the scent of leather, old kavage and sword oil was similar.

Antas stood before the platform, waiting for him.

Hanstau steadied himself, and walked toward his captor, looking him in the eye.

Antas watched him with lowered lids. "You speak our tongue?"

"A little," Hanstau said. "Not too well."

"Enough, though." Antas gave a nod of satisfaction. "Come. We will eat, you and I. We will exchange truths. You understand?"

"Yes," Hanstau said.

Antas walked toward another opening. Hanstau followed, only glancing back when he heard the chiming of bells. Catha was weaving a strip into the tent ties.

This was a smaller area of the tent, clearly Antas's sleeping area. There were weapons and armor thrown about, piled on saddles and saddle bags. Against one wall of the tent was a raised pallet, large enough for two.

Off to the side, was something different. Hanstau stared in surprised at an actual table, with wooden stools.

"Sit." Antas gestured, as he sat on one of the stools, adjusting his sword out of the way.

Hanstau sat, and Catha approached with water and cloths for the hand-washing ritual. Hanstau whispered a quick prayer to the God of the Sun for protection.

There was a small lamp on the table, with an open flame. Hanstau could clearly see that Antas was studying him. He lifted his chin ever so slightly.

Catha began to bring out food, and kavage. Antas seemed content to eat in silence, and Hanstau had no intention of trying to start a conversation. The food was normal camp fare. Flatbread, some kind of roasted roots, and grilled meat. Hanstau spotted the little red flakes on the meat, so he expected the explosion of spice on his tongue.

The food was good, the kavage was hot, but it all tasted like ash in his mouth. All he could think of was the brooding man across the table and the huge bed so close at hand. It felt like every breath he took; every move was being tested and weighed.

Catha was clearing the bowls when Antas spoke abruptly. "Do you know what 'Warprize' means?"

It was on the tip of his tongue to say something rude in Xyian, but he'd been warned. "I know of Queen Xylara," he said carefully. "And the Warlord, Keir of the Cat."

Antas nodded. "You and I," he made a gesture toward Hanstau. "You are my Warprize."

"No," Hanstau said.

Antas considered him through narrowed eyes.

"I did not aid your people," Hanstau said. "You did not take me from a battle." His voice cracked a bit at the look in Antas's eyes, but he kept on. "And between us, there is no… heat."

Antas was silent for a long moment, then he gestured to the pallet. "You. Me. We share."

"No," Hanstau kept his eyes on Antas.

"No share?" Antas frowned.

"No man with man share," Hanstau stumbled a bit. He'd known that this was common among Firelanders. The Queen, Master Eln, both had mentioned this, and been blunt as to its prevalence on the Plains. Hanstau really didn't take issue if others wished to—

"Man with woman share?" Antas asked.

That caught Hanstau by surprise. He looked away as heat rose in his face.

Antas grunted, as if he'd learned something that pleased him. But then he glared at Hanstau. "You, my Warprize."

"No," Hanstau started, but Antas cut him off.

"Warprize," he said, the threat clear. "If not—"

There was a jangle of bells, and then raised voices from the main tent.

Antas scowled, rising as Hail Storm came through the opening, Catha in his wake.

Antas and Hail Storm exchanged harsh words over Hanstau's head. Hanstau shifted on his seat, not wanting his back to the warrior-priest.

Hail Storm still didn't look well to Hanstau. There was a brightness to his eyes that spoke of a low-grade fever. But the stump of his arm looked much better, less swollen, and the redness had receded.

The two men snarled at one another, Catha hovering behind them. Hanstau couldn't catch every word, but he got the gist. Hail Storm had broken the bells, pushed past the token-bearer, and Antas was taking him to task for it.

Hail Storm couldn't have cared less. He seemed dismissive of Antas. "No matter," he spat. "We must speak of the young."

"We can do so later," Antas growled.

Hail Storm's eye flickered in Hanstau's direction. "You can court your so-called Warprize later," he said. "Order the theas to bring me their young warriors. Those that will go through the rites next year."

"Even Warlords do not 'order' theas," Antas growled. "Especially concerning the young."

"You will if you want them trained." Hail Storm moved as if to cross his arms, hesitated, and then let them drop to his side. "They will give them to me to be… enlightened as to new ways. Powerful ways."

Something about those words made the hair on the back of Hanstau's neck prickle. The very air around them changed, thickened with disapproval. For a brief moment, he thought to see if he could focus. See the golden power, see if it gathered near Hail Storm. No one would know—

'Don't assume' Reness's advice echoed.

Hanstau stilled.

"I will suggest the theas talk to you. Suggest that they send young ones for your training." Antas growled. "No more."

"As you choose, Warlord," Hail Storm gave a mocking bow, spun on his heel and left. There was silence until the bells at the entrance chimed again.

Hanstau let out his breath slowly, and looked up to find Antas standing there, watching him.

"You do not like Hail Storm," Antas gestured after the man.

"He is a bad man," Hanstau said, trying to find other words for his revulsion. "He is without truth."

Antas nodded, but there was no agreement in his eyes. "I will do what needs to be done to protect the Plains," he said slowly, as if trying to make sure that Hanstau understood every word. He stepped closer, looming over Hanstau. "I will claim you as Warprize," he said, reaching out to caress Hanstau's face.

Hanstau jerked away.

Antas swiftly clamped Hanstau's jaw, and forced his head back. "You will be my Warprize." He leaned in, his breath hot on Hanstau's cheek. "Or Hail Storm will make you."

Hanstau froze, pinned by cruel blue eyes.

A jangle of bells at the door, and Catha appeared. "There is a Singer without. One Quartis, sent from Eldest Elder Singer Essa."

Antas hissed in a breath. "I will welcome him. See this one back to his tent, well cloaked. Keep him hidden."

Catha nodded, disappearing to get the cloak.

Antas released Hanstau's jaw, only to reach down and grab a handful of tunic. He pulled Hanstau up, almost off his feet, toes just touching the ground.

Hanstau grabbed for the man's arm.

Antas pulled him close, and whispered in his ear. "Him or me, understood? Him or me."

"Understood," Hanstau strangled out the word.

"Consider my truths well," Antas growled, and released him.

Hanstau stumbled back a bit, almost tripping over the stool. By the time he regained his balance, Antas was gone.

Catha and the guards hustled Hanstau back to the tent, stripping off the cloak from his back as he stepped within.

Reness frowned up at him from her pallet.

"Shoes," barked the guard.

Hanstau toed them off, and kicked them toward him. The guard swept them up with a grunt, and then left, tying the tent flap behind him.

"You're shaking," Reness whispered, rising slowly from her pallet. "What happened?"

Hanstau stared at her mutely.

"Here," she said firmly, in what had to be her 'mother' voice. "Come here." she took his arms and pulled him down to her pallet, urging him to stretch out. She pulled over blankets, covering them both, even though the tent was warm. She crooned to him as one does to a babe, and Hanstau let her. Undignified, but a comfort.

He lay face up, staring at the tent above them. Reness put her hand on his heart, and her head by his. Hanstau closed his eyes, and felt the tremors slowly fade.

"Better?" she asked.

Hanstau let out a breath under the shelter of the soft wool, and breathed in the spicy scent of gurtle wool. He let it out slowly, nodding.

"Tell me," she commanded.

He did, from the start. In Xyian, in a muffled whisper.

Reness listened, stopping him only once in a while to have him explain a word.

At the mention of the young ones, her hand pressed on his heart. And stayed that way as he described Antas's threats.

The re-telling brought a quaver back to his voice, much to his shame.

Reness didn't seem to notice. She listened to the end, and then considered for long moments while Hanstau focused on breathing. On warmth and blankets and the feel of her next to him. Pulling every ounce of comfort he could from his surroundings.

"He would teach children his ways." Reness's voice was flat.

Hanstau turned his head to look at her. "Wild Winds called it blood magic. I do not know details, but whatever his source of power, the Plains hate it. And hate the wielder, or so Wild Winds said."

"And Antas would allow it," she said, her tone dark.

"He said he would speak to the theas, that he couldn't force them." Hanstau shifted his head to get a better look at Reness. "Is that tradition?" he asked.

"More than tradition," Reness replied, but continued without explanation. "You said a Singer was here?"

Hanstau nodded. "They said 'Quartis'. From the eldest Elder Singer."

"Well." Reness shifted her head closer to Hanstau's. "That's a saddle that will rub him raw."

"Why?"

"He is not following our ways," she explained. "If you are indeed his Warprize, he should be affording you the respect and courtesy that you are entitled to."

"Such as?" Hanstau asked.

"Have you been presented to his warriors? Offered a guardian? Have you been courted by other Warlords?" Reness shook her head against his shoulder. "At the very least, you must be offered a chance to leave the Plains and return to your people. He has not."

"He will not." Hanstau realized with a sickening feeling. "Not until he controls me."

"Which he will not do," Reness said with more confidence than Hanstau felt. "He can't publicly claim you as Warprize without giving you certain rights. We can use that against him."

"Reness," Hanstau looked at her doubtfully. "I am not sure Antas is someone you can finesse."

Reness rose up on her elbow, looking down at him. "What is 'finesse'?"

Hanstau sighed.

CHAPTER ELEVEN

Joden shielded his face against the fierce gale blowing snow and ice into his eyes.

He walked against the wind, unable to see, leaning in against the storm in order to stay on his feet. The winds howled, and battered him back. Where had the storm come from?

He'd been singing, or at least, he thought he'd been singing. He'd been struggling against the wind for so long he'd lost all track of time. There'd been people, and flames and bare earth. Now there was only the thick snow against his bare legs, the harsh blasts, and the cold.

It bit into him, and he felt every inch of his nakedness. He tried glancing around, looking for tents, for other warriors, for shelter.

So very cold.

Horses. If he could find a herd he could shelter in their midst, share the warmth of the herd. Where there were horses, there were camps. He drew a deep breath; the cold hurt his lungs. He threw back his head and warbled for a horse, and listened.

But all he heard was the howl of the winds, and his own harsh breathing. No hoofbeats, no neigh of acknowledgment. Nothing.

A cry echoed back to him. A human, the warble of a scout.

Joden peered through the blinding snow, blinking against the ice crystals forming on his lashes. "Here," he bellowed. "Here, here!"

A man stumbled out of the snow, a warrior, his leathers

tattered and shredded, hanging from his body. His head down, hair covered in ice, he ran right into Joden. Joden reached out, grabbing him by the shoulders to keep them both from tumbling down into the drifts.

The man lifted his head, blinking to see.

"Iften," Joden gasped in horror.

The blond looked terrible, wasted and pale, ice encrusted on his eyebrows and beard. For a moment recognition flared in those eyes, then hope, then—

Hate.

Iften pushed him away, jerking back to stand there, his face twisted in a scowl. "You! Oath-breaker. Liar. Faithless one, you betrayed—"

Joden stepped toward the man. "Iften, we need shelter," Joden shouted to be heard over the storm. "Join with me and—"

"Never," Iften screamed, and threw himself away from Joden, lost in the blinding snow. "Never, never, never," his screams became one with the wind. Even his footprints disappeared.

Joden stood, dazed, trying to think. Iften was dead. Cursed by the Warprize, killed by the Warlord Keir.

Joden hunched down, wrapped his arms around himself and tried to shelter in place. The drifts grew around him as he stared at the melting snowflakes on his arms.

Was he dead?

But he was cold, so cold, and the winds weren't stopping. He rose to his feet, struggled through the drifts that had mounded around him, and struggled on against the blasts. Dead or not, he needed to find...

A light flickered ahead.

Joden blinked, staring hard. It had to be an illusion.

No, it was there, one of the lights left outside a winter lodge in the worst of the storms. Joden started for it, struggling through drifts, the wind bringing tears to his eyes.

The winds faded, the snow eased. The doorway down into the lodge beckoned. Joden went down the stone steps, and pushed past the oiled leather that served as the first door. He stopped to shake the ice and snow from his hair and wipe as much damp from his skin as he could. Old courtesy, taught to every child. He shivered as the winds outside strengthened, and then pushed through the inner hanging door.

A wave of merriment, heat, and music swept over him, as good-natured laughter urged him in.

The lodge was crowded, filled with warriors of all ages. Wreathed in smiles, they pulled him in, laughing and welcoming. Sitting, standing, all were sharing in a meal, with smoke rising from cooking pots. Somewhere drummers beat a joyous pattern.

Joden was so tired, he couldn't make out the words, didn't understand what they were saying. He just basked in the joy they radiated and let them guide him deeper into the lodge. Food and sleep, and then he'd worry about the rest.

The crowd parted, forming a path, and gentle hands pulled him along, toward the place of honor. A wooden platform was there, as it was in every lodge, but the painting on the wall behind it was bright with color, and the hangings that surrounded the platform made it feel like a tent.

A brazier burned brightly in the center, and five people gathered around it, one sleeping by its side. Of the four seated there, three were clearly warrior-priests, and they were all Elders. Joden expected to make his bows and retreat back into the crowd.

One of the five was sleeping on a pallet, just below the painted wall, covered in blankets. But the other four all turned to greet him with smiles, and made a place for him close to the heat. Hands urged him onto the platform to sit, and the man to his right grinned and handed him a mug of steaming kavage.

Joden sat on the offered pallet and reached for the mug with a nod of thanks, only to find his hand close on nothing.

The mug crashed to the ground.

Silence filled the lodge.

"Ah," said a male voice. "You are not yet with us."

Joden looked over to his left, to see a thin man, with a thin, angled face. His black hair gleamed in the light, as did his dark eyes, one of which was surrounded by the tattoo of a bird's wing. He was smiling at Joden with an open, yet curious look.

"Singer," Joden said. "I do not understand."

"Nor do I," said the man with a laugh. "But understanding comes. We will talk, you and I. And we will see."

The activity around them rose again, but muted by the hangings. The others seated with them returned to eating, sharing bread and kavage and roasting long skewers of meat over the brazier.

Joden looked at his hands. "I feel the heat," he said. "Why can I not drink?"

"What is your name, warrior?" The man asked.

"Joden of the Hawk."

"Be known to us, Joden of the Hawk. To your right is Twisting Winds. Next to him is Summer Sky. Beside me is Stalking Cat." The man reached for his kavage.

"And you are?" Joden asked.

"Uppor of the Fox." the man glanced at Joden.

"But you are—" Joden stuttered to a halt. "You are the Trickster. I have sung of you, how you stole from each of the elements to create the horses of the Plains. But you are a Singer? You—"

Uppor wrinkled his nose as Summer Sky laughed and pointed at him. "The stories, I fear, have grown in the telling."

"Then I am dead," Joden said. "And these are the snows." He looked to where the mug should be, shattered in a pool of kavage. There was nothing there.

"No," Uppor said. "You are not yet with us. You walk between. Unlike the sleeper there," he nodded toward the pile of blankets. "For some, the way is harder than others. Especially when death is brutal, swift and unseen."

Summer Sky's joy faded from her face. She leaned over to adjust the blankets on the sleeping man. His hand slipped out from the covers, the fingers moving in a slow squeeze. Summer Sky smiled softly and then tucked it once more within the blankets.

"Wild Winds," Joden breathed.

"Known to you?" Uppor asked. "A friend?"

Joden opened his mouth, but no words came.

"Ally, then, perhaps?" Uppor lifted an eyebrow.

"Perhaps," Joden said.

All four of them turned to look at him, expectation in their eyes. "Tell us," Uppor commanded. "Tell us your truths, Joden of the Hawk."

Joden rubbed his face, feeling the roughness of his own palms against his skin. "I don't know where to begin," he admitted.

Uppor nodded. "Every beginning is an ending. And yet, every ending is the beginning of something new." He paused, shaking his head, his smile wry. "Choosing? That is the hard part."

"Have you heard of the coming of the Warprize?" Joden asked.

"Tell us," Uppor said.

So Joden did, through what felt like a night and a day, although the heat never waned, and he felt neither tired nor hungry. His words flowed, and those around him stilled and listened until it was only his voice to be heard in every corner of the lodge.

As he spoke, he stared at the painting on the wall of the lodge opposite him, so bright and colorful. As he spoke, it seemed the picture changed to reflect his tale, as armies moved over the lands, as warriors struggled to survive. A woman in a red dress, a four-ehat hunt, and—

"A Warprize," Uppor breathed the word with reverence.

The images moved on, of a woman and horse encased in metal, and a pillar of light that seared and burned.

And when Joden spoke of wyverns, they filled the air, black darts against a blue sky, tall mountains behind. He blinked, hesitated, as mounted warriors on winged horses fought back.

"And then?" Uppor asked.

Joden glanced away, to find the picture changed to a large tent alone on the Plains. "I met the Ancients," he continued. "And they spoke of taking the old paths to becoming a Singer." Joden sat for a moment, watching himself go through the rites, only to collapse at Essa's feet. "I took the old paths." He repeated as memory flooded back.

"Ah," Uppor added wood to the sullen coals in the brazier. "A Warprize," he said, shaking his head. "Last time, that did not end well."

"Lara is a true Warprize," Joden said hotly.

Uppor raised a hand. "I am sure she and Keir have the best of intentions," he said. "But trust me when I say that those do not always lead to the best of consequences." Uppor snorted a laugh. "And the Ancients. Did those little dried turds tell you the consequences of your path?"

"Yes," Joden said. "But—"

"Not in any detail," Uppor finished for him. He reached out with his dagger, adjusting the wood, stirring the coals.

"No," Joden admitted. "But they offered knowledge."

"Of course they did," Uppor growled. "As they have so often in the—"

Stalking Cat laid a hand on Uppor's arm to stop his words, and shook his head.

Uppor heaved a sigh. "I am reminded of the last time I raised my hand to interfere. It too did not end well."

The flames in the brazier were leaping up now, the heat pounding Joden's face.

"Did they at least speak of sacrifice to you, Joden?" Uppor asked.

"They did," Joden said. "And I am willing to make a sacrifice, if it aids the Plains."

"Willing sacrifice, willingly made." Uppor said. "Why?"

"Why?" Joden said. "To offer my knowledge to the people, to aid those that would lead them."

Twisting Winds held moist clay in his hands, working it as he listened. Joden watched as he formed a small bowl, and then set it in the flames to harden.

"Why?" Uppor asked again, as the bowl changed colors in the flame.

Joden frowned. "Because change must come; because our ways will no longer sustain us."

Summer Sky took the clay bowl from the flames, and poured water into it. Clear and cold the water flowed into the bowl, lapping at the sides.

"Why?" Uppor asked again, as the water splashed within.

"I would see our people flourish," Joden said.

Stalking Cat produced a sheaf of stargrass and threw it on the fire. Sweet smoke started to rise.

Uppor took a deep breath of the sweet smoke, and Joden followed his example. Only to find the man looking at him with knowing eyes. "Why?"

"Because I want the truth," Joden snapped. "Because truths have been withheld, hidden from all. I want to know what was, and how this came to be. And how we change without changing."

Uppor laughed out loud, and glowed gold within the smoke. "Change without changing," he chortled. "If only it were so."

The smoke filled the lodge now, puffing from the brazier. Joden could only see Uppor seated beside him, his palms up lifted, glowing brightly.

"We wish you well on your path, Seer," Uppor's voice echoed.

"May the fire warm you. May the earth support you. May the water sustain you. May the winds take you where they will." The smoke continued to build as did the sound of the storm.

Out of the smoke, Uppor leaned in closer, his dark eyes intent. He dropped his voice to a whisper. "Tell the Guardian I wait for her." He pulled back, and disappeared into the clouds of smoke.

Joden coughed as the sacred smoke grew thicker and then started to swirl. Everything vanished and the heat faded.

"Uppor?" Joden called, but his voice was lost as the winds howled into the lodge, extinguishing lights and stealing the breath from his body.

Joden staggered up. The pallet was gone, the walls were gone, and the ice cut into him once again. Once again he raised his arms to protect his eyes from the sting of the pellets.

He was alone, naked, wandering the snows.

The winds lashed out, swirling around and around, trying to force him back, strong enough to knock him from his feet. Whatever respite he had was gone. There was only him now, and the struggle.

Joden pressed on against the wind, staggering through the drifts, fighting to… fighting to… fighting against—

He stopped and closed his eyes. "Some Singer I am," he muttered, then shook his head. "He could have just told me."

But the winds laughed in his ear as they circled around him in a tempest of snow and ice. *'How then would you learn?'*

Joden stretched out his arms. "Where the winds will," he said.

He was turned, pushed, and started running with the winds, leaping drifts, almost losing touch with the earth below. There was something white ahead, a glowing expanse of rippling white cloth, waiting, ready—

He took one last leap, spread his arms and let the winds take him through the white light and into the darkness.

CHAPTER TWELVE

As she struggled for another handhold, Amyu decided that mountains held little truth.

A place that looked close was in fact hard to reach. A path that seemed straightforward was in fact steep; the brush that you thought to push through fought back. The rock that looked trustworthy would slide away under your foot. The root that you grasped to pull yourself up gave way.

The climb she thought would take little time was taking far longer.

Mountains were not to be trusted.

Amyu set her jaw and kept at it, out of sheer stubbornness. That flicker of white was still there, above her. Pure white and fluttering. Taunting her.

What was worse, it was now right above her, at the top of a wall of rock and roots. She would have to climb the sheer face to reach it, at the risk of falling.

Tired, hot, Amyu checked her footing, leaned against the rocks, and took a drink from her waterskin. She winced at the grit under her nails and the itch of sweat on her scalp.

She could turn back.

She *should* turn back.

Shifting carefully, she looked out, towards Water's Fall. Unlike the rest of the mountain view, this one was blocked by thick green trees, heavy with needles instead of leaves. Birds darted and peered at her from the branches, scolding as if astonished to see a human this high. There was a small breeze, just enough to stir the trees. She lifted her hair off her neck to let it dry.

Even if she started down now, she'd be another night on the mountain. A cold, hungry night, but she'd at least be headed down, and back in the city before—

A snatch of song drifted through the air.

Amyu jerked her head up. That sound had stopped during the climb, but there it was again. Faint, irritatingly familiar, and yet she couldn't name it.

It didn't matter. She had to *know*. She secured her waterskin, and headed up.

Nothing worked with her, not rock, not branch, not root. She lost the sound of the music in her own rough breathing. Muscles straining, she blinked against the sweat in her eyes.

The bit of white was still there.

Amyu reached up again, and tested another hand hold, and then another until finally, finally, she reached and felt an edge with her fingers.

She heaved herself up and over, on her belly on the cold worked stone, breathing hard.

The white was… cloth.

Amyu stared, disappointment washing over her. She scrambled to her feet, cursing her stupidity. It was the corner of a piece of cloth that had somehow gotten twisted into a thick cord, leading to a bigger bundle of cloth in the depths of the cave.

She blinked against the darkness. Cloth, stupid cloth that—

—was pure white.

Amyu stilled. Any cloth left for any time wasn't going to stay that clean. That white.

And this was no cave. As her eyes adjusted, Amyu saw that the opening looked more like a hall of the castle, only wider and taller. More of a passage, not a cave. She took a step further in, but the deep shadows didn't let her see more.

The bundle in the cave shifted.

Amyu jumped, her dagger out in an instant. A creature had gotten tangled and twisted in the cloth.

She took a few steps closer.

A moan, and more movement made it clear it wasn't a creature. It was a human, a man. The cloth was twisted around him, holding his arms close to his body. The man struggled weakly against the restraint.

"Wait, wait, don't move." Amyu said as she knelt next to him. "I'll help."

A faint moan was the only response.

She hesitated, unsure as to what to do. Cut the cloth? Try to unwind him?

But the man was tightly wrapped, and heavy enough she'd never be able to untwist the cloth without his aid.

Amyu grasped the cloth at the top of his head, pulling it up and away. She carefully inserted the tip of her dagger, and slit the cloth down slowly.

Black hair, brown skin was revealed as the cloth parted.

The man tossed his head. Fearing to hurt him, Amyu dropped the dagger and tore the cloth to free his face. Her heart froze in her chest.

She knew this man.

Joden?

Joden of the Hawk?

Amyu rocked back on her heels, jerking her hands away.

Joden of the Hawk.

It wasn't possible, and yet here he was. He was thin, his lips cracked and dry. It was Joden, but his face… he was clearly exhausted, starved, and unaware.

Amyu sucked in a hard breath in amazement and wonder.

She'd met Joden for the first time when he'd stood before the Council of Elders. He'd been so brave, so strong, defying Antas of the Boar and explaining his truths to the Council. For the first time, she had seen a new kind of courage, one that had nothing to do with the weapon in a warrior's hands. Joden had radiated power through his words and his truth.

Seeing that in him had given her the courage to defy her Elders and their command to kill the Warprize. Amyu had faked the attack and protected the Warprize with her own body as the tent around them erupted in chaos and violence.

But how had Joden come here? Last she'd known he was on the Plains, with Simus of the Hawk, about to undergo Singer Trials.

Joden's mouth moved, bringing Amyu back to the moment. The sound was faint, and there were no words. He was singing.

"Joden?" Amyu reached out to cup his cheek.

Cold. Stone-cold. Thin, and his normally rich brown skin was pale. His lips were parched and dry, his eyes closed.

Water. He needed water and warmth.

Amyu tore the cloth the rest of the way down his naked body. How had he gotten so twisted and trapped in the cloth? She would need to—

Joden took a sharp quick breath, and stiffened. The next instant, he started to thrash about, his arms and legs flailing wildly, his head tossing back and forward.

"Joden," Amyu cried, putting her hands on his shoulders, trying to hold him still. She watched in horror as the spasms continued, only to end as suddenly as they had begun.

Joden lay still now, as if dead. If he breathed, she couldn't see it. She pressed her hand to his chest, but it was cold to her touch.

"Elements, no," she whispered, more plea than prayer. "Not this warrior. Please, please don't let him be dead." Amyu swallowed hard, biting back fear and horror. Child of the Plains she maybe, but there was no one else here. If he was not dead, Joden could not be allowed to suffer. Mercy. She had to grant mercy.

She picked her dagger back up, gripped it tight to still her trembling hand.

She'd never done this before. She'd been trained, but she'd never killed anyone.

With her free hand, she reached for his right hand. His fingers were curled and cold in hers.

"Joden," she called out. "Joden of the Hawk."

There was no response, no change. She forced herself to reach over, to take his left hand.

"Joden," she called again, loudly. Nothing. No flinch, no movement.

Her fear grew, but she followed her training. She reached over and grasped his left foot. "Joden of the Hawk," and her tears started to flow down her cheeks. *Elements, please—*

Silence.

She sobbed, and reached for Joden's right foot, squeezing hard, trying to remember all she'd been taught about a death strike, about avoiding the rib and piercing the—

There was a throb under her fingers.

"Joden?" Amyu blinked against her tears.

He was staring at her, and his chest moved with a breath.

Relief flooding through her, Amyu reached for his hand. His fingers moved in hers, still cold but alive. She half-sobbed, relieved and shaken.

His mouth moved in the barest of whispers. "T-t-they're l-l-lovely," he whispered, his half-opened eyes now focused on a spot behind her.

Amyu blinked back her tears. The hairs on the back of her neck rose, when she glanced behind there was nothing there. "What are lovely, Joden?" Amyu asked. "What do you see?"

"Airions," Joden's eyes fluttered closed. "H-h-horse-h-h-hawks."

"What?" Amyu demanded sharply, but Joden's eyes were closed and he didn't rouse.

Which left Amyu weak with relief, frustrated, and with

more questions than answers. She ground her teeth, and sat back on her heels.

She couldn't kill him. Joden was respected, his truths honored. It wasn't her place to make that decision. If he'd been openly wounded, or asking for mercy, that was one thing. But this was Joden of the Hawk, and she would not be the one to silence his voice. Those tremors may be a passing thing. With food, warmth, and water he'd recover. She'd get him down the mountain and take him to the Warlord.

She jerked to her feet, and made a quick search of the passage. Her eyes adjusted, she walked back as far as she could, checking for signs of animals and possible threats.

The passage ended in a sheer rock wall. There were no side passages that she could see, and no debris that might indicate it was an animal lair. Satisfied, she sheathed her dagger and returned to Joden.

He was sleeping, his chest rising and falling normally. She made a nest out of the white cloth around Joden, leaving enough room for both of them.

She filled a bowl and managed to get water into him without spilling too much. He swallowed for her, but did not awaken.

After that, Amyu shook out her blankets, and got one under him with much tugging and shifting. Thin he might be, but Joden was still a strong warrior, and almost a dead weight. It took doing, but she got the blanket under him, enough to get him off the cold stone that could seep a man's heat away.

Finally, she stripped down, put her weapons within easy reach, and climbed into the nest, covering both of them with her remaining blanket.

She put his cold hands crossed on his chest, and then covered his body with hers. She shivered at the touch of his frigid skin, but she pressed in tighter, willing her body heat into him.

There was no way to figure how long it would take to warm

him. A fire wouldn't do much good in this cavernous space, but she'd see to that later. For now, this was her best choice.

His breathing was soft against her neck, and his heart beat was steady in her ear. She'd have answers when he woke.

How in the name of all the elements had he come here? Amyu frowned as she shifted a bit, trying to get more comfortable. How could he have climbed the mountain ahead of her, leaving no trail? Even if he had, where was his gear and supplies? And the cloth? Where had that come from?

Amyu let out a slow breath, and tried to rein in her impatience. Answers would come, once Joden woke.

She'd every intention of keeping watch, alert and awake. But the climb had been long and the blankets were warm. As Joden warmed beneath her, her eyelids kept closing… closing…

* * * * *

The call of a night-flyer roused her at dusk.

Joden was now on his side, wrapped around her warmth, his head cradled on her breasts. He was warm, his arms lax. His breathing was strong and regular.

Amyu sighed, enjoying the moment. She needed to waken, to hunt and get fuel for a fire. But she stole a few precious moments wrapped in the warmth of another.

Especially this man. After the confrontation with the Council, she'd only caught glimpses, or served him kavage when he'd talked with Keir or Simus.

And she'd best stop mooning over him, and get to work.

She eased out of their nest, trying not to let the colder air touch him. Joden frowned, but did not waken, curling into the warmth she'd left. He didn't waken.

Amyu dressed and armed herself as quickly as she could, eyeing the setting sun. "Joden," she said softly, just in case he could hear. "Joden, I must hunt, for fuel and food, if I can find prey."

To her surprise, Joden sighed. "P-p-prey," he lifted a shaky hand to point off to the left. "T-t-there." he whispered as he fell back asleep.

"Joden?" Amyu asked, but there was no response this time. She studied the man for a moment, and shrugged. "I will return as quickly as I can."

She climbed down swiftly, and then hesitated before heading in the direction he had indicated. It couldn't hurt. One place was as good as another.

* * * * *

Amyu crawled back up to the passage much later, then heaved up her pack using the rope she had tied to it. It was heavy, with a full waterskin, firewood, and six dressed mountain rabbits.

Her fear eased when she saw that Joden still lay in the cocoon of bedding, clearly warm and sleeping. He stirred at her arrival, but did not waken.

She bit back all her questions, and set to work.

First was starting a fire. She'd found two flat rocks that she'd brought back with her, so she built the fire on top and around them. Once the flames rose, she filled her pot was water and placed it close to boil.

She unbuckled her sword, keeping it close beside her. Then she knelt and finished cleaning the rabbits. The meat would cook on the flat stones, the bones would go for a broth. Her stomach rumbled at the thought of fresh meat.

She had a thought that they could use the uncured skins to protect Joden's feet, secured with strips of cloth. Not much protection, but better than nothing for the trip down the mountain.

She eyed the white cloth. She'd cut it, make a kind of tunic from it for Joden, belted at the waist. She bit her lip. What if it was sacred cloth of some kind, for a ceremony?

She shrugged. Well, if it was, it was too bad. It would have to serve their needs.

She shook her head, and focused on her work. The animals had a series of burrows on the side of the mountain, and had been easy targets for her rocks. They hadn't seemed to even recognize her as a threat. That thought made her shift uneasily, and she glanced over at Joden, still fast asleep.

How had he known? And he'd mentioned airions. How did he know of them?

Once the meat was ready and the bones simmering in the pot, Amyu cleaned her dagger and her hands and indulged her curiosity. She rose, and went to examine the passage.

It went back into the mountainside a fair way, only to end in a sheer rock wall, reminding her of the mountainside at the top of the highest tower of the castle. She searched, but it was all stone, the bricks of the wall going right up to it. No doors, no openings. Silent, solid rock.

Amyu knew the dead were sometimes buried in stone in Xy. Othur's body had been placed in something called a crypt. But there were no dead here, no places in the walls for bodies in boxes.

Amyu huffed out a long breath. It didn't matter. She had failed in her search for airions, but even that really didn't matter. She'd a new goal: to make sure that Joden reached Keir and Xylara safely.

She returned to the fire, to find the stones almost hot enough for cooking. She didn't want to wait, brushing off the embers and placing strips of the meat on the rock. The sizzle made her mouth water.

The pile of blankets erupted, as Joden stiffened and went into convulsions.

Amyu froze.

Joden's arm worked free, knocking over the pot of water, setting the coals to sizzling.

Amyu moved then, to push him back from the flames, to

try to restrain his body as it shivered and jerked under her hands.

It may have only been a few breaths, but it felt like an eternity before he relaxed, sighed and seemed to slip back into sleep. His breathing was normal now. Amyu's was not.

After a long moment Amyu covered him up again with the blanket, then set about rebuilding the fire, refilling the pot and setting the bones back to boil after cleaning off the worst of the dirt.

Her hands did the work routinely. But her thoughts raged.

They might kill him if she took him back.

How many times has she seen it? Theas escorting the old, the sick, the feeble away from camp, returning alone? Or taking the mis-born babies out into the wide, wide grasses, returning with empty arms and grieving eyes?

And as her time had come and gone with no babes of her own body, she'd known her failure to the Plains, and her duty. Only the intervention of the Warprize had prevented her from going to the snows.

A fierce need to protect him rose suddenly in Amyu's chest. She nodded to herself as she placed the pot on the far side of the fire from the sleeping Joden. She'd take him to the Warprize, and Master Eln. They'd not let any kill Joden outright.

And should any warrior bar her way, she'd buy the time he'd need.

As good a way to lose her life as any.

CHAPTER THIRTEEN

"There is power in death," Hail Storm said.

He spoke to the young warriors seated before him using a formal teaching tone. He kept his voice low so as not to be overheard by the theas hovering just out of earshot. The theas had agreed to treat his words as if he were under the bells.

They had met well away from Antas's main camp and the surrounding thea camps. The less that knew of this, the better.

Antas had ordered the theas to bring the young ones to Hail Storm to be tested. But none of them were pleased, and they expressed it with crossed arms and frowns as they watched. Suspicious, as always.

The young ones before him listened with the wide eyes of youth being told secrets.

Children on the verge of adulthood, who had not yet been through the Rites of Ascension, but were eager to be out from under the control of the theas. Old enough to go to war. Young enough to be shaped to his hand and his will.

Hail Storm sat before them, using a thick cloak to cover his arm, to appear wise and noble and remote as a warrior-priest should. These children had seen the glow of the power of the Plains. They had the potential for power, and certainly, the innocence he required.

No real problem to introduce them to the ways of blood magic. Except for their overprotective theas.

Hail Storm wasn't stupid enough to challenge theas. Antas may have decided to risk it, but Antas was a fool. Theas were terrors in defense of their charges, and Hail Storm would not risk their wrath.

Persuasion. Seduction. Those were methods he would use. Slower, admittedly, but far more powerful.

"The glow you see now is only the beginning," he continued, letting his gaze meet each child's. "For even as there is light in the day, there is darkness in the night. Both are the natural course, following each other over the Plains."

These young warriors leaned forward, fascinated.

"A new threat to our way of life calls for new ways." Hail Storm explained. "You would have been tested at your Rite of Ascension, and that is a season or two off." Hail Storm forgot himself and gestured with his hand to sweep widely over the wide sprawling grasslands. "But the Plains needs warrior-priests and you have within you the potential for that power."

The faces of the young told him he'd made a mistake. They'd focused on his arm, where the hand no longer existed, the cloak draping over, revealing the stump.

Hail Storm dropped his arm, silently cursing his own stupidity. He drew a breath to repair the damage, to explain—

"Hail Storm," one of the theas approached. "The young have their duties."

Meaning that he'd had them long enough, he supposed. He gritted his teeth, but graciously nodded his head in agreement. "This time again tomorrow," he said.

"If the Elder wills," the thea responded, and gestured for the young to rise. They ran off, each to their own theas.

The thea gave Hail Storm a slight bow, and followed after.

Hail Storm watched them depart and seethed. Yet he did not show his hate, his fury at their insolence. He sat, waiting until they were all gone before he rose to his feet.

Or attempted to rise. The stump put him off balance. What was once a fluid motion, filled with grace was now an effort. He grunted, staggered up—

His hand itched. His *missing* hand itched. Fiercely, painfully, if he closed his eyes he could see where the twinge was, reach to scratch—

But the hand was not there, and the pain was merciless.

He clutched at the stump, but that brought no relief, so he fumbled in his pouch, for a small handful of dried mushrooms that he crammed in his mouth.

He stood there for long, terrible moments, sucking on the fibers, until at last the pain receded, little by little.

He opened his eyes to find himself standing in the grasses, all alone. No one had witnessed.

The pain was gone. All that remained was the familiar floating sensation.

He took a deep breath and let it out slowly.

It was taking more and more of the mushrooms to deal with the pain, and he'd few left. He hadn't thought when he'd fled the Heart to gather any supplies. But then he'd never thought to have his tattoos stripped from his body, never thought he'd lose his powers, never thought that a simple wound to his arm could bring such festering.

The Storyteller spoke, his green eyes glowing with light. "... but may all the Gods, and all the elements grant that you get exactly what you deserve."

Hail Storm's lip curled. Damn that city-dweller. He'd destroyed the warrior-priests, destroyed any hope of restoring the Plains, destroyed any hope that Hail Storm would be supreme in the power the elements granted.

But there were other powers.

Hail Storm straightened, and started the long walk back to Antas's camp.

The grass caught at his trous legs as he walked. He'd naught else but a cloak and sword, for by tradition, a warrior-priest wore nothing but their tattoos. The sight of his own skin, mottled and pale, shorn of their colorful magical protection was disturbing. Yet, to wear a tunic would be an admission of... failure.

Hail Storm stopped for a moment, sucking on the mushrooms. This rage he held was not letting him focus, and he needed to plan. To think.

There was power in the Plains that he could reach, for death was a constant. Even the place where the gurtles were slaughtered for meat was a source, even if it was a weak one. There were other places where warriors had died that were stronger.

Stronger still was to drain the life of a warrior as they died at his hand.

He paused again, as the memory came of Arched Color's death at his hands. Her naked body, her eyes glazing... he shuddered, and had to stop again as he hardened in his trous.

He stood, not moving, letting the passion fade.

He doubted that he could kill again like that, at least not in Antas's camp. As an Elder warrior, Antas should have more respect for him, more deference. But no, Antas had cured him, hadn't he? Hacked off the injured limb and left him to survive or not as the elements willed.

Hail Storm grit his teeth. What would it be like to drain a warrior of Antas's strength?

He shook his head, and forced his feet to move. Such thoughts were unrealistic and dangerous. He needed the protection of Antas's camp for now. Needed to strengthen and heal.

And then there were his... experiments.

Hail Storm watched as the warrior lifted his severed arm, and tossed it into the fire.

The arm lay there, reddened by the coals, charred at the end. His fingers... its fingers moved. Hail Storm reached with his power, and watched as the singed fingers formed a fist.

Hail Storm's eyes narrowed at the memory. He'd started

small, with dead birds. Used his power to make them move. Just a twitch at first. But soon his skill had grown. Soon, he would try—

He lifted his head at the sound of hoofbeats.

A mounted warrior came over a rise, clearly intent on intercepting him. Hail Storm watched as the rider grew closer.

He watched as the horse abruptly reared, and refused to move closer.

The warrior dismounted, leaving the horse standing in the grass, and approached the rest of the way on foot.

"The Warlord Antas requires your presence in his tent," the warrior said abruptly with no greeting, no respect. "The Warlord Ietha has arrived, and he would have you there when he summons his Warprize."

Hail Storm stared at the warrior, who insolently stared back.

Rage built in Hail Storm's breast at the insult, but lashing out would serve no purpose. Killing this fool would be noticed. So he simply nodded. "I will come."

The warrior turned on his heel, and strode back to his horse, mounted and rode away without another word.

Hail Storm stood, and focused his anger.

So be it. He would cooperate with Antas, and control his Xyian pet. He'd take the abuse they gave him. He'd be the Eldest Elder Warrior-priest that Antas needed him to be. Gather a new Council, even.

But he'd also gather his power in the meantime. And who was to say where that may lead?

After all, there was no reason a horse had to be alive to be ridden. And much death lay at the Heart of the Plains.

He glanced at the sun, headed down to the horizon. He resumed his slow steady pace. It would take time to return to camp.

Antas would just have to be patient.

As would he.

Sudden rushed footfalls from behind had Hail Storm turning on his heel, his sword in his hand.

One of the young warriors from the teaching session ran up, and threw himself to his knees before Hail Storm. "Eldest Elder," he said breathlessly. "I am Jahal of the Boar. I would learn of the power from you." He bowed his head, his blond hair falling around his face.

Hail Storm looked around, but saw no one following. "Excellent," he said, sheathing his sword. "Your theas?"

"I snuck away, Master," Jahal explained ever so earnestly. "They are fearful," he raised his head and looked at Hail Storm through his bangs. There were the scraggly beginnings of a beard and mustache on his face. "I do not fear. I wish to know."

Hail Storm allowed himself a small, pleased smile. He would have to keep the lad hidden and isolated but that could be done. He reached out, and placed his hand on top of Jahal's head.

"Welcome, warrior-priest-in-training."

* * * * *

Cadr was disappointed to discover that magic was rather like work.

Oh, it was interesting, that was to be sure. In the morning, Lightning Strike and the others had taken over a tent, setting up for the ritual. There were discussions about compass points, and how best to proceed. There been no problem with him watching, he'd even helped set out the bowls of the elements and the larger bowl of water in the very center of the tent.

But after that, Lightning Strike had sat on a gurtle pad in the center, with four other warrior-priests-in-training around him. They closed their eyes and sat in silence.

"Disappointed?" came a soft voice, and Cadr turned to find Sidian at his shoulder.

Cadr shrugged, then nodded. "I guess I was expecting… more."

Sidian nodded. "Well, they are reaching out to Snowfall, and they are trying to do it without attracting unwanted attention. Think of it as whispering over the grasses. It may be some time, even days, before they succeed. So until then, we stand watch to protect them. And prepare."

Cadr nodded.

Gilla had taken her warcats hunting. Others gathered fuel and water. Cadr's still-healing wounds meant he wasn't much for the heavier work. Instead, he tended a fire, with kavage and a kettle of soup, and bowls of flatbread near to the ceremony. He also offered to sharpen weapons for any that needed.

Sidian had the others watching for intruders and wyverns, seeing to horses, and packing gear and preparing. Lightning Strike and he had agreed that they would need to break camp and move once they had spoken to Snowfall.

Hours later, Gilla returned with a horse laden with two dressed deer.

"They are still at it?" She asked as she brought the meat to the fire.

Cadr nodded. "They take turns," he said. "Whatever they do, it takes a lot of out them. They stagger out, exhausted, eat and drink, and then return."

"It does," came a new voice and Cadr looked to see Rhys approaching the fire. "It takes a tremendous amount of energy."

"You can do that?" Gilla asked, a slight blush on her cheeks.

"Not that, exactly," Rhys grinned. "That is wild magic, and it's not something I can use. But I draw my power in different ways, and my skills are more—"

"Sidian!" came a call from the tent.

Sidian came at a run, and Cadr, Gill, and Rhys followed. In fact, everyone in earshot came, forcing them to roll up the tent sides.

Cadr peered around Sidian, and then gasped.

Snowfall stood over the bowl, or at least, the image of Snowfall, formed from water. She was frowning at Lightning Strike.

No. Cadr realized his mistake almost immediately. She wasn't frowning at Lightning Strike, she was frowning *with* him.

"Let me try," came her voice, like rippling water over stones. "Simus, stand here."

And then the image folded and expanded. Simus of the Hawk took shape, a big man, taller than Snowfall. His arm was wrapped around Snowfall's waist.

"Don't move," Snowfall said, looking up at him, her lips brushing his cheek.

"Why would I want to?" Simus laughed, rubbing his nose in her hair.

The room went silent, except for a strangled choke that came from Lightning Strike.

Snowfall and Simus were bonded.

Cadr huffed out a breath of surprise at their ear-weavings. He'd seen them together in the Heart, so it wasn't that much a of a shock to him.

It was to the others, that much was clear.

"Snowfall?" Lightning Strike's voice was almost a squeak.

Snowfall turned toward Lightning Strike, giving him a nod. "Yes. I have bonded with Simus of the Hawk. Wild Winds will want to know—"

"Wild Winds is dead." Lightning Strike said harshly.

Snowfall's lips parted in a small gasp. Even though her image was colorless as water, Cadr could see the pain wash over her. Cadr dropped his gaze, and he wasn't the only one. Others looked away, reminded of their own grief.

"Dead?" Simus frowned. "How?"

Cadr took a deep breath and pushed forward, to kneel before Simus's likeness. "Warlord, I would report."

"Cadr," Simus's voice was deep. "What happened?"

Cadr described the attack, of not being able to find Hanstau, of taking up Wild Wind's body and being led by the dead.

Lightning Strike started in then with the pyre lighting, the appearance of a portal, and Sidian and Rhys.

"How do we know," Snowfall said, her voice both calm and pointed. "How do we know you are truly a warrior-priest?"

"From all I have heard, and all you have been through, I understand your doubts." Sidian removed his tunic, baring his ritual tattoos. "It has been many a year since I have done this," he said as he spread his arms.

Patterns of red, black, and blue appeared, the riot of colors that were the traditional tattoos of a warrior-priest. They covered his arms, chest and face. But then they faded again, and Sidian stood before them with only the scars. "Where I have traveled, they were dangerous to have. And I have since returned to find them dishonored."

"You are Eldest Elder then," Snowfall glanced at Lightning Strike as if seeking confirmation.

"No," Sidian said. "Long has it been since I have had access to the power, much less used it. I am a teacher, nothing more. Nothing less." He shook his head, those white bushy eyebrows meeting over his nose. "And with this Hail Storm I have heard speak of, you will need aid." He exchanged a glance with Rhys.

"Come to Xy." Simus said, and Snowfall nodded. "We are headed there, to the fortress at the border. Liam of the Deer awaits us, holding it in defense of any that might come against Xy.

"Liam of the Deer?" Sidian asked. "I know that name. And he will know of me."

Lightning Strike stared at Snowfall as if he could not make sense of her. "I do not know," he said slowly. "I do not know who to trust, now."

Simus opened his mouth, but Snowfall raised a hand to press her fingers over his mouth. "Lightning Strike, please consider." She gave him a rueful smile. "I know this seems over-swift."

"When you left here, you could barely speak his name." Lightning Strike's pain was clear.

Snowfall nodded. "As Wild Winds asked, I looked deeper. And saw something—"

"Marvelous," Simus drawled out the word.

Snowfall cast him a look.

Simus grinned, but then grew serious. "Lightning Strike, in bonding with Snowfall, I am pledged not just to her, but to all that share her history. We both know of the hatred between Keir and the warrior-priests. But our world changed the night of the Sacrifice. Come to Xy."

Lightning Strike straightened. "It is more than my voice. We will consider."

Simus frowned, but Snowfall nodded. "This same time, tomorrow."

"Agreed," Lightning Strike said, and gestured with his hand. The water images collapsed down to splash around the bowl.

They talked that night, Lightning Strike making sure that all truths were considered. Cadr and Gilla mostly just listened as meat, drink, and talk were passed about.

Even Sidian had something to add. "I knew Liam long before he was a Warlord. Always one of honor, and his truth was always strong. If, as you say, this Keir of the Cat hates warrior-priests, Liam would not be one to see us killed without honor." Sidian glanced at Rhys.

Gilla stood at that point, and crossed her arms to glare at Sidian. "There are truths you are not telling," she accused. "Something you know that we do not."

Sidian sat silent for a long moment, then shrugged. "Ezren

said you were clever, Gilla. Yes, we have not spoken all our truths but not to conceal. To protect."

"What?" Lightning Strike glared.

But it was Rhys that spoke. "We have dealt with one that engaged in blood magic," he said. "I have been checking, to see if any of you bore the taint. You do not."

Gilla narrowed her eyes as she spoke. "When Ezren Storyteller was among us, he told a tale of Orrin and Evelyn. How they defeated an evil sorceress. One who created horrible monsters from the dead. He called them odium."

"We were there," Rhys confirmed. "Both of us."

"There is another thing," Sidian admitted. "If we go to Xy, if things turn out badly, we can escape. Rhys knows how to create portals. I would not bring him to the Plains, unless I knew he could get home again."

Everyone reacted at that. "You can go anywhere you wish?" Lightning Strike asked.

"Well, to a place I know well," Rhys said. "This, these Plains? You may see landmarks, but all I see is grass."

"Still, it is a way to flee," Sidian said.

Lightning Strike stood. "Are there any that would add to our truths?"

No one offered more; many shook their heads.

"I do not know if there is any safety anywhere," Lightning Strike said. "But Antas killed Wild Winds and that is enough for me. I say we take the chance, and travel to Xy. Under the protection of Simus and Liam and Keir, maybe we can grow to what Wild Winds wanted us to be." Lightning Strike looked around. "What say you?"

"Heyla!"

* * * * *

Hanstau looked up when one of their two guards entered, and

threw a bundle down at his feet.

"Antas summons you," the guard growled. "He would present you to the Warlord Ietha and others this night."

Hanstau's stomach tightened, and his heart started beating faster. He glanced at Reness, standing off to the side, but she was staring at the guard with an odd look.

"Hurry," the guard said, ignoring Reness, gesturing at the cloth.

Hanstau reached for the bundle to find a hooded cloak, boots and the Xyian robes he'd been wearing when they had taken him.

Hanstau flushed, for the man clearly wasn't going to turn away. So he stood, striped off his tunic and trous, more aware than ever of his soft belly. At least this one was male.

"Hanstau," Reness spoke, in the language of the Plains. "I do not fully understand your ways."

"How so?" he asked, pulling the trous on, grateful for the distraction.

"We have been in this tent together for some time, but you have made no move toward me, no request to share my body."

Hanstau froze, his gaze firmly locked on the ground, heat rising on his neck. He risked a glance at the guard, who was smirking at him.

Reness took a step shifting behind the guard. "You have given indications of interest. And you have taunted me with glimpses of your nakedness, and those small white toes of yours. Yet you do not speak. Do Xyians not ask?"

"I—" Hanstau was frozen, his heart speeding up. "Reness, I—" he stammered.

The guard snorted, taking a great deal of pleasure in Hanstau's discomfort.

Reness moved again, coming up behind the guard, and slightly to the side. "You excite my heart," she said simply. "I wish to share our bodies. I wish to see if I can curl those precious toes of yours."

The guard snickered.

Reness struck swiftly. With a crack, she broke the guard's neck.

CHAPTER FOURTEEN

Joden awoke to darkness and the warmth of a woman.

He was stretched out alongside her, wrapped in blankets. His head was on her shoulder, his hand on her stomach. Her scent surrounded him, her skin warm against his.

His body felt odd, strange, aching in every muscle, with a tightness that promised cramps if he moved. His eyes felt gummy and gritty. He blinked, trying to clear them. But the effort was too much. Instead he lay still, trying to absorb the pain and trying to remember... but memory wouldn't come.

Whoever she was, she was sleeping, her breathing soft and her heartbeat rhythmic under his ear. She cradled him in her arms. There was kindness there, a strong sense of caring.

He had no idea who she was... but then he wasn't quite sure who he was, for that matter.

A sound came to him then, a scraping against stone.

He opened his eyes.

Winged creatures filled the stone corridor, dancing in their excitement, their saddles and harnesses bright and gleaming. Winged horses with the features of hawks, sharp beaks and claws.

Airions, he knew, and yet knew not how he knew.

Wings flashed as they moved, feathers flickering and stretching up and out. Fabulous creatures, of various colors, strong and healthy, their crests raised in their eagerness to fly. Joden marveled at the size of their claws and beaks. Both looked strong enough to cut through flesh and bone.

Their riders walked among them, talking, laughing, checking

their tack and the reins, tightening buckles and chains.

The closest airion tossed its head, flared its wings, and uttered a shrill cry, clearly impatient. The sound echoed on the stone, but did not rouse the woman that slept in Joden's arms.

"Hold there," a woman cried, then emerged from between the beasts, laughing and smiling, wearing the leathers of a warrior. "I'm coming, I'm coming." She pulled herself into the saddle, making an odd gesture over her lap as she settled down.

Her appearance was striking; not beautiful really, but memorable. Something teased at the back of his mind. He knew her somehow.

A male warrior mounted the creature beside her, and then all the airions were mounted. The woman was clearly in charge. All looked to her for command.

"Fly, my magi," she called out. "Fly for Xy!"

With her shout, the great creatures surged toward the opening, launching themselves and their riders from the edge of the stone, flying out into the great white light.

Joden jerked up, throwing off the bedding, struggling to rise. He wanted to follow, see them in flight see their wings spread in the glorious sun and—

"Joden, no!"

He staggered forward as the sun blinded him, seeing the last few launch, dip down and then rise into the sky, their flight spiraling higher, and higher. He shaded his eyes against the sun, shuffling forward, straining to see—

Warm arms wrapped around his waist. "Joden, no, stop."

He staggered back and looked down. He was at the very edge of the stone, and below him was nothing but a sheer drop.

"Step back," the woman urged, pulling at him.

Joden blinked again, and the sun was gone. The sky was dark, the stars blocked. Now the wide expense was filled with trees, their branches blocking the view.

Where had they gone?

The cave grew silent, with only the sound of his companion's ragged breathing. "Come," she urged. "Back to bed."

Joden closed his eyes, and shivered in pain. His muscles cramped and every joint ached as he shuffled back, letting himself be pulled down to the bedroll and covered up. He was grateful for the warmth and the comfort. Sleep tugged at him as he curled under the bedding. He could rest for a bit longer, slip back into sleep. The edge of it crept over him—

"Scared the life from me," she said, although through half-closed eyes he could see her smile. She scolded as if she knew him, or he knew her.

Did he?

She kept calling him 'Joden' as she stoked up the small fire, feeding it bits of wood from a nearby pile. It felt like that might be his name, but it was like fog settling on grass, with the tips of the blades hovering above wispy clouds of mist.

She was lovely as she worked, her breasts taut, her skin glowing in the light. She was brown of hair and eyes, with skin paler than his own. Her right arm carried the tribal tattoos of her bloodline, her left arm was unmarked. Which meant, which meant…

He could not remember.

Joden buried his face in the blankets, to hide his confusion. He breathed, taking in the scents of their bodies.

"We'll get some more sleep," she said, her voice soft and so achingly familiar. "Dawn is still a few hours away," she glanced out over the edge, her face puckered with worry. "I'll have to gather more wood and hunt again."

Joden frowned.

She caught his look. "Joden?" she seemed amused and yet there was caring there. "You usually rouse, and then fade back to sleep before my next breath."

Joden pulled the blanket away from his mouth. "Who are you?" he asked.

Except the words didn't come. "Wh-wh-wh-" The word 'who' caught in his throat like a bone.

"Joden," the woman inched forward, reaching out.

Joden heaved a breath, and then another. Memory returned. He was Joden of the Hawk, Warrior of the Plains, hope-to-be-Singer—

—the old paths.

Flashes of images, of the snows, of visions, all of it flooded into his mind, stampeding over him. The shock of it brought him upright with a jerk, spilling the blankets aside, the cold air hitting him like a blow.

"Wh-wh-wh—" His throat cramped as he strained, his eyes wide with the terror that seized his heart. Pain washed over him, in every fiber and muscle in his body, fueled by his panic.

Where were his words?

* * * * *

A sense of relief washed over Amyu when she saw the sense in Joden's eyes.

Until he spoke.

"Wh-wh-wh—" Joden's face distorted, the muscles in his neck taut. It hurt to see, and yet he still struggled to speak.

"Joden," she moved closer, afraid that—

"Wh-wh-wh—" Every muscle stiffened, his eyes screwed shut with the effort. With a gasp, his head snapped back, and he collapsed into convulsions.

"Skies," Amyu swore, and jumped forward to aid him. Not that there was much she could do. She'd learned in the time that she'd watched over him that it was best not to restrain, and to watch that he didn't do harm to himself, or choke on his own spit.

But the contact of skin to skin did make a difference, and

so she waited, stroking his face and arms, warming his hands. Until the shuddering and jerking faded. She covered him then, and crawled in beside him, pulling him close.

She drummed his back gently, humming an old lullaby that her theas had sung, over and over.

All she could do was wait.

Joden finally lifted his head, blinking at her. Confused, but there was recognition in his eyes.

"Wait," Amyu said. "Don't try to talk." She slid out of the blankets, into the chill air.

"W-w-w—" Joden's face screwed up.

"Stop," Amyu commanded. "Don't try to talk. Water first." She fumbled with a small bowl and filled it from the waterskin.

Joden shifted, leaning on his elbow. He took the bowl with a shaky hand and drank eagerly.

"Easy," she said as she refilled the bowl. "There's plenty. But too fast, and you'll sicken."

Joden nodded even as he finished the bowl.

"Now listen," Amyu commanded, relieved when Joden let her push him back down on the bedding. She pulled the covers up around him. "I'll tell you my truths, and then you tell me yours."

He nodded, his eyes intent on her face, but his hand fumbled in the bedding. She reached out and took it, his fingers were cold against hers.

"You are in Xy," she said. "High on one of the mountains close to the City of Water's Fall."

Joden's eyes went wide, his fingers tightened on hers.

"I am Amyu of the—" she bit her words off but his gaze had moved to her shoulder. Oddly, that didn't hurt as it usually did; she wouldn't have to explain herself to him. "I am in the service of Xylara, the Warprize." She took a breath, and plunged on. "I came up here, seeking airions—"

Joden's eyes widened, and he looked out toward the sky.

"And I found you," Amyu continued. "Here, in this cave, wrapped in this cloth." She grabbed a corner of the white material to show him.

Joden's fingers tightened again, then relaxed as he frowned, letting his gaze drop to the cloth. Amyu waited for a moment, then continued on.

"I don't know how you got here," she admitted. "But as I was about to give up my search, I heard you singing. When I climbed up here, you were delirious, cold and naked, with only the cloth, nothing more. I have watched over you for two days now and this is the first that you have been alert enough to understand me."

Amyu looked away. "Singer, I must tell you that you have been very ill. You have these spells where your arms and legs tremble and shake and you throw your head around like a wounded animal. I need to get you back to the castle, to Xylara and the Warlord Keir. The last any of us knew of you was when Yers arrived, telling of your disappearance." Amyu hesitated. "Yers claims Simus has betrayed Keir."

"N-n-no," Joden said, his lips twisted as he shook his head.

"Hush," Amyu reached out to cup his face. "So the Warprize said, and Keir has agreed to wait until he speaks with Simus directly."

Joden eased onto his back, still clutching her fingers. He coughed, clearing his throat. "I kn-kn-kn—" his face twisted again, as he struggled desperately for sound.

Amyu waited.

"Kn-kn-know you," Joden spat the words. "R-r-rescued W-w-w—"

"Yes," Amyu nodded. "I saved Lara." She smiled down at Joden. "Now let's see if I can save you."

* * * * *

Joden was grateful as Amyu gave him more water, then unwrapped cold cooked meat she'd set aside. He ate and drank carefully, aware that it had been a long time since he'd eaten. There was broth as well, thick from stewing overnight.

After, Joden struggled to stand and, with Amyu's help, staggered to the edge of the cave to make water.

As he relieved himself, he stared out at the trees, thick with green needles. They hadn't been there before, when the airions had launched.

Had it been a dream?

"Joden, are you done?" Amyu said, and he realized that she was supporting more of his weight. Her head came up to his chin, her brown hair caught under his arm. She was stronger than she looked.

His legs trembled as they returned to the fire. He was glad to settle back into the bed, the blankets still warm.

Amyu reached for her leathers. "I must hunt," she explained as she dressed. "We need more wood and water as well. There is good hunting close," she waited a breath, watching him for a moment, as if expecting him to react. When he didn't, she continued. "And a stream. I will not be long, and there is little to threaten you here. Still," she held out her dagger to him.

Joden lifted a shaky hand to take the weapon, then had second thoughts. He shook his head, pulling his arm back into the blankets. "Y-y-y—" he tried then sucked in a harsh breath.

"It is easier to skin the creatures with the dagger," Amyu agreed, giving him a slight smile. "Just promise me you will not leave the bed. I fear you falling."

Joden grunted.

"I have so many questions, as I am sure you do as well. But the needs of the body and belly come first. Sleep, if you can. I am sure that with food and rest, things will get better."

Amyu took up her sword and pack and he watched as she carefully started the climb down from their perch.

He'd every intention of trying to force words out, of trying to stretch out his aching muscles, maybe walking back and forth in their shelter.

There was a fogginess to his thoughts that dragged at him as well. For the first time, Joden had fragments of memories of the past, like a cloth had wiped the thoughts away. He remembered some, not all, but Simus a traitor to Keir? No. But he needed to think. To remember.

His words. They caught in his throat, like seeds he had swallowed the wrong way. He rubbed his neck, not feeling any difference. But his words… his speech…

Fear caught him, held him breathless.

'Fear closes your throat, makes it hard to breathe. Fear weakens your hand and blinds your eyes. Fear is a danger. Know your fear. Face your fear.'

The old teaching chant rose in his mind, and Joden focused on his breath. There was nothing to fear here; he was throwing lances at enemies out of range. He concentrated on his surroundings, consciously relaxing his body.

The bedding was warm, and his eyes were heavy. Amyu had urged him to rest. He'd sleep for a while, then he would try to speak again.

He remembered her, remembered her courage in defying her Elder. What kind of strength did it take to stand alone against tradition?

His last thought as sleep came over him was of her brown eyes, lit up within. She was so hopeful.

Elements, let her be right.

* * * * *

Joden woke to find Amyu naked by the fire, spitting some kind of rabbit on a stick. There was already another cooking, and a pot of stew. A pile of wood and a full waterskin were beside her.

He must have made a sound, because she glanced over and gave him a smile. "I wish I could offer kavage," she said. "But that will have to wait until we return to the castle." She finished with the rabbit, wiping her hands on her thighs. "I found some wild onion to add to the pot. Now, while we wait," she seemed nervous as she gestured to a small jar, set in the ashes. "I've warmed a bit of sweetfat." She turned toward him. "Would you let me try to balance your elements?"

CHAPTER FIFTEEN

Amyu grew even more nervous when Joden nodded his agreement. Her fingers shook so hard she feared she would drop the jar.

She'd done this before, with her tentmates back in the thea camps. But Joden was a warrior, not a child.

Joden didn't seem to notice her worry. He eased over onto his stomach, and she pulled back the bedding to reveal his back, His skin was a warm brown, and there were scars from old battles.

Amyu pored a bit of the warm oil on to her hands, and then straddled his buttocks. His skin was chill against her thighs. She rubbed her palms together and the sweet scent of the oil filled the air mixing with the teasing scent of the grasses of the Plains under the high sun. Amyu put her hands to each side of Joden's neck, feeling the tension there.

She took a deep breath, trying to make it look like she knew what she was about. "We are of the elements. Flesh, breath, soul and blood." With soft strokes, she started on Joden's neck and shoulders. "The elements within you have become unbalanced. Let my touch aid you, center you once again." She leaned in and whispered the ritual words.

Joden sighed, and his breathing slowed.

Amyu worked his shoulders in silence, then started down his left arm. She massaged his muscles as she worked, but she also moved the arm, trying to ease the stiffness in the joints. Joden let her have her way, moving as she commanded with just her touch.

She worked her way down to his wrist, flexing the hand and his long, strong fingers. "The soul is made of fire, and sits within the left hand." She whispered the ritual words as she worked over his knuckles and kneaded his palm.

Joden mouthed the words with her, but he didn't speak.

She finished his arm with a few soft strokes, and moved so she could ease the bedding over him to cover that side, and keep him warm. She moved back to his shoulders, placing her hands in the ritual position. "We are of the elements." She repeated. "Flesh, breath, soul and blood." With soft strokes, she started again this time working on Joden's right side until she reached his hand. "The breath is made of air, and sits within the right hand."

Joden took another, deeper breath, and let it out slowly. She felt him relax under her, which was good. She covered that side as well, and then eased off him to kneel beside. Which was also good, because she could feel her wetness in her depths, and the tight ache of her nipples.

Balancing the elements was a healing ritual, and it often led to sharing between warriors. But she'd not shared with another since it became clear that she was barren. The repeated act had become desperate and painful, and no one was willing to breed with her.

She hadn't felt this heat in a long time, and she wouldn't risk Joden's rejection.

She arranged the blankets again to expose his buttocks and long, muscular legs. Which didn't cool her own heat.

She distracted herself with more of the sweet oil, rubbing her hands together to warm them. Then she took a breath, placed her hands at the base of Joden's spine, and recited the ritual again, and started to work his left side.

Joden's breathing was even and strong, and again, when she worked his joints he moved with her silent commands.

She also noticed something else that made her frown as she

worked. Usually, working the flesh like this, there was a warmth that grew from the body. Joden seemed warm and relaxed, but it was as if a deep chill had set into his very bones. It seemed to cling and resist her warmth.

Amyu shook her head at her fancy, for it had to be that and nothing more. "The blood is made of water," she said, and she heard an answering murmur from Joden. He was echoing her words. She paused slightly, turning her head to hear better. "—And sits within the left foot."

Joden's lips moved as he soundlessly repeated the words.

Good. Perhaps that problem was fading. She covered his left side, and started again on his right side. Again, Joden repeated the words, faint and half asleep.

"The flesh is made of earth and sits within the right foot." Amyu recited the final words. "Let the elements be balanced within and without. Flesh, breath, soul and blood, we thank the elements for their gifts."

Joden's murmur was faint, and his sigh was deep and grateful to her ears. The pleasure that washed over her had nothing to do with her physical desire and everything to do with her ability to aid him.

Amyu checked the pot. The meat was cooking well, and those small wild onions she'd found added to the scent. She wrapped the bones in leaves and thrust them into the coals; they could suck the marrow out once they'd cracked. It would be a while yet.

She added more wood to the fire, and then hesitated. She could keep watch, or—

Joden shifted, blinking at her, then lifted the blankets inviting her in.

Amyu didn't give it another thought. She crawled over and in, to be wrapped in his heat, and his arms, and the scent of sweet oil.

Joden fell back asleep, and she yawned, and nuzzled his neck. She'd forgotten the pure pleasure of the touch of skin on skin in the warmth of a bedroll.

She stared up at the stone ceiling of the cave and gave some thought to the morrow. She needed to get Joden down the mountain, and to the Castle of Water's Fall. She started to think it through, to plan…

Joden pressed his fingers to her lips, as if he could hear her thinking.

Amyu chuckled, smiling against the warmth of his fingers, and nodded, allowing herself to drift off to sleep.

* * * * *

She woke to the smell of the rabbit and onion and Joden shifting in the blankets.

Amyu pushed back the bedding, shivered in the colder air and reached for her leathers. Joden rose as well, moving toward the edge, his steps surer and stronger. She watched but made no effort to aid him.

The stew was thick and bubbling, and the bones roasted through. She carefully pulled them from the ashes, and set about getting ready to eat.

Joden sat back in the bedding, pulling a blanket over his shoulders. He took the smaller bowl she'd filled, and ate slowly, picking out the larger pieces with his fingers. She did the same, blowing on the meat to cool it. They traded the waterskin back and forth as needed.

She let him get halfway through his food before she spoke. "Tell me your truths, Joden."

He paused, staring at the bowl, then nodded. "I d-d-don't remember m-m-much…"

It was painful to listen to him trying to form the words, freezing up, shaking his head, at one point slapping his knee hard in the effort to force the words out.

At that point, he had set the bowl down, so focused on the effort to speak. He grew so agitated that Amyu feared that he'd fall into more convulsions. She nudged his knee, and pointed to the food. He sighed, nodded, picked up the bowl and started to eat again.

The few times she tried to finish his words, or guess what he was trying to say, just added to his frustration. Anger flashed in his dark eyes. On one hand, she was glad of it, for it showed her that his strength was returning. But she was also ashamed of herself, for she was no better than the well-meaning ones that tried to give her suggestions on how to get pregnant. She resolved to stop. To be patient, to wait, and to listen.

And slowly, painfully, he told her his truths. How he remembered being with Simus, meeting Snowfall, and then leaving the camp with Singers for his Trials. He wouldn't talk about that, which was fair. Amyu suspected that Singers held secrets of their own.

He had memories of being attacked by a wyvern, and killing the beast.

He had no memories of climbing the mountain, no memories beyond when he'd woken in her arms.

"They say it happens," Amyu said. "The theas used to speak of injuries that could cause a loss of memory. Usually in battle, and usually a head wound. What ever happened to you, however you arrived, that could be causing you to forget."

"And s-s-speech?" Joden demanded.

"I do not know," Amyu admitted. "But the Warprize is a healer, as is Master Eln. They will know."

Joden shrugged, and finished his bowl. Amyu reached for it, and refilled it from the pot.

"This truth I do know," she said as he took it. "We cannot stay here. The hunting will not last, and this meat is not enough to sustain us." She scrapped the rest of the pot into her bowl. "The path down is very steep. It will take us days to descend even if the weather holds." She chewed for a bit, thinking. "There is enough of that white cloth to fashion you a tunic. I can use the extra strips and the rabbit skins to protect your feet."

Joden gave her a deep look. "W-w-why w-e-r—" He stopped, took a breath. "Why y-y-you here?"

Amyu winced. "I was searching for airions."

Joden raised an eyebrow.

So she tried to explain. And while he never expressed doubt or scoffed at her, as her words tumbled out it seemed sillier and sillier. A foolish dream. She'd wasted time and effort and betrayed her Warprize all for—

"S-s-saw them." Joden said.

"What?"

* * * * *

Joden would have laughed at the expression on Amyu's face if she hadn't been so serious.

"S-s-saw them," he insisted. "T-t-take flight."

The next hour was filled with frustration on both their parts as he tried to explain, tried to get the words out. To make her see what he had seen.

But his gifts as a Singer were made mockery by his words clutching and cramping in his throat. The pain of being unable to express himself brought him to a standstill with his head in his hands.

"Enough," Amyu shifted closer, taking his hands from his face and holding them. "Joden, I understand you saw something. But I do not think it was in the here and now."

Joden lifted his head

"The trees," she explained. "You said you could see clear out and down the valley as they took flight."

"Y-y-y—"

"Trees take time to grow," Amyu said, and he ached for the grief in her voice. "I don't know how long it takes, but it is not moments." She tightened her grip on his hands, staring out into the darkening sky. "It might have been a lingering echo of what was. Nothing more than a dream." Her disappointment reflected in her eyes.

Joden shook his head, but he didn't have the strength to argue. He wished he could offer her more.

Amyu heaved a sigh, then shook her head with a wry smile. "Why don't you walk and stretch while I take these things to the stream." She stood, and started to gather up the bowls and pot. "We'll save the extra meat. When I get back, we'll get ready to leave in the morning."

Joden rose to his feet, nodding his agreement.

Amyu took up the waterskin to refill, and headed to the edge to climb down.

"A-a-amyu," he said, then took a breath.

Amyu glanced back, her eyebrows raised.

"Y-y-you w-w-will r-r-return." he said slowly, taking care with every word.

"If I get permission," she said ruefully, and with that she was gone, climbing out of sight.

* * * * *

The worst part of it would be getting Joden down the cliff face to the path below.

At least, Amyu hoped that would be the worst of their journey.

They fashioned a tunic from the white cloth, with a hole for Joden's head, and a strip to belt it around his waist. Amyu tried not to let the white of the cloth bother her. That was the traditional garb of one who was offering their lives as a sacrifice, or about to seek the snows.

But it was what it was. She didn't want to cut their blankets, since they'd spend at least one more night on the mountain. Maybe two, depending on their progress. Besides, the cloth wouldn't stay white long.

The rabbit skins she'd rubbed with ash and dried. Not the best method, but the skins only had to last until they were off the mountain. Those and strips of cloth would serve as shoes. Joden's soles were tough, as were any of the Plains, but these paths were not the grasses of the Plains. Any protection for his feet would help.

She used the longest strips of white cloth to ease Joden down over the edge. Amyu braced herself, wrapping the longest strip around her hips, using both hands to let it out. Joden sat on the edge, and at her nod, eased himself over the edge, grabbing for whatever hand holds he could find.

Amyu grunted as her feet slid on the stone. Her biggest fear was that he would have convulsions and collapse, leaving him a hanging deadweight. She was trembling and wet with sweat when Joden finally gave a shout that he was on the path.

Breathing hard, she let the strips fall after him, and gathered up her pack with the bedroll. Out of habit, she kicked the ashes of the fire to be sure it was cold.

She took one last look around at the stone work. True, she hadn't found airions, but she believed Joden. He'd seen something.

"Permission or not," she whispered. "I will return."

She lowered the pack to Joden, and then climbed down. "I will take the lead," she said as she swung the pack onto her shoulders. "This is not the Plains, Joden. The path is narrow and steep. Here's hoping down is easier than up."

Joden nodded, and gestured for her to lead the way.

The path was even more difficult than she remembered, and it didn't take long for her to realize that down was harder on her knees and ankles. She slowed her pace, not willing to risk a fall. Amyu bit her lip. Their trip descent was going to take longer than she had thought.

Joden was a warrior, so there were no complaints. But he stopped once in a while, to rest or catch his breath. She made sure to stop and wait for him, never getting too far ahead, giving him the time he needed. Thankfully the day was bright and the sun high and warm. That was one worry off her mind.

When the path got particularly bad, she stopped and let Joden use her shoulder for balance. Once he made it past the hard part, he stopped to breathe.

"Harder than it looks," Amyu said.

Joden just nodded.

As the day wore on, Amyu started to think about shelter, and finding food. They were drinking as they went, and soon the waterskin would need refiling as well. She walked further ahead on the switchback path, just below where Joden was walking. "Watch this part," Amyu said. "The way here is washed out and old—"

Looking around, she tried to orient herself. Hadn't there been a cave just—

A sharp cry; a rattle of stones.

She jerked around to see Joden falling toward her.

CHAPTER SIXTEEN

Joden tried to focus on his footsteps, he truly did.

Amyu was right, this was not a walk through a wide expanse of grasses. Here he had to watch each step, and test the footing with care. Each stone, each root, each branch all seemed determined to cause him to stumble. For the first few hours he managed well enough.

But his thoughts were stampeding horses, running where they would, distracting him.

Where were his words?

His breath caught in his throat, and he swallowed hard not wanting Amyu to hear his grief. A Singer without words, without song, was not a Singer.

If he wasn't a Singer, what was he?

Nothing. He was *nothing*.

Joden stopped on the path, his heart heavy in his chest, his vision blurred as he faced the truth of that.

This place was so strange, with the trees that swayed in the breeze, clinging to the sides of the slope. The taste of the air itself was different and disorienting. Joden stood, breathing, trying to find comfort in the midst of strangeness.

Ahead, well, below him, Amyu paused on the path and looked back.

She was lovely in the sun, her brown hair caught by the breeze. Strong and determined to get him to Keir and Lara.

Keir…

Joden looked out, through the trees. He could see the stone

walls of Water's Fall in the distance. Amyu had said that Yers claimed Simus had betrayed them. Never. The Heart of the Plains would wither to dust first. But why couldn't he remember…

"This is a hard part," Amyu's voice cut through his thoughts. "Let me help you."

And she did, tucking herself in under his arm, taking some of his weight as they maneuvered past a fallen branch. She released him after that, walking ahead. For a time, Joden was able to focus and they made good progress down the slope.

But his galloping thoughts circled round, and round.

Why couldn't he remember?

The fog around his thoughts continued as he trudged, slow and careful down the path.

"Watch this part," Amyu said. "The way here is washed out and old—"

-the old paths-

Memory returned, and with it a cold wind that blew through his body, freezing his heart.

Was this the price? The cost the Ancients had warned of? What use was a Singer that could not sing of truths?

Blinded by pain, betrayed and angry, Joden took a step and his foot found emptiness. He lurched, swayed and… fell.

* * * * *

Amyu braced herself to stop Joden's fall, and instantly knew it was a mistake. But it happened so fast; one moment he was above her, the next knocking her feet out from under her. She was down and tumbling after Joden in a breath.

She'd fallen before on the Plains, tripped, stumbled, fallen from horses, tumbled to the grass but on firm, flat earth.

The mountainside was relentless and unforgiving. It knew only down.

She flailed as she fell, trying to catch herself against the rocks and brush as the mountain threw her with no regard to paths or obstacles.

She tried to curb her fall, to slide as much as she could, grateful for her leathers. But she'd hit something hard and gone sideways, and there was no thought of control. All she could do was desperately reach out to try to grab something to stop her fall.

Until an eternity passed and she found herself face down in leaves and branches, up against a tree.

Bruised, battered and breathless, she lay there, struggling to gather her wits. A deep breath made her sob. It hurt to breathe, to think—

A moan came to her ears, and it wasn't hers.

Forgetting her pain, Amyu scrambled to her feet. "Joden," she called out, looking down the slope, hugging her ribs.

A crumbled pile of white lay further down the mountain, sprawled below the path

Amyu lunged forward, then stopped herself. He was directly below her, but she'd need to go slow or she'd cause more harm than good.

Her pack was still on her back, but empty. The waterskin was gone. The bedroll was half unrolled and flopping behind her. She dropped it on the path to deal with later.

She moved down the mountain, discovering new aches and pains as she limped. But nothing was broken that she could tell and she ignored her pain as she reached him.

"Joden," she knelt at his side, pulling away branches and leaves. He was curled up on himself, but to her joy he was breathing. "Joden," she said. He was wedged at the base of two trees. She wasn't sure she could lift him. If she could find those cloth strips she could—

Joden moaned again, and turned his head slightly to stare at her.

"Joden?"

His face screwed up. "S-s-snows t-t-take t-t-t-his m-m-mountain." He spat and coughed then started to curse again, a low steady stream, haltingly naming every element and then some.

Amyu sat back on her heels, staring and then covered her mouth. The combination of his faltering words and the cursing was too much. Relief made her giddy and she started to laugh.

Joden gave her an offended look, but then he coughed and choked on his own laughter. They both sat there, covered in leaves and sticks and bruises and laughed themselves speechless.

"Enough, enough," Amyu coughed and groaned. "Need to breathe." She shifted back slightly. "Can you stand?"

Joden shifted, and groaned and rose to his knees. He used the trees to pull himself up and held out a hand to aid her. She took it, and accepted his help, groaning and clutching her ribs as she did.

"B-b-b," Joden gave up, and made a gesture as if breaking something.

"No," she straightened slowly and took a deep, cautious breath. "Not broken. Nothing grates. You?"

Joden twisted at the waist, breathing deeply, then shook his head.

"Praise the elements," Amyu said. "Let's get back on the path, and see what we see."

They helped each other up the sharp incline littered with leaves and rocks, and then stood panting together. They were both filthy. Joden's tunic was still suspiciously white to Amyu's eyes, but the foot coverings they had rigged for him were tatters. She was in better shape, although the slash in her leathers had grown.

Amyu caught her breath first. "I think," she said slowly, dragging leaves and sticks out of her hair. "I think that there is a cave just down a bit, where I rested on the way up." She hesitated.

Joden raised an eyebrow.

"I drove off a predator in the night," she admitted. "It was a good cave, though, and with the two of us—"

Joden nodded, and then gestured up the path.

"I'll see what I can recover," Amyu said. "But let's get you to the cave first. You can get a fire going. We will be warm, at the very least."

The cave was where she remembered it and thankfully empty with no signs that any animal was living there.

The scorch marks were still there, though.

She left Joden with a pile of tinder and kindling and a few long, dry sticks. It would take a long time to build a fire that way, but if she didn't find the pack…

Amyu didn't want to think about that.

Sometime later, she wasn't really any happier. She'd found the blankets, her pack, and the waterskin. The stopper had come lose, the water was gone. But it was whole; she could find more water in the morning.

The pack was torn, its contents scattered beyond finding. Only a glint of metal in the setting sun had given away the old battered metal lantern.

With the last rays of the sun, she headed back to the cave, to find light and warmth spilling out the entrance.

Joden sat by the fire, a smug look on his face and a pile of wood he had gathered by his side. She showed him her finds, and he reached for the blankets, spreading them out by the fire.

"We'll be hungry," she sighed. "But we will sleep warm." She grimaced. "Sore and stiff come the morning, though."

He nodded and shrugged. "B-b-b—" he struggled. "B-b-b-"

She waited.

He grimaced, sucked in air, and tried again. "B-b-better t-t-than d-d-dead."

"Truth," Amyu said. She went back outside and set up the driest sticks at the mouth of the cave, to give warning. She placed her sword on her side of the bedding and made Joden take the dagger. Better they each have a weapon.

They both stripped, checking their scraped raw skin and bruises. Nothing openly bleeding, for which Amyu was grateful. They did not need the scent of blood in the air.

Joden fed the fire, and they settled in together under the blanket, close for warmth. They both lay on their sides, facing one another.

Joden pointed at the scorch marks on the ceiling. "S-s-story?"

"Are you sure?" Amyu asked. "I am no Singer."

"B-b-b," he took a breath. "B-b-better than wo-wo-worrying."

"Well, then," Amyu said. "I had scattered sticks—"

She told him everything, her fear, the terror, the golden light and how it exploded in fury. Joden listened, his eyes half-closed as she went through the tale, his head pillowed on his arm. When she reached the end, she smiled, and in jest gave the ritual ending. "May the people remember."

"We will remember," Joden whispered back without effort, and then his eyes widened.

Amyu held her breath.

"R-r-r," Joden scowled at the stutter's return, slapping his thigh in frustration.

"Relaxed," Amyu whispered, sharing his disappointment. "It's when you are relaxed that the words come, or so it seems."

Joden shook his head, his sorrow clear to her.

"Give it time," she whispered, then hesitated again. Did she dare? She took a breath.

"The theas's old pain remedy," she offered tentatively. "If you would share?"

Joden looked at her, really looked at her. He was older, wiser, a warrior of many campaigns. He wouldn't want—

"Please," Joden whispered back

Heat coiled within her. Still, she felt awkward and foolish. But for the first time in a long time she wanted this, wanted to share bodies with another.

With Joden.

Amyu leaned closer and kissed him.

His lips were warm and dry. Perfect to her way of thinking. He tasted of smoke and dust and something uniquely himself.

He let her control the pace, and she kept it slow, just lips at first. But then she could not resist, and she reached out to stroke her palm over his arm, long slow caresses.

He reached out for her and did the same, following her lead. Her palms tingled as she ran them over his bruised and battered body. She opened her eyes, to see if maybe the tingle had something to do with the golden sparkles, but it was just her and him under the warmth of the blanket, to her relief. Somehow, it meant more that way.

Her aches melted under his touch, and her bruises seemed to fade, Amyu knew well enough that when they woke, they'd hurt. But for now, there was rich slow pleasure between the two of them.

Joden's hands felt as warm as hers, and far more skilled. She arched her back against them as he teased her breasts with his breath, and her nipples with tongue and teeth.

Her hands were not idle. She reached for him, stroking his length with her palm.

His own fingers dipped lower, and when he felt her heat, he pulled her on top as he rolled to his back. The blanket fell back, exposing her heated back to the cooler air.

Those wonderful hands cupped her buttocks, spreading her out. But then he paused, hesitating.

Amyu looked down into his worried eyes. "Joden," she pleaded.

"F-f-foalsbane," he managed. "I-I-I haven't—"

She laughed, but it was more a groan of pure frustration. "I have never borne, Joden.

Never once conceived."

Still he held her, poised above—

She took matters into her own hands, then arched down to demand her own pleasure.

Joden relented, met her stroke for stroke, but the control was hers, the delight was hers, the pinnacle was…

The peak hit, and she threw back her head, crying out at the joy. She rode out the waves, rocking back and forth until Joden's cry of delight joined hers.

They melted together, Joden pulling the blankets up as she rested her head on his chest.

"… probably made enough noise to scare off any predators," she whispered in Joden's ear.

Joden's chuckle rumbled through her as she faded off to sleep.

* * * * *

Amyu found a clear running stream early, so water was no problem. Food was a different issue.

She talked with Joden, about whether taking the time to hunt versus getting off the mountain as soon as possible. His words were broken, but his thoughts were clear and he understood their predicament. He stumbled and used more gestures than words. In the end, they agreed to choose speed, with care on the paths. It seemed the right choice, except when their stomachs rumbled.

But the water ran crisp and clear and they could drink as much as they pleased. Joden's makeshift shoes fell apart over the next day, but Amyu didn't think it a bad thing. It forced him to step with care, to slow down. She feared another fall more than hunger.

He seemed to feel the blame for their predicament and the slowness of the pace. It was in his eyes, sometimes as he hesitated on the path. Or the way he looked away when he heard her stomach rumble. But he made up for it in the nights.

As they reached the lower levels, the path got easier and wider. Amyu had cause to regret the end.

It had been so long since she'd shared, she'd forgotten the pleasures of the flesh. But there was something about Joden, something about the care he took with her. He made her feel… alive.

She would treasure each and every one of the nights they'd spent together. Joden was a respected and powerful warrior of the Plains. A Singer-to-be. He'd not—

Amyu stopped. The wind had brought a scent to her, achingly familiar. "Is that kavage?" she asked, taking a deeper breath.

Joden nodded.

They both hurried down the path, Joden right behind her, stumbling out into the field where the cows were grazing. Amyu could see the cheese cave, and a campfire with an old battered kavage pot, a group of Plains warriors gathered around. The smell of kavage grew stronger.

"Amyu!" came the shout, and Rafe of the Wolf headed toward her, with a wide smile. "The Warprize sent us to find—" he stopped dead in his tracks, his eyes wide.

"Joden?"

CHAPTER SEVENTEEN

Joden stepped toward Rafe, mentally practicing the words in his head. *'Greetings, Rafe. Greetings, Rafe.'*

Rafe, a familiar face, with his dark hair, wide smile and the faint scar that ran down the side of his face. "Joden!" Rafe's eyes were wide with astonishment. He reached out to clasp Jodan's arm, joy suffusing his face at seeing an old friend.

Joden reached out as well. *'Greetings, Rafe. Greetings, Rafe'.*

"G-g-g," the words caught in his throat.

The warmth in Rafe's eyes turned to concern, but in his despair, Joden didn't see it. He grimaced trying to force the words out, but nothing, nothing…

He was nothing.

* * * * *

Amyu caught the sound in Joden's throat, knew what it meant.

Rafe backed away in horror as Joden's eyes rolled up and he started to convulse. Amyu was quick enough, getting her arms around Joden and lowering him to the ground.

The other warriors gathered and stared as Joden thrashed. Amyu got one of their blankets out and covered him, for warmth, yes, but also to block him from their prying eyes.

"What has happened?" Rafe's voice was hushed as he knelt on the other side of Joden.

"I do not know," Amyu said, watching carefully to see if she needed to turn Joden on his side. But the tremors were slowing, and his breathing was becoming easier. "I found him so, in the heights of the mountain."

Rafe shook his head. "That makes no—"

One of the other warriors knelt at Joden's side, her dagger flashed in her hand. "The fire warmed you," she began the mercy ritual.

The three other warriors had gathered round, all women from Rafe's tent. They responded with the rote words. "We thank the elements."

Amyu grabbed the woman's wrist. "No," she snapped.

The woman looked out at her from under her black bangs. Her green eyes were dismissive as she raised an eyebrow. "He is ill, and deserves mercy. I am Fylin of the Snake, warrior of the Plains. You are but a child. Leave this to us—"

"No," Amyu said again, squeezing Fylin's wrist hard. "I will challenge, if you do."

"You cannot—"

"Try me," Amyu bared her teeth. "He needs food and drink, and not your stupidity."

"Fylin, hold." Rafe reached over to put his hand on their locked ones. "Look," Rafe continued. "He's stopped shaking."

Amyu looked down. With her free hand, she touched Joden's chest, feeling the strong heartbeat. His face was relaxed, as if sleeping.

She looked up to find Rafe watching her. "He will wake soon, and be well."

"This has happened before?" The woman with the short curly hair asked, kneeling beside Fylin.

"Yes," Amyu said. "Repeatedly." And then cursed herself for saying so as the others exchanged glances.

"This is not the way of the Plains," one whispered.

"True, Soar." Rafe said. "But it is the way of the Warprize. Fylin, remember when you all tended me during the plague?"

They nodded.

"That was not the way of the Plains either, yet the Warprize saved many of us." Rafe straightened, his face set. "Unless Joden chooses or asks for mercy, we will aid him and Amyu." he said.

Fylin shrugged sullenly, and pulled her hand back, sheathing her dagger.

"Let's get him to the fire," Amyu said. "Do you have gurt? We've had little food."

Rafe and two of the women helped carry Joden to the fire, while others went to get food from packs. Amyu wasn't sure she trusted their intentions, but her bigger concern was to get Joden conscious and get something in his belly.

Not to mention hers.

The first sip of kavage was wonderful, warm and bitter on her tongue. Joden roused after a bit, and sat beside her, blanket over his shoulders. He didn't try to talk, didn't meet her or anyone's eyes. He shook his head at the food, but took a mug of kavage.

Amyu's worry grew.

She stepped away from the fire and nodded to Rafe, who followed her. "We need to get Joden to Master Eln," she said quietly. "And get word to the Warprize."

Rafe nodded. "Easy enough. That's where she is most days, tending to the old lady, the cheesemaker."

Amyu swallowed hard, remembering Kalisa collapsing as she'd fled. Well, she'd face that when she had Joden safe.

Rafe looked over at Joden. "Can he ride?"

Amyu nodded, then thought better of it. "Not alone, in case he has a fit."

"That frequent?" Rafe asked.

"No," Amyu said. "That unpredictable." Although that wasn't quite true. She could tell when they were about to happen. "Why not get the horses ready. He can ride behind me."

"As you say," Rafe nodded.

Amyu cast a worried glance at Joden, staring into the fire, but nature called. She gestured to the Xyian small house set on the other side of the cave. "I will just be a minute."

Rafe nodded, and walked off, calling to the horses.

But it was more than a moment. Between her nerves and the journey, she needed that time to gather her wits about her.

When she emerged, Joden was gone. The others were gathered at the fire, and would not meet her gaze.

"Where is he?" she demanded.

"He made his choice," Rafe answered her glancing toward the path. "He has chosen the snows."

Amyu started to run.

* * * * *

Joden waited until Amyu had slipped away, and then rose, shedding the blanket. He took the dagger out of his belt, and faced Rafe.

"I-I-I choose s-s-snows," he said simply.

Rafe rose as well, his face a mixture of grief and understanding. "Safe journey to the snows, Warrior, and beyond." he said in the traditional response.

Fylin nodded her approval.

One did not argue with a warrior's choice, and for that Joden was grateful. He turned, and went up the path to that large boulder that marked the path. It was a good place, quiet, private and filled with sun. Another moment and his pain would be ended.

Why had he even come down the mountain?

It was time. Past time. He was nothing now, a burden, a Singer without words. It was a short walk to the boulder. The rock was warm as he put his back against it. He took a breath, allowing himself to grieve for what had passed. For his failures. Whatever the Ancients had intended, he was well and truly punished for his pride.

He could not even speak the ritual words. His thoughts would have to serve. Joden lifted his face to the sun, put the dagger point to his throat, and closed his eyes. 'The fire warmed me. I thank the elements.'

Running footsteps, headed toward him.

Joden sighed, and opened his eyes.

Amyu stood there, breathing hard, staring at him. The sun brought out the highlights in her hair, the tan of her skin, and the anguish in her eyes.

"Don't," she said, her voice shaking and out of breath. "Please don't."

He'd put that pain there, in the eyes of a warrior who had only offered kindness and aid.

He couldn't look at her, so let his gaze drop away. But she deserved to know the truth. His truth. He brought the dagger to his lap, opened his mouth and tried, one last time.

She stood there, so patient, as he struggled for words, for sounds that made sense.

It was torturous, but he got it out, finally. *'I am worthless. Nothing without my voice, my words, my songs. I will gladly go, to end this....'*

When the last of his stuttered, stammered words fell from his lips, Amyu nodded.

"We of the Plains say that only the sky is perfect." Her voice wasn't quite steady, and he noticed her hands were shaking. "But that isn't really true. The Tribes expect perfection from each member of the Tribe. The broken or flawed are seen as a burden, to be shed as a snake sheds its skin."

She looked up at the sky, and Joden took the moment to watch her, standing in the sun, her long hair hanging down her back, her face so solemn.

"How many newborns with partial limbs or harelips are sent to the snows by the theas? How many of the young ones who fail to pass the Rites of Ascension, like me? I was expected to take myself off to the snows as soon as my usefulness to the Tribe was ended." Amyu took a step closer to Joden. "How many older warriors broken or flawed by battle ask mercy on the battlefield?" She broke off. "But I would not know, would I? Having never been permitted to enter battle since I am a child."

Joden shook his head, but Amyu was having nothing of that.

"Oh no, Joden of the Hawk, in the eyes of the Plains I am a child and a burden, barren and unworthy." Amyu's voice broke. "You say that you are worthless, and nothing. The snows, you say, and as an adult and a warrior of the Plains that is your choice and your right."

Amyu took another step, quiet strength in her very being.

"I may be just a child," she said. "But hear a child's truth. I think this is a mistake."

She lifted her chin, as if to defy the world on his behalf. "I think you act too soon. The snows are always a choice, but they will wait, Joden. The Warprize is a healer, isn't she? And Master Eln? Who knows what healing they may have for you? What harm in delay when there may be a chance that this, that this problem, will change?"

"W-w-worse," he tried to explain.

"Or better." She answered. "But death is final. There is no turning back."

Joden considered her, then looked down at the blade in his hand. There was truth in her words. And, elements help him, he did not want to add to the pain in her lovely brown eyes. She deserved so much more.

"You did not kill Simus when he was injured in battle. You had hope for him," Amyu added quietly. "Have hope for yourself."

But there was a difference. Simus had still had his leg. Joden reached up to touch his throat.

"Also," Amyu added dryly. "If you go to the snows, I will

have to drag your body back down the mountain and tie it to a horse and haul it to Water's Fall, because no one will believe our story that you were here."

Joden laughed, strong and hard with no restraint. And when he was done he smiled at Amyu, who smiled back.

"Stay your hand, Joden of the Hawk. Walk with us yet awhile."

"W-w-with you," he said, standing and sheathing the dagger in his belt.

A shadow passed over Amyu's face, but it was gone in an instant. "For as long as you wish."

They walked down the path, emerging from the trees to find Rafe and the other warriors standing by the campfire. Rafe's face lit up when he saw both of them.

Amyu walked up and gave him a nod. "We will go to Master Eln in the morning."

CHAPTER EIGHTEEN

To his shame, Hanstau squeaked when Reness killed the guard.

It happened so fast. One moment the guard was smirking, the next Reness was lowering the body to the ground.

"Careless," she growled softly. "Stupid. He—"

Before she finished her thought, the tent flap opened, and the other guard poked his head in. He stared at Hanstau, who stared back, frozen in horror.

Not Reness. She rose from the ground, dagger in hand, and plunged it into the guard's throat. He jerked, and she grabbed his collar and pulled him in to lay next to the other one, twitching his last.

Before Hanstau could draw a breath, Reness was beside him, her fingers on his lips.

"We must move quickly," she whispered. "But first there is a choice."

"You killed them," Hanstau stared at the bodies, unable to believe his eyes.

"I am a thea," Reness said simply, as if that explained all.

"But our plans," Hanstau sputtered. "We were going to try to finesse—"

"I do not finesse," Reness said. "A choice, Hanstau," she continued and raised his chin so his eyes met hers. "We can slip away, and get to horses. Or we can warn—"

"The children," Hanstau whispered, his heart pounding in his chest. "We must protect them."

"Good," Reness nodded approvingly. "Help me." she knelt by the guard and started to strip his armor and weapons.

Hanstau hesitated, then went for the boots.

"Antas will have war drums near his tent," Reness whispered as they worked. "I will escort you. Those who know will expect you to come, dressed as a healer and fully cloaked. I can use the drums to signal the thea camps. Or—" she hesitated over the lacings. "Or I will go, and you can flee alone. You might have a better chance—"

"And be a city-dweller wandering lost on the Plains," Hanstau muttered, shifting off the guard's leather trous. "Might as well kill me now."

Reness coughed back a laugh.

"No," Hanstau said. "I go with you. If nothing else, I can ward your back."

"Once I drum the signal, they will come for us," Reness said, her face grim. "It will rest with the elements whether we live or die."

"Better that than becoming Hail Storm's puppet," Hanstau said. "Just promise—"

"I will send you to the snows," Reness reached out over the guard's body and touched Hanstau's cheek. "Know this truth, Hanstau of Xy. You excite my heart. If we should survive this, I truly wish to discover if I can curl those precious toes of yours."

Hanstau gulped, and flushed. "That would be…" his mouth went dry.

Reness's smile turned feral. "Yes, it would be. At the very first opportunity." She drew a breath. "Now let us dress. There isn't much time."

* * * * *

The Token-Bearer stepped forward, the Warlord's token in hand. "Rise and hail Antas, Warlord of the Tribes and Eldest

Elder Warrior to the Council of Elders."

Quartis rose with the rest, bowing his head, and waited for Antas to enter.

Singers were the knowledge of the Plains, or so it was said. His master Essa had sent him to this camp with instructions. *'Watch, observe, learn more than they do.'*

He'd learned more than he'd expected.

Antas would have it that his hold on his people was firm. But the air in this command tent felt overheated and nervous. All was not as it seemed, and for days Quartis had tried to learn more. He'd been treated with every courtesy, but every move had been watched. And all mouths were silent in Antas's camp, with few willing to voice truths. Even to a Singer.

A wisp of cooler air preceded Antas as he entered the tent, followed by his Second Veritt and the Warlord Ietha. They made their way to their seats on the wooden platform. Quartis had been placed prominently before the platform, but not on it. Clearly put in his place.

"Be seated, all," Antas stood as they all resumed their seats. "I have called senel to speak of events, and to make my decisions. Let us share kavage as we talk."

Catha, the Token-Bearer and three others started to pass through the crowd with pitchers and wooden bowls for the handwashing ritual.

Quartis washed and dried his hands, thanking the elements quietly. He was a Singer, and had been for many seasons. His skin seemed to crackle with tension, and unspoken threat in the air. He'd kept his thoughts off his face and out of his voice.

But it was interesting that Antas hadn't offered to listen to anyone's truths. And his token wasn't placed in the center of the room for any to use. Instead, it was by his side.

Ietha also did not seem comfortable. The tall dark-skinned woman had the slightest of frowns, and seemed to be looking about. She leaned over to Antas. "And your Warprize?"

Ah. Quartis had not yet glimpsed the Warprize that Antas claimed, nor talked to any warrior who had.

Once again cooler air surged into the tent. Hail Storm strode down the center aisle, cloaked and scowling, his face red and mottled, stripped of tattoos. But there was something that lingered in the air around him, something very dark. Quartis could have sworn that the flames in the braziers dimmed as he passed.

It had to be his imagination.

Hail Storm strode to the front, and Veritt rose and bowed, offering his seat. Hail Storm didn't acknowledge him, just sat with a swirl of his cloak.

"Welcome, Hail Storm, Eldest Elder Warrior-Priest," Antas's expression didn't change. "I was just about to tell the senel that my Warprize will be joining us later." He glanced at Hail Storm, who gave him the slightest of nods. Antas settled back, seeming more confident. "After our discussion."

Ietha leaned back as well, but didn't seem all that satisfied. Neither was Quartis. If in truth, Antas had claimed a Warprize, that individual was entitled to certain ceremonies, certain rights. A Guardian, at the very least. Still, if the Warprize appeared this night, that would answer many questions.

If.

Quartis accepted kavage and gurt with a grateful smile and took the opportunity to glance around. Warriors filled the tent, both Antas's and Ietha's but no theas that he could see. The theas had kept their camps at a distance from the main one, and while they had not spoken much, it was clear to Quartis that they were not pleased with this break in tradition. Either by Antas or Keir.

Still, no theas at this senel was no theas. How much support did Antas truly have? Essa would want to know.

Antas started asking questions concerning the status of

the army, the camp, and the herds, the usual start to a senel for an army on the move. Quartis listened with half an ear while watching faces.

The warmth of the tent, the familiar scents of kavage, all were comfortable and yet dangerous. Quartis could not afford to lose focus. The attack would come soon enough.

And it did.

"So, Singer Quartis," Antas's smile did not reach his eyes. "You have been here many days, but you have not yet taken my words to your master. Here sits the Eldest Elder Warrior, and the Eldest Elder Warrior-Priest. The Eldest Elder Thea will join us in the next day or so." Antas shifted in his seat slightly. "Eldest Elder Singer Essa should join with us, so that we may form the Council again."

And he knows full well all you need is a Singer,' Quartis thought, as he took a sip of kavage. "Eldest Elder Reness has joined with you?" he asked. This was the first he'd heard of that.

"Soon," Antas said crisply.

Quartis bowed his head in respect he didn't feel. "I have waited, Eldest Elder, to meet your Warprize, and see that proper honor is given." Quartis said. "You have spoken many times of your desire for him. But I have yet to know his name."

"He is of Xy," Antas shifted in his seat again. "He is not used to our ways. He needs time."

Xy? Quartis struggled to keep his frown off his face as he signaled for more kavage from the servers, giving himself a moment to think. The only Xyian on the Plains that he knew of was the healer with Simus, and he had gone off with Wild Winds.

"What matter that?" Ietha crossed her arms over her chest, and glared at both Quartis and Antas. "We have those gathered that are needed for a Council. Take word to your master so that he may come quickly."

Quartis sipped fresh kavage, sat down his mug, then gave

her the look all Singers give when someone tried to tell them what to do.

Ietha flushed, the red flare of heat dancing on her dark cheeks.

"I will take word, once I have met the Warprize," Quartis said, keeping his voice respectful. "But I am glad to have seen Hail Storm," he gave the warrior-priest a low nod. "Although I regret to learn that you are injured." Quartis made a vague gesture toward Hail Storm's missing arm. He'd heard the tale of Antas's 'mercy' with the ax. Would to the elements he'd seen it.

"I live," Hail Storm was polite but there was an edge to his tone. "I am the only living warrior-priest. As Eldest Elder it is my duty to the Plains."

"Wild Winds lives," Quartis said casually.

If the air in the tent had been tense before, it was now the silence before dark, sullen, storm clouds. Silence that went on, and threatened to go longer until Antas broke it.

"Wild Winds is dead," Antas growled. "There was an encounter with my warriors. Wild Winds did not survive. A terrible accident." Antas cleared his throat. "That is where I found my Warprize."

"I see," Quartis kept his voice neutral. "And has the Warprize been presented to your men? Offered a Guardian? Taken nothing except from your hand?"

Hail Storm snorted. Antas went red in the face. "Singer," he snapped. "You go too far!"

"He has a point." Ietha said pointedly, her anger fixed on Antas. "If, as you say, you hold with all traditions, then your Warprize should receive all honors."

Antas turned on her, and—

A thundering BOOM filled the air.

Startled, everyone froze as the vibrations of a war drum echoed in all chests.

WARNING, boomed the drums in a familiar call.

CHILDREN DANGER WARLORD BETRAYS THEAS FLEE

Silence, the tent, the camp, the entire world was silent. Everyone was wide-eyed, and—

Warbles began in the distance from the thea camps, acknowledging the danger.

Antas was on his feet, roaring. "Seize that drummer!" he screamed.

His warriors rose, crowding, spilling out of the tent and into the night. Ietha jerked to her feet. "What means this?" she demanded of Antas.

Her warriors milled about adding to the confusion. Quartis rose with the rest, and was swift to leave the tent. Warriors were headed to the right, presumably where the drums were.

Quartis went left, to where the deepest shadows lay, and he didn't stop.

Antas was still shouting. "Where is my Warprize?"

Quartis kept going, sticking to the shadows, pausing to avoid being seen by rushing warriors.

"Where is my Singer?" Antas bellowed.

'Not yours,' Quartis smiled grimly to himself and kept moving.

He was in the herds in moments, but didn't take to horse just yet. He paused for a moment to catch his breath. He'd left his gear in the tent assigned him, but he had his weapons, his horn, and his life.

He watched the camp in the darkness, listening to the sounds of fighting. He considered going back, to aid Hanstau and possibly Reness, but he shook his head regretfully. The information he carried was too critical. He wished them well, but Essa must be told.

He turned to mount.

A scream of defiance came from behind, from the center of the camp. Quartis glanced back, to see the tops of the nearest tents erupt in flames.

He allowed himself a fierce grin. Besides, it looked like they were doing just fine.

Quartis mounted, and fled.

CHAPTER NINETEEN

Hanstau's heart beat hard in his chest as he followed Reness. He didn't even realize that they'd reached the drums.

"Antas's guards are derelict. Sloppy." Reness muttered her disgust with the guards into his ear as she pushed down on his shoulder.

"I'm just as glad," Hanstau murmured.

"Stay hidden," she said as she reached for the drumsticks.

He knelt, pulling his cloak and hood tight around himself. He faced away from her, watching her back. But there wasn't much movement in the area. All the focus seemed to be at the front of the command tent, with light and talk spilling out. They had not been spotted, but Sun God above, he wasn't sure how. His heart still raced, blood pounding in his ears.

Reness took a breath, planted her feet, and struck the drum.

His heartbeat was nothing in comparison. The sound thundered through his bones. The silence after seemed to echo in his ears, as if waiting for—

She struck the drum again, pounding out a signal, dropped the sticks, tugged at his cloak and they were off and running between the tents. No hope of hiding in shadows, they were forced into the open to avoid tent ropes and stakes.

Warbling rose in the distance, seeming to come from all around the camp.

He heard Reness grunt as they ran. He risked a glance to see her feral, satisfied smile.

Warriors boiled from every tent. From behind, Hanstau swore he heard Antas bellowing his rage.

Reness guided him, heading for the edge of the camp. He could see horses just beyond the last of the tents, a large herd. If they could—

A shout of recognition. Two warriors barred their path, weapons ready.

Reness didn't change stride, didn't make a sound. She moved forward, sword and dagger out and then somehow, she was past the warriors. The warriors fell back, cursing and shouting.

It wasn't clear in the darkness but Hanstau smelled blood. Reness didn't stop.

Neither did he. He ran right past them, following her.

But there were more warriors now, he could hear them. His hood fell back as he ran, his breathing harsher and harsher in his ears. There were running footsteps behind him, a jerk on his cloak—

Even as he fell, he saw Reness turn, her eyes gleaming with rage and battle lust. She turned back and plunged into the warriors around them.

Hanstau rolled away, and then watched wide-eyed as Reness fought what had to be four, five warriors. Admiration rose, for she was a fine wild sight. But then fear washed over him. He struggled to rise. She'd be killed. No, no, he couldn't let this happen, but there were so many—

His despair overwhelmed him, and he almost sobbed. His breath caught as he tried to beg them to stop, not to hurt her—

Light exploded around his boot. Hanstau froze in astonishment. Golden light. Golden power. He sucked in air and with breath came hope. He could—

An image came to him from the power, of warriors engulfed in flame, burning, writhing, agony… *burn them?*

NO. Hanstau rejected the horror he saw in his mind's eye.

No, no. He cast about for another target, anything but—

The tents. Burn the tents!

With a WHOOSH and a crackle, the tents did just that.

All of them.

All around them.

Two of the warriors stayed on Reness, another grabbed Hanstau's shoulder from behind. The others ran off, yelling warnings, pulling down tents to smother the flames.

Reness was fighting hard, but these warriors were wary and experienced, moving to circle her like wolves. Hanstau's captor had an arm around his neck, pulling him up. Hanstau felt him take a breath, ready to shout—

Hanstau jerked the dagger Reness had insisted he carry out of its scabbard. He stabbed blindly back at the warrior's face. The blade hit bone, then slid into something softer.

His captor screamed.

Hanstau pushed harder, twisting his body away, twisting the dagger, turning to face his enemy.

His captor cried out again, the blade buried deep in his eye.

Hanstau yanked it out, intent on another strike, but the man collapsed at his feet.

Hanstau stood there, numb, breathing hard, staring down at the dying man.

"Hanstau," Reness's voice cut through the fog, and he blinked to see her at his side. The others were dead, and chaos reigned around them. "Come," she said.

He sheathed the dagger, and they ran together toward the herds.

* * * * *

Amyu's eyes popped open, staring at the night sky. Her heart racing, she lay still for a long breath.

Joden's breathing was soft and regular against her shoulder.

He didn't stir.

Something had woken her, something... she turned her head slightly, taking in their quiet camp.

Rafe and the others lay in their own bedrolls, still asleep. Fylin and Soar kept watch, their weapons at the ready, but they showed no signs of alarm. Neither did the horses, or the cows.

Amyu drew a deep breath, and let it out slowly. A dream, perhaps. Nothing more.

She closed her eyes, settling back, willing herself back to sleep. They'd leave in the morning, and seek out the Warprize and Master Eln. It would be a long day, and she should rest. She focused on Joden's breath. In and out, in and out...

Her heart slowed to its normal rate. Her breathing eased, and she fell back into sleep.

* * * * *

Simus roused, half-asleep, as Snowfall sat up, letting their blankets fall back. He grumbled, fumbling for them and for her.

"Power," she whispered. "Someone's using the power."

That brought him up, alert, sword in hand. "Where?" He demanded.

"Not close," Snowfall rose, reaching for her armor. "And further south, deep in the Plains."

Simus stood, considering. "Who?"

"I don't know," Snowfall shook her head, the beads of her weaving jangling softly.

"A threat?"

"Maybe," she pulled on her leather trous. "I will stand watch."

Simus sighed, and reached for his own trous.

* * * * *

Cadr was grateful when they finally stopped to make camp.

Lightning Strike kept them at a steady pace the last few days, but wouldn't call a halt until the sun was past the horizon. Cadr agreed with pushing on, but his aching ribs were just as happy to dismount from his horse.

"We'll risk a fire," Lightning Strike said as they started to pull saddles from the horses.

"I can help with that," Rhys offered.

"We've enough fresh meat," Gilla frowned, looking around for her warcats. They'd disappeared into the tall grass. "We can hunt tomorrow morning—"

All of the warcats' heads emerged from the tall grass, all facing the same way: south.

Lightning Strike's face went pale and he turned, wide-eyed, toward the south.

As did everyone else around them.

Cadr frowned, looked around as well, but there was nothing to see. Gilla and Rhys looked just as puzzled.

"What?" Gilla demanded.

Rhys shrugged, but Sidian answered her, his voice distant and distracted. "Power," he said. "A flare of power."

"Someone just used magic," Lightning Strike whispered.

"Like the sacrifice?" Gilla asked, shading her eyes.

"No," Lightning Strike said. "Not that strong, but—" he cut off his words. "It's gone."

The warcats lost interest, fading once again into the tall grass.

"I didn't see anything," Cadr said.

"It wasn't seen with the eye," Sidian said, still staring in that direction. He glanced at Lightning Strike. "I thought you said that all the warrior-priests that were left were here?" he asked.

"They are," Lightning Strike said. "All those that followed Wild Winds are all that survived the night of the Sacrifice."

"Hanstau," Cadr breathed. "It has to be Hanstau."

"The Xyian?" Lightning Strike asked.

"Yes," Excitement bubbled up in Cadr's chest, a relief of pain he hadn't known he was carrying. "The one Antas took. It has to be him. He is alive." Cadr turned on Lightning Strike. "I have to go, to rescue him. Where? Where was he?"

"Cadr," Sidian shook his head. "It doesn't work that way."

"You can't be sure," Lightning Strike said. "It could have been Hail Storm."

"Or against Hail Storm," Night Clouds added grimly.

"But I could, maybe I could find—" Cadr stopped when he saw the faces around him.

"You are still injured," Gilla said. "Even if we knew where—"

"Could you scry?" Cadr demanded.

"The surge didn't last long enough," Sidian shook his head, his arms folded over his chest. "There is nothing left to focus on."

"You think he's dead," Cadr said flatly, spinning to stare at Lightning Strike.

"I don't know, but—"

"But I had the same spike of power when I lost control back when Wild Winds was teaching us." Night Clouds held out his hands. "That amount of power…" he let his words trail off, with a shrug of his shoulders.

Cadr gave the south one last glance, then turned away. "Let's see to that fire," he said gruffly.

Later, after the others had settled into their tents, Cadr sat alone by the dying fire, poking at the coals with a stick.

Lightning Strike appeared, and sat next to Cadr. The fire danced on his tan skin, his dreadlocks falling forward to hide his face. His partial tattoos around his neck gleamed in the light.

They sat in silence for a moment.

"I have failed my Warlord," Cadr said softly. "I failed to keep my charge safe."

Lightning Strike nodded. "As I failed my master. As I fear

to fail my fellow warrior-priests."

Cadr frowned. "You will not fail them. You are taking them to safety."

"Am I?" Lightning Strike shook his head. "What use will Keir of the Cat and Simus of the Hawk have for half-trained warrior-priests?"

"You trust Snowfall," Cadr said.

"I do," Lightning Strike sighed. "But the doubt lingers."

Cadr offered his stick. "Poking at coals seems to help," he said.

Lightning Strike snorted, but accepted the offer.

"I know this much," Cadr said firmly. "I have served under both Keir of the Cat and Simus of the Hawk, and they listen to a warrior's truths. Even if it is not their truths.

"Are you certain they will listen?" Lightning Strike asked ruefully.

"Are you still a warrior-priest?" Cadr asked.

Lightning Strike poked at the coals as Cadr waited. Finally, he looked at Cadr, his eyes glittering. "I don't know," he admitted.

Cadr nodded.

Lightning Strike threw the stick into the fire, and rose to his feet. "The watches are set. We'd best sleep." He hesitated slightly. "I know something that might help with your pain. Would you share with me this night?" He reached out his hand.

Warrior-priests never shared with warriors, never forged bonds, never gave their names. So it had been for as long as Cadr knew. He reached out, and took Lightning Strike's hand.

"I would," Cadr said. "With pleasure."

* * * * *

Hanstau sat silent in the tall grass, watching. After a few hours of walking, Reness had decided to warble a thea camp for supplies, and a rider approached leading horses.

Reness wanted him hidden, but in all honesty, he wasn't sure he had the strength to stand even if he wanted to. Hanstau felt dazed, bruised, and everything around him seemed distant.

The rider approached, and Reness greeted her as an old friend. "I've brought the supplies," the thea gestured to the horses behind her, loaded down with supplies. "Saddles, blankets, tents, food, and waterskins."

"My thanks," Reness took the reins of the horses. "What news?"

"All the theas have taken their children into hiding," the thea shifted uneasily. "The camps are moving off, and we are going to scatter to the winds to prevent Antas from pursuing. None will support him now."

"Did Hail Storm get any children?" Reness demanded.

"There was only one teaching session." the thea said. "Antas will have no further access."

Hanstau couldn't see her eyes, but he could read the shame in the way she avoided Reness's gaze. "But there is a lad missing from Elder Nancer's camp. Nancer fears he has gone to Antas."

"Or Hail Storm." Reness shook her head.

"Come back with me," the thea urged. "Join our camps. You would be welcome, and there is strength in our numbers."

"No," Reness said firmly. "I have other plans, plans that involve staying away from Antas. I have not yet decided which direction I will take." She squared her shoulders. "Make it known to the other Elder theas that Wild Winds is dead."

"Skies," the woman breathed.

"There will be a Fall Council of Elders," Reness said. "And I will be there."

"As you say," the woman said. "I will spread the word." She looked up at the night sky. "I should be off. Antas hasn't stirred from his camp, still dealing with the consequences of fires. You should not be pursued."

"My thanks again for responding to my call." Reness said.

"An honor, Eldest Elder," the thea mounted. "May the elements be with you," she added and rode off. Hanstau stayed where he was until Reness spoke.

"Come," she said softly. "I will not be easy until we put some more distance between us and Antas." She knelt at his side, frowning.

"In the dark?" Hanstau heaved a sigh, eyeing the tall horses behind her.

"Not far," Reness said. "A few rises, and we will keep the horses at a walk."

Hanstau nodded and rose to his feet. Reness helped him mount, and wasn't that shameful? But he didn't even have the strength to be embarrassed.

They rode in silence, Reness leading the way, which left Hanstau alone with his thoughts.

Well, worries, really. About the golden light that had seemed willing to fry warriors like so many eggs. About how easy it would have been to do just that, in his anger and fear.

About whether Reness would still want him. It was easy enough to say in the confines of a prison but now? Surrounded by handsome, muscular Plains warriors?

Hanstau looked up when he realized his horse had stopped moving. They were between two rises, next to a stand of alders.

Reness was already dismounting, and pulling the packs off her animal. "There's a stream here," she said softly. "Within this grove. We'll set the tents, eat, and sleep."

Hanstau fretted as they worked to make camp. He could help with the basics, carrying food and seeing to the horses. But he wasn't much help with the small tent, even when Reness explained that it was actually two smaller tents combined into one.

She had him build a small fire as she finished. "Just enough for kavage," she said.

Hanstau nodded, and set to work, finding the tinder and a striker. Easy enough to get a small spark, and sit and feed it tiny bits of wood and dried grass.

Reness settled next to him, and dug out a small pot, and some dried meat. She handed him a share, and for a long moment, they both sat in silence, chewing and waiting for the pot to boil.

"Give me your dagger," Reness said softly. She was close enough to him that he could feel the heat of her body against his side. She took it, and tried to pull it from its sheath. The blade was stuck.

"Tsk," Reness clucked. "You are supposed to clean it, you know. On the grass or the clothes of the enemy."

"I'm sorry," Hanstau sighed.

"No matter," Reness stared at him. "I will clean it for you. But, Hanstau, what troubles you?"

Hanstau opened his mouth, but the pot favored him by boiling, and he managed to busy himself with the kavage. Once they were settled back, warm mugs in hand, Reness nudged his shoulder, and gave him a questioning look over the edge of her mug.

Hanstau sighed. "Reness," he started, then rushed on. "I am no warrior. I am not muscled, not tanned, not strong. I am a stout, balding healer of Xy who, tonight, broke his sacred oath to bring harm to none."

Reness leaned in closer. "He would have delivered you to Antas."

"Or Hail Storm," Hanstau shuddered. "But I could have found a way to—"

Reness kissed him. Her lips were warm, and soft, and wonderful. Hanstau closed his eyes, and kissed her back.

Reness broke the kiss. Her breath danced on his cheek. "You are who you are, Hanstau of Xy, and you are who I want.

I have a need for you. A need to learn all of you."

Hanstau opened his eyes, and stared into hers. Her eyes reflected the stars.

"Hanstau of Xy, would you share with me this night?" she asked.

"Yes," he said, his mouth dry.

"Good," Reness's smile was bright. "Now, take off those boots."

CHAPTER TWENTY

Antas was fond of the scent of death and smoke on the battlefield.

Just not in his own camp.

The sun was just rising, just enough to see. Smoke and stench filled his lungs as he stood with his Token-Bearer and his Second, and considered the damage. All around them his warriors sorted through smoldering tents, stomping the few flames that remained.

Antas knew that every eye watched and every ear listened.

"Report," he commanded softly.

"Every tent was hit," Veritt said just as quietly. "Even the small ones. Some only scorched, some completely destroyed. An attack from within."

Catha nodded, her arms folded over her chest, her head down. "The dead were all at Reness's hands," she said. "Your Warprize is nowhere to be found." She glanced at him, as if expecting him to explode. "We assume he fled with Reness."

Antas nodded, calmly. Now was not the time for rage. He'd save that for later. "Hail Storm?" he asked.

"No sign," Veritt said. "He disappeared in the confusion."

"And the Singer?" Antas asked.

"Gone as well," Veritt said. "But he only left with what he had on him. His tent was burned slightly."

"Hail Storm." Antas raised his voice. "It had to be. Only a warrior-priest would have the power to do this. He has betrayed us."

He looked at Veritt and Catha, but from the corner of his eye he could see nods and scowls on the faces around them. Good. Let their hate be focused elsewhere.

"Yet he was seated next to you when the drums sounded," a dry voice spoke from behind him.

"Ietha," Antas said, and made sure he was smiling before he turned.

Warlord Ietha stood there, surrounded by her people, her arms folded over her chest. "You held the Eldest Elder Thea captive?" she demanded, as if she didn't already know the answer to her question.

"No," Antas said. "I offered the warmth of my tents and asked her to stay to discuss the situation, and listen to my way of thinking. I wanted to persuade her." He shrugged. "I admit that I had forgotten the extent of her stubbornness." He sighed, and rubbed his hand over his face. "And perhaps I was stubborn in my own way," he admitted.

A snicker of laughter rose around them. Ietha's mouth quirked in one corner. "Perhaps?"

Antas shrugged again, then gave her a sheepish grin. Which was too much too fast, as Iaetha frowned again.

"To hold an Eldest Elder against their will, is not the way of the Plains, Antas."

"Ietha," Antas shook his head. "How could I hold her against her will? A thea? No, if she truly wished to leave she would have been gone or dead on her own blade."

There were nods to that, and he hurried on, making a wide gesture to draw their eyes to the camp. "The damage is done now. Hail Storm must have plotted with Reness against us."

Ietha considered him.

"Who else could use his power in such a way?" Antas demanded. "And after all that we had done for him. Offered food and shelter and—"

"Cut off his arm," Ietha added drily.

"Saved his life, from the sickness within him," Antas said. "Caused by a city-dweller, coming to the Plains."

"Yet he has fled," Ietha said. "With Reness."

"And my Warprize," Antas growled. "We are betrayed."

"He was seated beside us in the tent," Ietha frowned again.

Antas shrugged. "Who knows the power of a warrior priest?"

"I am almost of a mind to cry challenge on you." Ietha hadn't moved, hadn't changed her stance, but the threat was there now, in the air between them.

The winds died, and it seemed as if the entire camp held still in anticipation. For a wild breath, he thought of pulling his sword, and running her through with a swift lunge, but sanity prevailed. He needed her and her warriors, and she knew that.

Carefully, Antas made a show of sighing, and slowly running his hand through his hair.

"I would have no warrior beside me that is not fully supportive of me, and my cause." He said mildly. "We think alike, you and I. We defend the traditional ways, and would resist the changes Keir and his like would force upon us."

"We do," Ietha said and with that the tension was gone. "Let us see to this mess, and then consider our options."

"Agreed," Antas said.

* * * * *

Hail Storm and his new apprentice traveled far enough during the night to be out of sight of the camps, away from any that might interfere with the lesson. Jahal had gathered supplies and two horses. The horses were ground tied now, and far enough away that they did not object to Hail Storm's presence.

They'd stopped to eat, and Hail Storm had the young one set snares. "For your first lesson," he said casually, and the boy's face had lit up.

They'd talked as they waited. Earnest and eager, the boy had revealed more than he'd known. About the theas being suspicious of Hail Storm's intentions. About how no other of his tent mates had been interested in the warrior-priest's words.

"But I am," Jahal assured him. "I want to learn."

Hail Storm nodded silently, and considered. The boy seemed malleable and easily influenced. He'd no fear that he could train him on this new path to power. Once he'd claimed the dark power for himself, the boy would lose the ability to use the elemental magics, and really have no choice but to join with Hail Storm.

But first, to let him make his first sacrifice.

"Kill it, and see what I see," Hail Storm demanded.

Jahal looked down at the rabbit squirming in his hands.

Hail Storm stood behind the boy, just to the side, watching.

Jahal's lips thinned, as he knelt and pressed the rabbit to the ground. He thrust his blade into its throat. The rabbit convulsed in his hands, its blood staining Jahal's fingers.

"You can see it," Hail Storm asked. "The life as it flows out? Capture that dark essence and make it your own."

"I can," Jahal's voice cracked in excitement. "I can see it, Elder."

Hail Storm was careful not to sniff at the boy's enthusiasm. There was little in the way of power from the death of the tiny animal, but it was a start. Once he'd learned the darker path, they could—

"I see both, the golden and the dark, all the power!" Jahal crowed.

Both? He sees both?

Rage flooded through Hail Storm, pure fury that made his vision go dark, blurring his sight. *He has what I've lost.*

Of its own accord, his hand pulled out his bone knife. A mere step and yank on the boy's hair and his knife plunged itself into Jahal's throat.

Even as the blade hit bone, Hail Storm regretted his action. Alive, unharmed, the boy was worth more to him... but what was done was done. He followed the body down into the grass, and as he had with Arched Colors, he drained the boy's power and life as he died.

Yet with Arched Colors he'd been pressed for time, and here, now, he could take the time to go further, to drain every bit of energy until the body was a dried husk of nothing.

Hail Storm knelt there, panting, feeling the exultation of the power he'd drawn within.

One of the horses snorted, scenting the blood.

Hail Storm froze. The packs. The supplies. They were still on the horses.

Mentally he cursed himself for a fool. The horses tolerated the boy, but they wouldn't tolerate his approach. He glanced over. They were a fair distance off, there would be no way he could reach them before they bolted.

But he'd power now, didn't he? And as he had done with that captive, he could use it well.

Hail Storm rose slowly to his feet, clutching the knife in his right. He turned, focused on both the horses, and reached out, clutching his fist tight.

Both horses jerked their heads up, their eyes rolling in their heads, but unable to move. Their chests heaved as they fought for freedom.

Hail Storm strode forward, focused on their struggle, letting his power flow out.

Sweat gleamed on their hides, foam flecking in the corners of their mouths.

Hail Storm stopped steps away, his own breathing ragged and hard. They were big animals, bigger than a human, and they were struggling. His control was slipping.

A moment's thought, and he released the one with the

saddle. It reared, screaming its fear, and galloped off.

The other fought, but Hail Storm's control held.

He drew closer, the blade in his hand. He couldn't subdue a living horse to his will for long.

But a dead one?

* * * * *

It took Quartis a few days to locate Essa and the others. While he had a general idea of the location, it wasn't like the Eldest Elder wanted to be found.

He passed the guards on watch, and then headed toward the main tent where they had gathered for the evening meal.

He pushed through the flap, and the laughter and music stopped.

"Quartis," Essa called from his elevated seat on the wooden platform. "What news?"

Quartis stood before him, bowed, and then started talking. There was much to tell, and halfway through someone pushed a mug of kavage into his hand.

At the end, Essa shook his head, and gestured for Quartis to sit next to him on the platform. "Eat," he said.

Quartis balanced his mug with a platter of fried gurtle meat and flat bread. The red flakes were thick, just the way he liked it. The spicy scent made his mouth water.

"Eldest Elder," Para stood. "What will we do?"

Essa shrugged. "Summer comes. It is the Season of War. Many of the Warlords have gone off to loot, to plunder, and raid, for the benefit of the Plains and the Tribes, as they do every summer. It is the way of our people. It is in our blood."

Quartis hurried to swallow. "Singers too," he said.

"Singers too," Essa said. "But this season, the warriors with Keir and Antas will sit idle in the heat, waiting for a confrontation that will not come for perhaps months. Maybe at the Fall

Council, maybe at the borders of Xy itself." Essa regarded the room. "Regardless they will gather at the Heart whoever prevails, and we will be waiting."

"So, we will do as we have always done. What do we normally do in this season? We gather. We sing, exchange news, and talk. But unlike other seasons of war, in this season we will not join the armies. We will scatter into the grasses, to stay safe and low until—" he broke off as one of the guards entered the tent, clearly agitated. "What is it?"

"Eldest Elder, the tent of the Ancients has appeared."

Quartis could feel the loathing rolling off of the Eldest Elder Singer as Essa rose to his feet. He pitied the man, even as he took another bite. To have to face those—

"Quartis," Essa commanded. "Come with me."

Quartis scrambled to his feet, swallowing and wiping his hands on his trous. He followed Essa out of the tent, and they both stood looking at a far rise where a tent stood alone against the horizon.

Essa swore under his breath, and started walking through the tall grass. Quartis followed.

It had been years since his Trial as a Singer. Quartis only had a vague memory of the Ancients when they had blessed him. The tent was as dark and hot as he remembered, and the three old figures wrapped in blankets had not changed.

Essa marched up to stand in front of them, and glared. "What?" he demanded. "It's not enough you have cost me a fine, potential—"

"Where is Joden of the Hawk?" Came a thin, quavering voice.

Essa gaped at them. "You don't know?" he asked.

The Ancients stared at him with three sets of glittering eyes. Quartis felt the very air grow thick and oppressive.

"You *don't* know," Essa breathed.

The silence was deafening. Quartis's heart pounded in his ears.

Essa folded his arms over his chest. "When we opened the grave, Joden was gone."

"Dead?" this voice was a cackle. Wavering and uncertain to Quartis's ears.

"We'd know," a third voice said. "We'd know if he were—"

"Silence," whispered the last voice.

"You are supposedly all powerful, all knowing," Essa demanded. "And yet you—"

"Be gone," the voices chorused, and with that Quartis found himself outside the tent, Essa at his side. Before he could even turn, he knew the tent was gone.

"What was that about?" he asked Essa.

"I have no idea," Essa said. He glanced behind, snorted, and then started walking back to camp. "But my decision is made. We will fade into the grass, and stay safe and distant from any and all disputes. Except for you, Quartis."

"Me?"

Essa nodded. "You, I am sending to the border of Xy. You will be my eyes and ears."

"To watch for?" Quartis pressed.

"Whatever is to come."

CHAPTER TWENTY-ONE

Joden awoke to Amyu in his arms, the camp stirring around them.

Amyu was warm, cuddled close, her head under his chin. He breathed in the scent of her hair, as he blinked against the morning. Something smoky in the smell, carrying a hint of the grasses of the Plains and the open sky.

Rafe knelt by the fire, stirring up the coals. Joden caught his eye.

Rafe smiled. "Toasted bread with gurt, and some hot kavage before we start," Rafe offered. "Then we will get you to Water's Fall."

"If he can ride," Fylin said, setting flat bread to warm on the stones.

"He can ride," Amyu said sharply. She moved in his arms and Joden released her with regret. She rose, tossing the blankets aside. Joden stood slowly, feeling every bruise, and started to fold blankets.

"We could load you up in that cheese wagon, and haul you to the city." Rafe made the offer with a grin, his eyes sparkling as he nodded toward the wagon over by two big wooden doors.

Joden stopped what he was doing, narrowed his eyes and glared at Rafe.

Rafe laughed, and shrugged. "Just as well. I have no idea how you harness horses to it anyway."

Amyu wore her leathers, and now stared at the mass of white cloth Joden had shed the night before. She frowned. "This is the worse for wear." She glanced over at the wooden doors. "I wonder if there is anything in there we could use."

Joden caught her eye, and tilted his head toward the doors with a lift of his brow.

"It's where they store their cheese," she explained. "Those saddles I told you about? They are in there as well."

"Locked up tight," Soar said as she brought out a sack of gurt. "Kalisa's..." she paused, frowning. "Sons of sons?"

"Nephews." Rafe said firmly. "They moved most of the herds to different grasses and locked up the barn. Not too happy, it seems."

Amyu flushed bright red.

Joden stepped close, and took the white cloth from her hands. "W-w-we can m-m-make this work." he said.

"Best not to shock the city-dwellers with naked Firelanders," Rafe laughed. "At least, not this early in the morning!"

* * * * *

It felt good to be riding again. The feel of the horse under him, the reins in his hand, the wind on his face, it was all familiar and welcome to Joden.

Rafe had taken the lead and the other warriors had surrounded Joden. Amyu had dropped back, behind and to Joden's right. He frowned at her, but she shook her head at him. He gave her a nod, and faced front. Now was not the time to make an issue of her status.

Not that he had the words to aid her, or argue in her defense.

The road ahead went through the trees, heading down to the valley before the City of Water's Fall. Rafe had said it would take a few hours, and he kept them at a good pace.

Joden tried to focus on riding, and not on the meeting to come. While it would be good to see Lara and Keir again, whether Master Eln or Lara could heal his affliction was not something he wanted to think about.

Had the winds done this? Joden strived to remember. He'd asked to take the old paths. He could remember singing to the others, dancing in the ring of earth. But the memories grew hazy and faint, until there was a blank in his mind. Joden shook his head, as if the motion would restore lost thoughts. He'd never felt this before, being unable to recall. It was a terrible, empty feeling and—

"Finally," Rafe called out ahead. "I can see the walls."

Joden lifted his head. They were coming out of the trees and the ruins of Water's Fall stood before them.

Ruins.

Joden sucked in a breath.

The great city was shattered, destroyed. The walls had fallen, mere rubble before them. The proud gates were gone, only angry black scorch marks in their place. The buildings were collapsed within, their roofs sagging or gone completely. There were no signs of life, other than the wyverns wheeling above in the sky, circling and circling—

"Let's run for a bit," Rafe called and urged his horse to a gallop.

Joden frowned, but said nothing. Did they not see what he saw? A glance told him that they didn't, or at least that they thought nothing of it. He looked back at Amyu, but she returned his look with one of concern, not shock.

Joden turned to stare again, only to find the city walls whole and well, with guards walking the walls, scanning the clear skies above.

His horse kept up with the others of its own will. Joden was too stunned to do more than keep his seat. What had he seen? He had seen it. It had been as real as his own breath. But now it was gone.

Rafe led them at a gallop, but he didn't hold them to that

pace long. He raised a hand, slowing as they hit the main road to the gates. These fields were usually under plow, with various crops. Lara had explained it to him and Simus one night. But now both sides of the road were lined with tents of the Plains, an army that spread out as far as the eye could see. Joden craned around, searching. Yes, there was Keir's command tent, and the dance grounds where he had displayed his Warprize to his men…

But that was in the past, and Keir's army had returned to the Plains and disbanded. There were no tents—

And like that, they were gone.

Joden's heart start to thump in his chest. He sucked in air, suddenly aware that he'd stopped breathing.

The winds. Had they taken his wits?

Tall plants, crops of some kind, danced in the breeze on both sides of the road. The tents, the army, gone as if the winds had taken them.

Joden sucked in another breath, and another, trying to focus on his horse beneath him, the sun and the sky, and—

Amyu coughed.

He glanced to his right. She had urged her horse up, slipping in beside him, worry on her face. As if she sensed his pain. Now it was her turn to raise an eyebrow in a silent question.

He nodded, and gave her a weak smile.

She frowned, but nodded back, and let her horse slow to resume her place.

What was happening to him? The past as clear as the present? Was that the future he was seeing? Joden's gut roiled and he rubbed a hand over his face. Were his voice and sanity both gone?

"Heyla," Rafe called out, waving toward the walls of the city.

Joden straightened in the saddle, and faced forward. It wasn't far now, the gates were growing closer. The guards on the walls had spotted them; Joden could see them moving about, preparing to allow them in. The tilled fields ended, as Lara had explained.

There were only the mounds to pass, the mounds left by the mass burials of the dead, bodies of Xyian and Plains warriors both.

Only, the dead were waiting for him.

They lined the road, quiet and solemn, garbed as they had been in life, with armor and weapons at their side.

Joden's horse slowed, and stopped.

The dead ignored Rafe as he passed, and the other warriors. But they turned to Joden, looking at him, all their attention focused on him.

Joden sat and stared. So many dead, so many lives cut short. Yet in death, they stood side by side, waiting.

Watching.

There were no words, but Joden knew. They wondered if their sacrifice was worth the price. Wondered what they had given their lives for.

They looked to Joden for answers.

"Joden?" Amyu's voice cut through his daze.

He caught the scent of her hair, and it brought him back to the world. She'd brought her horse close to his, so close their legs touched. The others were ahead of them, quizzical looks on their faces.

"Joden?" Amyu repeated. "Are you well?"

"The dead," he kept his voice low. "All around us."

Her eyes went wide, and she glanced around, shifting in her saddle. So did Joden.

The dead were still there, still waiting.

"Let me have your reins," Amyu said softly.

He nodded, but couldn't seem to make his hands work. He felt her warm fingers on his as she slid the reins from his hands. He clutched at his saddle with a tight, desperate grip.

Amyu urged her horse forward, and nodded to Rafe. Rafe took the lead again, but this time at a slow walk. The other warriors took up positions around them, and their little procession headed toward the gates.

Joden felt his horse start to walk with the rest, heard the guards call out, heard the great gates start to swing wide to admit them. But he only had eyes for the dead, silent and watching.

The dead, lining the roadside.

The dead, who knelt, their heads bowed, as he passed. Row after row of endless, silent witnesses.

"Our dead travel with us, ride along beside us," Joden recited the ancient words in his head, words he'd heard from his theas. "Unseen and unknown, but knowing and seeing," he choked as he continued the litany. "Until the longest night, when we mourn our dead, who are released to journey to the stars."

Yet these dead were still here.

Joden kept his eyes open, and met the gaze of every warrior, every man and woman. It was the least he could do, maybe all he could do.

He endured until Rafe lead them through the gates, and then he closed his eyes.

It was enough.

* * * * *

Amyu's gentle hands led Joden into the Healing House. She didn't question him, or ask him to open his eyes, just calmly put his hand on her shoulder and warned about steps and low doorways. He was grateful for her quiet strength at his side.

There were exclamations, and various people speaking all at once, but Master Eln's voice cut through the confusion. "Bring him in here, Amyu."

Amyu moved and he moved with her, sensing the walls of the hallway.

"Joden?" came a shocked exclamation. "Amyu?"

Joden opened his eyes. Lara, Warprize and Queen of Xy stood there in tunic and trous, confused and anxious.

Behind her, Joden caught a glimpse of an old woman lying on a bed, staring at the ceiling, with others standing around her. There was something familiar about that profile, something—

The old lady turned her head, taking them in. Her eyes reminded him of the Ancients.

A soft exclamation from Amyu and he was being tugged further down the hall, to the door where Eln was standing. Joden caught a last glimpse of the old woman as Lara shut the door and followed them. "Joden?" she started. "How did you—"

"Questions can wait," Eln said, ushering them in. "We need to see to injuries first. On the table, Joden."

Joden pulled up short, jerking Amyu back.

Eloix lay on the table, her back wounded, raw and festering. Master Eln stood over her with a handful of bloodmoss, his face grim. Amyu knelt by Eloix's head, and yet she was guiding him in. Master Eln was behind him.

Yet they were there, at the table. Master Eln plunged his hand into the wound, and the bloodmoss withered away.

Joden reeled back, swaying. Amyu moved to support him, even as Master Eln moved in from the other side. Lara's hands were on his back.

"Joden?" Amyu said, her worry clear. "What are you seeing?"

"Y-y-you tried b-b-bloodmoss on El-l-loix?" Joden closed his eyes, and shook his head, willing the image away. But the vision was still there.

"Amyu told you?" Eln sounded resigned. "I'd hoped it would counteract the poison of the wyvern sting."

Joden watched as Eloix plunged her dagger into her own throat. "S-s-she didn't let you g-g-give mercy." he looked at Amyu.

"She considered me a child," Amyu said, her brown eyes open and staring at Joden. "And I did not tell you that."

Joden was shaken, but he caught the glance that Lara and

Eln exchanged.

"Let's get him on the table before he falls," Lara said. "We can start on answers then."

* * * * *

Amyu pressed herself into a corner of the room, and watched as the two healers examined Joden. She was grateful that their focus was on their patient, but she knew her reckoning for her actions was due. Any delay in that was welcome.

Still, for now all that mattered was Joden.

"Sweet Goddess," Lara frowned as they stripped Joden of the white cloth, little more than rags now. "What happened to you?"

The healers were looking at his body, only Amyu was focused on Joden's face. His expression was one of pain and sorrow. "I-I-I," he grimaced as he tried to force out the words.

Lara froze. "Joden?"

Master Eln was pulling down bottles and jars from his shelves. He looked over his shoulder with raised eyebrows.

"Joden doesn't stutter," Lara said grimly. "At least, he never has before." She turned, and those fey blue eyes pierced Amyu like an arrow. "What happened?"

Amyu tore her gaze away, and looked at Joden. Joden sighed, then nodded his permission.

"I went into the mountains, searching for airions," Amyu started.

"We will speak of that later," Lara's words were crisp and firm, but without heat.

Amyu nodded. "I failed. I'd just decided to give up, when I…" she hesitated, then made a decision. "When I saw a flutter of white. I climbed higher, and—" she kept to the essentials of the tale.

Lara and Eln listened in silence. Amyu couldn't tell if they believed her or not, but that mattered very little.

"That is all I know," Amyu said finally.

"Let us check you over," Eln said. "And treat these cuts. Not much we can do about the bruising…"

With relief, Amyu saw that they were going to drop the issue for now. They went over Joden's body, using bloodmoss and ointments and various creams.

Finally, Master Eln stepped back. "Well, you are clearly in a weakened state. You need food, water, warmth, and sleep." He hesitated. "There is no sign of a head wound. Do you remember any blows to the head?"

"N-n-no," Joden managed, and tried to continue, but Master Eln cut him off.

"And you say that the stammer started before the fall, is that right? Are you sure?"

"Y-y-yes," Joden took a breath. "I-I-I wo-wo-wo—"

"Joden is a Singer," Lara said. "He's never had trouble with speech before this."

Joden started again. "I-I-I—"

"Well," Master Eln talked over him. "The convulsions are a concern. When did the first one occur?"

"I-I-I d-d-don't-" Joden said.

"Then I suspect that—"

"Stop that," Amyu stepped forward, furious. "Stop cutting him off. Joden can talk, you just have to give him time to get the words out."

Both Lara and Eln stared at her, and then glanced at one another. Master Eln bowed his head in her direction. "I am sorry. You are correct, of cour—"

"Apologize to Joden," Amyu snapped.

"I offer my apologies, Joden of the Hawk." Eln inclined his head again, this time talking directly to Joden.

Joden nodded back. "F-f-forgiven." He gave the healer a

small smile. "F-f-frustrating."

"Infuriating as well, I imagine," Eln said. "So. Let me try again. This started before you fell?"

"Y-y-yes. I-I-I wo-" Joden grimaced, but fought on. "Wo-wo-woke this way."

Eln waited to make sure that Joden was finished speaking. "I am not sure about the cause. Especially with no head wound, and no sign of a brain storm." Master Eln hesitated. "Sometimes, rarely, I have seen where there has been a blow to the heart - not a physical blow, mind, but one of…" Eln stopped. "You are a warrior of the Plains, Joden and I would offer no insult but where there has been such pain of the heart, speech has been affected."

"What is the remedy?" Amyu asked, her heart almost bursting in her chest. "With all your skills, why aren't you reaching for a jar or ointment or one of those awful teas?"

"The only remedy we know of is time," Lara said sadly.

"And that is not a complete cure," Eln warned. "The damage may be permanent."

Joden's shoulders sagged, and he nodded.

Lara's face was the picture of grief, reflecting Amyu's own pain at the news. She wasn't sure how Joden could bear this.

But then Joden straightened, and took a deep breath. "At-at-at l-l-least c-c-can still t-t-t," he hesitated. "S-s-peak." He gifted them all with a smile.

Amyu's heart broke a little more as her eyes teared up.

Master Eln cleared his throat. "As to those awful teas," he said, reaching for another jar. "I have one here that will aid with the bruising, and help you sleep."

"And you, young lady," Lara turned on Amyu. "I see those bruises you are trying to hide beneath your armor. You took the same fall as Joden. Let's see to you."

Amyu swallowed hard. The reckoning had come. She knew her duty. She knelt at the feet of the Warprize, and pressed herself to the floor, her hands out in supplication. As required of a child of the Plains who had disobeyed her thea.

There was silence above her; all she could hear was her pounding heart and her harsh breath against the stone floor.

"Amyu, stand before me." The Warprize commanded.

Amyu rose, afraid to look her in the eyes.

The Warprize's voice shook, "I confess I was furious when I realized where you had gone, but I was angry because I feared for you. I was worried sick. The mountains hold their own dangers, as you have learned."

Amyu nodded, still staring at the floor.

"I have told you before, and will tell you again, you are an adult in my eyes. I may not agree with your choices," and now Amyu felt fingers under her chin. Lara lifted her head so that Amyu had no choice but to look her in the eye. Lara was smiling, and had tears in her eyes. "But I also know what it is to go after something you want more than life itself."

Now they were both crying.

"So let's see to you," Lara stepped back, and gestured. "Get out of that armor so we can treat your injuries."

"I can promise you," Master Eln said drily. "It will involve those awful teas."

CHAPTER TWENTY-TWO

It was only after she had been treated with bloodmoss, had creams and ointments rubbed on every bruise, and been handed a cup of vile tea that Amyu worked up her courage to ask. "How does Kalisa?"

Master Eln snorted as he handed a cup of the same tea to Joden. "The only thing wrong with her is old age and attitude, neither of which I have a tea for." He glared at Amyu. "Drink."

Amyu took an obedient sip, then shared a glance with Joden, who shared a grimace with her.

"I fear it comes down to just that," the Warprize said softly, casting a look at the door behind her. "Her family told me they had never seen her so angry as she was before she collapsed. She's not really been coherent since they got her here, and she's not eating. I fear her time is near." She narrowed her eyes at Amyu. "I haven't pressed for more information. She gets upset and agitated when we do. Why were you asking her questions about airions?"

The door burst open, and Prest ducked into the room. He dropped his armful of chain armor, leathers, and weapons on the table. "Joden," he said, then nodded to Amyu. "Rafe told me of your need. We are of a size."

"P-p-prest," Joden exclaimed. "Wh-wh-wh—"

Prest waited patiently.

"Wh-what are you doing here?" Joden finally got the words out.

"Guarding a stubborn Warprize, who insists on coming to

the Healers without proper escort," Prest growled. "One that needs to return shortly to nurse the babes."

Lara gave them an impish smile. "I sneak down in healer's robes and a cloak and no one is the wiser. But he's right, I need to get back to the castle. Answers can wait. I will say my farewells to Kalisa's family while you dress." She slipped out the door.

"Rafe said your leather trous were torn." Prest handed Amyu a bundle from the pile. "This is from him, he is closer to your size."

Amyu took the bundle with a nod of thanks.

"I must keep an eye on my charge," Prest said. "She is as slippery as a snake, and I do not trust her."

"She is the Queen of Xy," Master Eln said with a huff. "Her people love her."

"I do not trust them, either," Prest said, as he disappeared out into the hall.

"I am going to make up packets of tea to take with you," Eln said, as he too went to leave. "Dress quickly. I need the room for people who are actually sick."

Joden started dressing, feeling better at the touch of cloth and the weight of the chain on his shoulders.

Amyu was quicker, pulling on leathers and tightening her belt. She fussed with the buckle, not looking up. "The visions," she said quietly. "You did not tell them."

Joden adjusted his own sword belt, making sure both dagger and sword were secure. He shrugged, not willing to try to speak.

"You saw Eloix die?" Amyu spoke in the barest of whispers.

Joden glanced at the table, which thankfully remained empty. He nodded.

Amyu bit her lip, frowning. "The next time it happens, put a hand on my shoulder. No one needs to know until you are ready to tell them."

"M-m-my thanks," he managed to get out.

Amyu gave him her soft smile. "Ready?" she asked, looking around the area.

Prest stuck his head in. "Come, quickly. The Warprize is ready to leave. Rafe and the others are waiting."

* * * * *

Joden felt more like himself with armor over his chest and a sword and dagger at his side. The weight of the chain and the leathers was a comfort.

Not to mention boots.

Even better was the lack of visions as he went toward the Castle of Water's Fall.

They'd slipped through the back streets with Lara leading the way, over Prest's protests. But even Prest had to admit that she knew the ways better than he, but that didn't stop him from grumbling.

Once through the gates of the castle walls, Lara took them through the gardens toward the kitchen. "I'll get Anna to feed you," she said as they crossed the yard, past a sparring circle. "I need to check on the babes."

A shriek split the air. Joden spun on his heel, and watched as two naked bodies tumbled off the roof and hit a small wooden structure, shattering it beneath them. Chickens squawked, and feather flew into the air.

"Joden?"

Heath rose first, moving stiffly, helping Atira to her feet. They were both laughing and shushing each other as they fled the scene, climbing the large tree and disappearing into a window above.

"Joden?"

Amyu was at his side, the others staring at him in confusion.

He gave them a weak smile, intending it to be reassuring even as he reached out and squeezed Amyu's shoulder. But Lara's frown deepened.

The door opened behind her, and Keir stepped out, a bundled babe in his arms. "Lara?" he asked then stopped dead. *"Joden?"*

Lara reached for the babe. "Kavage," she said firmly. "Kavage and food before any questions."

Keir's astonishment faded from his eyes, to be replaced with concern as he took in Joden's appearance. Keir gave a sharp nod. "Follow me." They all followed within.

The kitchen was filled with people, noise, and wonderful smells. Joden's stomach rumbled even as the noise overwhelmed him.

Then the room went silent and dark, the absence of light and heat almost as disorienting. The fires were unlit, except for one lone candle casting shadows about the room.

Anna, seated at a table, weeping alone with a nightshirt in her hands.

Her pain hit Joden like a blow.

Noise flooded back into his world, bringing light and sounds and scents. Anna stood before them in her glory, in her kingdom, but not happy to see them invade.

Joden stared at the contrast of the vibrant woman before him with the sorrowing one in his vision.

"Out with ya," Anna commanded, wooden spoon in hand, her chins all wobbling as she scolded. "I'll send up the nooning shortly."

Joden swayed, then a warm body pressed against his side, and without thinking he reached for Amyu's shoulder.

Amyu stood close, strong and solid. He took in her scent, her presence, more powerful than those hated teas.

She glanced up, giving him time. When he returned her look, she waited for him to take a step, and then stayed close as they followed Lara and Keir out of the kitchens and into the halls.

Joden took steadying breaths, and concentrated on moving his feet. The stones around them were grey and cool, lit by arrow slits along the way, but at night he knew—

The hall went dark as the night, with no torches to light the shadows. The assassins leapt at Heath from behind.

Joden squeezed Amyu's shoulder, feeling her leather armor under his fingers, her solid bones beneath that.

The corridor grew light again, with no blood, no blades.

"Kayla had just started to fuss," Keir was telling Lara as they walked. "Keirson is with the wet nurse."

"We can eat and talk in our chambers," Lara said. She glanced back at Joden. "Privately. Joden has much to tell us."

And no words to tell you with, Joden thought.

* * * * *

Marcus waited for them in the chambers. He allowed Keir and Lara to pass, and Joden. Amyu was not surprised when he blocked her way. "We will talk later about the pain you have caused Herself," he growled.

Amyu nodded.

Marcus huffed, allowed her in, then blocked Rafe and Prest. "Herself is about, feeding," he announced. "Go about your own work."

The Warprize may have adopted many of the ways of the Plains, but she was still of Xy.

The wet nurse was already in one corner nursing Keirson, but that was acceptable. "She does not speak the language of the Plains," Lara said, avoiding the Xyian tongue. She settled in one of the chairs before the hearth where a small fire burned, just enough to take the chill from the stone.

These chambers had not changed, and yet it felt strange to Amyu. Different. But her real focus was Joden. She stepped forward, and saw to it that he settled in one of the more comfortable chairs, facing the Warlord and Warprize.

The Warlord leaned forward, his blue eyes intent. "Joden, how do I come to find you in Xy?"

"Amyu," Marcus jerked his head at her. "Aid me with the nooning."

"No," Amyu stood by the arm of Joden's chair.

All three looked at her in astonishment.

"At least," she amended. "Not yet. I will tell the beginning of the tale from my truth. Joden can speak after he has eaten."

There was a clatter at the door, of servants and dishes. The smell made Amyu's mouth water.

Keir leaned back in his chair. "As you say," he said mildly. "Tell me your truths."

Amyu took a breath, and felt the slightest pressure of Joden's hand against her hip. The smallest of things, but it gave her confidence.

"I went into the mountains, searching for airions," Amyu started, using the same words she had given to Master Eln and the Warprize. But this time she left nothing out, about the caves, and the animal attack, and almost giving up until she saw a flutter of white and heard a snatch of song.

Lara rose to trade babes with the wet nurse. "You heard singing? Coming from Joden?"

She returned to her chair with Keirson in her arms, and put him to her shoulder, patting his back. "Are you sure?"

Amyu shrugged. "He was unconscious when I found him, Warprize." She continued to describe his condition and the actions she had taken. She told of Joden walking toward the edge, but didn't mention the visions. That was Joden's part of the tale to tell.

She kept an eye on Joden as she talked, making sure he ate and drank as he listened, occasionally nodding his agreement.

Once she was sure he'd eaten his fill, she wrapped up the tale with meeting Rafe and the others.

Marcus shoved a plate at her, with a mug of kavage.

"Joden?" Keir leaned forward. "How did you get there from the Plains?"

* * * * *

He'd dreaded this.

Joden took a sip of kavage, and then stared down into it. Whatever else he was, he was no coward.

The babe in Lara's arms started waving his fists around. Lara moved her face away, avoiding those tiny hands.

Joden smiled at Lara. "Th-th-the T-t-tribe h-h-has g-g-grown. Th-th-the t-t-tribe h-h-has f-f-f-" he closed his eyes, and screwed up his face. "F-f-f-lourished."

Lara returned the smile a thousandfold.

Joden lifted his head, and looked Keir in the eye.

"I-I-I," he paused and took a breath, fighting panic. How was he going to—

Amyu settled down on the floor with her meal, just in front of his chair. She leaned back slightly, putting pressure against his leg. With no other obvious sign of support, she started eating.

Joden puffed out that breath and tried again. "T-t-the T-t-trials of S-s-singer," he forced out. "I ch-ch-chose an old path."

There was a flicker of pained sympathy over Keir's face, but then he settled back in his chair and waited.

Joden frowned, more to himself than anything, trying to decide what to say. "I-I-I c-c-cannot tell all. B-b-but the winds t-t-took me wh-wh-where they w-w-willed."

Marcus had taken Kayla into his arms, and the wet nurse slipped out the door. He brought the babe to Keir, who took her with a smile of thanks. Kayla was fussing, and Keir put her to his shoulder and drummed her back softly.

"And Simus? When did you leave him?" Keir asked.

Joden struggled on, telling of Simus's trials and Snowfall's appearance. It took what felt like hours, but he didn't give up. Keir had to know, and had to hear it from Joden.

"Y-y-yers w-w-wrong," Joden said finally. His head was pounding, and his neck and shoulders ached with the strain of trying to speak. He was tired and frustrated, but his truth needed to be said. "S-s-simus is l-l-loyal t-t-to y-y-you."

Keir stood, taking the babe to a cradle nearby. His face was grim, his silence speaking more than words.

Keirson started to cry as Lara rose. "This boy," she said, shaking her head. "I swear he hates to sleep. Like he might miss something." She rocked him for a bit until he settled, then put him in the cradle next to his sister.

Everyone held their breath, but Keirson settled quietly.

Lara turned, her voice hushed. "Enough. The babes need their sleep, and I think everyone could benefit from rest. I, for one, am taking a nap."

Joden rose, as Keir gestured toward the door. "Come. Let's see to a room for you."

Joden took a step, then hesitated, looking back at Amyu, still seated on the floor. She gave him a nod of encouragement, and it was enough.

Joden nodded back, ignoring the glances of the others. He turned and followed Keir. They eased out of the door quietly, but once it was closed behind them, Joden shook his head.

"S-s-spar?" he asked.

Keir's face lit up. "There's a practice ring outside the kitchens."

* * * * *

Amyu rose quietly as the others left. The Warprize had already eased herself onto the bed, and the babes were sleeping. She'd follow Joden and see to it that he—

Marcus was in front of her, dirty dishes in hand and a glare in his eye.

CHAPTER TWENTY-THREE

Amyu was grateful that Marcus let her change into tunic and trous and tie back her hair before marching her down to the scrubbing room off the kitchens. He was in little mood to let her do anything else, already grousing at her as they walked.

The large stone room held wooden tubs for washing, with long, narrow windows high on the walls. Sunlight streamed in through the steam as the kitchen maids poured heated water in the tubs, chattering as they worked. They looked up when Marcus entered, raising eyebrows, and clearing a space for them. There was no lack of understanding glances Amyu's way.

"What were you thinking?" he groused as he plunged the dishes into one of the tubs. "Herself just giving birth and has two new babes to care for, and you traipsing—" he gestured for Amyu to wash.

Amyu stayed silent, and concentrated on each dish. Never mind that Anna's staff would have washed these as well, especially since they were close to finishing their tasks. Amyu knew that this wasn't really about the dishes.

But she wasn't going to prolong the lecture by missing a spot.

"Herself all flustered, with not having enough milk—"

That got Marcus some dirty looks from the women around them. Men in Xy didn't talk about babies apparently, or breasts or the milk they contained. Amyu noticed some rolling eyes in their direction. Of course, men in Xy also did not wash dishes.

Which puzzled Amyu. They ate, didn't they?

But the maids' disapproval didn't stop Marcus's sharp tongue. At least he was drying as he scolded.

"—finding out you caused the old cheesemaker to collapse. Herself is fond of her—"

Amyu flushed at that. She'd no defense against his truths. She had caused the old woman's rage, as angry as anyone she'd seen without a sword in hand.

"A woman just giving birth, finally having to send someone to find your sorry carcass and—"

The maids had finished and scurried out, leaving just her and Marcus. The pile of dishes had diminished, but quite a few remained. Amyu poured more hot water in, and set to work with a will as Marcus continued to rant. At least he hadn't decided they'd do dishes for the entire castle.

Shouts from outside, and the sound of sword on sword, coming from the narrow windows just above her head.

"Hisself and Joden, no doubt," Marcus rubbed a pitcher dry. "The practice circle is just outside."

Amyu lifted up on tip-toe, catching a glimpse of Joden through the high window.

He was circling Keir, laughing, his grin wide. His bronze face glistened with sweat, and his laugh… his laugh boomed out as Keir lunged and missed.

Amyu dropped down and stared at her wet hands.

"Good for them both," Marcus said gruffly. "Work the body to ease the worries."

Amyu turned her head to look at the scarred man next to her, calmer now that he'd had his say. "He almost went to the snows." she shared.

Marcus's scarred lips thinned, but he said nothing.

"He is broken," she admitted in the quiet room. "Like us." She picked up a wet bowl and picked at a bit of dried food with her nail. "I fear for him."

"Dishes don't wash themselves," Marcus said pointedly.

Amyu stared down at the bowl. "How did you bear it, Marcus?" she asked, then froze, shocked that those words had come from her mouth.

Silence.

Maybe she hadn't actually said the words out loud, and praise all the elements that—

"How did you?" Marcus asked. Quietly, without anger or shame.

Amyu didn't look at him. "The Warprize gave me hope. I thought to find... more. To prove my worth is more than an ability to bear children."

She risked a glance to find Marcus nodding his agreement. She dared to breathe.

"I had a reason," Marcus said quietly. "People who I needed to protect. I lived for them, not for my own self. I lived for the Tribe, but it was not without pain or cost."

Amyu stared down at the bowl again, watching a soap bubble pop.

"Dishes won't wash themselves," Marcus said again.

She nodded, and started back to work.

"He will need to find his own reason," Marcus continued. "But the loss of a voice for a Singer," he shook his head. "That is not easy to overcome."

Amyu's eyes teared up. She nodded, and for a while they worked in silence.

A movement at the door had them both looking up. Rafe stood there, his irrepressible grin in place. "Marcus, may I speak with Amyu? Under the bells," he added, trying to look apologetic.

Marcus sniffed but nodded.

Amyu dried her hands and stepped over, but Rafe pulled her further away to stand in the doorway. Fylin, Soar, Ksand and Lasa stood there, just out of sight, all with an air of excitement.

They were holding bundles and saddle bags stuffed to bursting.

"Amyu, we have permission from the Warlord to go back to your mountain path and explore," Rafe kept his voice down, his joy obvious. "Come with us."

Amyu blinked in surprise. "You don't believe in airions," she blurted out.

"Truth," Soar's eyes sparkled as the rest chuckled. "At best, we find some sign of them. At worst, we escape these stone tents for a few days."

"Days?" Amyu asked.

Rafe nodded. "There are no orders yet, but every warrior will march with the Warlord when he returns to the Plains. Sooner rather than later. The Warlord will want every able-bodied warrior with him." He shrugged. "I think he will call senel soon. But we will take these few days and explore, and find your airions. Come with us."

"No, I—" the words were out of her mouth without a thought, but then she hesitated. This might be her last chance to find the creatures. And yet…

She looked down the hallway, toward the open door and beyond. Joden still sparred with Keir in the sunlight. He was still laughing.

"Something more important than flying, eh?" Rafe asked.

Something in her heart twisted.

Fylin frowned. "He is to be a Singer—" she started.

"And I am a child," Amyu said the hateful words first defiantly, hoping to ease her pain. It didn't, but it caught Fylin by surprise.

"My thanks, Rafe." Amyu turned away from the open door. "But I think I need to make amends." She tilted her head slightly toward Marcus, dishes finished, waiting with his one eyebrow raised.

"As you say," Rafe said with a knowing grin, and they were off.

Amyu took a breath. It was the right thing, after all. To make amends for her disobedience. But oddly, she didn't have even a twinge of regret about not going with them.

She returned to Marcus's side. "What next?" she asked.

"Nappies," Marcus smirked as he produced a wooden washing paddle. "And you will aid in the night feedings."

Amyu sighed.

* * * * *

Lara lifted her head from her pillow, watching Keir slip into their room, fully armed and armored, the hilts of his swords poking up over his shoulders. He caught her eyes and padded in, casting a wary eye on the babies. He raised an eyebrow and tilted his head toward the cradle.

Lara nodded.

Keir made a show of slowly retreating to the garderobe. Lara smiled, and let her head drop back, enjoying these quiet moments of peace. All too soon the babes would need tending. She stretched under the blanket, reveling in the moment.

Keir returned, wearing only trous, his bare feet quiet on the stone floor. He climbed under the covers, and pulled her into his arms. He pulled the covers over their heads like a tent, and kissed her.

"I heard you sparring with Joden," she whispered in his ear. "Only a warrior of the Plains would think 'rest' means the same as 'fight'."

Keir gave her an unrepentant smile. "Joden needed it as much as I. He was far more relaxed by that than by talking."

"Did he fight well?" she asked, knowing that would be a concern.

"Yes," Keir said. "Whatever happened has not affect his skill with a blade."

"Give him time," Lara leaned closer to nuzzle Keir's neck.

She loved the scent of his skin. "His problem speaking may be a passing thing."

"Time may not be on our side," Keir said slowly.

Lara pulled back, watching his face. "Do you still doubt Simus?"

Keir was silent, his eyes hooded.

"Well, I don't," Lara said firmly. "Simus would never betray you. I know what Yers said, but I—"

Keir laid a finger on her lips, and Lara realized that her voice had risen. She hushed. They both waited, but no sound came from the cradle.

"Simus is loyal," Keir said. "That is a truth. But it is also true that we do not know the extent of the warrior-priests' power. Now a warrior-priestess challenges to become his token-bearer, and he allows it? What if he is influenced, or even controlled?" Keir moved his hand to stroke her cheek, his skin warm against hers. "What if he leads an army to the border, and suddenly attacks Liam?"

"Liam of the Deer has warriors, both of the Plains and Xy," Lara said.

"Liam of the Deer has some warriors," Keir said. "But mostly the skilled workers we sent to repair that old tower. And if Antas follows on Simus's heels?"

His hand stopped stroking her cheek, and Lara reached for it to grasp it in her own.

"Now Joden brings word that Wild Winds is dead, because of a vision he saw," Keir said. "What weight do I give to that truth? And if so, who leads the warrior-priests now?"

"Joden said they were dead, except for those that followed Wild Winds," Lara reminded him.

"Forgive me if I do not mourn for those dead," Keir's voice was flat, his anger clear. "But who in this do they support?" he continued. "All I have is questions. And…" His voice faded away.

He rolled over onto his back, and pulled the blanket down from their heads. The cooler air made Lara shiver. She shifted closer under the blanket and put her head on his shoulder.

"And all the answers are to be found on the Plains," she finished for him.

"I do not want to leave you," Keir's voice was a cracked rumble under her ear. His arms tightened around her. "I do not want to leave them." His pain was clear.

She brought her hand up to lay on his heart.

"It is not the same as the thea camps," he said. "In the thea camps all cared for all. There was no meaning, no connection with—" he struggled with his words.

"There was love, but not like this." She lifted her head, and her curls escaped to fall around his face.

He nodded, then looked awed. "They change every day," he whispered. "Their eyes focus, their tiny hands reach. Already, their spirits shine. I see you in them, in so many ways."

"As I see you," Lara pressed her lips to his. "Keir, we always knew that you would return to the Plains."

"In the Fall," he said with just a hint of desperation. "When they were older and you were fully healed. Not now, not so soon—"

"You must go," Lara said. She lifted her hand to brush back her curls. "And we will go with you."

"No," Keir's arms tightened around her.

"My Council supports us, what with the promise of trade routes opening up, and the money flowing from Crown," Lara said. "Heath will serve as the Warden of Xy, and keep the kingdom secure."

"No," Keir repeated. "I want you here, safe, within stone walls, with as many strong warriors as I can spare."

"You can't spare any," Lara said. She smiled down into his blue eyes. "I followed you once before, my Warlord. I will do so again, with babes in my arms if I must."

"Flame of my heart—"

"Hush," she said. "We can argue it out tomorrow. Let's enjoy our peace while we can." She put her head back down on his chest. "Do you think that Amyu knows she is in love with Joden?"

"Lara," Keir said. "He is a Singer. In the eyes of the Plains, Amyu is—"

Lara lifted her head and glared at him. "She is no child."

"In your eyes," Keir said.

"Firelanders," Lara grumbled.

"City-dweller," Keir rolled them both over and pressed her to the bed. "Let's not think on them." He smiled. "Let's think on us."

Lara wrapped her arms around his neck and pulled him down. They kissed for long, slow, glorious moments.

A whimper, and then a cry, joined by another little voice, came from the cradle.

They both groaned.

* * * * *

By that evening, Joden was exhausted. Exhausted from the effort of speaking, of struggling to get the words out. Exhausted from the emotions of the day, not to mention sparring with Keir.

Anna had one of her maids take him to his room, but only after she'd had him bathe, and fed him again.

He recognized the room as Marcsi opened the door. "Th-th-this," he forced out, grimacing with effort. "W-w-war—"

"The Queen's old room," Marcsi smiled as she went straight in, checking the fire and pulling a pot from under the bed.

Joden put his armload of armor and weapons on the bed. Anna had given him tunic and trous to wear for sleeping.

Marcsi lit the candles on the mantle. "Sleep well, my lord," she bowed out and closed the door behind her.

Joden sat on the bed with a sigh.

He knew this room, remembered it from the tour that Lara had given to Keir and his warriors. It felt like ages since then.

He glanced at the window. He remembered that it overlooked the city, and the fields and burial mounds beyond the walls. Where the dead had been standing.

He didn't look out.

He set about preparing to sleep, grateful for the warmth of the fire, and the smaller bed. It was one of the huge soft ones that Simus had told him about. Not as comfortable as gurtle pads, but Joden was fairly certain he would fall asleep on a bed of rocks this night.

He organized his armor and put the weapons within reach. He stripped off the tunic and trous and slipped within the bedding. City-dwellers were still such puzzles. Imagine wearing clothes to bed.

He settled, and closed his eyes, feeling that he was missing something. He reached out next to him, thinking…

Amyu was not there.

He pulled his hand back. His bed was empty, and his chest ached.

Of course she wasn't there. She'd been kind, getting him down off the mountain, and to Keir and Lara. Even kinder when she'd asked him to wait to go to the snows. So young to be so steadfast, not even a true warrior in the ways of the Plains. But in truth she was under no obligation to him, and what did he have to offer her?

He wasn't even sure who he was anymore.

Joden rolled on his side, facing the fire.

Keir had listened, but he wasn't sure Keir had believed. He could see the doubt in those eyes, and the flicker of hate at the mention of warrior-priests. He'd tried making it clear to him, that Simus was loyal, and that he supported Keir, but the words, the words would just not come.

Joden rubbed his face, feeling his frustration like a lump at the back of his throat. He owed it to Keir to stand with him. He needed to return to the Plains to find Essa. Even if his path to Singer was denied, even if he'd lost that chance, Essa needed to know what had happened.

Joden closed his eyes, and felt sick at the idea of trying to tell the Eldest Elder Singer his tale, stuttering and struggling for words that didn't come.

Amyu was right. The snows could wait. He'd struggle through this, and then... well, he'd leave that to the elements.

But he hoped she'd find her airions. He hoped she'd fly.

Joden turned, and closed his eyes. He listened to the beat of his heart, the crackle of the fire, the sound of his breath. In and out and in... sleep finally came.

At least, until the dead called.

"Joden of the Hawk," whispered an ancient voice. *"Come to me."*

CHAPTER TWENTY-FOUR

Joden threw back the blankets, pausing only long enough to pull on the sleeping trous.

"Come," the ancient voice called again.

He knew the halls from that tour long ago but even if he hadn't the call made his path clear. The corridors were dim and silent. No torches burned, no guards barred his way.

The doors to the chapel were open, candles flickering at the base of the statue of the Xyian Goddess. The stone floor was cool beneath his feet, the room empty. Joden still thought it odd that they worshiped people in this way. The eyes of the stone woman seemed to follow him as he circled around it.

"Come."

Past the statue was a flat surface for worship, and behind that a passage barred by an iron gate. It pushed open easily at Joden's touch. White stone steps disappeared down into the darkness.

Joden started down.

It was colder here. He could see his breath. His skin prickled with a chill as he descended. There were no torches, no lanterns, but the stone itself glowed with a dim light.

Deeper he went, and the corridor branched off to his left and right. But the call was straight ahead and he continued, past stones engraved with writing he could not read. Another odd custom, not to return the flesh to the elements, but encase them in hard rock. He paused at one, running his fingers over letters seemingly freshly cut. Was this—?"

"Come."

Joden dropped his hand and obeyed, going deeper within the mountain, following an urge he could not deny. Here the stone felt older, the carved letters worn, more symbols than words. Crowns, swords, horses, and airions that reared up, their wings spread wide.

The corridor narrowed, the walls rougher, the graves more frequent and the steps more worn in the center. Joden walked on until he reached a doorway, and stepped down into a round room with a domed ceiling. There was an elaborately carved stone box in the center, its side covered with robed figures, clearly weeping. On the ceiling, circling airions were carved.

Beyond the stone box, a man sat on a throne, formed from the very rock.

"Welcome, Joden of the Hawk."

The voice had an empty, echoing quality to it. The man wore a kind of armor Joden had never seen. Pure metal that encased his entire body, with a helm that framed his face. On his lap, over his knees, was a sword of crystal glimmering blue.

"Do not think to disturb the others that sleep here, wise one. They will not rouse to your call." The man had the same grayish light to him as did the surrounding stone.

"I do not seek to disturb them." Joden stepped forward. "I do not seek—"

The warrior chuckled. "Such as you always seek." His voice was a dark rumble against the stone. "It is your nature, your very breath."

"Maybe," Joden admitted, feeling his questions all start to pile up behind his tongue.

"A Seer, newly come into your power." The man regarded him with flat eyes. "No control, no understanding. Who says the powers have no sense of humor?"

"What do you call me?" Joden demanded.

"You are with us, but not of us," the man continued.

"The dead," Joden said.

"The dead." The eyes closed for a moment, then re-opened. "The dead, unseen and unknown, yet knowing and seeing."

"Those are ritual words of the Plains," Joden said. The cold stale air filled his nose and throat.

"Are they? Are you certain?"

"Who are you?" Joden demanded.

"Xyson."

Joden frowned. "Lara, she read to us from a book. *The Epic of Xyson*, she called it."

"The same." the stone corners of the man's mouth quirked. "That Warprize of yours, she has quite the temper. Gets it from me, I suspect."

"So all these," Joden gestured back behind him. "They will all—"

"No," Xyson said. "The dead of Xy that lie within have gone beyond the snows, leaving only echoes. Only I remain."

"You are of Xy," Joden said. "How do you know the way of the Plains?"

"You walk in two worlds now, Joden of the Hawk. You speak with the dead, but the dead do not always speak the truth. You should always wonder about the dead's reasons."

Joden narrowed his eyes. "What are your reasons?"

The specter laughed but then grew solemn. "To put right a wrong I created." Xyson glanced up, as if looking through stone. "We have little time," he said. "Even now, the stones suck the heat from your flesh and life from your heart. Even now, the guardian seeks the snows, one who has not kept to their oaths."

"There is time," Joden said trying to ignore the cold creeping into his feet and legs.

"Two things I will tell you, Seer. Long ago there were two sisters, who loved as all women do, with their hearts and not their minds. They fell in love with two brothers, both powerful warriors within their tribes. But for the complications of their people, all would have been well. But conflicts arose and one of the brothers died and the other… broke two kingdoms for his love."

"Two kingdoms?" Joden asked.

"Xy, and what you now call the Plains," Xyson answered. "Tore the fabric of the world. Tore the power from its roots."

Joden wrapped his arms around his chest for warmth, tucking his hands within. "The Ancients said something about the Chaosreaver—"

"Who left only destruction in his path and the cold and the silence," Xyson nodded as he recited the words. "Those dried up turds still live?" he shook his head. "I am not surprised. Hate, like love, lingers." He paused. "You have awakened old powers, Joden. Set in motion a chain of events you do not control. You bring change."

"Keir started it," Joden protested.

"One man with an idea makes no difference," Xyson trailed his fingers over the flat of the blade in his lap. "But when another agrees with him? That shakes the world, for good or ill. Like water cascading down on rocks. The rocks will surrender to the water eventually." Xyson sighed. "People can be perfectly rational, but then love turns to madness and hate."

"How do you know this?" Joden asked. "About the sisters? About the Plains?"

"I was part of the… complications." Xyson shifted in his chair. "Question the motives of those around you, Seer."

"That is vague enough to be a Singer's answer."

"My father always said that the young never listen. How right he was," Xyson chuckled. "For if they did, mistakes would never be repeated, hate would never build, and no one would risk the pain of loss for the joy of love." He glanced over Joden's shoulder, then spoke hurriedly. "When the destruction came down upon us, a guardian was established within Xy, the burden laid on her long ago. Her oaths have become distorted, for the guardian has turned bitter with age and pain. The loss of her powers, the loss of her lover." Xyson dropped his gaze to the sword. "For the second thing—"

"We haven't finished the first," Joden protested. "What does this mean, that you—"

"Silence," Xyson rose, an imposing figure, with sword in hand. The blue flamed and the crystal glowed clear. "If your watcher wishes to fly, tell her to re-forge the sword."

"But—" Joden protested.

Xyson lunged.

Before he could react, the point of the sword touched Joden's chest. He was thrown back, against the flat stone coffin. His head hit cold stone and he knew nothing more.

* * * * *

Amyu never knew what prompted her to check on Joden between feedings, but she roused the entire castle in her terror. Heart racing, she had every castle guard, every warrior searching every inch.

Until someone shouted, and she ran into the chapel. The alert guard pointed at the open gate.

"The crypts?" She grabbed up one of the torches from the wall and lit it from the candles.

"It's kept locked." The guard was young, his face pale and frightened. "It's a maze down there. Wait and I'll get—"

Amyu plunged down the steps, torch high. She paused, listening.

Nothing. No sound, no light, just cold harsh air that stole her breath.

"Joden!" she called, and waited.

Nothing. Then she heard a faint noise, like crystal ringing on stone.

"Get aid," she shouted over her shoulder and ran toward

the sound, then skidded to a stop. She forced herself to think, to use her wits. No use for two of them to be lost. She closed her eyes, remembering Othur's burial here in the—

There were lanterns at each crossing of paths, high, on chains.

She dashed back, lit the lantern at the base of the steps, and then ran toward the sound. Each crossing, she lit the lantern, reaching high with the flaring torch. Leaving a path behind her of light and warmth, a path back to the living. Praying to every element that Joden lived.

"Joden," she called again, but there was no response.

Another lantern and then another. Amyu cursed, fearing she had lost—

That sound again, a faint ringing. She flew down the last dark passage to stumble down a small set of stairs and into a round room.

Joden lay on the stone coffin before her, wearing nothing but trous, sprawled and unconscious.

She darted to him, torch high, reached for—

She stopped, her fingers hovering over his neck. No, no, for a moment she stood frozen, afraid he was dead and as cold as the stone.

A statue of a man sat opposite on a throne, silent and dispassionate, a stone sword on his lap. Its gaze was cold, and her fear rose.

Amyu prayed, and let her fingers rest on Joden's pulse point. He lived.

All her breath rushed out, and her shoulders sagged with relief, but it was short lived. His heart might beat, but he was cold, so cold to the touch. She cupped his face, his brown skin a contrast to her cold, pale fingers.

Noise behind her, and voices. "Here," she called out. "He's here."

Heath burst into the room, his men behind him. Heath

froze at the sight, and cast his eyes around the room. "Xyson's tomb?" he sounded astonished. "How did he—"

"We need to get him to the Warprize," Amyu snapped out an order. The guards came forward and gathered Joden up, careful to support his head. Six of them carried him out, Heath leading the way.

Amyu followed.

* * * * *

Joden's senses were filled with Amyu even before he woke.

He was cradled in her arms, in blankets, in warmth with her scent in his lungs. Her heart raced under his cheek, thumping wildly, and her scolding voice filled his ear.

"… idiot, but I am sure you are aware of that. So stupid to wander in and sleep on a tomb, but you know that as well. What you don't know is that I need you to wake up now, wake up and tell me that you are—"

Joden turned his head, still half-asleep and nuzzled her neck.

Amyu gasped. Much to Joden's dismay, she pushed back out of his arms and started to climb out of the bed. "Warprize, he's awake."

"Excellent. We just finished feedings the twins, so—" both women stood glaring at him.

Joden threw the blankets back and stood, wobbling slightly. "M-m-m," he gave up. "G-g-go."

"You are not going anywhere," Amyu scowled. "I am not done yelling at you."

"K-k-kalisa," Joden said. "D-d-dying."

Lara and Amyu exchanged a glance. "I'll order horses," Lara said.

* * * * *

They took two horses, and clattered through the night to Master

Eln's. Joden wasn't sure Lara was up for riding, but Keir solved the issue by mounting and then taking her in his arms.

Amyu had swung up in the saddle and offered Joden her hand before he could say a word. He almost protested, but her glare was enough to get him to swing up behind her in the saddle. He wrapped his arms around her waist, and took advantage by burying his face in her hair. She turned her head slightly, but she made no protest. She covered his hands with one of hers and then urged the horse forward.

The night was clear, the moon high. No one barred them as they trotted the horses through the main streets, taking the fastest path.

Master Eln's house was clearly awake. Every window bore a light. An apprentice opened the door, and called for help with the horses. Master Eln appeared in the doorway. "I was just going to send word," he said. "She doesn't have long."

Lara nodded, dropping her cloak in a chair and heading down the hall. Amyu followed, then Joden with Keir behind. They entered the room where Joden had seen the old woman. It was warm, and the air stung with the scent of herbs and ointments.

She was lying in bed, eyes closed, face pale. A young woman sat at the bedside holding her hand, with a man standing behind, his hands on her shoulders.

"Anser, Mya, I am so sorry to disturb you," Lara started.

Mya had tears in her eyes. "It can't be much longer," she choked on the words. "She hasn't roused since yesterday, and—" she sobbed. Anser leaned in, letting her bury her face in his tunic.

"Auntie's lived a long and good life," Anser started, but Joden raised a hand, stepping to the bedside. Anser looked at him questioningly.

"G-g-guardian," Joden called.

Kalisa opened her eyes.

CHAPTER TWENTY-FIVE

Joden watched as Kalisa's eyes flooded with awareness, then narrowed with loathing, focusing on him. "Lord of Light, spare me," she rasped. "A Seer." She coughed as she struggled to lift her head from the pillow.

"Auntie," Mya moved, supporting her and offering a cup of water. "Save your strength," she urged.

"G-g-guardian," Joden struggled with the word. "Y-y-you m-m-must—"

"Must?" Kalisa glared at him, ignoring Mya. "Who are you to say 'must' to me? A Seer newly come to power," she scoffed, and then cleared her throat. "Have you come to scold me? Berate me?" Kalisa's lip curled as she spoke. "I will not aid you, Firelander. Or the stupid child at your side."

Gasps rose around him, but Joden stayed focused on Kalisa. "Y-y-your oath as G-g-guardian re-re-requires you r-r-release y-y-your charges," Joden fought to slow his words and get his tongue out of the way. "O-o-or you will w-w-wander the snows, l-l-lost—" he drew a breath, trying to finish his thought. She'd wander lost in her own hate.

"Who are you to tell me what my oath requires?" Kalisa's eyes raged at him, spit foaming in the corners of her lips. "Who are you to tell me, a Guardian of Xy, anything?"

"Xy-xy-xyson," Joden could barely force out the word.

"Xy-xy-xyson," Kalisa mocked him, then her lip curled. "Bastard always was a meddler." Her face crumpled in pain. "If he'd only left us alone—" she hacked again, as if her pain caught in her throat.

"Drink," Mya urged, but Kalisa pushed the cup away, water slopping over the sides.

"I have warded my charges for years, watching over the generations, day after day, month after month," Kalisa's eyes filled with tears. "Weary decade after decade, waiting for one to bear the sign. Every son, every daughter in my line, but my warrior blood faded through the generations."

Anser was staring at her as if he'd never seen her before. "Auntie, how long have you lived?"

"Cheesemakers." Disdain dripped from Kalisa's words. She snarled at Anser and Mya. "All of them. None bear the gift and never will."

"Auntie," Anser said, straightening his spine. "You don't mean that."

Kalisa stared at Lara. "But your babes, now. Your children and those that will follow—"

Lara, pale and trembling, drew herself up. Keir was behind her. He stepped forward. "What about our children?" he demanded.

"They were born on the night the power returned," Kalisa's eyes grew distant, and her voice dropped to the barest whisper. "Too early to know, too early to tell, but they may bear the gift."

"She had a fit that night," Mya whispered. She sat on the bed, her arm wrapped around Kalisa's hunched back. "On the night of the royal births."

Amyu shifted next to Joden, stepping forward closer to the bed. "Do you mean the golden light?" she asked. "I can see it."

Kalisa snarled, "I know. I can see it in you, child. You have the gift."

Amyu leaned forward. "Please, Elder, show me. I can learn to—"

"I swore an oath," Kalisa trembled with rage. "Never to use

it again, never to touch what was left. I could take up the power, rid myself of this withering, aged—" She coughed again holding up her swollen hands. She curled her lip at Eln and Lara. "Joint cream and teas. Bah." She closed her eyes and covered her face with her hands. "I can't, I can't—"

"But I can," Amyu started.

Kalisa screamed. Joden reached out to steady Amyu as she flinched back, his hands on her shoulders, wishing he could shield her from this.

"You?" Kalisa shrieked, dropping her hands, rage in her eyes. "Never. Never will a filthy Firelander touch my charges." She coughed, clutching at her chest. "They were created for Xy and Xy alone. I will keep them safe and free of your taint. Only the pure blood of Xy will fly these skies. Never, never, never—"

She clutched at her heart and gasped out the last few words.

"Uppor w-w-waits," Joden said. Keir stiffened but Joden kept his eyes on Kalisa.

She paused, then her face crumpled. A long moan came from her, that seemed to take all her breath. "Uppor, beloved," she wept. Then she gasped, and threw her head back.

Eln moved then, with Lara, to aid Mya. They eased Kalisa back down on the bed. There was a rattle, a struggle for another breath.

"Gracious Goddess, Lady of the Moon and Stars, be with her in the hour of her death," Lara recited the words, as Mya started crying.

"Gracious Goddess, Lady of the Moon and Stars," Anser took up the chant. "Full of forgiveness, forget her offenses and her flaws."

Kalisa's breaths were harsher now, and slowing. All attention was on the bed, but Joden caught a glimpse of Keir easing out of the room as all of the Xyians gathered around and continued the chant.

"Gracious Lady of the Moon and Stars, full of mercy, see her true repentance." Lara glanced back at Joden.

He knew he should leave out of courtesy. Amyu walked toward the door. But he held back. When she died, would he see…?

Joden stepped back, toward the door but kept his eyes on the bed.

"Gracious Lady of the Moon and Stars, full of kindness, incline your ear to our plea."

One last harsh breath and then… silence.

"Gracious Lady of the Moon and Stars, full of glory, guide her to a place in your garden

and let her dwell there in peace." Master Eln closed Kalisa's eyes, and gently pulled up the sheet to cover her face.

Joden stood silent, but there was nothing to see. No wisp of a ghost, no change in the room.

"I don't understand," Mya said, looking lost and bewildered. "Where did that anger come from? She never once spoke of it, never expressed it to us. How could she be so hateful?"

"Some of the herbs I gave her for pain," Master Eln said quietly. "I didn't expect they would affect her. I only meant to make her more comfortable."

Joden caught the glance that Eln exchanged with Lara, and knew Eln's words were not the truth. But they had the desired effect.

"Oh," Mya's face cleared of confusion, and Anser relaxed. "She had a long and fruitful life, but a hard one, seeing to all of our family."

"Let me get you some tea," Master Eln gestured to the door. "And then we will see to her."

"We will lay her in the family burial grounds," Anser helped Mya rise.

Joden slipped out as Lara stepped forward to make her farewells, with soft words and hugs. Amyu was waiting down the hall. They went out together into the morning air.

The cooler air felt good, but Joden was far more concerned with Amyu. Her face was pained, her eyes anxious. "She hated me," she said. "How can someone hate like that?"

Joden wrapped an arm around her, offering as much comfort as he could. Amyu leaned into him and put her head on his shoulder.

Keir was a step away, leaning against the outer wall of the building, his arms folded over his chest. "Uppor," he said. "She knew Uppor? Uppor the Trickster of the Plains?"

Joden nodded.

Amyu looked up, wide eyed. "So old," she said. "Did her hate build over all those years? Such that she took her secrets to the snows? Did her hate blind her so to our need?"

"And you can see the power?" Keir's voice was flat and abrupt. "Like a warrior-priest?"

Amyu stiffened in Joden's arms, then stepped away to face Keir. "I do see the power," she lifted her chin. "I do not know how to use it, or what it means, but yes. I see it. That does not make me a warrior-priest."

Keir's eyes were dark and brooding. He glanced at Joden, then looked down at his boots.

Joden tilted his head slightly. Amyu nodded, and stepped back. "I'll see to the horses," she said, and walked off.

Joden waited, looking at Keir, who hadn't moved, his arms crossed over his chest.

Joden shifted then to take the same position next to his friend.

Keir looked up.

Joden raised his eyebrows.

Keir shook his head. "Her hate was so real," he said quietly. "She was striking to kill, Joden."

Joden nodded.

"Keekai once told me that blind hatred of the warrior-priests is a dangerous thing," Keir added with a rueful shrug. "Well, more than once."

Joden snorted, remembering the Elder in question.

"And now our children may be touched by—" Keir paused and seemed to swallow hard. "They may be warrior-priests, Joden. I do not know what to think. What to do."

"I do." There was a rustle at the door as Lara emerged. She walked to Keir's side. "We figure this out," she held up her hand. "Together."

Keir straightened away from the wall, and put his hand to hers. They laced their fingers together, tight. "Together." He nodded, his voice strong.

Lara leaned into him for a hug. "I feel so tired. As if drained of all life and hope."

Keir wrapped his arms around her, and Lara put her head on his chest as she continued, "I knew her all my life, and yet I didn't really know her at all."

"Come," Keir said as Amyu walked up leading the horses. "Let's return to the castle."

* * * * *

Amyu thought the Warprize looked exhausted when they reached the main doors of the castle.

The Warlord looked haunted.

The Warprize lifted her eyes up the spiral staircase with a sigh, and put a foot on the first step. "Let me," the Warlord said, and swept her up into her arms. She wrapped her arms around his neck and put her head on his shoulder.

They were silent as they climbed the stairs to the floor of the royal chambers. The Warlord turned as they reached the doors to their rooms chambers, the Warprize already asleep in his arms. Marcus had opened the doors, and stood waiting.

"I want to think on this," Keir said quietly to Joden. "Let us talk in the morning. There is much to consider."

Joden nodded.

Amyu hesitated, but Marcus let the Warlord enter and then caught her eye. "See to him," Marcus said jerking his head toward Joden. "Return to your duties at the nooning."

She bowed her head in obedience as Marcus closed the door.

Joden gave her a soft smile, and then yawned. She shook her head, took his arm, and they walked together toward his small chamber.

It was as they had left it. Rumpled bed, blankets tossed on the floor. The fire had burned down and the air was chilled.

Amyu knelt, stirred the coals, and added tinder, waiting for the flames to catch. She could hear Joden moving behind her, removing armor, climbing into bed.

The fire crackled and she added a few logs, careful not to extinguish the flame, knowing full well she was stalling. She wasn't sure if he'd want her to stay; she wasn't sure she should if he did. The events of the night had whipped her hard. She ached from the cold, the fear, and emotions that had been poured over her head.

Finally, she rose, and turned. He was naked, seated on the side of the bed, the blankets half over his legs. He looked up at her with tired, brown eyes.

She took a few steps forward, close enough to catch the scent of his skin. "Do you need anything?" she asked, expecting kavage or gurt as his request.

"Y-y-you," Joden said, taking her hand.

CHAPTER TWENTY-SIX

Joden didn't know if Amyu was aware of the tears streaming down her cheeks. She looked so tired and so defeated. "Seer," she said, her voice a cracked whisper. "She called you a Seer. What does that even mean?"

Joden put his hands on her hips, and tugged. Amyu stepped closer, between his legs and put her hands on his shoulders.

"I failed," she said, sniffling. "Joden, I will never fly, no one will. She locked them away somewhere, and who can say where, or how to free them?"

He reached up then, and started to work one of the clasps on her leather armor. Amyu choked back a sob, and started to help him. "You can't," she started, and then hiccupped. "We can't," and now she was crying in earnest. "We are two broken people and we can't—"

Joden reached up, and tried to dry her tears with his thumbs. Amyu gave a weak, wet chuckle, wiping her own face. Heaving a deep sigh, she shed her leathers, letting them fall in a heap.

Joden chuffed at her, reaching for her armor and folding them neatly as she unbuckled her sword belt. She placed it on top of the pile and then started to crawl into the bed.

Joden shifted back, lifting the covers for her. There wasn't much room, but they fit themselves together. Amyu tucked her head under his chin and put her hand on his chest.

Her hair smelled like the night sky on the Plains. Part smoke, part sweet grasses, part open sky. He took a deep satisfied breath, then made sure the blankets covered them both.

"What happened down in the crypts?" Amyu asked.

Joden hesitated, but Amyu lifted her head. "Tell me," she said. "However long it takes, I need to know."

He nodded, and took a deep breath as she settled back against him. "Xy-xy-xyson called me," he started, fully expecting Amyu to fall asleep as he struggled with the words of his story. But her eyes were bright and her patience seemed to have no end.

He explained, struggling through to tell her the part she really needed to know. "He s-s-said 'i-i-if y-y-y-our w-w-w-atcher w-w-wishes t-t-to,' he grimaced at the effort, but he forced the words out. "f-f-fly, t-t-tell h-h-her to re-re-reforge t-t-the s-s-sword."

Amyu frowned. "Joden, I don't doubt your truth," she said slowly. "But I was there. I saw the sword shatter." Her frown deepened. "I had the hilt in my hand," she said.

"W-w-what h-h-happened t-t-to i-i-it?" Joden asked.

"I don't know," Amyu shrugged. "I handed the hilt to Anna, but then the Warprize went into labor, Atira was attacked, and then saved the Warprize from being killed. I am not sure what happened to it."

"F-f-find," Joden said firmly.

Amyu's face crumpled. "To what end? How do you re-forge a crystal sword?" She put her head back down on his shoulder. "Did he tell you that?" she asked, her voice muffled in his skin.

"N-n-no," Joden admitted softly.

Amyu sighed, and relaxed against him, seemingly going to sleep. But Joden's thoughts raced like a herd of horses.

What had Xyson said? *A Seer, newly come into your power'* Joden frowned, staring up at the stone ceiling above him. What was a seer? There was no mention of that in the songs that he knew, the stories that he'd heard all of his life. Warrior-priests, certainly, but not by that title. But Xyson had said something more. *'No control, no understanding.'*

No understanding, that was a truth. But control? He could control it?

How?

Joden drew a deep breath, but let it out slowly, not willing to disturb Amyu's sleep. There were no teachers, no tales to aid him in this. He'd have to enter the sparring circle with the visions, trying to command them as they came. Or maybe figure out how and when they came and see if he could create them—

He rolled his eyes. Might as well try to bridle a galloping horse, and the rest of the herd while he was at it.

Joden narrowed his eyes at the stone above him. Best to go to the source. He should go down into the crypts, confront Xyson and ask his questions. The only way to get to the truth of this was to—

Warm fingers pressed on his lips.

Joden shifted his head, to see Amyu's bright brown eyes looking at him as she frowned.

"Don't even think it," she whispered.

Joden raised an eyebrow.

"Going back to the crypts," Amyu said. "Wandering in the dark, almost freezing to death down there again." She shifted, reaching up to cup his face. "Enough, Joden," she said. "We'll go," she promised. "In the light of day, with a guide." She sighed again, still tired and worn. "We will figure this out, somehow."

Joden felt her shift against him, felt her sorrow in the hand that touched his face. He so much wanted to offer comfort, to reassure her, but the idea of trying to speak, made him tired before he even drew a breath to try.

Amyu shifted again, and he felt her hand lift, about to be drawn away. He reached up and pressed it close.

Maybe he didn't need words.

Joden turned his head and tickled the palm of Amyu's hand with the tip of his tongue.

Amyu sucked in a breath, wide-eyed, but she didn't pull away.

Joden smiled, leaned over, and kissed her. It was long, slow and sweet, just lips soft against one another. He released her hand, and reached to stroke her neck, just below the hairline. Amyu shivered against him.

He shifted then, pulling her with him, so that they faced each other on their sides. Now his hands were free to touch, long slow strokes down the length of her arm, and her hips.

Amyu lifted her chin, granting him access to her tender throat. She moaned as Joden explored it with his mouth. Her skin was soft and delicious, invading all of his senses. He took his sweet time, keep his hands just below her breasts, his thumbs rubbing the central spot between. Her nipples had hardened, and they were a delight to behold, begging to be touched. But Joden held off, leaving them hungry, leaving her in a state of suspense as she writhed in his arms.

He chuckled against her skin as Amyu reached, trying to force his hand down to the center of her heat.

Amyu narrowed her eyes. She changed tactics, reaching for his length. It was his turn to gasp at her touch.

She laughed at her victory, but he turned the tables by taking a nipple in his mouth and grazing it with his teeth. She moaned, grabbing his head to try to keep him there. "Joden," she panted, and he heard her plea. Joden rolled onto his back, bringing her up and on top of him, straddling his hips.

Amyu rose above him, the blankets falling back, letting the cooler air touch their over-heated flesh. Now she leaned on him, her hands on his chest, her breasts swaying above him.

Joden reached up, kneading and squeezing, and rubbed her nipples hard with his thumbs.

Amyu pushed against his hands and started to thrust with her hips against him. She moaned in frustration, then reached with one hand to arrange things to her satisfaction. With a triumphant cry, she sank down, taking him in to both their pleasures.

Joden arched his head back, lost in her heat, lost in the delight that swamped his senses.

Amyu clamped down, then drew up, and then down again, and there was no way he could hold out against her. He could only meet thrust for thrust as the light exploded behind his eyes.

Amyu cried out her climax, shuddering around him, and he followed her into sweet release.

When his reason returned, and his vision cleared, he found Amyu on his chest, a soft warm blanket. He eased out of her, and gently pulled her on to her side, cradling her head on his shoulder. With his free hand, he pulled the blankets back over them.

Broken, she'd called them, and Joden acknowledge the truth as he slid into sleep. But broken together. That made all the difference.

* * * * *

Amyu hesitated at the darkness leading down to the crypts, but Heath held his torch high as he strode through the gate. "This way," he said with a confidence she didn't share.

Joden followed, so Amyu did as well, carrying her own torch, and one to spare. Shadows danced just outside of the pool of light. She'd no desire to be trapped down in this warren of tunnels with no light and apparently talkative dead.

She'd also no wish to find out if the dead spoke to any other than Joden.

"Here." Heath was lighting the lanterns as he went, which eased some of her fears. He held the torch high and pointed. "Xyson is buried down this way."

Their steps echoed against the stone in a way that Amyu hadn't remembered from her frantic rush down theses paths. Her heart had been racing so fast in fear, she might not have heard them. But she did now and felt the damp chill of the stone. She might not be able to see her breath, but she felt it on her face as they moved down the narrow passageways.

Heath continued on in silence, lighting sconces as he went, until he stopped in front of a stone that looked newer to Amyu's eyes. He stood there, his face still, and ran his fingers over the words carved there.

"O-o-o," Joden grimaced, then tried again. "Y-y-your f-f-father?"

"Yes," Heath said quietly. "You said you were called," he continued, staring at Joden. Amyu could see the question that burned in his eyes.

Joden shook his head. "I-I-I d-d-do n-n-not h-h-hear h-h-him," he assured Heath.

"No," Heath's shoulders relaxed, and he smiled sadly. "Of course not. My father would go straight to the gardens of the Goddess. He is at peace. Still," Heath grimaced, "I would give much to speak with him again."

Joden nodded.

Heath straightened, and continued walking. "It's just that, with Keir having to decide his course of action, I feel the lack. I turn to talk to him, turn to ask him something and it takes me a moment to remember that he isn't there." Heath glanced over his shoulder. "You know?"

Joden nodded.

Comforting even without words, Amyu thought as they kept walking. Joden didn't need words sometimes. He had such expressive eyes, and his hands… She flushed, suddenly very glad to be at the back as her face flushed with sudden heat.

The sharing between them had been lovely. Warm and comforting and oh so pleasurable. Her nipples tightened under her clothing at the heat of memory.

"Do you think the Warlord will decide soon?" she asked, not

really wanting to know, but she needed to think on other things.

Heath was silent for a while, lighting another lantern. Joden glanced back at her, looking puzzled. Amyu frowned. Had Heath not heard her? Or worse, would he not speak to a child? Amyu stumbled and caught herself. Heath had not seemed to think that of her, but he was bonded to Atira and she—

"I think he must," Heath spoke, to her relief. "All of his plans require peace between the Plains and Xy. He really has two choices. Head to the border or stay and defend from within these walls if he is attacked." Heath paused, lowering his voice. "Will he have to fight a war at the border, to defend Xy? Or will he have to attack the Plains themselves, to secure his position?"

Joden had also stopped and Amyu was at his shoulder. She could feel the heat of Joden's body against her, even as she stared at the both of them. "You think it will come to that," she said flatly.

"I do not know," Heath said. "I do know that the City of Water's Fall is in a fever, commanded by the Queen to make swords, weapons, armor, bolts, arrows, and everything else an army on the move needs. Lara has opened the treasury, and is willing to pay well for quality work, and Sun God help anyone who tries to pass off shoddy workmanship."

Heath looked up at where his torch licked at the ceiling above them. "And then there is the matter of the wyverns."

"G-g-gone," Joden said.

Heath shook his head. "Everyone is assuming that since they have flown off they are no longer a threat. I do not plan to make that mistake. Regardless," he continued. "Keir is going to make a decision soon, probably within a few days."

"You think he will go," Amyu said.

"I think it is not in the Warlord's nature to sit and wait." Heath grinned.

Joden snorted, "Tr-tr-truth."

"I suspect that Lara will go with him," Heath said. "Taking the babies with her. My mother is working herself up into a state at the very idea." He turned, looking down the passage.

"It's not much further," Heath continued walking. "We don't want to lose the torches."

Amyu gave Joden a push forward. He threw a grin at her, but moved quickly enough to satisfy her.

They went for a while in silence, until Amyu blurted out her burning question, "Will you go?"

"With Keir?" Heath shook his head. "No. I am Seneschal of the Castle of Water's Fall." Amyu could see the weight of his words on his shoulders. "I will hold this castle, and the city for Xylara." He paused at a crossing of tunnels, then plunged ahead. "Atira has said she will not leave me, as we are bonded." He stopped. "We are here."

Amyu stood at the top of the steps leading down into a round room with a domed ceiling. She remembered the elaborately carved stone box in the center, where she'd found Joden sprawled, shivering and convulsing. But she lifted the torch higher, and gazed at the airions carved on the ceiling, circling with wings wide, carrying riders.

Riders.

Her breath caught in excitement. There above her, airions and their riders soared. Riders in saddles, like the one she'd seen in the cave. Amyu stood on tip-toe, watching the light and dark play over the carvings, trying to take it all in. Surely they were real, were not the thing of—

Joden's voice brought her back to reality.

"N-n-nothing," he said, his voice echoing on the walls. Joden was standing by the seated statue of a man, a stone sword in his lap. He leaned over, and splayed his hand out over the statue's chest.

"He is not here?" Heath's voice held an odd note.

"M-m-more l-l-like em-em-empty." Joden said, pulling his

hand back. "G-g-gone."

"I am not sure if I am disappointed or relieved," Heath said. He held the torch close to the statue's face, looking at the carving. "What was he like?"

"D-d-demanding," Joden said. "C-c-commanding. K-k-kingly."

"Like Lara," Heath laughed. "But don't tell her I said so."

"Look," Amyu pointed overhead. "Look at that."

"Well," Heath said. "Airions."

"With riders," Amyu pointed urgently. "See? Not just legends." She lowered her gaze to stare at Heath. "Xyson told Joden that if we wanted to fly we need to re-forge the sword. What does that mean?"

"I have no idea," Heath said with a shrug. "You should talk to Atira. She is working in the smithy of Dunstan, an old friend. She wants to make swords someday." Heath smiled with obvious pride, but then gave Amyu a frown. "Where is the sword? Or what's left of it."

"I don't know," Amyu said. "I had the hilt—"

"Mother will know," Heath said. "Come."

They retraced their steps, extinguishing the lanterns as they went. Amyu was grateful to leave the cold and narrow tunnels.

Heath led them to the kitchens, which were wonderfully warm, noisy, and crowded with preparations for the nooning. Anna was in her usual glory, ruling the overheated hearths.

"Wandering the crypts," she scolded Heath after he explained, her chins wobbling. "For what fool reason did you do that? Sit. You will need warming up from that cold stone."

Amyu found herself seated on a long bench, Joden beside her, with a mug of hot kavage and bread and butter on a wooden platter.

"Eat," Anna commanded.

"We just have a question," Heath protested.

"Which I will answer as you eat," Anna said firmly.

Joden didn't hesitate. He took a slice of bread, slathered it with butter, and took a bite.

"Good," Anna patted him on the head.

Amyu choked back a laugh, but Joden just looked smug. Heath rolled his eyes at both of them, but settled on the bench and grabbed his share of bread.

"Mother, do you know where the Crystal Sword ended up?" Heath asked.

"Of course," Anna said, and went to her spice cabinet, her keys jangling. She pulled out a basket, and set it before him.

"You put the Crystal Sword of the House of Xy in a bread basket?" Heath asked as she set it before him.

"Safe, wasn't it?" Anna asks. "All the shards are there, I saw to that."

A clatter arose from the staff, and then the sound of shattering crockery. Anna frowned. "What's that then?" she moved off, intent on the source of the racket.

Amyu looked in the basket. The hilt was there, but so were the shards of blue, some little more than slivers.

"Keep it," Heath pushed the basket closer to Amyu. "Not much use now."

Marcus came in with a tray, glaring as always. "You there," he pointed his chin at Heath. "Hisself wants you."

Heath crammed the last of the bread into his mouth, and took his mug with him.

"You," Marcus's glare focused on Amyu. "You will take baby duty tonight. Rest up. Keirson is cranky and refusing to sleep. You'll probably be up all night."

"Yes, Marcus," Amyu said.

"Joden," Marcus continued. "You are to rest as well. Master Eln is coming to see the babes this evening, and will be checking on you. Hisself will likely wish to talk as well." He filled his tray with more kavage and left as abruptly as he had come.

The kitchen was in chaos around them, but the staff ignored them. Joden leaned over, pressing his arm to hers. "N-n-ap," he nodded in the direction of his room, raising his eyebrows, his eyes hopeful.

Amyu nodded, suddenly dry mouthed. "Yes," she whispered, suddenly fiercely glad. She'd have him for a time, but she knew full well he was not hers. The Plains would call him back. But she would steal this moments with him, take whatever days she could get and enjoy the sweetness.

The rest, she'd leave to the elements.

* * * * *

To Joden, it seemed the next few days passed like birds on the wing.

Keir was considering his options, and he called on Joden to sit in on the discussions. "I need your ears to hear truths," Keir told him privately.

And so Joden listened to Warren and Wilsa of the Lark. He heard talk of warrior numbers, both Xyian and of the Plains. Detros was brought in with Heath, to talk of the castle and the city, how to secure the walls and withstand a siege.

Lara and Heath reviewed the costs. Joden's head whirled at the way they talked of coin and tallied up numbers on papers. Keir also seemed overwhelmed at times, but they both learned as best they could, and trusted the Warprize's judgment.

The hardest truths to hear were those of Yers, still suffering from the head wound, still convinced that Simus had betrayed them. Joden could see Keir struggling with that idea, but each day no word came, and each day Joden feared that Keir lost more confidence in his old tent mate.

It was then that Joden would stand and stretch and pull Keir from council rooms and down to the sparring circle. Keir would agree, thinking it was mostly for Joden's benefit. Joden was gaining strength and muscle back quickly. But sweat and movement helped a warrior see clearer. Tired and pleased, Joden would return to the room, to find Amyu there, waiting.

There was such joy in her touch, in the scent of her skin, and his pleasure was reflected in her eyes as well. The babes were still her first duty, but they took their pleasures where they could, as often as they could. It loomed over them at times, the uncertainty of it all. But they had this now. Together. And each day, Amyu grew more important to him, to his life. Broken together.

But this morning, Keir called a halt to the talks. Instead, he and Joden had gone to the sparring circle early, and worked themselves into exhaustion. Joden knew his old friend, and could see that even as he wielded his weapons, his thoughts were elsewhere.

Which let Joden get in a few more 'killing' blows than he could normally score on Keir. And he took them shamelessly, when the opportunity was offered.

"Enough," Keir finally said. They racked their weapons, and then headed to the well, stripping down to trous and splashing cold water on themselves. Joden tipped a full bucket on his head, letting the water pour over him.

The doors from the kitchen opened. Lara, Marcus and Amyu emerged with blankets and fussy, crying babies. Anna had little Meara by the hand, encouraging her to walk. Aurora, the youngest of Lara's handmaidens ran ahead, calling for her dogs.

Lara looked frazzled. "Your son will not sleep," she said. "I thought maybe the warm sun might—"

"Here." Keir dried off, and then took Keirson from Marcus. He put his son on his shoulder and started to drum his back.

"Thankfully, he didn't wake Kayla," Lara took the girl babe from Amyu, and cooed to the sleeping child. She settled on the blanket, rocking her babe. "So," she said tiredly. "Have you beaten each other enough to reach an answer?"

Keir shook his head, pacing with Keirson.

Aurora came pelting back, the dogs chasing her. Meara sat at Anna's feet, and they ran up and licked the giggling child.

Joden finished drying himself, rubbing the cloth over his chest. He caught Amyu staring, and managed not to grin when she caught his eye and flushed. He loved that he could do that to her.

Keirson let out a piercing shriek. Keir looked at his son with wide eyes.

Joden laughed, and stepped forward. "L-l-let m-m-me," he said.

Keir gave over the baby with a shake of his head. "Watch your ears," he warned.

Joden cradled Keirson close to his chest with both hands. The babe's face was bright red, his eyes scrunched closed, tiny fists waving in the air.

"Mmmmmm," Joden hummed, deepening his voice.

Keirson's tiny eyes popped open, staring into Joden's.

Joden smiled and drew a breath, gently blowing on Keirson's face. The babe blinked, and yawned. Pleased, the words of the old lullaby came into Joden's mind. He gentled his voice and sang.

"Helya, tiny warrior,
Heyla, cease your cries
Heyla, the moon is rising
Heyla, close your eyes."

Keirson yawned, and settled into Joden's hands, his face pushed into Joden's chest. Joden waited a long breath, but Keirson didn't stir.

Joden looked up in triumph, only to find everyone staring at him, their mouths open.

It took him a moment to realize…

His voice. He could sing.

CHAPTER TWENTY-SEVEN

It hadn't gone away. Joden's words still came out broken. If he tried to talk, just talk, the words and sounds caught in his throat as bad as ever. He could substitute words sometimes, trick his tongue that way, but names were always a problem.

But to his utter joy and relief, he could sing. And if he sang the words instead of speaking them, his speech flowed.

When they had realized that he could sing, Lara and Keir had hustled him back to their chambers, summoned Master Eln and made Joden demonstrate.

Lara and Master Eln had no answers as to why. They made Joden try over and over again, for hours, until Joden dripped of sweat and his vision blurred. He'd stumbled to his room, collapsed into bed and fallen asleep immediately.

The next day as they ate the morning meal, Keir had asked him to open the senel with song.

Amyu hadn't come to him in the night, no doubt busy with the babes and her duties. She'd hovered at the edges of the room as he'd worked with Master Eln and Lara. He'd hoped to see her before this moment, but in the flurry of getting ready there had been no time.

Now Joden stood next to the throne of Xy and tried to calm his stomach and his shaking hands. The throne room was filled to capacity, with Xyians and Plains warriors alike. The fancy dress of the nobles blending with the armored warriors made an odd contrast, but the eagerness in all faces was clear. It seemed the two peoples were coming together, at least here and now. That was good to see.

If he could just calm his own fears. He felt the sweat gather on his scalp and the middle of his back.

The great doors swung open. Kendrick, Herald of Xy, stepped into the room. The old man was leaning on his staff a bit more, still looking as unsteady as a new colt, but he seemed determined to do his duty.

The crowd turned, and cleared a path from the doors to the throne. Joden noticed Heath, and the Castle Guards scanning the people, but there was no indication of trouble.

Kendrick lifted his staff with effort, and pounded it three times on the floor. "Lord and Ladies, all hail Keir, Warlord of the Plains, Overlord of Xy, and Xylara, Queen of Xy, Warprize… and Master Healer."

Joden heard Lara's chortle of delight above the wave of amusement that swept the room.

Keir was dressed in his finest armor, all black leathers and polished chain. Lara looked radiant in Xyian blue and white, the crown of Xy on her head and jewels sparkling at her throat. They both stepped into the room together, Lara's hand on Keir's.

Xyian and Plains warrior alike knelt as Lara and Keir approached, and rose as they passed by. When they reached the two thrones, Lara accepted Keir's aid as she walked up the two steps to stand before her throne. Keir then took his place in front of the other one.

Joden licked his lips, knowing what was coming.

"I call this senel to order," Keir said, his voice carrying over the crowd. "We will speak of events and announce our decisions. Know that we have considered all truths in deciding our best course." Keir paused. "But first, in our tradition, let us thank the elements. I call on Joden of the Hawk for a song.

All eyes turned to Joden.

He stepped forward. He had practiced this.

As he had in the past, he let his gaze scan the crowd, seeking their attention. He raised his hand, palm to the sky, and opened his mouth to speak the ritual words.

The words froze on his tongue. *He had no voice.*

In that moment, he spotted Amyu. She was in the doorway off to the side, back behind the crowd, watching with Marcus at her side. Her eyes were bright with hope. Bright for him.

He found his voice. "May the skies hear my voice. May the people remember."

It wasn't perfect. His voice sounded too high to him, too sing-songy. Almost as if he mocked the ancient words. But elements above, his words flowed and the people understood him.

The response rose from the room, "We will remember."

Joden didn't hesitate. He drew a deep breath, and let loose with an old song, one he'd learned from the theas, praising each element in turn. His voice was strong, deep, and clear.

Relief flooded through him, and a joy so profound he almost wept. Instead, he continued with each refrain and verse, praising the fire, water, earth and air.

When he was done, when the last note hung in the air, he opened his eyes and sought for Amyu. She was still in the doorway, her face filled with tears of joy.

But why did he also see pain in her eyes?

"Our thanks, Joden of the Hawk, soon-to-be-Singer and well deserved," Keir caught Joden's eye, his face solemn but his gaze reflected Joden's own joy.

Joden bowed his head and stepped back to his place beside Keir's throne.

Lara seated herself on her throne, and Keir followed her example. "We wish to let all know that Xykeirson and Xykayla are well. They are strong and thriving." She chuckled ruefully. "Keirson especially has very healthy lungs."

The crowd's laughter joined hers. Yet Joden could see relief in many eyes. She'd been wise to reassure them.

"We also extend our deepest thanks to the people of Water's Fall," Lara said. "Our warriors are now prepared, and fully supplied thanks to their efforts."

"We depart for the border with the Plains in two days," Keir said. "We will take a force of Plains and Xyian warriors with us." He paused, surveying the faces around him, and then continued, apparently satisfied with their reactions. "We have had no word from Liam of the Deer or Simus of the Hawk in some time. We do not know what we will find there, but we will be ready for all things. Supply wagons will travel with us."

"As will Xykeirson and Xykayla," Lara's voice was as sharp as a sword. Joden could see disapproval in some Xyian eyes.

"If they go, I go," another voice chimed in. Anna stood there, defiant, back by the door with Marcus. Anna's stout arms were crossed over her chest. "And none to say me nay, either."

That caused a stir, but Joden frowned at something else. Amyu wasn't where she had been, standing next to Marcus. Where was she?

"Heath will act as Warden of Xy in addition to his duties as Seneschal the Castle of Water's Fall." Lara said firmly, speaking over the murmurs. Heath stepped forward and bowed to her. Lara smiled. "He and his bonded, Atira of the Bear, have our full faith and trust."

"Lord Marshall Warren and Wilsa of the Lark will be traveling with us. Wilsa will serve as my Second," Keir said. He was the picture of confidence, seated on the throne. "They have sent word that they have routed the bandits and will arrive shortly. Forces will remain here and at the border to ward Xy." Keir looked over at Heath. "As to the wyverns…" he gestured to the younger man.

"We have found age-old weapons called balista stored in the ancient tunnels," Heath said. "I have men working to figure out how to install them on the various towers. In addition, every man on the walls has crossbows and bolts and alarm horns. We will be on watch for when, or if the creatures return."

Joden shifted his weight slightly, anxious to have this senel over. He needed to go find Amyu, but he could not leave his post.

"Despite this activity, we do not feel that it should delay the departure of the trade mission to the Kingdoms of Nyland and Cadthorn," Lara continued. "Lord Korvis, how go your preparations?"

Joden sighed as the man puffed up like a pigeon, and resolved himself to wait until the senel had ended.

* * * * *

Amyu wept to hear Joden's voice ring through the throne room. Glorious, strong and clear.

He was a Singer.

She'd tried to avoid the truth of it even as he had worked with Master Eln and the Warprize.

He was a Singer.

She was a child.

Her heart filled with joy, but she felt the cracks as well, forming bitter, hard shards.

"I'll check on the wet nurse," she whispered to Marcus, unable to stop her tears.

He gave her a look with his one eye that told her he'd seen through her excuse, but he gave her a sharp nod.

All was well in the royal chambers. The smiling wet nurse was grateful to give up her watch. The babes were sleeping quietly, which was a blessing from the elements. Amyu took up one of the clean nappies, sat down and indulged in quiet tears.

Joden had found a way to deal with his voice, and she shouldn't - couldn't - cling to him. He would become a Singer, upholder of the traditions and the ways of the Plains. He was destined for glory, to stand at the side of the Warlord and the Warprize, and yes, become Eldest Elder, of that she had no doubt. For him, for all that would be, she was so happy and so proud, and yet there was a blade caught in her heart, making it hard to breathe.

Amyu muffled her face with the cloth and let the sobs come freely.

But weeping endlessly is not a warrior's way. She dried her face with a determination she did not feel, and yet anger boiled in her gut. Anger at a problem she could not solve, a flaw within her that she could not fix.

Marcus slid into the room, casting a careful eye toward the cradle. "Xyians," he muttered. "They are still talking trade routes and will be at it most of the night." He took in Amyu's face. "Go. Eat. I will take watch."

Amyu nodded and headed toward the door. Marcus stepped aside to let her through. "You could try talking to him," Marcus offered. "Talk to Joden about—"

"As you did Liam?" Amyu lashed out.

Marcus stiffened. She'd never seen him so stricken but she couldn't find it in herself to care.

"I will protect him from himself," Amyu hissed, fully expecting Marcus to draw his daggers. "As you protected Liam. I know Joden's worth, and I will not let him waste it on me." Heart pounding, she continued recklessly on, "But do not tell me that all will be well. Any more than it is for you."

She didn't wait for his reaction. She slid out and eased the door closed, so as not to wake the babes. Her anger bubbled as she pounded down the stairs, but it faded with every step, leaving only pain.

The kitchens were being cleaned and settled for the night, but Amyu found a table full of warriors. Marcsi was serving them kavage, bread, and cheese and the talk was lively.

"Rafe?" Amyu called, and his head popped up from the table.

"Amyu," Rafe gave her a grin. "Come and sit. We missed the senel, didn't we?"

"It is still going on, but the Warlord announced that he would leave in two days' time. Now they speak of Xyian matters." she slid into a space on the bench next to him. "Did you find anything?"

Rafe shook his head. "No, no airions. We found the cave you were in, but little else. Still the mountain is beautiful, and we learned much of climbing."

"And falling," Ksand grimaced.

Rafe laughed. "True enough," he said, taking a moment to stuff his face with a meat pie. "Good," he mumbled around his mouthful. "Two days will give us enough time to prepare. Lasa lost her dagger in a tumble, and we left Fylin with Master Eln to stitch up a deep gash. Couldn't use bloodmoss, too dirty." Rafe took a long drink from his mug. "Let us tell you, that mountain is a force of the elements in its own right."

Amyu let their talk wash over her as they described their adventure, chiming in and talking over each other. She even worked up enough of an appetite to eat a bit of bread and butter.

Horns sounded, and everyone lifted their heads. "End of the senel." Rafe started to rise. "Best we report to the Warlord."

They all rose. Amyu followed them out of the kitchens, but took another path as they headed to the royal chambers. She'd left a few tunics and the basket of shards in Joden's room. She'd get them quickly, and be done.

The room was the same, unchanged, still smelling slightly of their bodies and sharing. Amyu opened the shutters and turned back. Joden had made up the bed and had folded her tunics off to the side, sitting them on a chair. On top of the tunics was the basket holding the shards of the sword.

Amyu took them up, and cast a glance about, looking for

anything else she'd left behind. But there was nothing left of hers, well, no things. But her dreams?

Anxious not to cry again, anxious to have done with her pain, she shut that thought down and turned toward the door.

Joden stood there, his face filled with questions

* * * * *

Joden stood in the doorway, his heart sinking as he saw Amyu gather up her things.

She turned, her arms full and stared at him before dropping her gaze. Her eyes were red and puffy and stricken.

"Singer—" she started.

"Amyu," he sang her name, not wanting to stumble over it.

Amyu frowned. "You don't need to do that with me," she said. "Not if you don't want to."

Joden nodded. "L-l-let t-t-there b-b-be t-t-truth b-b-between u-u-us."

"Good." She straightened and looked him straight in the eye, her sweet brown eyes sad and determined. "Here is my truth, Joden of the Hawk. You are a Singer, destined for greatness on the Plains and beyond. You have taken the old paths, and shown your willingness to sacrifice for your people.

"A Singer must be an example to the People," her voice cracked. "A Keeper of the way of the Plains, of our traditions." She drew a ragged breath. "This, what is between us, is not of our ways."

"A-a-amyu," Joden's heart shared the pain he saw in her eyes.

"You are a Singer—" Amyu's voice was shaking.

"N-n-not," Joden shook his head. "M-m-may n-n-not." He shook his head in frustration, then sang the words, "A Singer's voice must be true, their words strong."

"And yours are, and will grow stronger. You are an admired and respected Singer-to-be," Amyu continued. "You can't have a child in your tent or at your side, in defiance of the ways of the Plains."

Joden stepped toward her, his arms open.

Amyu took a step back. "Look me in the eye, and deny this truth," she challenged.

Joden lowered his own gaze and his arms, and could not speak. His throat closed with pain, his stomach knotted. As a Singer, he should be the first to urge her to the snows. But she stood before him, lovely, vibrant, her pained brown eyes wet with tears.

"The Warlord departs in two days," she said. "You will ride with him, in all honor. I will remain in Xy. A child. An outcast."

Joden shook his head. "W-w-we w-w-would p-p-protect—"

"And lose honor in so doing," Amyu said. "The Warlord can't risk losing all he has worked for in defense of one barren warrior," she continued. "I have a worth here." She looked down at the basket of shards. "I just haven't found it yet."

"W-w-worth t-t-to m-m-me," Joden said. He couldn't bear her pain any longer and opened his arms again.

Her face crumpled and she walked into his arms, crushing the basket and tunics between them. Her voice was muffled in his chest as he put his chin on the top of her head. "You have seen me as I am, not as child or as failure. I thank you for that truth. I will carry it with me as long as I live."

Joden hugged her tight, taking in the scent of the Plains in her hair.

But then Amyu stepped back, and he let his arms drop, letting her go. She gave him a watery smile. "But here is another truth. I am too much the coward. I need to stop here. I will not come to you again, and I beg you not to come to me."

She pushed past him to the door, and he turned to watch it close behind her. He sank down on the bed, his legs losing all their strength.

He had found his voice. He could still achieve his dream, at a price.

He'd lost his heart's flame.

CHAPTER TWENTY-EIGHT

The power of death was everywhere.

How had he never seen this before? Hail Storm mused on the nature of this new gift of the Plains as he trotted his dead steed over the wide grasses.

Perhaps it was because he'd been trained only to use the golden light that had been so rare and growing scarcer before the Sacrifice. He'd learned blood magic only by mistake, and had never shared his discovery of its use with the other warrior-priests. He had resorted to it when the elemental power of the Plains had gradually diminished. A shiver of delight went through him at the memory of killing Arched Colors. Her body had writhed under his in pleasure, pain, and her death throes.

He'd give much to be able to do that again.

And Mist, that old bitch. She'd supported him until the Sacrifice, and then tried to kill him. Instead, he'd killed her, absorbing her life essence in the process.

The stone-handled dagger at his side throbbed with his memory of that moment.

The darkness, the power of death, was there under the grass, deep in the earth. Like a hidden treasure he'd passed over many times. What was around him wasn't as strong as a true death at his hands, but it was plentiful. He wasn't going to have to kill small animals or birds for power. The source was wide and vast and untouched.

The elements could rage at him all they wanted. He had what he needed.

Access to power gave him choices.

Hail Storm frowned down at his empty hand. There was no need for reins. The dead horse went exactly where he sent it. But it only moved when he willed it.

He could turn back. Cache the supplies and the saddle and let the horse drop where it stood. Return to Antas's tent, worm his way back into favor. Build a network of support from within and betray him at the first chance. Hail Storm smiled at the idea of killing Antas and draining him dry. Fitting revenge for the loss of his arm.

But in truth, that would take time and the outcome was uncertain. Too many people to try to control, too many doubts as to everyone's loyalties.

Besides, Wild Winds was dead, which meant that somewhere there was a group of young warrior-priests in training. Young. Malleable. He just had to find them, and court them with fine words, gestures of support, and promises of power. Some, not all maybe, but some would be lured to him and the knowledge he could teach.

A thump brought him out of his musings. The horse had stumbled ever so slightly. He looked down to see that the sinews of the leg were wearing at the hoof. He cursed, and eased the creature to a walk.

A dead horse was obedient, but not truly sustainable. The flesh had worn away under the saddle, and the smell left much to be desired. Hail Storm didn't let the reek trouble him, but it had drawn scavengers when he'd camped for the evenings. And the dead horse never moved without a command, never grazed, only stared at him over the fire, light glittering in its clouded, rotting eyes.

Still, it was better than walking and carrying his packs. He'd have trouble replacing this mount when it fell apart. Living horses sensed his presence from afar and would not come close.

He'd not be able to lure one to its death at his hands.

But maybe he didn't need to. His eyes narrowed as he considered the possibilities.

There was so much death in the land, so much corruption. Where prey had been taken, where the very grasses of the Plains shriveled and died, all that was power for his taking. It was as if a cloth had been torn away from his unseeing eyes. With no access to the elemental power, other sources made themselves known.

What if he could imbue the horse's carcass with enough energy that it didn't need the physical body? What if he didn't need to constantly focus to make it move on its own? Hail Storm considered that thought with the greatest of joy. There was enough power that he could build up as he went, and then he could find a place where deaths had been frequent and—

The Heart.

Hail Storm lost his focus and the horse stopped moving.

The Heart. The dead warrior-priests. He remembered their bodies scattered everywhere. There was a source of power, most likely fresh and undiminished, just waiting to be tapped. To be used. To be used against Antas of the Boar, against Keir of the Cat, against any that would block his demand for power.

The young warrior-priests would return there, sure as the sun would set. The armies would gather for the Fall Council. The Council would be reborn, and beneath its tent he would claim mastery of the Plains and its people. He could raise up a new generation of warrior-priests, and their powers would not be mocked, would not be dismissed. They would be feared and obeyed and he would be their Eldest Elder.

In the meantime, he must learn and grow. Practice his new arts. Be certain of his strength and skills.

He turned his mount toward the Heart.

Everything would be decided there.

* * * * *

Cadr felt relief when Lightning Strike called an early halt. Gilla's warcats had flushed out and killed three deer. More than enough for their needs.

Cadr slid from the saddle with a grateful sigh. He was healing and there was less pain, but every once in a while, a twinge caught him off guard.

They'd stopped by a gully with a pond and flowing stream, protected by thick alders.

"Our regular watches," Lightning Strike said. "We can dig a pit for the meat, and dry some for the journey."

"I'll set wards," Rhys said quietly, and he and Sidian walked off together.

"I'll gut," Cadr offered. A messy job, but with the pond close he'd be able to wash himself after. A few of the others moved to help, and it didn't take long before the carcasses were cut up. Cadr hauled the offal out a distance from the camp. The cats followed him, making odd chirrips and mews, eager for their reward.

The pit was finished, and the fire started. It would have to be tended all night once the meat was racked for drying. Cadr went to the pond, stripped and plunged into the icy water, using the sand to scrub himself. It felt good to get clean.

The sun was lowering when he returned to the fire, his armor and gear in his hands. The warmth felt good as it dried his skin.

Rhys was seated there, and kept averting his eyes from Cadr's nakedness, just like a city-dweller would. Cadr chuckled, but Gilla gave him a shove, so he donned his leather trous.

They all set to work cutting the leaner bits of meat into strips for the drying rack. Lightning Strike and others set up tents.

Cadr sighed with satisfaction. He'd take a night watch, eager to make up for his lack while he'd been recovering.

Night Clouds and Moon Waters approached the fire, their arms filled with ogden roots for roasting.

"Oh, these will taste good," Gilla said, starting to clean the roots.

"There's more," Moon Waters settled next to her, pulling her dagger. "Plenty for all and enough left in the ground to grow."

"Night Clouds," Rhys piped up. "I have an idea I want to try. Would you show me how you scry?"

"Sure," Night Clouds wiped his hands on his trous. "I've a scrying bowl in my pack." He trotted off, returning in a moment with a bowl filled with water. He knelt beside Rhys, and placed the bowl on as level a space as he could find. "What shall I scry?" he asked.

"The Heart," Lightning Strike came up behind them, soaking wet from bathing, his gear in his hands. He shrugged at their looks. "Easiest to focus on. That's what we all learned at first."

Cadr went over and stood shoulder to shoulder with Rhys, just as curious as anyone. They both leaned over the bowl, looking down.

"The Heart," Night Clouds whispered. He was staring at the bowl, talking under his breath. The water was still and dark within. For long moments, nothing happened, and then Cadr squinted. There was an image, a vision.

Suddenly he was looking at the Heart, as if standing on the rim. The circular grey stone arched around either side, and there in the center lay the body of a dead wyvern, covering half the stone. Ravens pecked at its eyes and back.

"Skies," Cadr breathed.

"I can see it too," Rhys said softly.

Lightning Strike came over, Sidion close behind. "Is that a wyvern?"

Cadr nodded. "The one that was killed, when Simus and the gathered warriors rescued the Elders."

Sidion whistled, peering down. "That is some creature," he said. "Is that a stinger on the end of that tail?"

"It's vivid and detailed." Rhys crouched for a better look. "I might be able to portal—"

"No," Cadr interrupted. "Night Clouds, can you change it? Show us the shore?"

Night Clouds said nothing, just turned his head slightly. The image fluttered and moved. The shore appeared, seething with wyverns. They were all tearing prey, and feeding young in rocky nests. The young ones had their wings spread, and Cadr could almost hear their cries for food.

"So many," Lightning Strike breathed. "I didn't realize."

"And vicious," Cadr said. "That sting is a deadly poison that eats flesh."

"No portal," Sidian said.

"No portal," the others agreed.

"Night Clouds," Sidian continued. "Does there need to be water in the bowl? To Scry?"

The image faltered and then disappeared. Night Clouds looked up, eyes wide. "I don't know," he said.

"Try it," Sidian suggested.

This gained them more attention as other warrior-priests gathered. Cadr gave way his place, more interested in making sure the roots got roasted. Gilla also backed away. But those not on watch gathered around, all talking as Night Clouds dumped the water from the bowl, and dried it.

It must have worked, from the soft exclamations that came after a while. Next thing Cadr knew, everyone was trying it, pulling out their own bowls. Then those with metal shields were using those, clearly pleased with the results.

It was only at Cadr's second call that they stopped and started eating.

"It takes more power," Night Clouds said as he blew on his ogden root to cool. "And it's harder to keep the image stable."

"I wonder," Sidian said. "Can you do it while moving?"

Night Clouds looked at him with wide eyes, and then jumped up.

Sidian laughed. "Finish your food, then try."

"Why do you ask?" Lightning Strike asked.

"For the next spike of power," Sidian said. "If they can get an image…"

"I could portal," Rhys continued. "Might link us to your Hanstau."

Cadr brightened.

"Might get us in more trouble," Lightning Strike countered then he shrugged. "Still, a good skill to learn while we continue on."

"To Xy?" Gilla asked.

"To Xy," Lightning Strike confirmed.

* * * * *

Hanstau lay back on the bedding, staring at the tent over him, safe and warm and toes well and truly curled.

Reness was out by their fire braiding her hair. He turned his head enough to see the curve of her back and the glow of her skin in the firelight. As she moved, lifting muscular arms, he caught glimpses of her breast. It roused him, as it had in the past, and always would, he suspected.

At least, for as long as this lasted.

Reness had found a small herd, and they had stayed within their midst the past few days, hiding from the world. Hanstau knew he should return to Xy, and take word to his Queen of all that had happened. But his heart wanted to stay here, with this woman, in this bubble of time for as long as he could.

He tried to feel guilty. He really did.

But in all honor, they needed to travel more directly so that they could—

The golden glow of power appeared in the corner of his eye.

Hanstau turned his head toward it, away from Reness, to see the glow pooled beneath horses' hooves. It couldn't be true, but the light seemed to dance around them, deliberately, as if celebrating light and life and joy. Foolishness on his part, surely.

As if it noticed him watching, the light danced over and gathered around his fingers. He held them up, looking at the glow that surrounded his hands against the dark of the tent.

"You are playing with the light," Reness said, crawling in beside him, and stretching out her long legs against his.

"How did you know?" he asked. "You can't see it."

"You get this look in your eyes," she chuckled. "Like fleeing prey."

"Er," Hanstau huffed out a breath. "I'm not sure—"

"Like you are looking at something dangerous and fascinating at the same time," she said. "Maybe like a child with its first real sword. Or—"

"Maybe you should stop there," he said dryly.

She huffed a laugh.

"But you are right," he said. "I am looking at something dangerous. I don't think I should try to use it again."

"Why?"

Hanstau frowned. His fingers still glowed. "Because." he said slowly. "Because what I did back there, it felt loud. Obvious. Frightening."

"You did the right thing," Reness said. She eased up to pull their bedding over them.

"Yes," Hanstau said. "I know that. But they were trying to kill you, and it was dire. My fear could have led me to do terrible things, Reness."

"How is it terrible, when they are trying to kill you?" she asked with simple warrior logic.

"It is," Hanstau said firmly. "And I am not going to try to use it again."

"Unless someone tries to kill us." Reness reached over to caress his cheek.

"Unless someone else tries to kill us," Hanstau agreed.

Reness smiled against his lips and kissed him, driving away any need for talk.

* * * * *

Antas stood on a rise, and watched an army approach.

It had taken time and precious supplies to repair the damage, deal with the dead, and calm his warriors.

Ietha had also required careful handling, and he still wasn't certain that she'd support him in the end. Antas flexed his fists. Talking with no action was starting to irritate him, and he knew if he lost his temper he'd lose support.

And now Reht approached, and all the messengers would say was that she wanted to talk. Reht was a short woman, short of stature, short of hair, short of temper. Antas wanted in the worst way to say exactly what he thought of that, but he kept his truths in his mouth and agreed to a meeting. He brought Veritt, his Second with him.

He could only hope it came to blows. Much more talk and he'd—

"Hail, Antas of the Boar, Warlord and Eldest Elder Warrior," Reht rode forward, ahead of her warriors.

That boded well. Antas stepped forward and boomed his own greeting. "Hail, Reht of the Horse, Warlord of the Plains. What brings you here?"

"I've come to join with you," Reht said. "I offer my support against Keir of the Cat."

Antas grinned. "Welcome," he said simply.

CHAPTER TWENTY-NINE

Amyu slowly climbed the last remaining stairs of the highest tower of the castle, her heart as heavy as her footsteps. She went up through the trap door, stepping out into the sunlight and clean, clear air.

She walked to the low wall that surrounded the top of the tower, and with a puff of breath, tried not to look at what she dreaded to see.

The City of Water's Fall stretched out below her, as it had in the past. Beyond that the fields and forests still sprawled out in the valley below. The long road still snaked down the valley from the main gates of the city.

Only this time, down that road marched the combined armies of Xy and the Plains.

Somewhere in their midst rode Joden of the Hawk.

The wind caught Amyu's brown hair, whipping it around her head. She caught the long strands in her hands, and bound it up in a quick knot.

She hadn't gone down to the castle courtyard to see them all off. It would have been more than her heart could take. Joden had honored her request, and he'd not come to her. Nor had she gone to him. She'd managed to avoid him as she'd aided the Warprize in preparations, thinking she'd done the right thing and yet—

He was gone, and she'd give anything for one last word. One last chance to say goodbye.

"We'll be able to see them for some time," came a familiar voice.

Amyu looked over to find the Xyian guard Enright sitting in his usual position, on a bench facing the low wall, working on repairing a bit of armor. His crossbow sat beside him, cocked and ready, and an alarm bell sat on his other side.

"Takes a while to move an army that size." He gave her a knowing look. "The sun will set before we lose sight." He shifted over a bit, making his wooden leg clack, and patted the bench next to him. "Have a sit."

Amyu sat. The sun was warm, and the stones beneath their feet radiated warmth. Around them bees buzzed in their large basket hives. The mountain towered above, its craggy walls stark and unforgiving.

"Someone you care about down there?" Enright gestured toward the army.

Amyu shrugged, then nodded.

"They'll be back," Enright said confidently. "Maybe not every one of them, I'll be honest with ya, but on the whole, they will be back. Triumphant, if I know the Warlord."

Amyu stared out, watching the long line of men and horses moving along the road. "Joden goes to finish his Trials and become a Singer, the Singer he was destined to become. Maybe even the Eldest Elder Singer. Keeper of our ways. Our laws."

"The laws that keep you here?" Enright asked quietly. "The laws that deems you outcast."

"Not outcast." Amyu still stared out over the wall without seeing anything. "Useless." Her voice sounded flat and odd to her own ears.

"Ya know that's not true," Enright said.

Amyu nodded but couldn't speak, her eyes welling up.

"Well then," Enright shifted again, then stood with a clatter. "I gotta use the privy," he said gruffly. "Might take me a bit, what with the stairs."

Amyu nodded again, keeping her eyes on the army, her

tears starting to fall.

"Here," a large white piece of cloth appeared in front of her face.

Amyu took the cloth, and Enright left, his wooden leg clacking as he made his way down. She was grateful for the privacy. She didn't want to weep, but the tears kept coming.

It all felt so hopeless. The Warprize had told her to keep searching for the airions, but she didn't truly believe that Amyu would find them. She also asked that Amyu learn to read and write Xyian. An honorable task, but... Amyu felt useless, and a failure and—

Footsteps came up the steps, and it was not Enright. Amyu mopped her face, and stuffed the cloth away.

"Amyu," Atira came up through the trap door and walked over to sit beside her. She looked around the top of the tower with a satisfied smile, then turned to Amyu. "I have been looking for you."

Amyu resisted the urge to look back out at the departing army. She met the warrior's gaze bravely. Atira was tall and fair of hair and face. She was the Bonded of Heath of Xy, and a well-respected warrior.

"Heath said that you need a sword re-forged," Atira said. "The Crystal Sword of Xy?"

"Yes," Amyu nodded. "Do you know how?"

"I don't," Atira smiled. "But I know someone that might."

* * * * *

Amyu followed Atira through the streets of the city, until she led her through a large wooden door. Amyu stood dumbstruck in the doorway of the forge, staring at the men laboring over red hot metal.

Atira glanced over her shoulder at her, and laughed. "I had the same reaction," she said. "Come, we will get closer."

It was as if all the elements danced at the big man's command.

The heat hit her first, like a blow to the face, heat so hot it dried the sweat that formed. The air held an acrid tang.

The room was huge, with stone walls and a high vaulted ceiling. Heavy wooden beams arched over the room. There were clusters of men and boys around the walls, working at tables. The noise battered at Amyu's ears. Each group worked on something different, but her eyes were drawn to the ones in the center.

The greatest heat came from the furnace in the middle of the room, where a circular stone ring sat, covered by an arched dome. She could see flame flickering within the openings. A young man worked some sort of odd wooden and leather thing up and down, and the fire at the center danced in response, crackling and swaying with his movements.

"That's the fire that Dunstan uses to heat the metal." Atira raised her voice to be heard over the noise. "The apprentice works the bellows, see? It keeps the fire at the right heat." She pointed to three men, working close by the fire. "See the anvil? That large metal piece there?"

"What are they doing?" Amyu asked.

"Making bolts for the new ballistae." Atira stared at the forge, desire raging in her eyes, awe in her voice. "Heath as Warden had given orders for hundreds of them."

"You have worked down here," Amyu said, knowing full well that Atira had.

Atira just nodded, seemingly lost in thought. "I am going to make swords." Her voice rang with quiet determination. "I will forge such blades that Singers will praise them for centuries to come."

"First you have to advance past making nails." A woman came up to stand next to them, a welcoming smile on her face. "Who is this, Atira?"

"Ismari, this is Amyu." Atira said, still staring at the flames. "She has questions about re-forging a sword, so I brought her here."

"A sword?" Ismari frowned. Amyu noticed that while she was Xyian she wasn't wearing skirts. And her hands were calloused and rough, with a few old burns. Her eyes were bright and curious. "Well, Dunstan is the expert, but he will be at the fire for a while. Show it to me, and let me see what I can tell you."

Amyu reached for the pack on her back, and pulled out the basket containing the shards.

Ismari took it, and her eyes went wide. "Is this the Crystal Sword of Xy? In a bread basket?" Her voice was hushed. She looked around, and pulled Amyu toward a nearby door, hustling her into another work area. "Let's not give the apprentices more to gossip about than they already have," she said.

Atira followed, but her steps dragged. Amyu gave the blonde warrior a questioning look. Atira shrugged sheepishly. "I don't get down here as often as I wish."

Ismari had pulled a thick black cloth out and spread it on the table. "Dunstan won't be long," she said. "Let's see what we have here."

Amyu dumped the basket on the cloth. Ismari winced. But she reached for the hilt and put it flat at one end of the cloth. "Let's see if it's all here."

It was. All the shining blue shards made a pattern, and Ismari had a gift for sorting them out. Once they were done, the sword was recreated, except in parts.

"Odd," Ismari stepped back. "I would expect some of the smaller slivers to be missing. But it all seems to be here, and would go back together if you had a way to bind them."

The door opened behind them, and Dunstan stepped in, wiping his hands on a cloth. "Atira, Ismari," Dunstan rumbled. "What—" he stopped dead. "Is that the Crystal Sword of Xy?"

Amyu sighed.

After explanations, Dunstan shook his head, his regret clear. "I know of no flame that would bind these parts together," he said. "And that is a shame. It has always been part of the Monarch's regalia."

"I do not know that word," Amyu said.

"Regalia?" Dunstan smiled. "It means the robes, the clothes, the jewelry, all symbols of the Crown."

"What he or she carries at every ceremony," Ismari said. "I've never seen this sword except in the hands of the King or Queen." Her fingers touched the hilt lightly. "And it feels wrong to see it like this, even though it shattered for a purpose."

"And no way to fix it," Dunstan put his hand on his sister's shoulder. "No fire, or any other element that I know of, could re-forge the blade. It's not the kind of work for a smith, that's for sure." He turned away, looking pained. "Let's find something better for you to carry it in than that basket."

* * * * *

Archbishop Iian smiled at Amyu from across a table filled with sand. "This will not be as hard as you think," he said. He picked up a jug of water and poured it over the sand.

"The Warprize wishes me to learn," Amyu said glumly. This was not a task she would have chosen. But she'd come to the nursery as instructed.

"This is how we teach our children their letters," Iian said, stirring the damp sand. He must have seen the doubt in her eyes because he continued, "I do not think of you as a child," he said firmly as he smoothed the sand. "This is just the best way to teach you. Take this stylus," he offered her a straight stick. "Now, this is how you make an 'a'."

Amyu watched, and copied him stroke by stroke as he went through all the letters.

"Now," Iian put down his stylus, and leaned forward. "Let's see what you remember. Write an "A".

He recited the letters and Amyu drew them out as fast as he spoke, with Iian clearing the sand in between. At the end, Iian leaned back and shook his head.

"Flawless," he said. "Your people's memories are amazing."

"So we are done?" Amyu asked.

"No," Iian smiled. "You must still learn to form the letters into words and then there is the order words go in, and how to write them down so everyone can read."

Amyu slumped in her chair. The shards of the sword clinked together in the leather bag tied to her belt. "Isn't it easier to just remember it all?" she asked, trying not to whine.

"It is," Iian said. "But we write things down to preserve our knowledge and information." He frowned at the sand. "Although that didn't work with the wyverns, did it?"

"Because there are no books?" Amyu asked.

Iian nodded, absently drawing a wyvern in the sand. "There should be records," Iian said. "Something that preserved that knowledge. Yet we have nothing. If we of Xy had perfect memories—"

"Joden thinks it was deliberately forgotten," Amyu said. She leaned her elbows on the sand table. "Long ago."

Iian sighed. "If memory can be distorted or lost, and paper and ink lost and destroyed, how are we to preserve knowledge? There must be a way."

"Even if it is remembered, the old can refuse to share their knowledge," Amyu said glumly. "Kalisa refused to tell us anything about the past."

Iian's frown deepened. "True," he said. He tilted his head to the side. "There are other, older people. Have you talked to Kendrick?"

"The Herald?" Amyu straightened. "Is he as old as Kalisa?"

"Maybe older," Iian stood. "Let's go ask."

* * * * *

Kendrick chuckled at their question. "I am not that old. But I have served four monarchs in my life time. Xyvon, Xyron, Xymund," a shadow passed over his face. "Othur was an old friend." His eyes looked sad and distant, but when he focused back on Amyu it was with a gentle smile. "And now Xylara is Queen, may the God of the Sun bless and keep her."

"So you don't know the old ceremonies?" Amyu tried not to let her disappointment show.

"Of course I know the ceremonies," Kendrick lifted his chin. "That is my charge." He gestured to the shelves around the walls of his office, filled with books and scrolls. "All of the Crown ceremonies, rituals and the bloodlines of the noble houses. All here."

Even Iian seemed stunned. The Herald's office was lined with shelves and all the shelves were crammed with books and scrolls and loose papers. Dust floated in the sunlight that streamed through the windows.

"Could you tell me of them?" Amyu asked. "Of the rituals that surround the crystal sword?"

"Rare for one so young to care," Kendrick said with a broad smile. "But I would be pleased to share my knowledge." He rose slowly, and tottered over to a shelf. "This is the most recent copy of the Regalia of the House of Xy."

The book was brown, its pages faded and curled with age. Kendrick brought it over and settled on a stool. "This was drawn by my predecessor," he said, leafing through the book. "Here." He put the book down, and pointed.

Amyu leaned forward, with Iian looking over her shoulder. The drawing was all crisp black lines. Amyu recognized the Council Room. The sword was displayed on the table, and on the wall behind was the tapestry of the airion.

"The Crystal Sword of Xy is one of the two most ancient artifacts of Xy," Kendrick said. "It was always displayed in the Council Room, set out on the Council table as you see here. The sword is only removed for the High Ceremonies," He continued. "The Coronation of the Monarch, the Marriage of the Monarch, the Confirmation of the Heir Apparent, and the Funeral of the Monarch."

"Two ancient pieces?" Iian questioned.

"Yes," Kendrick turned the page. "The other is the Xyian Ring."

This drawing was stark in comparison. The ring was a plain band, with a stone set in the center.

"The Xyian Ring was always worn by the Monarch," Kendrick said. "Originally, the sword was always carried as well, but that practice ended before my time."

"I had forgotten the Ring," Iian said.

"Many have." Kendrick shook his head. "Lara's father, Xyron, wore it until he sickened. It kept falling off his finger as he grew thinner. I offered the ring to Xymund, but he felt that it was not worthy of him. He wanted something grander. Something that befit a king." Herald sniffed. "Never mind its history, its age, or significance. He talked of melting it down, having it refashioned, and bid me store it until he had decided on a design."

He stood, and reached deep into a high shelf, moving scrolls and papers out of the way. "Here it is," he said, pulling out a small wooden box.

Amyu stared at the ring, a gold band and blue stone that matched the sword. "They are the same color," she said.

"At every High Ceremony, at some point in the ceremony the monarch holds high the Sword, displays the Ring and recites the Call." Kendrick turned back to the book and pointed to markings below the picture. "'Let the protectors of Xy arise to my call.' In suitable, stirring tones, of course."

"Of course," Iian said.

"There have been no changes in the rallying cry." Kendrick started to thumb through the book, looking for something. "But there have been variations in the gestures over time."

"Why isn't Xylara wearing it now?" Iian asked.

"Xylara wore it for her hasty Coronation." Kendrick frowned. "I made sure of that. But it slid off her finger and she wasn't going to take it to the Plains. Something about 'taking nothing from my Warlord.'"

"Take nothing except from the hand of the Warlord," Amyu corrected.

"Ah," Kendrick nodded. "A ritual of the Plains, no doubt." He shrugged. "I have been meaning to speak to Xylara since her return, but with all the ruckus, I hadn't had a chance."

Iian looked around the small room. "Do you have apprentices? Assistants?"

"No," Kendrick sighed. "Othur and I talked of it, but Xymund had no interest beyond his own glory. I haven't bothered Xylara, but with the birth of the babes."

Iian frowned. "We must take action to preserve—"

"Could I take it?" Amyu interrupted. She didn't want to be rude, but they might talk forever. "I have an idea."

"The ring?" Kendrick's bushy eyebrows climbed up with horror. "But—"

"On my authority," Iian said.

Kendrick looked at both of them as if their wits had been taken by the wind. "Let us talk to the Warden of Xy," he said firmly, closing the ring box with a snap.

* * * * *

Amyu released her horse into the herd of cows grazing at the foot of the mountain. Kalisa's family was nowhere to be seen, and the cheese cave was locked up tight. That suited Amyu. She didn't want to have to answer any more questions.

She'd answered plenty in the last few days, enough that they still rang in her head. She'd been honest in telling Heath and Atira that she'd had an idea about how to summon the airions using the sword. She just hadn't told them everything.

It had taken time to convince them. Days in fact, but that had been fine. She'd needed time to prepare and gather items for her own ritual.

There'd been arguments against her of course, with everyone pointing out the flaws in her idea. That she didn't have the Blood of Xy in her veins. That the sword and the rallying cry were for the people of Xy, not some mythical creature. That no sign had been found by Rafe and the others. That this was a foolish idea, and that she'd lose the Ring of Xy in the brush and that was a hell of a way to treat an ancient artifact of the House of Xy.

That last had been from an indignant Kendrick, quivering with worry at the very idea.

In the end, Heath had shrugged. "The skies favor the bold," he quoted as he gave her permission.

She cached her saddle, and took up her pack. She'd plenty of food, and all the gear she would need. This shouldn't take as long this time, as she wasn't searching. She knew exactly where she was going.

Amyu adjusted the straps of her pack, shifted to make sure it sat right. With a deep breath, and a shiver of excitement, she started up the path.

CHAPTER THIRTY

Even knowing the way, it took time. It was easier, being familiar with the path, but she still took care.

It was also easier not having to worry about Joden… but she wasn't going to let herself think about that. Or dwell on the pain. She concentrated on her feet and the path. Amyu wasn't going to risk a broken limb or worse, losing the Ring or the Shards in a fall.

But after a few nights in the open she came to the small cave. The dried sticks were still out front of the opening, and the inside was still clear and clean of debris.

The scorch marks were still on the ceiling.

Amyu put aside any memories of Joden, resolving to lock them away, and to focus on other things. She made camp, setting out her gear and her bedroll, and got a fire started for hot kavage. It was early yet; she'd hunt later, to supplement her dried meat and gurt supplies.

For now, she settled on her bedroll, dragged her pack toward her, and with a deep breath she pulled out the battered lantern.

She had an idea, and now was the time to try it. Away from prying eyes and questions she really didn't have answers for. It had been something Dunstan had said.

'No fire, or any other element that I know of, could re-forge the blade.'

She set the small lantern down in front of her, and sat cross-legged, staring at it intently.

No element he knew of.

What if there was another element?

She held her breath, feeling a tingle through her body at the very thought. All her life, she'd been taught by the theas of the four elements that ruled the Plains.

Was it possible the golden light was an element that no one around her could see, or touch, or use?

Was it possible she was special?

Part of her rejected that thought in an instant. But part of her... part of her dared to think it.

Kalisa had said that she'd foresworn the power, and that meant that she'd used it at some point. As hard as it was for Amyu to believe, Kalisa had somehow seen it in her.

Amyu hugged herself as she stared at the lantern. 'If you want to ride a horse,' she whispered. 'You have to get up on the horse.'

She closed her eyes and summoned the memory of being in the dark. Alone. A creature outside, with claws and fangs and...

Light. She needed light. But to set her weapons down, to fumble with flint and striker was unthinkable.

Another stick cracked, as if the creatures were gathering themselves up to rush her.

Light, her mind screamed, but she crouched low, frozen in fear.

Small golden sparkles started to gather at her feet.

Amyu opened her eyes.

Golden sparkles danced before her face, glittering little stars.

She breathed out, and then sucked a breath in astonishment. She reached out, and her hand tingled as if they were not there and yet really there at the same time.

The gold gathered on her fingertips, and traced her movements as she moved her fingers.

"Here," she whispered. She lowered her hand, and put the sparkles in the lantern. "Stay here."

The sparkles fell off her fingers and gathered into a ball in the lantern, glowing brightly. More sparkles joined them, until the light, the power all rested within.

A deep sense of satisfaction washed over her, but then her stomach rumbled and brought her back to reality.

She closed the small metal door, and light gleamed out from the metal. "Stay," she whispered. "Stay for me." She stood, taking up her bow and arrow.

When she returned, dead rabbits in hand, the cave still glowed with the light of the lantern.

Amyu set about spitting the meat, but she couldn't help the excitement building inside. She could use it, control it, see it. What else could she do? She bit her lip, thinking, remembering the light, the fire and heat and—

She happened to look up. The scorch marks were above her, glaring down, the black a stark contrast to the stone in the light of the lantern.

Amyu settled back on the bedroll, and watched the flames of a perfectly normal fire sear the meat. With regret, she tamped down her excitement. Fire was an element. It was both friend and foe. A force to be used, a danger to be feared. That was true of the other elements as well.

She'd go slow. Be cautious. Wary.

But the excitement was still with her when she stretched out to sleep. Her stomach was full, the lantern gleamed, and her dreams were filled with flying.

* * * * *

The sparkles had faded within the lantern during the night, but that didn't dim Amyu's excitement. She packed up her gear, wrapped the remaining meat for her nooning and started up the path, light of step and heart.

Until she rounded a bend and memory struck her like a stone.

Joden standing there, bruised and battered, his eyes crinkled in the corners by his smile. He pulled leaves from the tangles in her hair, standing close enough that she could smell the scent on his skin. He smelled of crushed pine needles, moist earth and spice. As he pulled at the tangles he let the leaves and sticks fall to the ground. They both started to laugh as they stood there, worn, weary, and alive.

He took care around the feather she had tied into her hair, carefully arranging it in front of her ear. His eyes warm and strong and—

It was like a physical blow to her heart. Amyu stopped in the path, pressed her hands to her chest, and let the pain wash over her.

Tears threatened. It had been the right decision to set him free, but her heart could barely beat in her chest. She made the choice; they both made the choice. Joden of the Hawk must become what he was destined to become and she—

She tipped her head back, and looked up at the mountain. At the trees swaying green in the breeze; at the blue sky above.

How in the name of the skies above and the earth below had that man become so important to her in such a short time?

Amyu stood for a while, letting herself feel all the anguish and heartbreak the memory brought. Then she dropped her hands to her side.

She had her own path.

She wasn't going to sit and weep and waste away for lack of him. She was going to keep moving. Keep breathing. Find her own way. The pain of losing him would fade. Amyu took a step along the trail and then another, dashing away tears.

The pain would fade.

But the regret? The regret would settle deep, forever in her bones.

* * * * *

She didn't make camp inside the tunnel-like cave where she'd found Joden. Instead, she went off toward the side, where she'd hunted game previously. Her thought was two-fold. If something went wrong, her gear and supplies would be safely out of the way.

If the ceremony she performed killed her, there would be evidence of her presence for searchers.

While that wasn't the most positive of thoughts, it was practical.

She spent the rest of the day cleaning out the large cave of debris, and the remains of their campsite. She wasn't sure of the reasons, but it felt right, and important somehow. She focused on that.

She didn't think on Joden.

A ceremony invoking the elements was usually conducted under the open sky. But as she swept the cave clear, it felt more important to face the wall at the back. She compromised by placing herself at the halfway point between the back of the cave and the open ledge.

That night, she hunted and ate, and then bathed in the chill waters of the small stream. On the Plains, she might do a ceremony like this naked but it was not a requirement. While she wished to honor the elements she invoked, she felt more comfortable armed and armored. So that was decided.

She lay down on her pallet, under the blankets, blinking at the night sky and thinking she would never get to sleep. She started to rehearse again all that she planned to do and say… only to wake at the first light of dawn.

She dressed, ate a quick meal, and then took up her backpack. She made the climb back up to the cave, and then stood on the ledge looking out. The moment was here, and she was quivering with what she hoped was excitement.

But it could well be fear.

The stone floor remained clear. She'd worried to death about the positioning of the bowls, finally deciding on a circular pattern for the five bowls, each an equal distance from the other, the sword in the center.

She set out everything she would need off to the side, and then pulled the leather bag from the pack. The shards clinked together as she pulled the hilt from the bag. She oriented everything to the looming wall at the end of the tunnel, treating that as north. The hilt she set down so that the handle pointed west, and then spilled the shards out.

It took her longer than she expected to piece the blade together as Ismari had done. The stone floor was cold and hard under her knees. It was almost the nooning before she finished. Sunlight was starting to creep in to the mouth of the cave, dispelling the darkness.

Amyu settled back on her heels, and studied the arrangement. It was as good as she could make it.

She thought about returning to camp, to rest and eat, but her nerves wouldn't let her. She'd done all she could, planned all she could, and she'd wait not a moment longer.

She raised her hands in supplication. "Elements," she cried out. "Hear my plea."

The sound echoed against the walls. Amyu swallowed hard, and reached for the first bowl. "Earth, element of the Plains," she called out, holding up the bowl and crumbling clean soil into it. "I beg your presence, as witness to my plea." She trembled inside but kept her voice steady. "Find me worthy of aid."

She replaced the bowl and reached for the next.

"Water, element of the Plains," she intoned as she drizzled water into the bowl. "I beg your presence, as witness to my plea. Find me worthy of aid."

The next bowl held crushed green leaves she dropped onto a live coal. A small tendril of smoke arose as she invoked the element of air. Then the bowl where she placed fresh tinder on the coals, and a tiny flame sprang up, dancing in the bowl.

Each time she invoked the element. Each time, she asked to be found worthy.

And last, the very last, she dared to break all tradition.

She held up the bowl and breathed the words. "Magic," she announced, and her words seemed to echo off the stone walls. "Element of the Plains. I beg your presence, as witness to my plea. Find me worthy of aid."

She gathered sparkles of power at her finger tips, and shook them into the bowl. The sparkles fell lightly, rolling around below the rim. This bowl, she placed at the top of the pattern, at the point farthest from herself.

The sword lay in the center, still shattered.

Amyu put on the Ring of Xy, and held her hands out, facing the sword. She took a deep breath, and then started the familiar chant. "Fire, water, earth, air," she paused, then again broke every tradition she knew. "Magic. Hear my plea."

The air around her crackled, and the hairs on her arms rose.

"Water, earth, air, magic, fire," she said. "Hear my plea." She continued, moving each element through the chant, honoring each in turn, weaving magic into her words. She'd honestly thought she'd be struck down by now for her daring, but it hadn't happened.

Yet.

The air around her seemed charged with excitement that might have just been her imagination. Only one way to find out.

"Death of earth, birth of water," she started then paused. The hairs on the back of her neck stood up. The bowl of magic was brighter, and the bowl of water held a vibration that had not been there.

Amyu continued, struggling to keep her voice steady. "Death of water, birth of air."

The golden sparkles swelled, and the column of smoke trembled. Something was happening.

Her voice rose, and her words spilled out faster and faster. "Death of air, birth of fire," she gulped.

It wasn't her imagination. The magic was growing within the bowl, and the other elements were responding. Her heart started to beat a wild rhythm.

"Death of fire, birth of earth." She cried out in her excitement.

The ritual words were completed, but everything seemed to hang in the air, suspended, waiting. Waiting for her to invoke—

Amyu cried out what was in her heart, without thought. "Magic," she cried, putting everything she dreamed in the words. "Weave a new pattern!"

The magic responded. A shaft of golden light shot out from its bowl to the bowl of fire. The flame within shot higher and brighter.

The magic shot out again, striking the bowl of water with a ringing sound. The water swirled, and rose, a pillar to match the flame.

The magic hit the bowl of earth with a deep ringing sound. It shook her bones.

A roaring sound filled Amyu's ears. She couldn't move, couldn't breathe, her arms outstretched in her plea.

Air now, and the bowl rocked as the smoke swirled like a twisting wind storm, surrounding the sword. The light crackled with energy.

"Elements, all, hear my plea," Amyu cried out. "Restore that which has been shattered."

The magic shot out, a glorious stream of golden light, and struck her full in the chest. The power flowed into her. Amyu breathed deep, trying to hold it in, trying to bear the pressure in and under her skin. She feared she wouldn't be able to hold it, but then her eyes dropped to the shattered sword at her feet, and she knew...

She brought her hands together, and threw the magic at the sword.

A burst of heat and gold and light filled the cave, overwhelming and blinding.

* * * * *

Hanstau jerked in his saddle, catching himself before he fell. His horse snorted tossed its head.

Reness was instantly on alert, scanning the herd around them for a threat. "What?" She asked.

"I don't know," Hanstau said, staring off in the direction of the sound. "Didn't you hear it?"

"No," Reness said. "The herd is not reacting," she pointed out.

"It was—" Hanstau shook his head. "Remember how I said that using the power seemed noisy? I think someone just—" he stared off in the direction the sound had come from. "Someone just used power. A lot of power."

"That way?" Reness asked.

Hanstau nodded. "What lies there?" he asked.

Reness snorted in amusement. "City-dweller," she teased. "That way is north."

"Xy?" Hanstau asked. They'd been wandering within the safety of the herd for so long, he'd lost all sense of direction. He flushed a bit. All sense of direction, of time, of propriety,

"Xy," Reness confirmed. "I've enjoyed our wandering, Hanstau. But now I think we must move with a purpose."

Hanstau nodded. "To Xy."

"To Xy," she confirmed, and put her horse's head in that direction. "But don't think this means there is anything less between us." She threw him a glance over her shoulder. "I claim you, my city-dweller."

Hanstau tried to stammer something intelligible out, but

no real words came. He settled for blushing.

Reness laughed, and urged her horse to a gallop, leading his by the reins.

* * * * *

Simus was just settling down to his nooning when Snowfall gasped, dropped her kavage and turned north. He was on his feet in an instant, and the warriors around them took defensive stances.

No sounds, no outcry arose around them. Snowfall was focused on a distant point, off to the north.

Simus took a step closer to his bonded, and waited.

"A flare of power," Snowfall said. "Far to the north. Would that be Xy?"

"Xy." Simus sheathed his sword, and the other warriors relaxed around them.

"Lightning Strike?" Simus asked as he bent to get her mug.

Snowfall shook her head. "Too far north for it to be them," she said absently, squinting off into the distance as if she could see if she just looked hard enough. "But who else could use power like that?"

"You told me that all Plains warriors are tested at the Rite of Ascension," Simus filled her mug and pressed it into Snowfall's hands.

"Yes," Now those grey eyes were focused on him, intent and lovely. Simus took a moment to enjoy their beauty even as he answered the unasked question.

"Have I told you of Amyu?"

* * * * *

Cadr first knew of it when Lightning Strike jerked in his saddle. He pulled his horse to a stop as the others slid from their saddles, taking out their bowls and shields.

Gilla rode up, whistling for the warcats, who bounded out of the grass to sprawl at the horses' feet.

"Got it," Night Clouds cried.

Cadr pressed in, everyone trying to look in the bowl at the same time. He caught a glimpse of a woman's back. She was kneeling in a cave, before ritual bowls. She cast a quick look behind her, but it was enough.

"Amyu," Cadr said, grabbing Lightning Strike's shoulder. "That's Amyu. That's Xy."

They watched as Amyu stood, taking up a strange sword that sparkled blue.

"But where is she?" Sidian asked. "Can you see more?"

Night Clouds nodded, frowning, staring at the bowl.

"Give us room," Lightning Strike said, and others moved back. Cadr stayed glued to his side. Sidian and Rhys both leaned in closer.

The scene in the bowl shifted to reveal the cave and the mountain side.

"What is—?" Lightning Strike exclaimed.

Sidian started to explain mountains, and caves. Cadr ignored them, kneeling at Night Clouds' side. "See that," he pointed, careful not to touch the bowl. "It's a path."

Night Clouds nodded, and the scene blurred as it rushed down the mountainside. The trees finally opened up, to show a wide grassy area, filled with large animals.

"What are those?" Lightning Strike asked.

"Cows," Rhys said. "They're like large gurtles. I can portal there." he added.

Cadr looked up at Lightening Strike. "Do we go?"

"We go."

* * * * *

Amyu held her position, blinking against the fading glare, waiting for her breath to return. An odd tickle burned between her shoulder blades. She glanced behind herself, but there was no one there.

She turned back, and looked down.

The sword was whole.

"Heyla," She cried, her voice ringing on the stone walls. But even as the sound faded, she stared at her hands. There was no change, no glow, all seemed as it was, all but the sword.

Giddy with joy, she reached for the sword hilt, almost afraid it would shatter again as she lifted it.

The blade was heavier than she expected, but it was straight and true and so blue within its depths it seemed to glow. She rose to her feet, forgetting everything else in her excitement. With a deep breath, she faced the back wall of the tunnel.

She held the sword up and stretched out her other hand with the Ring of Xy displayed. "Let the protectors of Xy arise to my call!" she proclaimed, and waited, breathless.

Nothing happened.

CHAPTER THIRTY-ONE

Amyu stood there, dumbfounded. Sword in one hand, the ring on the other, feeling the fool.

She cleared her throat, and called again. "Let the protectors of Xy arise to my call!"

Nothing.

She blinked. Then she cursed. She cursed the mountain, cursed the sword, the ring, the city-dwellers, the entire idea that she could find the airions.

Then she stood in the silence. She consciously slowed her breathing, letting her anger fade, and considered.

The ritual had worked, the sword was whole again. She could wield magic, that she had proven. She took a breath, letting that confidence flow back into her.

But Kalisa had talked of her bloodlines, like the bloodlines of a Tribe. Even the Warprize was of the Blood of Xy. Maybe one had to be of the Tribe of Xy to summon airions.

Her shoulders sagged. She let the blade fall, catching it with the open palm of her ringed hand. At least she had this much that she could take back—

The blade hit her palm, and the back of the ring.

The entire cave rang with the sound. Like the wardrums of a Warlord, it shook Amyu's body to the bone.

Amyu lifted the sword, and turned her hand, to see the blue stone of the ring glowing.

Giddy joy passed over her as the vibrations faded from the cave.

"There have been no changes in the rallying cry," Kendrick started to thumb through the book, looking for something. *"But there have been variations in the gestures over time."*

Variations. *Changes.*

She faced the wall again, grinning like the fool she wasn't. She held the sword before her, point up. "Let the protectors of Xy arise to my call." She cried out, and then struck the sword with the stone of the ring.

The tunnel rang, trembling with a subtle roaring sound. The wall before her turned blue, glowing with the sword and the ring, and then it faded. As the rumbling passed, Amyu could see light at the end of the tunnel, white and clear.

Something moved, blocking the light. Something big, something charging her way—

Amyu threw herself to the side as she heard claws scrabble on stone. She pressed herself tight to the wall, hardly daring to breathe.

The creature stopped at the ledge, turning its head to look at her. The horse body was there, the head more horse than eagle, but with a sharp hooked beak. No grass eater, this. All four legs ended in talons. Golden colored, with black eyes that seemed to take her all in with one glance. The warmth of its body swept over her, along with the familiar smell of horse. The hair was the same on its body, but the mane, the tail were made of bright gold feathers, and the wings—

To her utter delight, it half-spread its wings, screeching like a hawk as it shook itself out. Feathers and horse hairs went flying. Amyu laughed, and sheathed the sword. "You are a beauty," she crooned as she rose, hoping against hope, stretching out her hand to touch the withers.

The airion extended its neck, huffing at her hair, taking in her scent. It reared, trilled an odd sound, turned back to the open space and folded its wings in. As if waiting.

Amyu held her breath. It couldn't want her to mount.

The airion turned its head and stared at her.

She took a step, then another, and without daring to think it through she buried her hand deep in its mane. An impulse of sheer joyous madness made her mount. Her legs were in front of the wings, and she settled back, as if born to—

With a deep cry, the airion surged up, and out, its wings snapping open as they left the cave.

Amyu cried out, in joy and terror, her stomach somewhere behind her. The air rushed passed, the ground spiraled below.

She was flying!

She gripped the mane tighter with both hands, and tucked her feet in, as if it were a horse she could guide. The wind streamed her hair behind her and stung her eyes. She blinked against the tears, still laughing. Triumph trembled through every muscle in her body.

With powerful down strokes, the airion rose over the tree tops, creeing its joy. It climbed, spiraling up, riding the air as easily as a horse rode the earth.

More trills from behind, and the sound of wings, and more airions filled the skies around them, dancing in the air.

Amyu laughed, amazed and delighted.

She was flying!

She could see the entire valley below her, and the city walls, and hear the distant alarm bells.

Oh, skies above. The wyvern alarm bells.

Amyu leaned in, suddenly anxious that they not fly any closer to the walls. "Down," she said, not sure if she'd be understood.

The airion did, it seemed. It clucked with seeming regret, tucked its wings in, and… fell.

Amyu shrieked, and lost her grasp on the mane. The airion's body was slipping out from under her. Her stomach gave a huge lurch. She'd fall and—

The wings snapped out and the airion slowed. The hesitation was enough for Amyu to regain her seat and her grip. Her heart racing, Amyu remembered the saddles in the cave, with the buckles and harness for the rider.

Sheer instinct gave her power. "Aid me," she cried out, and the magic responded as if a saddle. Golden light wrapped around her waist securing her to her mount.

The airion creed, pulled in its wings and once again they plunged to earth, down toward the field where the cows were starting to run, mooing their distress. Amyu gulped against the feeling of having no weight, but then the wings spread again, and she grunted as the creature slowed.

Light as a feather, the airion settled down to the earth. Amyu released the golden straps, and dismounted, falling to her knees. The world spun as she laughed and emptied her stomach. She'd found them. Against all odds, she'd found—

"Amyu?" a voice called.

She was on her feet in a moment, her blades out. She stared at the group of people coming toward her. "Cadr?"

"What are these?" one of them asked, pointing.

Amyu turned to see her airion, the golden one, leap for a cow, and bring it down with a bite through its spine. The herd was setting up a ruckus, scattering into the woods as shadows passed over the field. She looked up to see more airions in the sky above her, circling. All different colors, their wings spread, their cries filling the air.

"Airions," she laughed, sheathing her weapons. She wiped her face, the taste of vomit and success in her mouth. "They're airions."

* * * * *

Quick introductions were made, with quick explanations as they watched the airions devour the dead cow.

"Look at those claws," the man named Rhys said. Amyu knew he was not of the Plains, but little else.

"Talons," another corrected him. Sidian. Older, and the bushiest eyebrows to rival Enright's. He wore the ritual scarring of a full warrior-priest. They all bore some partial tattoos of warrior-priests, except Rhys, Gilla, and Cadr.

The other airions had joined the golden one at tearing at the carcass. Amyu wasn't going to get close to them while they were feeding. But she and the others looked their fill, and it was glorious. She was still lightheaded, from the discovery and the flight.

She had flown. Amyu's smile was so wide her face hurt.

"Can anyone ride them?" Lightning Strike asked.

"I don't know," Amyu continued to stare as she described her first flight and the drop. They all nodded at the description of the saddle.

"Makes sense," Cadr said. "What if you were injured in mid-air?"

"We've so much to learn," Amyu said. Then she frowned, something other than flying invading her thoughts. "Where did you come from?" she asked. "Did you meet the Warlord coming from the Plains?"

"Well," Lightning Strike shrugged. "We didn't exactly walk."

Amyu opened her mouth to demand more, but the alarm horns were sounding from the walls again. "They think it's a threat," she frowned. "We need to get word to them."

Sidian shook his head. "You need to go tell them." He said with a grin. "Might warn them about us, too."

"I'll take a horse," she started but just then the golden airion danced over, its wings half-spread, clacking its beak and tossing its head.

"Oh, lass," Sidian laughed. "How can you resist making an entrance like that?"

* * * * *

Amyu kept her mount clear of any crossbow shot, flying high over the city, heading to the castle. The air grew colder the higher they went, and it felt like she was losing her breath, but better that than a bolt to the chest.

She circled the highest tower, seeing Enright ringing his alarm bell, until she saw Heath and Atira burst through the trap door, swords at the ready. She warbled then, using the calls of the Plains, calling 'friend' and 'scout reporting'.

Atira sheathed her weapons, but it took sometime before the others lowered their crossbows.

She urged the airion down then and it obeyed, its wings beating as it landed, raising a cloud of dust.

Amyu released her magic, and dismounted with much more grace than before. She couldn't help grinning at the looks on their faces while they were all staring at the golden creature beside her.

Who promptly nudged her shoulder and creed. She reached up, and scratched under its mane.

All eyes shifted to her, then, and she tried for a more dignified look. "Heath, Warden of Xy," she started formally, but then her joy was too much for her. "I found them!"

Other people flooded the area, Warren, Wilsa, and more guards. They all froze and approached cautiously.

"You did," Heath laughed with her. "How did you—"

Amyu pulled the sword from her back. "Warden," she said solemnly. "The Crystal Sword of Xy is whole again."

That brought a gasp from everyone, at the sight of the sword in her hands. It glittered blue in the sunlight, and the stone of the ring flashed as well. Amyu noticed that Enright was using his white cloth to wipe his eyes.

"The protectors of Xy have arisen," Amyu said as she gave the Sword and Ring back to Heath.

"Them?" Heath exclaimed. "There's more?"

"Yes," Amyu said. "Of various colors, including black. They are with the others. We didn't want them flying off toward the walls, for fear they would be harmed."

"Is it tame?" Atira asked, eyeing the sharp beak and talons.

"So far," Amyu said. "But we have much to learn. The others are willing," she grinned again, remembering the look of horror on some faces. "Well, some are."

"Others?" Heath asked.

Amyu took a deep breath. "The warrior-priests in training," she said.

Atira and Wilsa stiffened.

Amyu continued, "The ones that Joden spoke of. They heard me call to the airions and used their powers to travel here. They will aid me, if you allow it."

"Warrior-priests," Atira's voice was flat and angry.

Amyu stared her down. "Yes. They seek their place, as I seek mine. As a barren woman of the Plains. As a child who disobeyed her elders. As a magic-wielder. As one who has given her oath to the Warlord and Warprize."

Atira dropped her eyes, glanced at Heath, and then nodded. "Truth," she acknowledged. "But they have not yet given their oaths."

"We will come to you," Heath said. "We will talk, and see what comes of that. What needs do you have?"

Amyu mounted the airion, and called her magic to form the straps. "We are in the fields outside of Kalisa's cheese cave," she said. "We need the saddles within, and new ones made," she frowned again. "And more cows. I do not wish to wipe out their herd."

"If they eat cows," Heath laughed. "Then more cows you shall have. We will come as quickly as we can, Amyu of the Skies."

Amyu jerked her head around to look at Heath. He bowed his head as a warrior bows to another. Her gaze traveled over all of them, and they all bowed their heads to her.

Emotion welled up in her chest. Pride, joy and something she dared call happiness.

Amyu blinked rapidly against her tears and urged her mount with her knees. The great creature creed and sprang up and off the tower, its wings spread as it dipped then rose gloriously into the sky.

Her heart was full. And maybe, just maybe, some of the cracks within were healing. But the largest crack? The largest flaw?

Joden was not here to see. To know. To share.

If she wept as she flew, only the skies were witness.

CHAPTER THIRTY-TWO

Joden was behind Queen Xylara as she rode out, waving to her people, using something called a sidesaddle. Cheers and well-wishes filled the air as the joint forces of Xy and the Plains passed through the gates of the City of Water's Fall.

"I know, it looks odd to you," Lara had wrinkled her nose at all of the Plains warrior's comments. "But trust me, it's the only way I am going to mount Greatheart at this point."

The crowd loved her, and there were just as many cries of support for Warlord Keir of the Cat, Overlord of Xy, who rode at the side of his beloved, waving to the crowd between worried glances at the saddle.

"Stop that," Lara said at one point. "I am not going to fall."

Keir just gave her a skeptical look.

Once he saw the gates. Joden kept his eyes on his horse's mane. It was a truth, but if the dead were waiting outside the city walls, it felt like more than he could bear. But he couldn't help himself, and after a few minutes, he glanced around.

The fields were empty except for the burial mounds.

He drew a breath, and sat a bit straighter, grateful and yet disappointed as well.

After an hour, they came to a rise, where wooden wagons were waiting under heavy guard. Rafe and Prest were there as well. The royal contingent pulled off the road, as the army continued on.

Lara dismounted quickly. "Are they still sleeping?" she asked as Keir aided her up onto the wagon.

"Yes," Anna said. "As sweetly as you could wish," she was settled in a corner with the babe's baskets beside her. "I swear the rocking motion soothes them."

Marcus turned where he sat next to the driver. "Let us offer to the elements for that," he said. "Now settled yourselves, and let's be off. The army is leaving us behind."

Lara nodded, and sat opposite Anna on a pallet of gurtle pads and pillows. "Anna, are you sure you—"

"You are not going without me," Anna said firmly.

Joden had to admire the woman's grim determination. A city-dweller her entire life, she was leaving her kitchens, her family, her world behind to care for her loved ones. There was a fierce commitment in her eyes, covering over her nervousness.

Keir was talking to the Xyian guard. "Keep them in the middle at all times. There will be Plains warriors in front and behind you."

"Aye, Warlord," The man said. "We'll keep them safe."

Keir gave a nod, and the wagon headed out, merging in with the mounted units.

Keir mounted. "The wagons will remain in the center," he said. "Have the scouts gone out?"

Prest gave a nod. "I have them ranging to the fore, the sides and behind. I also assigned watchers to the skies to watch for wyverns."

"Warren and Wilsa have the front," Keir's mount stamped under him, expressing its impatience, and he patted its neck. "I will travel with each unit in turn, but I will spend each night with Lara at the wagons." He gave a rueful smile. "At least, that is my intent. We will see what the skies will."

A murmur of assent. One never knew what the need would be when the armies marched.

"We are limited," Keir said. "The Xyians march well, but we must travel at their pace." He looked out after the army, moving slowly past the rise. "Also, we bear supplies for Liam and Simus and any other Warlord that joins with us. Those wagons slow us as well." Keir looked at Joden. "Which is where you come in, Joden. Our travel will be slow, and I worry that Xyian and Plains will not all rub along smoothly. Especially since they are all men, although I think they have learned there is a price for disrespect to our warriors. If you would, be my eyes and ears where I cannot be. Let me know what you learn."

Joden nodded. He served Keir before in this manner, and would again.

"One last thing," Keir frowned. "There have been no messages from Liam or Simus for some time. If a messenger comes, get word to me or Lara immediately."

Prest cocked his head. "You fear news of betrayal."

Keir shook his head. "I can deal with betrayal," he said. "It is the silence I fear."

* * * * *

Joden had deliberately lost himself in the preparations for the march to the Plains. It was easy enough to do. The familiar thrum of the warriors around him had let him forget, even ignore his heartache.

He'd honored Amyu's request. He'd not sought her out after she'd left his room. He had not tried to get a glimpse of her during the days, and the nights…

Well, she'd said nothing of his dreams.

She'd haunted his dreams. Her scent, her hair, her face as she's taken pleasure in both their bodies. But even more, her wry wit and sparkling eyes. She was so very special, so very precious to him. Yet as a Singer, a would-be Singer, he should not feel this way. He should be the first to urge her to the snows as one who would never become a warrior and a drain on the Tribe's resources.

He stilled himself, reminded himself that she was safe in Xy, worthy in Xy, and she would be well. He kept that thought clear, and tried to fill the emptiness with other things.

Thankfully, preparedness had a call of its own, and he'd kept his mind on the sharpening of weapons, checking over his armor, and standing at Keir and Lara's side.

But now, on the march? He had time, and then some. Time to think on things he did not wish to think on.

Like everything that had happened so quickly since he'd entered the Singer Trials.

And what he had lost taking the old paths.

He kept trying as he rode, to break the pattern of speech, to go over and over what he intended to say, only to have the words catch when he spoke. The singing worked, although he hated it. It sounded false to his ear, and felt false on his tongue. Chanting worked as well. He could sometimes trick his tongue, substituting another word for the one he'd intended, but not before he had tripped over the first sound.

As the days passed, he found himself angrier and angrier. This was what the Ancients intended? The loss of his voice? This was the gift of the old paths to being a Singer? How could that possibly be true? Joden scowled at the horizon. One thing was certain, he'd not go to the snows until he got some answers from the dried little turds.

He tried to let the anger go, but it sat deep in his belly. Sparring helped when they camped for the night. So did listening to the woes of others as they marched.

It was known among the Plains warriors that he was a Singer-to-be, and so held words in confidence. And while the tales of his affliction had certainly spread, it had an odd effect, one that Joden had not anticipated.

Apparently, when you can't talk, people trust you with their most private truths.

"It didn't matter how often I went up there," Prest said. The bells in his horse's mane chimed as they rode off to the side, far enough away from the other warriors to be seen but not heard. "Every single time, my head would spin, my knees would knock, and I would have to crawl over to the trap door and slide down a few steps before I could stand." Prest shook his head. "To think that Amyu is braver than I am. Even Enright, old and fat and crippled, is braver than I," Prest brooded.

Joden frowned and opened his mouth but Prest continued on. "Ever have I faced my fear in the past, but this has defeated me. A horse is as high off the ground as I ever want to be." He drew a deep breath. "But I have been thinking, Joden—"

Joden didn't even try to speak. He just raised an eyebrow.

"Maybe that is the way of things," Prest said. "Maybe not all fear can be controlled or permanently conquered," the younger man mused, as if trying to convince himself. "Maybe they can only be faced, over and over and each time, conquered anew."

Joden grunted, and for long moments they rode in silence.

Prest looked over at Joden. "Maybe that is a new kind of courage. A new kind of strength."

A hail came from the road. One of Prest's scouts had returned.

Prest leaned forward to remove the bells. "My thanks, Joden. Your truths are always welcome." He tucked the bells in the saddle bags, and urged his horse toward the road.

Joden quirked his lips into a smile and followed. It seemed the less he talked, the more they seemed to solve their own problems.

* * * * *

Between listening to the talk among Xyians and Plains warriors, and dealing with his own inner turmoil, it took Joden a while to notice. But after a few weeks, it occurred to him that

Rafe and the women of his tent were always nearby. As if they were taking turns.

Rafe grinned, no apology in his face or his voice when confronted. "It's the Warlord's command," he said, guiding his horse next to Joden's. He gave a sharp whistle, and the other warriors of his tent appeared, surrounding Joden.

"You noticed?" Fylin said.

"Took you long enough," Soar added, frowning.

"We had a bet going," Rafe said. "She lost." He appeared quite pleased.

"The Warprize told us that you were our special charge," Lasa said with a gentle smile.

"The Warlord's and the Warprize's command," Rafe said.

Lasa continued, "She wanted our eyes on you at all times, in case you had—" she caught herself.

"In case you had the falling sickness," Ksand finished, rather cheerfully. "She told me what to watch for. Master Eln told us how to make sure you didn't swallow your tongue. But you haven't fallen once," she added, and her disappointment was clear.

Joden looked at Rafe, who nodded. "Yes, the Warlord, the Warprize, and Master Eln all took us aside and told us to watch over you."

"There was one other," Lasa said slyly.

"True," Rafe laughed as Joden's eyebrows went up. "Amyu threatened us if we let anything happen to you on the march."

Joden blinked. 'Amyu?' he mouthed.

Rafe laughed. "Sure enough."

Joden couldn't help smiling at the thought. Amyu, afraid to put herself forward, threatening warriors for him. Warmth bloomed in his chest as the image rose before his eyes.

Rafe chortled, clearly enjoying the look on Joden's face. "So, we don't have to hide our duty any longer. Who has this watch?"

"I do," Ksand said.

"And Soar has dish duty for ten nights," Rafe crowed, and plunged his horse ahead with a laugh over Soar's protests.

* * * * *

Joden knew it to be a truth. Someone's always worse off than you.

"The headaches are better," Yers told Keir as they rode together. "And my vision improves. Maybe Master Eln is right, although lying in the dark in his healing rooms for days was a hell worse than the snows."

Keir nodded. "I think even Lara would agree that the healing can be more painful than the wound."

Joden noticed that Yers didn't nod back; that he seemed to be keeping his head perfectly still, looking straight ahead at all times.

"There was little I could do but think," Yers continued. "And I thought on Simus."

Keir waited as their horses walked on.

"I rescinded my oath, as is tradition when one can no longer support one's Warlord," Yers said. "I offered challenge for Warlord, as is tradition."

Keir stayed silent, and Joden wasn't about to interrupt.

"Simus defeated me," Yers said. "And there is no shame in that. The shame," he took a breath. "My shame was in my approach. I should have tried harder to make him see the danger in allowing a warrior-priestess to stand at his side."

"Yers, at any time did Simus say to you that he would rescind his oath to me?" Keir asked. "Withdraw his support?"

Yers was silent for a time. "No, Warlord. But I fear Snowfall's influence over him. Whenever have the warrior-priests offered us anything but scorn? There is no truth in her, for all her oaths."

"No messengers have come." Keir shook his head. "There is nothing to do but wait and see." He looked at Yers. "I know you declined to serve as a warleader, but if you are feeling better—"

Yers shook his head, then winced. "No, Warlord. I am aiding Wilsa as best I can, when I can. I thank you, but I must decline."

"Very well," Keir said. "But when the time comes, when Simus approaches, be with me to witness his truths."

"I will," Yers said, and then moved off, leaving Joden and Keir alone.

Keir reached into his saddle bags and pulled out a strip of bells. The other warriors melted back as Joden gave Keir an inquiring look.

"So much hate," Keir said. He gripped his reins tightly, and his knuckles whitened. "For so many years, I have considered the warrior-priests the greatest enemy to change on the Plains. My greatest enemy. Now word comes that some of the warrior-priests are dead, at their own hands, and one of my staunchest allies rides with a warrior-priestess at his side. What is worse," Keir's voice cracked. "Our children may have been touched by their evil."

Joden opened his mouth, but then closed it. Keir hadn't noticed, and nothing Joden could say would aid him.

Perhaps the best gift Joden could give his friend was the silence in which to find his own path.

"I hate the warrior-priests," Keir's voice was almost a hiss. "For what they have done, and not done for our people for years. Hidden their powers or lack thereof. Refusing to change, to the benefit of all the Tribes. I loathe them, and will never forgive their arrogance and treachery."

Joden watched as Keir's fists relaxed their grip on the reins.

"But," the reluctance in Keir's voice was clear. "But maybe my greatest enemy is my hatred, that blinds me to the truth." He looked over at Joden, clearly seeking reassurance.

Joden hesitated, then shrugged.

"There is truth in that, friend." Keir grimaced. "And 'wait and see' seems to be the only option." He leaned forward to remove the bells. "Come. I feel the need to be with Lara this night."

* * * * *

"She never once complains," Marcus said quietly over the dying campfire.

The others had all bedded down for the night, leaving Joden and Marcus alone by the fire. Joden lifted an eyebrow.

Marcus jerked his chin toward the tents. "Anna. Poor lady is uncomfortable, unhappy, and as miserable as a person can be. But she never once has made a complaint, or said a word of her suffering." Marcus shot Joden a look, a glint of humor in his one eye. "Even Herself complained on that first journey."

Joden smiled at the memory.

Marcus continued, "Odd how even city-dwellers find the strength to endure when they act out of love."

Joden blinked, glanced at Marcus and then just as quickly decided to poke the coals with a handy stick. Marcus had a temper and he was known for his sharp tongue and sharper daggers. Silence was the best option.

Marcus must have caught the look, because he glowered. "I know what you are thinking," he growled.

Joden shrugged.

"You are thinking of Liam of the Deer." Marcus stated flatly. "I know full well he holds the border for the Warlord, and I know full well he is at the keep we are heading to." Marcus stood up. "I will not see him, will not speak to him. Our bonding severed when my ear melted away, and it is past time the damn fool saw the truth."

With that, Marcus stomped away, and disappeared behind the tents, where he had placed his pallet.

Joden gave the coals another poke, and wondered how long Marcus could fight against his own truth.

* * * * *

Prest appeared the next morning before the kavage was even hot. "My forward scouts have reported," he said as he slid from his saddle. "Wellspring is a day's march."

Wellspring. Joden felt his heart turn over in his chest.

The plague village.

CHAPTER THIRTY-THREE

The stone well was all that remained of Wellspring.

Joden walked beside Lara and Keir as they slowly approached the place where the village had stood. The field was covered in thick green plants with purple flowers on tall stalks. The air was filled with their perfume. No trace was left of the pyres of the dead that had covered the area, or the smoke that filled the air. No trace, except in their memories.

"We didn't stop here on our way to Xy," Lara said.

"You were asleep in my arms," Keir said. "We rode past. I saw no reason to wake you."

Lara frowned, running her fingers over a few flowers. "I don't remember this lavender being here before. But we were here later in the year."

Keir stood next to the well, his jaw clenched, a muscle pulsing in his cheek. He reached out to Lara. She reached back, and stepped closer to hug him and bury her face in his chest.

"S-s-safe?" Joden had to ask.

"Yes," Lara lifted her head to face him. "As far as I know."

"D-d-disrespectful?" Joden asked again, gesturing to the area around them. "T-t-to c-c-camp h-h-here?"

"No," Lara said, but her voice held doubt. "But the memories…" her voice trailed off.

"We will march on," Keir said. "Our dead are beyond the snows, and in the stars. But the living carry burdens of pain and sorrow. Joden, I would ask that you sing for our dead this evening. After we make camp."

Joden reached out and touched the stone of the well. It felt cold and rough under his fingers. He found himself nodding yes before he could really think about it.

"You honor us. I will give the command," Keir said, and tugged Lara away. They walked off together through the flowers, their arms wrapped around each other's waist, Lara's head on Keir's shoulder.

Joden watched them, an odd longing in his heart, mingling with his sorrow.

"Would you drink, good sir?" came a cheerful voice from behind him.

A Xyian woman with a lovely smile stood there, a bucket and rope in hand. She dropped the bucket into the well. Joden heard it splash into the water.

"Clear and cold on the hottest day," the woman continued. "It's how Wellspring got its name." She started hauling on the rope, bringing the full bucket up with ease. Water sloshed over the stones as she set it on the wall.

Joden dipped a cupped hand and drank. The water was as she said, crisp and sweet. "My thanks," he said, the words flowing easily.

He looked around, at the village around them. It was as it must have been before the Sweat, before it burned. People going about their business, calling out well-wishes for the evening meal. The gates were shut tight for the night.

"Have you lived here long?" Joden asked.

"All my days," she said. "With my Ma and Pa and now my husband and firstborn. We have a fine place…" her voice trailed off, and her eyes grew wistful. "But I cannot find them, for some reason."

"Where are they?" Joden asked quietly.

"I do not know," her voice was small and pained, her smile gone. "I felt ill, and I lay down with my babe and…" She looked over her shoulder. "There are voices calling me from the gardens, but I can't go. I can't find her."

The village wavered, and started to fade.

"What is your name, lady?" Joden asked.

"Meara," she said. "Meara of Wellspring."

Joden drew in a breath. "Meara," he said, and knew what he had to do. "I can tell you of your babe."

Her eyes went wide as he told her what had happened, and that Lara had taken the babe into her care. "They did not know her name," Joden said. "So they named her after you."

"The Queen gave her my name?" Meara asked, covering her mouth with the tips of her fingers. "And she is well?"

"Well and happy," Joden said.

"Show me," Meara demanded and held out her hands.

Joden took them in his. "Meara, I don't know how—"

"Show me," she begged, and gripped his hands tight.

A vision rose up before his eyes, of Meara and Aurora in the kitchen gardens of the castle under Marcsi's watchful eye. They were playing with the dogs, Aurora running, Meara toddling behind and laughing. She giggled as she plopped on her butt, the dogs wagging their tails and licking her face.

Joden blinked to find Meara crying, clasping her hands to her breast. "Oh, she is beautiful and brimming with health and joy," she said, weeping silent tears.

"You're crying," Joden said.

"I weep for what we have lost, Seer," Meara's voice broke. "I weep for the days I will not see her grow, for the nights I will not watch over her. She will not hear my voice or see my face but I hope she knows of my love."

"I will see to it," Joden promised.

The village faded away from around them. Meara looked over her shoulder again, then scooped up her apron to dry her eyes. "My family, my loved ones, they call me. They have been waiting so long." She smoothed her apron down, and smiled at him through watery eyes. "Thank you, Seer. I am grateful."

She turned away, took a few steps and then stopped.

"They tell me, Seer, to tell you," Meara turned back, her eyes distant as if seeing something beyond him. "The Sweat waits. It will return. Warn the House of Xy."

Joden went cold. "When?"

"I do not know," she said with a shake of her head. "But it will come. Blessings on thee, Seer."

Before he could say a word, she took another step, and was gone.

"Joden?" a worried voice this time. He turned to find Ksand staring at him. "Joden, are you well?" She gave him a squinty look. "Are you going to fall down?"

"N-n-no," Joden said, then smiled at her disappointment.

"Come then," Ksand said. "The army moves on without us."

* * * * *

Lara stared at him, white-faced. "She did not tell you when?"

Joden shook his head. "S-s-she d-d-didn't kn-kn-know."

Lara pressed her lips together, then shook her head. "There's not much we can do," she said. "We will spread the word, and make sure that everyone knows the signs. If any sicken we will know. There are healers in with the Xyian forces, and there's fever's foe aplenty in the wagons." She gave Joden a weak smile. "At least we are warned."

Joden nodded, and went to step from the tent, but she stopped him with a gesture. "Joden, about tonight—" she hesitated, and he could see the blush rising on her cheeks. "I remember the ceremony from before, but we have Xyian warriors with us. I think it would be best if—"

"N-n-no s-s-sharing," Joden said solemnly.

Lara relaxed with a nervous laugh. "No sharing."

* * * * *

The stars were out when Joden took his place before Keir and Lara, and faced the crowd. It was all Plains warriors. Warren had come to Keir with an offer from his men to take the watches so that all could mourn. Which was a kindness, but additional pressure Joden didn't really want or need.

Voices had been lowered as they went about the business of setting out tents and building cookfires. All were affected by the memories of this place and the losses they had suffered.

The torches and fires were lit, and a dancing area cleared before the platform. The drummers were ready. The dancers were ready. That left only the signal to begin.

Joden raised his face to the stars, and lifted his right palm to the sky. "May the skies hear my voice," he chanted, a wave of relief washing over him as the words came out strong and clear. "May the people remember."

The response rose, "We will remember."

Joden lowered his arm and spoke again, "Birth of fire, death of air."

One of the dancers knelt, and blew on the coals within a brazier, feeding fuel that caused flames to leap up and dance.

"Birth of water, death of earth," Joden chanted.

A second dancer knelt, dipping her hands in the brazier at her feet and letting the water trickle back down.

"Birth of earth, death of fire." Joden filled his lungs and chanted the next part, letting his voice rise to the skies.

The third dancer knelt, raised a lump of dirt, breaking it up to let the clods fall back into the brazier.

"Birth of air, death of water," Joden sang the words, letting them ring out.

The fourth dancer knelt. He too blew on coals, but the fuel he added caused a thin trail of smoke to rise up.

The four dancers stood, bowed to their elements, and waited.

"We gather tonight in remembrance of the dead," Joden spoke-sang, keeping his voice deep and projecting as far as he could. "All life perishes. This we know. Our bodies arise from the elements, and return to them when we fall."

There was a deathly silence as he paused. All eyes turned to him, and Joden felt the power he wielded over them, felt the impact his words were having. He gestured, and the drummer started a beat then, a slow but steady pulse.

"But we are also more than our bodies," Joden reminded them. "This we know. That which is within each of us, lives on. Our dead travel with us until the snows, when they rise to the stars. They do not—"

He cut himself off from the traditional words, but then continued, "They do not linger here."

No one seemed to notice. He took a deep breath, seeing some of the faces around him relaxing in the firelight. He nodded, to reassure one and all, then took up the ritual words, "How can we mourn then? How can we sorrow for what must be? If our dead are with us, and we will join with them when our bodies fail, how then do we weep?"

The drummer's beat continued, slow and steady.

"We grieve for what we lost. For the hollow place within our hearts. For the loss that is felt each time we turn to confide a secret, to share a joke, or to reach for a familiar touch." Joden kept his voice steady, but his anger grew. Anger for the loss of so many lives to something that could not be fought. Anger at old hatreds that had shaped the Plains in ways that no one knew. Anger at his own loss. "This is our pain, the pain of those left behind. This is our rage, that death must exist at all. Let us share it."

He raised his fists, and the other warriors roused and stood, raising theirs as well. Joden felt their pain and grief, and their anger like a wave over his body.

"Death of earth, birth of water," he chanted as if it were a curse, and the crowd joined in their voices and their pain, repeating the words. "Death of water, birth of air, death of air, birth of fire, death of fire, birth of earth."

Over and over until the earth seemed to shake. Joden opened his fists, and the crowd went quiet, opening theirs.

"Dance with me," he sang. "Death and pain are a part of life. But not all of it, People of the Plains! Joy is also there, to be enjoyed and shared! Rejoice! Dance with me!"

The crowd as one started to step to the drum beat. They formed patterns they'd known since the thea camps, lifting their hands to the skies and pounding the rhythms on the earth with their feet. Keir and Lara were also standing, their hands high, dancing with each other. Xyian warriors were pulled into the dance, welcomed by those of the Plains.

This then, was the true power of a Singer. To bring the people together, to aid them in their sorrow and their joy. Joden's tears streamed down his face, but he did nothing to stop them.

"Heyla," Joden roared.

The crowd roared back their response. "HEYLA!"

The drums continued, and Joden repeated the call and response for long glorious moments under the night sky.

Joden dropped his hands, and the drums ceased.

The warriors froze, all eyes on him.

Joden dropped his words into the silence. "May the skies hear my voice," he chanted. "May the people remember."

"We will remember," came the response. With that, the warriors started to disburse to their tents, with a quiet reverence.

Joden stood sweating, exhausted, filled with his own joy as he watched them leave.

He was no longer the man he had been.

Maybe, just maybe he was something more.

He started toward his tent, passing various warriors that whispered thanks, or gave him nods of respect. He returned them, but didn't linger.

There were whispered invitations to share as well, but he declined those with a shake of the head and a regretful smile. The euphoria he'd felt was fading, and he ached. He might be something more, but at a cost. The sacrifice of his voice. The sacrifice of Amyu at his side.

That hurt the worst. Her face flashed before his eyes, brown eyes welling as she pushed him away. The price of his dream.

Joden shook his head, clearing his thoughts, tired and drained and too weary for words.

He stripped, made quick work of a wash, and crawled into his one-man tent with a sigh of thanks. Dawn would come, and with it more questions, more challenges. He took a deep breath and let his body ease into the gurtle pads below him. Perhaps Prest was right. Perhaps it was an obstacle to be faced every day. He yawned, and pulled up the blankets.

Joden turned, and closed his eyes, deliberately seeking sleep. He listened to the beat of his heart, the crackle of the fire, the sound of his breath. In and out and in… sleep finally came.

Until he heard his name called.

"Joden of the Hawk," whispered an ancient voice. *"Come to us."*

CHAPTER THIRTY-FOUR

Joden opened his eyes, to find himself in the bright winter lodge with the dead. But the braziers were filled with sullen coals, everyone around them bedded down for sleep.

Joden sat up, letting his blanket fall around him. There was enough light for him to see Uppor next to him, his thin face and slanted eyes filled with worry.

"Uppor," Joden said. "I do not understand."

Uppor gestured for him to lower his voice, and leaned his head closer. "Nor do I," Uppor said with a grim hush. "Events and the winds swirl about us. It passes out of my understanding." He shrugged. "All we can do is what we can do. Beyond that, it is in the hands of the elements."

"Why did you call me?" Joden asked, keeping his voice low.

"Why did you come?" Uppor countered, then shook his head. "No, forgive me. This is not the time for ritual responses."

"Is it ever?" Joden rubbed his face.

"How else?" Uppor laughed quietly, then grew still. "You know of one named Hail Storm?"

Joden jerked his head up.

"He has slain the Ancients." Uppor glanced around then lifted his hand and touched Joden's forehead. "See."

* * * * *

Hail Storm stared at the lone tent on the horizon and considered.

There were no horses around, no smaller tents. No warriors

around at all, in fact, and that was unusual.

Still, it might be a source of news, or supplies... or power.

Hail Storm licked his lips, and headed his dead mount in that direction.

No one hailed him as he approached. Hail Storm dismounted, threw open the tent flap and stepped inside. He was met with a wave of heat, reeking of old kavage and fermented mare's milk. Braziers burned brightly in each corner. The heat dried his nose and stung his eyes.

"Shut the flap, shut the flap," came a quavering voice. "You are letting out the heat."

At the far end of the tent, on the traditional wooden platform, were three bundles of blankets. In each, sat a... person.

They were old, ancient, wrinkled with spots and very few wisps of hair on their heads. Their eyes were milky and rheumy with age. Hail Storm couldn't tell their sex, and their skin seemed so faded it was hard to tell what color it had originally been.

They sat facing him, waiting.

Hail Storm gathered himself, and stepped closer. He too could play the waiting game of silence.

Three sets of eyes glittered at him, and the silence stretched on.

Hail Storm gave up. "And who might you be?" he demanded.

No answer.

Hail Storm frowned. "I am—"

"Hail Storm," the one on the far left spoke with a soft whisper. "Eldest Elder Warrior-priest."

"Hail Storm, stripped of power by the Sacrifice," the one on the far right cackled, high-pitched and irritating.

"Hail Storm," the one in the center spoke with a quaver. "Wielder of blood magic."

Hail Storm narrowed his eyes, his rage just below the surface. But he kept it there, simmering. There was a pallet centered before them. He swept forward and knelt there, not waiting for an invitation.

He placed his hands on his knees and waited.

"We are the Ancients of the Singers," they said in unison.

"Impressive," Hail Storm said.

"Hail Storm is confused," the one in the center spoke with a quaver. "What is this, perhaps?"

"Ancients," came the cackle. "This is not the way of the Plains."

"How can this be?" continued the whispering one in mocking tones. "The elderly among us, no longer useful to the Tribe, they go to the snows."

"It would seem that the Singers have secrets," Hail Storm said.

"There are songs that Singers do not sing," The Ancients chuckled. The one in the center grinned, bare gums all that showed. "Tales we do not tell. Songs and stories handed down from Eldest Elder to Eldest Elder. Stories not told to children."

Hail Storm cocked his head to one side and considered. "Tales you have not shared with Essa, perhaps."

Three pairs of eyes suddenly sharpened, focused on him.

"You haven't passed down your knowledge, have you?" It was Hail Storm's turn to chuckle. "No wonder Essa was always in such a sour mood." He considered them for a long moment. "I assume you want something," he said.

Their glares grew fiercer.

"The Council restored," the left one said, in a voice as clear as a bell.

"Xy destroyed," the right one said, with a sweet innocent tone.

"Our knowledge preserved," said the one in the middle, with a deep timber.

"Do you always change tone like that?" Hail Storm asked. "I admire the technique."

...The stony silence after his words was ice cold.

"Let me guess," Hail Storm continued. "You did something that didn't turn out the way you had planned. The skies know I am well aware that can happen." Hail Storm glanced around the tent. "Essa and his ilk not obeying your commands?"

"We are the Ancients," all three said together. "We are to be obeyed."

Hail Storm nodded. "Odd, isn't it, that we think that change will bring more of the same? Or keep things the way they are?" He shook his head. "Change is hard, and painful and unpredictable. It tears at patterns we thought fixed and unmovable, in ways we can never foresee." Hail Storm gave them his sweetest smile. "But change does bring new ways. New patterns. New opportunities."

"We are the Ancients," all three said together. "We control knowledge. We hold the power."

"Well, as to that," Hail Storm rose to his feet and pulled his knife. "Let us see who has the greater power, shall we?"

* * * * *

Joden blinked at the suddenness as the vision cut off.

"So he has gained in strength, using blood magic long lost on the Plains," Uppor said.

Joden sat in silence, listening to the words, considering all the things that Uppor was not saying. The lodge was quiet, the coals in the braziers hissing softly. "So we have lost their songs," he said.

"I am not sure it's a loss," Uppor replied. "You are not bound by the hatred they may have contained."

"They wanted a pawn," Joden said, and then seeing Uppor's confusion explained. "A piece in a game played by Xyians."

"Ah," Uppor said. "See, even the dead do not see all things."

"Why are you telling me this?" Joden frowned, studying

Uppor. "Why should I believe you? You are Uppor the Trickster who stole lightning from the sky—"

"Uppor the trickster, Uppor the thief." Uppor flashed a grin but it faded quickly. "Because you are the only one who can stop him. No obstacles lie in his path, and the deaths he has planned will only fuel his fire." Uppor glanced around, then leaned closer. "Joden, a Seer's gifts differ. Some see the future, see a path to what must be. Some see only the past, weaving through memories imprinted in soil and stone. Some walk in both worlds, the living and the dead. You seem to have some of each, and little or no control."

"Can it be controlled?" Joden asked.

Uppor nodded. "Over time, but you do not have time." Uppor looked at the painting on the wall. Joden followed his gaze.

It was a map, of the northern part of the Plains and the valley of Xy. Bright sparks appeared in Xy and on the Plains, all heading to one spot on the border. A tiny Liam stood at the top of a tower, his long hair blowing in the wind, his arms folded over his chest.

"Forces are gathering, Joden," Uppor gestured to the map. "Forces that will determine—"

The four bedrolls around the brazier stirred.

"Muck," Uppor said and from the tone Joden knew it for a curse.

Blankets were flung back, and the four warrior-priests rose from their pallets, staring at Joden. From their faces, they were not pleased.

Twisting Winds rose to his feet, lifting his hands. "Learn, Seer. Magic is a blade that cuts both ways."

Summer Sky rose, and lifted her hands. "Learn, Seer. That which was taken is restored. That which was imprisoned is now freed."

Stalking Cat rose and spoke, lifting his hands. "Learn, Seer.

Embrace the old. Preserve the new."

Then, to Joden's shock, Wild Winds rose from his pallet, lifting his hands. The warrior-priest looked old and tired, but his eyes glittered with strength. "Learn, Seer," his voice was rough as if with disuse. "The path between life and death is forbidden. Walk it at your peril."

They all dropped their hands together, and the winds started to howl. The lodge around them wavered and shifted as the snows began to blow.

Joden felt himself slipping away. He reached out, and grabbed Uppor's wrist. "Kalisa?" he demanded.

Uppor's face crumpled. "She wanders the snows," he called as the winds roared around them. "I hope in time she can forgive us."

Joden shook his head, and shared his sorrow. "The one she needs to forgive is herself," he shouted, releasing Uppor's wrist and letting the winds carry him away.

He woke, sweaty and shaken in his tent.

* * * * *

It took Joden forever, stumbling over his words, trying to explain his vision to Keir and Lara. Marcus was there, and he reached out, and put a hand on Joden's arm. "Breathe," he said, offering kavage.

Joden nodded, took that deep breath, and then started using the sing-song voice. It was important that Keir hear and understand.

Keir did listen, intently. He asked questions, asked Joden to repeat the chant of the warrior-priests.

In the end, Keir leaned back, and considered his kavage. "Joden, the sparks on the map. How were they placed?"

Lara rustled through her satchel, pulling out paper and her writing supplies. Joden spread a sheet over the ground and pointed for her to draw. "Here," he said. He drew a line with his finger, and Lara marked it. "The line is the border of Xy." He pointed to various location, where Lara placed dots. But Joden shook his head. "These were bigger. Brighter."

"And who do you think each is?" Both Keir and Lara leaned forward.

"Us," Joden pointed to each in turn. "Liam, at the border." He gestures to the three sparks on the Plains. "Antas? Simus? And as to the north, perhaps Heath?"

Keir studied the map. "We cannot move faster than our current pace, for many reasons."

"The children" Lara said. "We are slowing you down."

Keir shook his head. "More the supply wagons and the Xyian infantry," he reminded her. "But truth be told I do not want to stand at the border without warriors at my side." He pointed to the spark closest to Liam's. "In case this is Antas and not Simus." He shook his head again. "We will keep our pace. If I am right, all these points will meet at roughly the same time. Then we will see."

"What if they get to the border first?" Joden sang.

"Liam will hold." Keir glanced at Marcus, who was checking the babies.

"What if the dead are trying to use us, use you, as a pawn?" Joden argued. "What if—"

Keir shrugged. "You are a wise and good man, Joden. You have always given me your truths, even when they were painful to hear. Continue to do so, and I will honor that." He rose to his feet. "But I would give a great deal to know who is closer. Simus? Or Antas?"

CHAPTER THIRTY-FIVE

Antas lifted his mug of kavage to his lips, and hid his grimace behind it.

His face ached from all this snows-be-damned smiling. Hours of talking had left him with a sore ass, a headache, and a desire to kill something.

All to good effect, at least. The senel was going well.

He took another sip, and glanced around the tent. The heat had built up within such that he'd ordered the sides rolled up. It also made sure that all who wished to hear could.

Ietha had relaxed enough that she was laughing and smiling with his Second. It wouldn't surprise him if they shared this night. That suited Antas. All the warriors looked well fed and comfortable. His Token-bearer had done well, keeping their guests' hands filled full of bread and meat and their mugs full of fermented mare's milk.

"A pity your Warprize has fled," Ietha said.

Antas put on a sad look of resignation as he lowered his mug. "I fear that my poor city-dweller has been misled," he said. The words came easily, since he'd repeated the lie so many times. "Who knows what Reness has told him. I never should have housed him with her, but with her wound we both thought it best."

"It is not right, that she came between you," Reht swayed a bit in her seat.

Loyalty and support, that was what he needed from these warriors. He'd come close to losing it the night of the fires. But he'd turned the herd his way.

"It is not right," Antas said. "But I live in hope that when I see him again, when we have defeated Keir and his ilk, that he will listen and come to my side."

Nods of agreement all around. Antas was deeply satisfied. He lifted his mug and drained it.

Only to catch a glimpse of the repairs and scorch marks at the top of the tent.

Hail Storm, of course. It had to have been. A warrior-priest was the only one who had that kind of power, and Hail Storm was the only warrior-priest alive. He'd taken his revenge, the *bracnect*.

"As to that, what next, Antas?" Ietha turned, her laughter fading.

Antas turned to her, and smiled yet again. "The repairs are almost done," he said. "The supplies that Reht brought have been distributed. My scouts report that Simus and his forces are ahead of us, headed north. The scouts also report that Singers are watching, from a distance, not approaching but not concealing their presence.

"The Eldest Elder Singer waits and watches," Ietha scowled.

"As ever been his practice," Antas agreed. "I propose that in the next few days, we also march for Xy."

Nods of agreement all around. Antas drew a breath. Now was the time.

"But it is not my intention to engage Simus," he said, which drew the surprise he knew it would. "I have told the scouts not to make contact, and to avoid any conflict. They will keep watch, and they will warn if Simus turns to attack us."

"Why?" Ietha asked.

"As Warlords, we give our oaths to the Council, and to our warriors," Antas said. "Their blood is our blood and their flesh our flesh. We are charged not to waste the lives of the warriors entrusted to us."

Keir of the Cat wasted the lives of his warriors. He fought Xy, and then allowed it to stand, not raiding or pillaging its wealth for the benefit of the Plains. He wasted the lives of the warriors lost in the filthy sickness of the city-dwellers, and then had the nerve to claim a Warprize and defy the will of the Council," Antas continued. Not quite the truth, but it would serve. "In doing so, he defied the Elders and the ways of our People. But his insult to our ways did not end with that.

"Keir also caused Simus to contest as Warlord, and look what devastation that brought down upon us. The Council destroyed, and these wyvern fill the skies, killing warrior and horse alike.

"All of this, Keir the Cat has done. He must be stopped." Antas took a breath. "But I will not waste lives in battle. I will not set the People of the Plains against one another."

The silence was thick.

"Instead, I will challenge Keir of the Cat. Let our strength and swords determine the winner. If I kill him, his people surrender to me. And if I die," Antas shrugged. "Then the elements have decided our fates."

There was an uproar, but not as much as Antas expected. Instead there were more thoughtful gazes, and considering nods.

Reht protested, "Keir is a mighty warrior, Antas."

"As am I," Antas said. "Am I not eldest Elder Warrior of the Eldest?"

There was debate, of course. Antas acknowledged many times that it was a risk. But he countered every argument, and talked more and more of conserving the lives of warriors.

He ended the senel with promise of more talk, and thanking all for their truths.

Once the tent was clear, and the sides rolled down, his Second came to stand before him.

"Sharing with Ietha?" Antas asked.

Veritt shrugged, then gave him a considering look. "You risk much," he said.

Antas dropped his voice, "I risk nothing."

Veritt raised his eyebrows.

"I will challenge Keir to combat to the death," Antas said. "I will offer this method to resolve our differences, and I will call on him not to spend the lives of his warriors. He will agree, for that is his weakness, Veritt. He will agree, and we will carve out a challenge circle between the two armies, and all will witness our fight."

Antas thumped his chest. "If I kill him, so be it. But if he looks to be winning, you will be there. You will cry out loud that he has betrayed his word and attack Keir's Second. That will give the signal for archers to fire. Keir and Simus will fall dead. If Keir's Warprize is there, so much the better. She will die too." Antas smiled and almost enjoyed the ache in his cheeks.

Veritt stood silent, his eyes on the ground. He shifted his weight, folding his arms over his chest. "This is not the way of the Plains," he said softly.

Antas nodded. "There is truth in that, Veritt and I honor it. But I would restore what we have lost, and I will do that at the cost of honor if necessary." Antas stood and put his hand on Veritt's shoulder. "Our sacrifice, for the good of our people. Besides, none but you and I will ever know." He paused. "I need to know I have your support in this," he said.

After a long moment, Veritt lifted his head, and look Antas square in the eyes. "I will do what must be done," he said.

"As your Warlord commands?" Antas demanded.

"As my Warlord commands," Veritt said.

* * * * *

Quartis arrived late to the hidden Singer camp. A senel was in progress, and he had to push his way through the crowded tent toward the front.

Eldest Elder Essa was seated on his platform, drinking kavage, and waiting.

Quartis made a bow, and then went to sit by Para.

"You're late," Para hissed.

Quartis rolled his eyes at her. "The Ancients?" he whispered.

"No sign," came the soft response. "And he's in a real snit."

Quartis sat down, accepted water for the washing ritual, and then took a mug of kavage. He tried to keep his head down, but Essa's eyes were on him.

"I call this senel to order," Essa announced, his voice cutting through the conversation. "I commanded that we watch and see what actions the Warlords took. I would have your reports. Garso," he gestured and a young woman rose to her feet.

"I was sent to the army of Niles of the Boar," she began and from there it was a normal report, talking of raiding and successful battles.

Essa nodded, and then questioned each Singer in turn as to the Warlord they had been assigned to. All was normal, until he reached Annith.

"I was assigned to Osa of the Fox," the Singer reported. "She did not take her army to the field."

"What?" Essa asked as the tent stirred.

"She gathered her army, and then gathered at least two thea camps." Annith said. "She kept them close until they joined with Warlord Ultie.

"This I can verify," Roci stood. "I was assigned to Ultie, and I linked up with Annith when the armies came together. They sit together, off to the west of here, sending out scouts but not engaging."

"They wait," Essa mused. "For events."

"As do we," Quartis said, louder than he intended.

"As do we," Essa nodded. "Report, Quartis."

Quartis rose, and nodded to his Eldest Elder. "I have watched for activity near the Xyian border," he said. "Both Simus and Antas head in that direction, separated by days. Simus's path is direct. Antas is slower, perhaps because of the damage his camp suffered. Perhaps by intent."

Essa gave him a nod, and Quartis sat back down, easing his dry throat with a sip of kavage.

"Thron, I sent you to the Heart," Essa said. "What say you?"

Thron stood. "Would that I could offer good news, Eldest Elder," Thron shook his head. "The lake is still surrounded by wyvern, who now feed their young in the nest. They are voracious in appetite, and it is only by the grace of the elements that I stand here. The Heart itself is empty of life, and there is an enormous dead wyvern rotting on the stone." Thron made a face. "It will take an army to clear the area, if the wyverns leave."

"And if they don't leave?" Essa asked.

"Then many warriors will die trying," Thron answered. "And their deaths will be agonizing"

Essa nodded. "My thanks, Thron." As the man sat, Essa rose to his feet.

"At this time of year, we would normally scatter to the various armies, to support our people and bear witness to events. But this is no normal year. At some point, Keir and Antas will confront each other, and it will be at the Xyian border."

Quartis waited as did those around him.

"We will watch, and wait." Essa said. "And when the moment is right, we will insert ourselves into the conflict. Taking no position. Judging, as Singers have judged in the past. The Singers must be witness to what occurs."

Essa considered them all grimly. "Neutral, but I do not trust their truths. I do not trust Antas. So only Quartis and I will go to Xy.

"Eldest Elder," Para stood to protest. "You must take some

of us to guard you."

Essa nodded. "Four others then, of your choosing, Para. The rest of you will scatter, and shelter with various Warlords." He rose and stood before them. "Para, you are the eldest and most experienced after myself. Most likely to be chosen Eldest Elder at my death. You will hide yourself with two others, and wait for word."

"Eldest Elder," Para tried to argue, but Essa cut her off.

"No," Essa said. "Too much is at risk. Before you depart, I will share what needs be shared." A pained look crossed his face, but then he smiled grimly. "In fact, I will share with all of you that which only the Eldest Elders have held. I will not risk my knowledge being lost."

* * * * *

Hanstau noticed a change in Reness the further north they went. She seemed more distant during the day, and there was a touch of desperation in their love-making at night. He'd thought it was the stress of watching for Antas and his warriors, but when he finally worked up the courage to ask, that was not the answer he received.

"I have a fear," Reness said, poking at the coals of their evening fire. "A fear that when you are once more in Xy, and with your people, and their walls and their ways that you… you will not—"

Hanstau reached out, and turned her to face him Her cheeks were wet with tears.

She lifted her chin away. "There, I have said it." Reness scowled. "I feel like a foolish child before her Ascension. Tell me your truths, Hanstau."

Hanstau sat quietly for a moment, letting his joy spread and settle in his bones. "I am no warrior," he said. "I have not served in campaigns."

"I know that," Reness said, and he could swear he heard a pout in her voice.

"I have been faithful to my lady wife before she died," Hanstau said. "I have learned my profession and raised our children, and served my Queen, so I have met my obligations to the Tribe of Xy."

Reness jerked her head around at those words.

"So I say this truth to you, Reness, Eldest Elder Thea, Warrior of the Plains and woman I love, I am sworn to you. Forever."

Reness stared at him, her tears forgotten. "Those are ritual bonding words," she whispered.

"Good," Hanstau lifted his chin. "I got them right then. Now, I believe you have something to say to me?"

"Do," she hesitated, her eyes wide with growing delight. "Do you know what they mean?"

"Yes," Hanstau mock frowned at her. "Well?"

Reness's smile was a pleasure to see, and her hands trembled as she reached for his. Damp and cold, and shaky, he took them into his grip. The golden sparkles surrounded both their hands.

"Hanstau of Xy, Healer, and man that I love, I say this truth to you. I am sworn to you." Reness leaned in, and pressed her forehead to his. "Forever."

Hanstau kissed her until they were both out of breath.

Reness broke away, chuckling. "This means your toes are mine," she teased.

"Yes," Hanstau. "My toes are yours, as yours are mine. But perhaps we could keep that under the bells." He shook his head. "I must tell you that I am not fond of that ear thing your people do."

"Your people wear rings?" Reness asked.

"Yes," he said. "A nice plain gold band on the ring finger." He splayed out his hand and pointed.

Reness leaned in, joy in her face and desire in her eyes. He could feel the heat of her body on his skin. "How do you feel about toe rings?" she asked slyly.

* * * * *

So, you have had some time," Heath, Warden of Xy said. "What have you learned?"

Amyu rose to her feet. They - the warrior-priests in training - had all agreed that she would speak for them.

Heath had called this senel at their camp, still close to where she had found the airions. The cows had been moved out, and she'd heard more than enough about the precious-bloodline-of-milk-cows to last her a lifetime. But Heath had soothed hurt feelings with bright coins, and other cows and sheep had been brought in to feed the airions.

So they had established their camp, and set about learning to fly.

They had all gathered around the main cook fire, with the airions around them, curled in sleep. The warcats were scattered about, apparently sleeping too, but Gilla kept a watchful eye on them. They could not resist trying to kill the airion's tails whenever there was so much as a twitch.

Heath gave her an encouraging nod across the fire.

Amyu took a breath, and began. "Flying is not as easy as it looks," she said. "Even with the saddles you brought us, it requires power to stay on the airion. The saddles help, especially if one loses their concentration." She glanced at Cadr.

"I tried," he offered. "On a horse, keeping one's balance is easy. But airions," he put out a hand and dipped it around in the air. "They do not stay level to the ground."

Everyone nodded in agreement.

Amyu continued, "There are other risks to being buckled in too tight, or having a girth snap. Too easy to tumble right off, and while they try to aid us," she gestured toward the golden airion. "You can fall far in a short time."

Heath frowned. "And if you were fighting wyverns?"

"That's another problem." Lightning Strike leaned forward. "Fighting on a horse there is only what is around you and under you. But with these creatures, there is also up." He shook his head. "We have had some near misses."

"But up is an advantage," Amyu pointed out. "And we can use the sun to our aid."

"How?" Heath asked.

The entire group started talking then, using their hands to try to describe moving through the sky, using the sun to blind the enemy.

Heath nodded. "I think I understand. What other problems?"

"Throwing a lance in mid-air," Amyu said. "We have tried using trees and stones as targets, and it is much different."

"And yet?" Heath asked, a hint of a smile on his lips.

"It is wonderful," Amyu said, still amazed at what the sky offered. "Dangerous and wonderful."

Heath nodded. "I am having more saddles made, and Atira is creating more lances. Do not rush this," he cautioned. "You are all of us that use the power. We will need you all."

"No," Amyu said, catching Heath by surprise. "We need to rush this. To push ourselves."

"Why?" Heath asked.

"We don't know," Lightning Storm said "But we all feel this sense of dread. That we will be… are… needed."

"But you can't tell me why?" Heath asked.

"It could be the wyverns," Lightning Storm suggested, but he looked at Amyu.

"I fear for Joden," she admitted. "Like sensing a storm on the horizon."

Sidian stirred by the fire. "We've no skill at augury," he admitted. "But both I and Mage feel it too. We have scryed the

Heart, and nothing has changed. The wyverns seem only intent on feeding their young."

Heath stared into the fire, then looked up. "Continue to train. Go at the pace you feel best, but try not to take unnecessary risks." He rose to his feet. "I end this senel. The watches are set. Let us seek our beds."

Everyone rose, and did just that. Gilla called the cats to her tent, and they loped behind her, with only a few last lingering looks for moving feathers.

Amyu paused, and stood watching the flames. If she thought of Joden, and she did more often than she cared to admit, her heart would race with an urgency she didn't understand.

She lifted her eyes to the night sky, and the stars peeking through clouds. "Be well, beloved," she whispered. "For I fear the dawn."

CHAPTER THIRTY-SIX

The messenger horns blew shortly after the nooning.

Joden was riding next to Lara's wagon. He jerked his head up to see four riders coming down the side of the road. The warrior in the lead was tall and straight in the saddle, his long hair flowing in the wind.

"L-l—liam," he said to Lara.

Lara stood as the wagon stopped, reaching out to balance herself on the shoulder of the driver. "Keir just left; he will have heard the horns."

Out of the corner of his eye Joden saw Marcus disappear deeper into his hooded cloak, and sink to the bottom of the wagon. Anna gave him an odd look as she tried to see who was coming.

"Warprize," Liam pulled his horse to a halt beside the wagon, just past Lara. "Simus approaches the border. He sent word that he is coming, and that his army would remain at the bottom of the embankment. He will come up the switchback trail." Liam was speaking to Lara, but his eyes were fixed on the cloaked figure in the wagon.

"Keir's not far," Lara said, signaling for her horse. "He will be here shortly, I imagine."

Liam nodded, still staring at Marcus.

Anna noticed. "Are those two still arguing about military tactics?" she asked Lara.

Lara ignored her as a warrior brought Greatheart over.

"What is that?" Liam asked, staring at the saddle.

"Never mind." Lara climbed into saddle from the wagon. She took the reins just as Keir rode up at a gallop with Prest and Yers.

"What word?" Keir demanded.

Liam explained. "I told Warren where to take up positions," he continued. "In case."

Keir nodded. "Prest, Joden, Yers, Marcus, join us."

"Not I," Marcus's voice was muffled by his hood. "I stay with the babes."

Liam scowled, but Keir just gave a sharp nod. "Let's ride."

* * * * *

They were just past the vanguard of the army when they saw Simus and his party riding toward them.

Joden recognized Elois and Tsor, most likely Token-bearer and Second. And the woman beside Simus was Snowfall.

And in Simus and Snowfall's ears glittered the ear weavings of a bonded couple.

Joden heard Keir suck in a breath even as he pulled his horse to a stop and dismounted. They all followed his lead, Prest aiding Lara from her saddle.

"Be ready," Yers hissed. His hand was on his sword hilt.

Simus and his people rode a bit closer and then they too dismounted, and walked forward. Simus's face was grim as he strode closer. Joden couldn't read his—

"LITTLE HEALER!" Simus ran forward and swept Lara into a bear hug, sweeping her off her feet.

"Ooopfh" Lara grunted, and then laughed as Simus spun her around. "Fool! Put me down."

"But you are no longer big of belly," Simus laughed. "Where are the—" his eyes went wide. "Joden?"

Simus slowly lowered Lara to her feet, and then stepped closer, his face filled with amazement. "JODEN!"

With two long steps Simus swept his arm around Joden and pounded his back. Joden hugged him back, grinning like a fool

"We thought you taken by the Singers," Simus said. "Or dead. Or worse. What happened? We had no word—"

A gentle, cool voice spoke from behind him. "Simus."

Joden looked over with Simus.

Snowfall stood there, her hands folded over her chest, an eyebrow raised. She nodded to their right.

Keir stood there, hands folded over his chest, his face a mask.

Simus released Joden, his smile gone. He turned to face Keir, pulled his sword, and dropped to one knee in one smooth move.

"I, Simus of the Hawk, Warlord of the North do hereby swear my sword, my truths, and my warriors to Keir of the Cat, Warlord of the Plains, Overlord of Xy," he took a deep breath. "And WarKing over all."

Joden sucked in a breath, even as Lara gasped out loud.

Keir's lips parted, his eyes glittering. He stepped forward and placed his fingers on the blade of Simus's sword. "I accept your oath. I will be your WarKing in all things. Your flesh is my flesh, your blood is my blood."

Simus bowed his head. "May the very air of this land grant you breath."

Elois took a step forward and knelt. She bowed her head to Keir. "I, Elois of the Horse, Token-Bearer, acknowledge the oath of my Warlord. May the very earth of this land support your feet."

Tsor took a step forward and knelt. He bowed his head to Keir. "I, Tsor of the Bear, Second, acknowledge the oath of my Warlord. May the very fires of this land warm your skin."

Snowfall took a step forward and knelt. She bowed her head to Keir. "I, Snowfall of the Plains, Bonded of Simus, acknowledge the oath of my Warlord. May the very waters of this land quench your thirst." She lifted her head, and looked Keir in the eye. "May the powers I wield serve you, WarKing."

Keir nodded. "Rise, all of you, and serve our people."

"HEYLA," Simus shouted, flashing a grin of white teeth against dark skin. "That's that, then." He jumped to his feet and sheathed his sword. "Is there kavage? I am dry as dust."

A grin the likes of which Joden had never seen split Keir's face. The WarKing reached out and hugged Simus, the two of them laughing and beating each other's backs in welcome.

They finally broke apart, laughing and breathless.

"Come," Liam said in a dry voice. "There is much to discuss.

* * * * *

Before discussions could be had, basic matters had to be seen to. Keir and Simus issued orders to their warriors, making camp both around the keep and on the Plains. Lara and Marcus settled Anna and the babes safely in a room at the top of the tower, with a strong guard around them of both Xyians and Plains warriors.

When they finally gathered in the Great Hall of the keep, they found a meal waiting for them. Joden was glad to see fresh loaves of hot bread, spiced gurtle, roasted ogden root, pots of kavage—

And Eldest Elder Thea Reness and Hanstau waiting for them at the tables.

Amidst exclamations of welcome, Warren stared at both of them. "Two armies crawling all over the Plains and you snuck through them?" he asked.

"She is a thea," Hanstau said. "Please pass the butter."

"You could have sent word," Keir complained as they ate.

Simus shook his head. "I didn't feel I could risk it. The Plains crawl with scouts. Some I figured were Antas and his allies, others may be Singers watching from a distance. It felt as if the entire Plains was watching us, and I would not risk a warrior. I didn't think it was necessary," Simus said but then he glanced at Yers, seated at one of the other tables. "But I can understand the doubts." Simus put his mug down and looked Keir in the eye. "Snowfall is my bonded," he said. "And I am hers. I trust her with my life. But you must judge for yourself."

Joden could hear the joy in Simus's voice and see it in his eyes. But there was something more. A sense of contentment from his friend. Or perhaps completion was a better word.

Keir gave Simus a nod of agreement. "Oaths have been given," he said. "I am satisfied."

Simus turned his head to look Joden in the eye. "You are awfully quiet for a Singer, old friend. What say you?"

Reluctantly, Joden opened his mouth but Lara, elements bless her, interrupted. "Joden's tale is long," she said. "And we have more urgent things to discuss."

Simus nodded. "Truth. Antas is not more than a few days behind us."

"No," Lara said firmly. "More urgent than that."

* * * * *

The room the babes were housed in was not large, but everyone squeezed in. Joden watched as Anna took a stance next to the babes' basket, guarding her charges with a suspicious eye. Lara made introductions. Anna seemed particularly unimpressed at the mention of 'thea'.

Reness just smiled at her. "What is that scent?" She asked.

"I tucked some of the lavender into the clean nappies," Anna said. "The scent will sooth the little ones."

"A good idea," Reness said, and Anna seemed to soften a bit.

"What fine warriors," Simus exclaimed. He picked up one of the babes and cradled it in his arms. "What did the elements name this one?"

"Xykeirson," Lara said. There was pride in her tone, but Joden could also hear her worry. "And this," she lifted the other bundle. "This is Xykayla."

Simus smiled as he rocked the babe in his arms. "The Tribe has grown," he said gently and with pride. "The Tribe has flourished."

"I need you to tell me—" Lara's voice trembled and her eyes were tearing as she turned to Snowfall. "If they are well. If they are safe."

Snowfall's surprise was clear. "Forgive me, Warprize. I do not understand. Why would you think there is something wrong?"

"Kalisa," Keir said grimly.

Joden listened as Keir explained the doubts and fears that the old Xyian woman had roused in them. Lara rocked Xykayla with a quiet desperation as Keir spoke, nodding at his words but clearly overwrought.

Snowfall listened intently, never interrupting, her lovely face expressionless. She waited until Keir finished, and gave it a moment before she spoke.

"WarKing, Warprize, please know that there is no way to tell if your children are gifted," Snowfall said. "Not yet, at any rate. They are too young to have the will to use the gifts." Snowfall stepped forward, and reached for Xykayla. Lara put her into her arms without hesitation.

Snowfall's lips curved in a small smile as she looked down into the babe's eyes. "I can tell you that I don't see any touch of the power upon them. Both of them," She added, looking at Keir.

"Neither do I," Hanstau said.

"You?" Lara asked.

"Yes," Hanstau said. "And you were right, Snowfall. I need training."

Snowfall frowned. "But weren't you north?"

Hanstau shook his head.

"Your Amyu, then," Snowfall said to Simus.

Joden jerked his head up. "A-a-amyu?" It caught him off-guard to hear her name.

Simus stared at him, but Joden ignored him.

"It seems she might have the gift as well," Snowfall said and explained about what she had sensed. Hanstau nodded beside her, but didn't interrupt.

"Warprize, I have never known a child hurt by the power of the elements." She placed the babe back in Lara's arms. "With the power returned in force, we will have to be watchful. But that is a truth of this world, yes?"

"Yes," Lara responded with a resigned sigh. Joden was pleased to note that both she and Keir seemed more relaxed.

"Enough, shoo, all of you." Anna took Xykeirson from Keir's arms. "These babes need their sleep."

"She's right," Lara said, and the others slowly drifted out of the room, and down the circular stairs to the Great Hall.

Simus put a hand on Joden's shoulder. "I think it's your turn to talk, my friend." he said, guiding Joden back to the benches.

"Yes," Joden sang. Simus's eyes narrowed.

But a ruckus at the door stopped them all.

A warrior appeared, flushed and breathless. "WarKing," he called. "A messenger from Warlord Antas."

* * * * *

Keir agreed to meet with Antas at noon the next day.

The messenger waited as they debated who would go. Lara was adamant about attending, and nothing anyone could say would dissuade her but Joden convinced her. "If you die," he sang. "Our WarKing would go into battle rage, and most likely die as well. Who then raises the babes?"

Lara's eyes welled up as she sputtered without an answer. Keir swept her into his arms, and kissed her face as she wrapped her arms around his neck.

"Prest, tell the messenger that Simus and Joden will stand at my side tomorrow." Keir said. "Pardon us," he added as he headed toward the stairs with Lara in his arms. "The hour grows late."

The others as well said their goodnights. Snowfall rose, touched Simus on the shoulder, and left with the others.

Simus poured out more kavage. "Tell me. What happened?"

Joden did. He sang to his friend, then dropped into his normal speech, fighting the words. He told him of the old trials, told him of the mountainside. As much as he tried to avoid it, over and over again he told of Amyu's aid, her strength, for she was a major part of the story. His story. Simus sat listening, intent.

"So you have not seen Essa," Simus said.

Joden shook his head.

Simus studied his mug. "Your eyes change when you speak of Amyu," Simus said.

It was not a surprise. Simus was an old tent-mate, and knew Joden better than he knew himself. Joden shrugged, dropping his gaze. "She is a child," Joden sang sadly. "And I am not as I was."

"And Snowfall is a warrior-priestess." Simus stood and stretched, then looked down at Joden. "Don't be stupid." He walked off toward the stairs.

Joden sat staring at the dying coals until their spark was gone.

CHAPTER THIRTY-SEVEN

Antas had quite a bit to say, and Joden didn't trust any of it.

It was a perfect day in all other aspects. They'd met between Simus's camp and Antas's, equal distance from both. Out of the range of hearing, but not out of bow range.

The grass was trampled by the movement of warriors and horses. The sun was high, the sky clear, and just enough breeze to cool the skin.

Simus stood just behind Keir, arms crossed, glowering. Keir was intent, listening to Antas speak about preserving the lives of warriors.

Joden was listening, but he was also watching. Ietha was clearly confident and strong in her support of Antas. But something in Veritt's stance gave Joden pause.

"If I die," Antas said. "Then my army leaves to raid elsewhere. If you die," Antas's smile was nasty. "I will give your forces a day before we attack. We—"

"Agreed," Keir interrupted Antas.

"Wait, what?" Simus sputtered.

"When?" Antas was smiling, confidence shining in his eyes.

"Now," Keir said. "Let us cut a challenge circle here and now and—"

Horns blew in the distance, and everyone looked over to see five riders bearing down on them.

"Essa," Antas growled.

"Essa," Keir confirmed, and the both took a step back, and waited.

Essa and the other Singers rode in at a gallop, the horses blowing as they stopped and dismounted. There was no sign of bright colors or silks; they were all armored, weapons ready. Joden eased behind Keir blocking Essa's view of him.

He really need not have bothered. Essa was focused elsewhere.

"Keir," Essa strode forward to stand before them. "Antas."

"Warlord Antas," Antas growled.

"Really?" Essa arched an eyebrow in a way only a Singer could. "Did you contest at the Spring Trials and I did not see?"

Antas puffed up but Joden could see him rein in his temper.

"What say you both?" Essa demanded.

Antas launched into his speech, and now Essa's eyebrows climbed to the top of his forehead. He listened, and waited, and when Antas was done he turned to Keir. "What say you?"

"I agreed," Keir said. "Let it be decided. Here and now."

Essa nodded. "It has ever been the way of the Plains to use the strength of a warrior's weapon to support their truths."

Essa looked coolly at Antas. "The death of one of you ends this conflict," he said. He turned his gaze to Keir. "The death of armies wastes the lives. Quartis and the others will prepare the challenge circle. My Singers will ride to your respective armies and warn them of what is to happen. Warn them also not to interfere. A trial to the death needs no Singer to judge. But we will witness."

Simus pulled Keir away. "A word," he said.

Keir moved, and Joden found himself eye-to-eye with Essa. "Joden?"

All the Singers stopped in their tracks, and stared, rendered speechless. Joden would have laughed, but there was no humor here.

"E-e-eldest E-e-elder E-e-essa," Joden let him have the full truth of his voice.

Essa's eyes bugged out for a moment, but then they narrowed into slits. He opened his mouth, and then snapped it closed, as if remembering his audience. "We have Singer matters to speak on, after this," Essa said.

Joden bowed his head, and followed Keir and Simus. The other Singers dashed to their horses, and started off with their messages. Quartis started cutting the sod to create the circle. Joden glanced back to see Antas and Veritt in a whispered discussion as Ietha stood off, calmly watching. Essa stood where he had been, looking aloof. But as Joden walked to his friends, he could feel Essa's glare on the back of his neck.

"What are you thinking?" Simus asked Keir in hushed tones. "You risk everything."

"The skies favor the bold," Keir said calmly, reaching for the waterskin on his saddle.

"Lara is going to kill you, if he doesn't," Simus pointed out.

Keir drank, then glanced up at the keep. It was too distant to make out anyone, but Joden was sure Lara was watching. "Best if this is over before she knows she needs to worry," Keir said. He turned back to glare at Antas. "I will kill him and end this."

"You're good," Simus said. "But he is, or was, the Eldest Elder Warrior."

"I fear treachery," Joden sang softly.

Keir fixed him with a stare. "Do you have a vision of this? One way or another?"

Joden shook his head.

Keir nodded in satisfaction. "Simus, leave. If I fall—"

"I am not leaving," Simus said. "Don't die."

Keir grinned. "I won't."

* * * * *

The circle finished, both Keir and Antas stepped into the circle and wasted no time. Keir, with his two curved swords. Antas, with sword and shield.

Antas moved fast, to block and swing. But Keir leapt to one side, and slashed hard, cutting Antas below the eye. Blood dripped down into Antas's blond beard. He roared his anger.

Keir grinned, took a stance, and waited for the charge. Keir's swords thudded on Antas's shield. The air whispered as Antas's blade failed to hit.

It was brutal, which was exactly as expected. Two warriors evenly matched as far as Joden knew. Antas was older and experienced; Keir was younger and stronger. They both hated each other with a passion, and Joden could feel it in their blows. Any outcome was possible.

Joden watched, holding his breath, transfixed as the two circled on another, looking for an opening. But a slight movement, caught his eye. Veritt, Antas's Second had shifted his stance, his arms folded over his chest. Joden looked away, but something felt… wrong.

Joden focused on Veritt.

Antas's Second was a troubled man if ever Joden saw one. The signs were subtle, but they were there. Twitchy, shifting weight, watching the fight with a desperation that made little sense.

"Ha," Antas shouted. Joden looked back as he scored a blow on Keir's arm, drawing blood. Keir never stopped, just charged in with a flurry of strikes against Antas's shield, forcing him back.

Essa and the other Singers watched, their faces neutral. Simus and Ietha were stoic as well, arms crossed as unconscious mirrors of each other. Joden gave them a glance, then stared back at Veritt.

Who was looking at the piles of sod beside him.

The sounds of the continued fight filled the air, the sounds of two men locked in deadly combat.

But Joden kept his eyes on Veritt and waited.

Veritt looked up, and Joden caught his eye. Veritt met them for a second, and then flicked past to look at Antas.

Joden didn't look away. He waited.

The fight raged on, with the sounds of scuffling feet, the ringing of sword on sword, and the clang of blows on the shield. Antas's breathing grew ragged as the fight went on. Keir was silent, but Joden knew his friend's entire focus was on killing his enemy.

Joden watched Veritt, who glanced at him every now and then. Joden made sure the man knew that his eyes were on him every time he looked Joden's way. Joden didn't look with hate, didn't glare or threaten.

But he was watching.

Veritt's glances grew more frequent as the fight went on. Joden kept staring. Veritt's nervousness seemed to grow, and then oddly he stilled, staring at the earth.

Joden didn't dare look away, although the sounds of the fight were changing. Antas seemed to be retreating, catching his breath behind his shield. Keir was having none of that, if the blows to the shield were any measure.

Veritt look up, and stared at Joden. He took a deep breath, eased his shoulders back and nodded at Joden. Just a quick nod that no one seemed to catch. Veritt had come to a decision, it seemed.

Joden nodded back.

A cry of pain. Antas was on one knee, his shield up. "Veritt!" he cried out.

Veritt stood like a rock, unmoving.

Keir lunged, and Antas dodged, rolling out of the circle to get to his feet. But he wasn't fast enough for the block. Keir's sword bit into his neck. Blood spurted out.

Antas snarled, charging Keir with the shield intent on beating him down. Keir stepped to one side, let him pass.

Antas stumbled, his sword and shield still up, but glaring at Veritt. "Veritt, you betray—

"Antas," Keir roared.

Antas swung back, and stood there, panting. "I will kill you," he screamed, and charged Keir.

Keir waited, dodged the charge, and hammered his sword into Antas's neck, almost severing it.

Antas's eyes rolled up. He staggered, fell, and died.

The only sound was Keir's breathing. Keir stood there, blood dripping from his weapons and wounds. Joden had expected elation, a shout of triumph.

But Keir looked down at Antas's body with satisfaction tinged with regret.

"What now?" Essa's voice was silk as it broke the silence. "What now, Keir of the Cat. Will you declare yourself WarKing?"

Ietha growled.

Keir looked up, and to Joden's eyes, looked more commanding then he ever had in battle.

"No, Eldest Elder Singer." Keir stepped out of the circle to face him. "It shall be as it always has been. When the grasses of the Plains turn red and the raiding season ends, the Fall Council will gather. I will attend, my warriors will have full saddle bags and be loaded with supplies for the needs of the theas. I will speak my truth before the Council, and then, yes I will ask the Council to name me WarKing."

"I will be there," Ietha snarled. "And I will raise my voice against you."

"Each will speak their own truths," Keir said calmly. "And the Council will decide."

Ietha turned on her heel and left.

"I would ask for assistance." Veritt gestured to Antas's body.

Keir went to Simus, who took one of his swords and started cleaning it with a handful of grass. There was joy in their eyes, but they kept their celebration of the moment to themselves.

Two of the Singers heaved Antas's body on the back of a

horse. Joden picked up Antas's sword and shield and walked over to offer them to Veritt.

Veritt took them. "My thanks," his voice was a soft whisper. "You helped me face my truths, Singer."

"Not Singer yet," Essa's voice came from behind them. "A word, Joden."

Veritt bowed his head to both of them. "I will take Antas's army. The raiding season is not yet over, and we will go to aid the other Warlords. I will see you at the Fall Council, Eldest Elder," and with that he led the horse off with its burden.

"Joden," Keir called, letting his pleasure show. "Come, let us return."

Joden nodded toward Essa. "I've Singer business," Joden called back, using the sing-song voice. "I will follow."

"You just don't want to face the Warprize," Simus rolled his eyes but his smile never faltered. "Don't be too long, for you should share in her wrath."

Keir mounted, and pulled his horse around to face them. "Farewell, Eldest Elder Singer," Keir said. He looked every inch the victor. "I will see you in Council."

"And have no fear," Simus grinned. "We will have the Council tent well repaired for you when we reach the Heart."

Essa snorted, but the two men just grinned, turned their horses and galloped back toward Xy.

As they mounted, Quartis gestured and the Singers bent to replace the sod in the circle. Joden watched as the grass covered Antas's blood.

"Joden," Essa asked, and there was pain in his voice. "Where did the old paths take you?"

"T-t-to t-t-the s-s-snows," Joden forced the words out. He faced Essa, well aware that Quartis and the others were listening as they worked. "T-t-then t-t-the w-w-winds b-b-blew m-m-me t-t-to X-x-xy."

Essa winced. "They took your voice," he said. It wasn't a question.

"And opened my eyes," Joden sang.

Essa's eyes widened. "You can still sing?"

"And chant," Joden said. "But my true, strong voice? The Warprize says it may improve with time, but I know the truth. It is gone."

"You must complete the rites," Essa said. "Become the Singer you were destined to be."

"Without a voice?" Joden shook his head. "S-s-speaking l-l-like t-t-this?"

"You can still sing," Essa said. The others rose from their finished task, all nodding their agreement.

"You have songs that need singing, Joden," Essa said firmly. "And the Ancients may teach you their songs. Come with us."

Joden opened his mouth to tell him, but then closed it. He blinked.

Behind Essa, the horizon was clear. The armies were no longer there, the grasses were wide and empty except for a lone rider.

Wild Winds lifted his hand and summoned him.

Joden took a breath, and knew what he had to do. He focused back on Essa. "I will come," he chanted. "I will come and tell you all. But first, I would celebrate with my friends, and say farewell."

Essa nodded, clearly not pleased. "Very well. But do not make us wait too long, Joden. The rites should be completed before the Fall Council. And the skies know when the Ancients will appear to us."

Joden nodded. "I will come." He nodded toward where Veritt's and Ietha's warriors were moving off to the east. "Avoid them," he suggested.

"I have a mind to travel west," Essa said. "I will take word to Osa and Ultie, and shelter within their camps."

"As soon as my business is finished," Joden sang. "I will seek you out."

* * * * *

The keep was alight with joy by the time Joden returned. The celebration was going strong, with drumming and chanting echoing from its walls.

But he was stopped at the gates by watchful guards. Joden was pleased to see that those on duty had sharp, clear eyes.

The Great Hall was filled with the smell of roast cow, baked bread and kavage. Xyian and Plains warriors alike greeted him with smiles. "Keir of the Cat, WarKing of the Plains," one crowed as he sloshed fermented mare's milk from his cup.

Joden smiled, and continued on to the high seat at the end of the hall, by the huge fireplace. Keir had replaced the traditional high table with the low platform. He sat at the center, with Lara on his right and Simus on his left. Marcus was serving kavage, a rare smile on his face. For a heartbeat, Joden looked for Amyu.

She was not there, and would never be.

"You," Lara called out, her expression a mix of joy and anger. "Joden, how could you let him take such a risk?" She and Anna were sitting side by side, the babes in their arms. Xykeirson and Xykayla were waving their arms, and staring at the commotion around them, fascinated.

Joden smiled as he walked forward, opening his hands wide to offer his apology. "The skies favor the bold," he sang.

"And the earth covers the stupid," Lara and Marcus said together.

All the warriors nearby laughed.

"We already tried that," Simus said. "It didn't work."

"Join us," Keir said gesturing to the platform. "We are another step closer to our goal."

Marcus stepped down off the platform, bearing a mug and

a pitcher of kavage. He offered the mug to Joden, and started to pour.

Liam appeared behind him, coming in from Marcus's blind side.

Joden didn't have time to react. Liam tossed his cloak over Marcus and struck his jaw, knocking him out.

The pitcher fell to the floor, shattering.

Marcus started to collapse, but Liam scooped him up and flung him over his shoulder. He stood for a moment, then patted Marcus's buttocks.

"WarKing. Warprize." Liam gave them both a nod. "I have supported you, and now I claim my prize." He turned on his heel and strode from the hall before any could say a word.

In the stunned silence, Anna turned to Lara with a frown. "That's not really about military tactics, is it?"

* * * * *

Later, when the fires had burned down and the celebration had ended, Joden turned to Keir and sang to him softly, "Will you stay here? On the border? Or return to Xy?"

Keir shrugged. "We have not discussed it. There is much to be done to prepare for the Fall Council." He glanced at the stairs where Lara, Anna and the babes had disappeared earlier. "Lara will want to attend the Council, but the dangers…" he shook his head.

Joden nodded. "I must go," he lied. "Eldest Elder Essa requires that I give a full account of what happened to me." Joden kept his tone dry, "It will take days. I may have to repeat my words more than once."

Keir chuckled, then grew serious. "But you will be at the Fall Council? You will seek us out?"

"As soon as my business is finished," Joden sang. "I will seek you out."

* * * * *

The next morning, Joden rode down the switchback trail, leading a re-mount piled high with packs and a tent. Keir had provisioned him well, he wouldn't need to delay his journey with foraging.

There was no sign of Veritt's and Ietha's armies. They had wasted no time leaving, as they had said they would.

He paused on the edge of the milling warriors. Simus's warriors were making plans to travel up the longer, sloping road to the keep and busy with their own tasks.

He sat for a moment, looking out over the wide expanse of the grasslands.

Part of him knew what awaited him beyond. Hail Storm needed to be confronted and stopped and not by an army. Joden knew his task, but there was no certainty that he could defeat the warrior-priest. Or whatever Hail Storm had become. He was willing to take on this task, willing to face his own death, for the Plains and his people of both lands.

His regret was Amyu. Not to see her again, not to tell her of his need, his want, his love of her. The ache was deep and wide and almost more than he could bear.

"I hope you fly, beloved," he whispered to the winds.

If the winds heard, they gave no sign.

The warriors called out greetings, and Joden raised his hand in acknowledgment. Wanting no questions, he headed his horse to the east, in the direction Essa had taken, until he was out of their sight.

Finally alone, with only the grass and the skies for company, he looked south.

Wild Winds sat astride a horse, waiting on a far rise. He turned his mount and headed toward the Heart.

Joden followed.

CHAPTER THIRTY-EIGHT

Marcus awoke in an instant.

His training kept him still and silent, with no change to his breathing. His eyes closed, his other senses provided the information he sought.

He was bound, spread-eagle, but not painfully so. There was a pallet under him, the scent of crushed grass in the air. His jaw throbbed with his pulse.

No sounds of warriors, or horses, no smell of a fire.

He was still armored, not stripped. No sense of the sun, but there was light on his eyelids, so—

"I know you are awake," came a dear, longed-for voice.

His eyes snapped open, taking in the tent above him, the sides all rolled up. The sun was waning but not yet set, and beside him, beside him—

Liam of the Deer sat crossed legged by Marcus's feet, two daggers in the grass next to him.

"Marcus," Liam's voice and face were stone-cold, but so precious. Marcus looked his fill for a long, sweet moment. Still so handsome, but with new crinkles in the corner of his eyes, and some grey in that long flowing hair. His chest still just as gorgeous, his belly still as taut. A hunger flooded through Marcus, but then steel entered his soul.

Marcus narrowed his eyes and growled, "I told you that if you—"

"Yes," Liam sighed. "You would take yourself off to the snows. And I will follow behind."

"What?" Marcus tried his bonds, but the leather straps held his wrists tight. "What do you mean?"

Marcus's eye widened, taking in the fact that Liam was dressed only in thin white trous.

He glanced around, seeing only grass in every direction.

"Do you remember," Liam asked. "When you were injured? Burned so horribly that none thought you would live? Keir of the Cat saved you then, his caring and your sheer stubbornness."

Liam's eye drilled into his, the bond weaving glittering in his ear. Marcus could not look away from the pain in those eyes.

"Keir brought you back to me," Liam continued. "I had understood, when you said you would serve him, I had understood when we separated so that you might serve. One last campaign, you said." Liam drew a deep breath. "Keir brought you to me, and I welcomed you in, and you rejected me. Rejected our bond."

"To protect you," Marcus whispered.

"I did not seek protection when we bonded," Liam said. "I sought forever. I thought we'd found it."

Marcus looked away. "You had honor and status within the People, and were overdue to take your place on the Council. I did not know if I would survive, and I could not let you throw it away. The fire burned my ear away, and with it, our bond."

"You never gave me a choice," Liam snapped. "Never asked. Never listened to one who deserved your first thoughts."

Marcus snarled, tugging at the bonds. "You wouldn't have listened."

"You never gave me the chance," Liam snarled right back. "So I stayed as a Warlord, offered support to Keir, hungered after any mention of you, even—" Liam snorted. "Even courted the Warprize so that I could learn more."

Marcus turned his head. Strong fingers brought his head back around as Liam leaned in.

"So I have claimed my prize," Liam whispered. "You, beloved."

Marcus jerked his chin up, away from Liam's touch. "No," he said. "I told you—"

"I know," Liam's voice was in his ear.

Marcus turned his head back, and Liam was there, ready. His lips were dry and soft and the kiss was agony. Marcus closed his eyes and returned it eagerly, like a man drinking from a dry well. Tears streamed down his cheek, and whether they were his or Liam's didn't matter so much as the love that—

Liam broke the kiss and cut his bonds.

Marcus blinked at the loss of Liam's mouth and the sudden freedom of his hands. Liam placed a dagger at Marcus's side, and then rose to move to his feet, sitting with his back to Marcus.

Marcus stared at his love, outlined by the setting sun.

"If you choose the snows," Liam's voice shook. "I will follow. I will not look on you again. The smell of your blood will tell me your choice."

Marcus sat up, took up the dagger. It felt cold in his hand, the blade sharp. He leaned down, and cut his feet free. "I could leave," he growled. "Return to the Warlord and the Warprize."

"Yes," Liam nodded, not turning his head. "So be it."

Marcus stood, hesitating. "What will you do?"

"I will go to the snows," Liam said.

"No," Marcus growled. "You are needed. Hisself needs you to—"

"No," Liam said. "If our bonding ended in fire, if you are no longer who you were, I should have done it long ago." Liam's back was straight and rigid. "At least I had hope before. If you leave, I have none."

"You stubborn, stupid man," Marcus shouted, his hands shaking. "I should kill you now."

"You already did that," Liam said. "When you rejected me."

Pain crashed down on Marcus, the regret, the guilt, everything that he had denied for so very long. He took a step, and then another, and then stopped. "I could not bear that," he gulped out, closing his one eye against the tears. "I defied the elements to stay alive. I cannot defy you."

There was movement then. He didn't dare look. But he could feel the warmth of Liam's body as he stood next to him. Marcus took a breath of his scent as warm fingers took the dagger from his hand.

"Flame of my heart," Liam whispered. "Look at me."

Marcus looked up, blinked against his tears. Liam was looking down, ever so much taller than he, with eyes filled with love.

Marcus reached up then, desperate for the reassurance that he did not deserve.

Liam leaned down, and kissed him, wrapping his arms around him, each losing himself in the other.

Marcus wept, with ugly sobs, wept out the pain of the years, and the desperate feeling of loss. He didn't deserve this, wasn't worthy of this warrior's love. But Liam would not let him go, kept tight hold as he drew them both back down to the pallet, and held Marcus as they both released the anguish within.

It seemed hours later, as the sun was setting, that they both lay naked in each other's arms. Marcus spoke as the sun reached the horizon and started to slip away. "The Warprize, Lara, she once told me that love never dies."

"Wise woman, that city-dweller," Liam said. "For a female." His hand drifted under the blanket, and Marcus caught his breath. "I prefer other prey," Liam nuzzled the spot where Marcus's ear should have been.

Marcus shivered.

"Shall we?" Liam asked.

"Yes," Marcus whispered. He reached for his beloved. "Yes."

* * * * *

Amyu's challenges made the days fly as fast as airions on the wing.

And that was *fast*.

"I wonder," Lightning Storm mused over their nooning. "If there is a way to shield our eyes with power."

Today's meal was a thick soup of pig and plants with dark bread. Xyian food tended to be bland, so they'd all added some of the red spice to the meal. Sidian was devouring his bowl. Rhys had decided to try it, and was cautiously dipping bits of bread in the broth. He seemed to like it, but his eyes were watering.

"But the bugs would hit it, right?" Rhys gasped a bit as he talked, and took large droughts of water. "So that's a problem."

Amyu smiled. Rhys had absolutely refused to mount an airion, but he was willing to aid them as best he could.

"Amyu, what do you think?" Lightning Strike asked.

Here was one of her challenges. Everyone kept asking her questions she didn't have answers to, expecting her to guide them. Amyu tried, but she lived in fear that someday they would discover she knew no more than they did. But they turned to her for leadership, and so she did her best. "Thinking about the shield would be distracting," she thought out loud. "And the wind isn't that bad. But worth a try."

The others nodded and started right then and there to fashion shields before their eyes.

One of the warriors that Heath had assigned to aid them slunk closer, offering more bread and kavage. Amyu took more, making sure to thank him with a smile.

There was another challenge. Weaving a pattern between Xyian and the warrior-priests. Or whatever they were now; even Lightning Storm wasn't sure. Two cultures trying to deal with strange creatures had brought some headaches. Some of the Xyians were none too pleased that they could not ride an airion easily.

Amyu sighed inside. That was really her final challenge. Flying itself. It was dangerous, and wonderful to ride an airion into the clouds. But it wasn't easy. She glanced over to where her Golden was sleeping. No not easy. But she'd never give up.

The days flashed by. But her nights... Amyu looked toward the south. At night, her thoughts were all for Joden.

Lightning Strike had put down his bowl of soup, and was trying to fashion a cover for his eyes that didn't glow with power. Amyu joined in the laughter, but then noticed that his bowl was vibrating.

"Lightning Strike?" she pointed. "How much spice did you add to your bowl?"

"Eh?" Lightning Strike looked down and gasped. "Snowfall?"

The soup spilled over, and an image of Snowfall rose from the bowl, wavering, with bits of meat suspended in the fluid.

"Aid me," Lightning Strike yelped, and two others of the warrior-priests moved to his side. Amyu could see the power flowing and watched as the image grew steadier.

"Lightning Strike," Snowfall said. She seemed to peer around. "Is Joden of the Hawk with you?"

Amyu jumped to her feet. "Joden?"

The image of the woman turned to face her. "Amyu?" she asked.

"Yes," Amyu took a step closer. "What is wrong?" she asked, dread filling her chest.

Snowfall frowned. "Joden of the Hawk left us after Keir killed Antas. He told Keir he would be with Essa. Essa has sent a messenger asking where Joden is, for he has not arrived in the Singer's camp. We'd hoped he was with you."

Fear flooded through Amyu. He'd been gone long enough—

"Scry the Heart," she commanded. "Now."

Warrior-priests scattered to obey,

"You think—" Snowfall's eyes were wide. "You think he went to the Heart? Alone?"

"I fear—" Amyu cut herself off, and stepped over to Night Cloud's side. He had an image, bright in the bowl. Amyu leaned in and her heart stopped. "Joden," she breathed.

"Tell me what you see," Snowfall demanded.

"Joden is riding toward the Heart," Amu shifted as others crowded around. "There is a man, dressed only in trous. He is surrounded by…" she trailed off, unsure what she was seeing.

"Odium," Rhys breathed. Sidian sucked in a breath as Rhys continued, "Those are the undead he has brought back and controls."

"Undead warrior-priests," Lightning Strike said grimly. "See? They are shorn of their tattoos."

"Skies above," Amyu swore. "That man is an idiot."

"We cannot reach him," Snowfall said. "The distance is too far. He goes to his death."

"No, he doesn't," Amyu strapped on her weapons belt. "Night Clouds, pull the image back. Rhys, open a portal."

"Portal?" Snowfall demanded.

"We will all go," Lightning Strike stood.

"No," Amyu turned grim. "We cannot risk all of us. I will go, get him out of there, and we will flee. We cannot leave Xy undefended."

Lightning Strike stopped, the conflict clear on his face. But he gave her a nod. "I will get you extra lances," he said and ran off.

"Keir agrees," Snowfall said. "But how will you—"

Amyu whistled.

Golden lifted his head, and rose up, stretching his wings in the sun.

Snowfall gasped. Other heads were trying to peer from behind her, and voices were raised.

"Lightning Strike will explain," Amyu said over her shoulder s she grabbed up her saddle. "I need to go."

"Will Golden fly through a portal?" Rhys asked.

"We'll find out." Amyu called as she raced to her airion. Heart pounding, she threw on the saddle and forced herself to slow her shaking hands.

"I'm coming, beloved," she whispered. "And if it's to both our deaths, at least I will be at your side."

CHAPTER THIRTY-NINE

Wild Winds never approached Joden as they traveled toward the Heart.

Each night Joden would make camp, and each night Wild Winds stood guard at distance on the southernmost rise. Leaving Joden to his thoughts.

Which left Joden to his thoughts. To his grief, over the loss of his voice. Those thoughts were confusing, for he had a voice, but it wasn't what it had been. Still, he had it, but it wasn't perfect, wasn't what it was.

It left him to thoughts of what was happening to him, or what had happened. Seeing the dead, the visions… Xyson and Uppor had both implied that he could learn control. So far Joden hadn't figured out how to do it, but there was an itch of curiosity deep within. What could he do? What could he learn? What could he *see*, if he was in fact a Seer?

But worse than the loss, worse than the itch, was his pain at leaving Amyu. She was right; if he would be a Singer with any honor she could not stand at his side. And yet, she was there, in his thoughts and dreams and sweet memories.

But in the nights, in the flames of his fire, he could see her lovely face and hear her laugh.

When he woke in the mornings to face the day, he wanted to gallop his horse past the ghostly figure and get this over with as quickly as possible.

Yet… the days and nights of steady travel, over the wide expanse of the Plains steadied Joden. The sun rose and set, the winds blew, and late at night the stars glittered in the sky.

Until finally, as they drew close to the Heart, Wild Winds stopped, looked back, and gestured Joden forward.

Joden rode up the rise and stopped his horse next to him. They were looking down at the Heart and the lake beyond.

"Learn, Seer," Wild Winds's voice echoed. "The path between life and death is forbidden," his eyes were bright. "Except to you. Walk it at your peril."

"W-w-w—" Joden started, wanting to ask all of his questions. But before he could get the words out, Wild Winds faded and was gone.

Helpful, Joden thought wryly. He took a deep breath, then studied the scene below him.

The lakeshore beyond the Heart was covered with wyverns, feeding their young. There were none in the air, thank all the elements. Two of the adults had their heads up, staring at the Heart, as if keeping watch. But they did not take flight. Elements keep it that way.

The Heart was still there, the dead body of a wyvern draped over it as Simus and Snowfall had described. The flesh was torn and rotted. White bone shone through places where the leather skin had burst. The wind was from the north for now, and Joden was grateful for that.

The mounds of the burial pits were obvious, not yet flat to the land. The grass there was green where Simus and his warriors had placed the sod. At first glance, all appeared as it had been left.

Except for the dead.

The hairs on the back of Joden's neck rose as the ghostly spirits of the dead warrior-priests turned and stared at him with a burning rage he could feel on his skin. Yet the anger was not for him.

"Joden," Hail Storm emerged from behind the dead wyvern to stand on the edge of the circular stone. He wore the trous of the warrior-priests, but his tattoos were gone, stripped from his body. One arm was but a stump, but with the other Hail Storm gestured. "Come and join me," he called, his voice echoing over the distance.

Joden urged his horse into a walk.

The dead spirits didn't move, but they turned as Joden passed. Joden could see their skin shorn of tattoos, their faces grim. Could Hail Storm not see this?

He rode closer, until his horse stopped, trembling, and refused to move any closer.

Hail Storm chuckled as he walked forward, stepping down from the Heart. "I am afraid you will have to walk," he said, stopping between two of the burial mounds.

Joden did. He had his sword and daggers, and he drew a lance before he set the horse free. He did not close the gap between them, but stood, waiting.

Hail Storm seemed amused. "I expected Snowfall," he said casually. "Or Simus's warriors, perhaps. Not you."

"I have walked the old paths," Joden said. "I have walked the snows. The dead rage against you, Hail Storm."

"Interesting," Hail Storm said. "But how will you stop me, Joden of the Hawk? Without powers of your own? How will you stop these?" He gestured toward the mound. "Come forth," he called.

The earth moved, bulged. The sod parted on old seams, and the dead bodies of warrior-priests rose from within, climbing out of the pits. There was rot and the stench reached Joden, making him cough and retch.

"You get used to it," Hail Storm laughed.

The dead bodies crawl out, rose and walked forward at Hail Storm's command. The spirits around Joden cried out in anguish and anger. But the rotten bodies moved forward, reaching for Joden.

Joden hefted his lance to throw.

Hail Storm laughed again, reached out as if catching a bug in his fist.

Joden froze, unable to move.

Hail Storm walked closer as the dead bodies surrounded them. He gently took the lance from Joden's hands, and unbuckled his sword belt, letting it drop to the ground. Joden strained, but could not move.

"Your Ancients gave me so much more power," he said quietly. "And the dead here? It's almost overwhelming."

Joden glared.

"I wonder what power I will drain from you?" Hail Storm reached out and stroked Joden's neck. His finger left an ice-cold trail and Joden shivered.

"Come," Hail Storm said. "Walk with me to the Heart."

Joden struggled, but his feet moved. He staggered behind Hail Storm.

The dead bodies followed, making no sound but the shuffle of feet through grass.

But the spirit dead followed as well, and the wind began to rise.

The wyverns were stirring, heads lifting, wings partially spread. They hissed and snapped, their long necks weaving back and forth like snakes.

"They will not approach," Hail Storm chuckled. "They fear me, fear my power over them. Come."

Joden fought for control of his body as they walked closer to the Heart. He'd weapons at hand, but couldn't raise an arm to wield them. Frustrated, he fought despair and his bonds.

"I will clear the Heart," Hail Storm didn't even look back, or pay any attention to Joden's useless struggles. "It will take my servants a while but there is time. All must appear well before the Fall Council. The Warlords, the Elders, they will approach thinking the only threat is the wyverns. Think of the power I will gain from their deaths."

"Wr-wr-wrong," Joden forced out the word.

Hail Storm looked at him in shock. "Was that the sacrifice required of you?" he asked, and Joden felt the bonds on him ease slightly.

"Yes," he finally had the breath to sing. "Wrong to use death this way."

"Were you told of the cost?" Hail Storm tilted his head, seeming almost as if he truly cared. "Isn't it wrong to ask that price of someone who wishes to be a Singer?"

Joden froze at the memory.

Uppor looked at him with knowing eyes. "Why?"

"Because I want the truth," Joden snapped. "Because truths have been withheld, hidden from all. I want to know what was, and how this came to be. And how we change without changing." The realization hit him like a blow to the heart. He hadn't asked to be a Singer. He'd asked for so much more.

"In truth, it does not matter," Hail Storm's voice brought Joden back.

The undead bodies shuffled to a stop all around them. Hail Storm frowned, and then seemed to concentrate on them to get them moving. He turned back to Joden and shrugged. "Life and death are one. I rather think it depends on how you use the power." He smiled again. "And I intend to use it, Joden." He gestured to the edge of the stone platform. "Here, I think. Come forward just a little."

Joden was forced forward, kneeling at the edge of the Heart. The dead wyvern was not far, its eyes gone from their sockets.

Beyond the wyverns were rising on their haunches, hissing and flapping their wings, but keeping back.

The dead spirits continued moaning around them, furious, their hands outstretched begging Joden for aid, for—

Hail Storm pulled a bone-handled knife from his belt, its edge glittering in the sun. He placed the cold, sharp edge against Joden's neck. "I doubt your sacrifice was worth the pain it brought you," Hail Storm said.

Joden looked past him, to the ghosts, who were asking for... asking for permission.

"I traveled to the snows," Joden chanted, crying out the words. "I walked the old path. Take the path, through me."

The spirits howled their delight, and fled to their bodies.

Hail Storm shook his head. "This is almost a mercy on my part." He leaned in and pressed—

A dead hand took his wrist, and yanked it away from Joden. A female warrior-priestess stood there, her rotting jaw in a grimace of joy. "Vengeance," was the sound that issued through rotting flesh.

"What?" Hail Storm staggered back, onto the Heart itself. "Mist?" he cried out in recognition, then tried to fend her off with his dagger.

Joden collapsed, free of restraint but drained of strength as the dead used him in a way he didn't understand. Like an open door, the snows blew through him and out of him and the dead spirits within their bodies shrieked and turned toward Hail Storm, arms reaching with sharp rotting fingers.

"No, no," Hail Storm snarled, scrambling back. He glared at Joden as Joden raised his head. "They come through you," he spat. Hail Storm raised his stump high. "Aid me," he cried out.

With strong sweeps of its wings, a wyvern rose in the air. It hissed as it leaped forward to Hail Storm's side, its stinger dripping foul poison. It swept its head in front of Hail Storm, knocking aside the dead that threatened him.

"Now," Hail Storm crowed. "Now I will have you."

Joden found himself locked in again, unable to move. Hail Storm approached, his dagger out, his eyes gleaming in anticipation.

A hawk cried above them, clear and loud.

"What now?" Hail Storm demanded, turning, shielding his eyes from the sun.

Joden managed to look up, blinking against the glare.

To see Amyu, on an airion, plunging down from out of the sun.

"A-a-Amyu?" Joden gaped at the sight, certain he was dreaming.

The airion struck the wyvern, sharp claws digging into its back. Amyu had a shield in one hand and reins in the other. She sat boldly in the saddle, as calm as she could be, a warrior in every sense of the word. Strong, confident, with a look of grim determination.

Joden's heart swelled, even as it beat faster in fear for her.

The wyvern heaved, no longer guarding Hail Storm as it lashed out at the weight on its back. The tail arched in, but Amyu blocked it with her shield. It hit with a resounding clang.

The wyverns around the lake stirred, taking notice.

The wyvern whipped its head back, but the airion clung on. After a moment of struggle Amyu barked a command.

The airion sank its beak into the wyvern's spine and snapped it in half.

The wyvern collapsed.

"No," Hail Storm roared, but it was too late. The dead warrior-priests were on him, reaching, grasping, pulling. He screamed once, a high-pitched wail of terror.

Joden staggered back, and watched in horror as they tore Hail Storm to pieces. In their midst, the one Hail Storm had called Mist stood triumphant, the stone-handled dagger raised in her fist.

Joden was conscious of Amyu landing close by, and dismounting. But it was the dead that had his attention, the dead souls in dead bodies, who turned to him now.

"My thanks," he said.

"Our thanks, Seer," came a great whisper and a wave of gratitude.

"Return now," he commanded. "The snows await, and beyond, the stars."

There was a sigh, first of reluctance and then acceptance. The bodies staggered back to the pits, and began to crawl within.

"Joden," Amyu was tugging his arm.

The last Joden saw was Mist and the dagger disappearing into the dark earth, and the sod replacing itself.

"Joden, come back to me," Amyu's voice sounded desperate, and there was another sound of a beak clattering. She was kneeling beside him, the scent of her hair surrounding him as he looked into her worried eyes.

"Beloved," his heart leaped as he reached up and took her help to stand. "B-b-beloved—"

"No time," Amyu jerked her chin toward the lake.

Wyverns hopped toward them from the lake, their wings half out with young ones underfoot, their long necks weaving back and forth, staring.

"Stay low," Amyu hissed as she pulled him away. "Golden, come." Her airion clacked its beak, casting threatening looks back, but it obeyed, following them on foot.

"You found them," Joden chanted, his voice filled with awe.

"Focus," Amyu warned, but she flashed him a smile, her eyes filled with joy.

The wyverns stopped at the dead beast, flapping their wings to perch on top. After long suspicious looks, they started to feed, tearing out hunks of rotten meat. But two of the adults were still focused on them, eyes bright.

"Don't run," Amyu panted. She had one hand buried in the airion's mane, urging him on.

"My horse," Joden sang, pointing ahead. His horse was

calmly grazing where he had left it. But next to it was a glowing circle of white. "What is—?"

"Friends," Amyu said. "Go, go."

* * * * *

They emerged to a crowd of over-joyed warriors, welcomed with shouts and back-pounding hugs for Amyu.

"Y-y-you w-w-watched?" Joden asked, too astonished to sing.

There was laughter at that, and explanations that tumbled from so many mouths that he just shook his head in astonishment.

Amyu watched him, and just when it seemed that the people, noise and news threatened to overwhelm him she stepped in. "Enough," she said. "Send word to Heath, and Snowfall, and tell them Joden is safe. If the Warlord calls senel tomorrow, Joden can tell his tale once, for all to hear. And hear ours in return." She tilted her head at Joden. "For this night, he is mine."

That met with agreement, and smiles, and a few knowing looks. Joden was willing to endure it all, when Amyu turned to him. "Come. Let's fly."

* * * * *

Golden flew them both up to the tunnel cave, winging back to land on the ledge.

"T-t-that was scarier than Hail Storm," Joden released his death grip on Amyu's waist and dismounted.

"I held you safe." Amyu released their packs from the harness, and slid from the saddle.

"Isn't he beautiful," Amyu asked as she scratched Golden under his jaw. The airion clacked in appreciation.

"N-n-not a-a-as b-b-beautiful." Amyu flushed and waited as he finished. "A-a-as y-y-you."

Amyu dropped their packs, stepped over, and pulled him

into a kiss. Joden returned it with enthusiasm, using his lips and hands to express everything his voice couldn't.

They parted, breathless, still clinging to one another.

Amyu stared up at him. "I have so much to tell you, so much I want to talk with you about. I will steal this night, and any other nights I can before you must go. It might not be right, it might risk you becoming a Singer, but—"

Joden put his fingers over her mouth and shushed her, shaking his head.

"Don't be stupid," Amyu said. "The Plains need your truths, and as a Singer."

Joden shook his head again, and took a breath. "I cannot live this lie, for there is no honor in denying what is. I love you," his voice trembled in the melody. He reached out and took her face in his hands. "That is the highest truth of all, Amyu of the Skies. I would ask you to bond with me in the traditions of the Plains, yes, even when our traditions dictate that you should go to the snows."

Amyu was crying. She turned her face into his palm, and kissed it.

"I will stand by your side, for to do any less is to deny the truth of my heart. And if I deny this about myself, how can I stand before our people and speak any truth that will be believed?"

Joden shook his head.

"Joden, beloved," Amyu flung herself into his arms, and Joden found joy in their lips coming together with heartfelt promises.

Until a noise at the cave entrance caught their attention. Golden had one of the leather straps of the packs in his beak, chewing it.

"Golden," Amyu scolded, stepping back and wiping her tears.

The airion froze, looking as guilty as an airion could.

"T-t-they u-u-understand?" Joden asked.

"Some words," Amyu said. "We are still learning, aren't we?"

She untangled the pack from beak and claw. Then she started to unbuckled the saddle.

Golden mantled his wings, clacking his beak.

"Hunt," Amyu said, getting a tight grip on the saddle. The airion slipped out from under it, and took off, wings flaring as it disappeared from view. She put the saddle upside down, and then brushed her hands off. "There is still so much to learn," she said. "About the airions, about the powers—"

"About each other," Joden sang.

Amyu gave him a smoldering look as she tossed his pack at him. "Just you set up our bedrolls," she commanded. "And we will start on that."

Joden grinned and hastened to obey.

Later, as their fire died, with the blankets thrown back to cool their hot, sweaty bodies, Joden turned to whisper in Amyu's ear. He sang the words he wanted her to hear. "So I say this truth to you, Amyu of the—

Amyu reached out, and placed her fingers on his lips. "No," she whispered. "Too soon," she curled in closer to him and smiled. There was no rejection in her eyes. "It's too soon, Joden. Ask me again, when we have lived with the changes in our lives for a time. Ask me again, after the Fall Council."

Joden pulled Amyu in close, and nodded.

"In the meantime," she continued, her voice rough with the need for sleep. "Let's talk about the stupidity of going to the Heart alone. What were you think—"

Joden stopped her mouth with a kiss, and then another, and another, until they found a different way to distract each other.

CHAPTER FORTY

When the grasses of the Plains began to dry, the wyverns rose with their young and scattered in every direction, returning to their territories. With warnings and watchful eyes, the Xyians were ready. Amyu, Lightning Strike, and the others rose on their airions to meet them.

Wyverns quickly learned a lesson in blood.

When the grasses of the Plains turned red as fire, Keir and Lara once again organized a march to the border. But this time, the wagons brimmed with food, and clothing and bedding and leather and all sorts and sundry that the thea camps would need to carry them until Spring.

The Xyian forces bolstered those at the border, commanded by Liam of the Deer, with Marcus at his side.

Anna insisted, and Lara agreed, that this time the babes would remain at the City of Water's Fall. Part of Lara's agreement was the wonderful portal magic of Rhys of Palins. But all agreed that this secret was one to be kept for now.

Simus was the first to arrive outside the Heart, to claim the place for his tent and Keir's and crow with delight when the Heart was cleared and the new Council Tent was raised over it.

Once again, the Heart beat with the life of the Plains, for every warrior, every thea, every Elder and Warlord came to witness this Council. Osa and Ultie were the last Warlords to arrive.

Gilla took one look at Osa of the Fox, and her mouth dropped open. "She's beautiful," Gilla whispered.

Cadr looked at her with concern. "Gilla, she's a Warlord,"

he hissed.

"She's going to be my bonded," Gilla insisted. Cadr just rolled his eyes.

Eldest Elder Singer Essa called the Fall Council unto session wearing his regular silks. The debates began the moment the last prayer to the elements was uttered.

The first matter was simple enough. Four Eldest Elders were required to conduct a Council, and so four Eldest Elders there must be. Reness was there, Eldest Elder of the Theas, proud and strong and ready with her opinions. Her bonded, Hanstau, was at her side when he was not teaching his healing skills and learning new ones.

For Eldest Elder Warrior, Niles of the Boar bowed to the will of the other warriors, and claimed the title. He had held the place after Antas's betrayal.

But the debates grew hot over the Eldest Elder Warrior-priest, for both Snowfall and Lightning Strike swore that they were no longer warrior-priests.

All the wielders of power were brought into the tent, and questioned. Lightning Strike refused to give in to their demands for the old titles. "We will stand as witnesses to ourselves, carving out new truths. Some may choose to ride the airions of Xy. Some may choose to return to the Plains," he said defiantly. "But in no way do we wish to return to the false truths of the past."

Just when Joden was certain that Essa's head would burst, Amyu rose from her seat behind Lightning Strike and Snowfall. "Let us be known as warrior-magi, then," she said. "And let the new title reflect a new truth."

There were head nods all around, which pleased Lightning Strike until he realized that he had been chosen to be the Eldest Elder. Snowfall insisted. "I have made other vows," she said, glancing at Simus.

Simus puffed up with pride.

Essa was offended that the words of a child had been considered in Council, but he had already been offended when Joden refused to become a Singer.

Quartis had held out the wyvern horn, now hollowed and polished. Joden shook his head, and refused the gift and the title.

"What are you then?" Essa snapped in the privacy of his tent. "Bad enough the Ancients are slain, and their songs lost. Now you refuse—?"

"M-m-my t-t-truth is my own," Joden shrugged and left without saying more. No amount of argument would change Essa's mind, and Joden wouldn't waste the breath.

He'd returned to their tent to find Amyu talking to Reness.

"I would offer her the Rite of Ascension," Reness said, "You have more than earned the right, Amyu. The other Elders support me in this."

"No," Amyu smiled to soften her rejection of the offer. "Although I thank you for your offer. But," she stood taller now, confidence in every inch of her body. "There is no need. I have proved myself to all, and—" her smile grew brighter. "More importantly, I have proved it to myself."

* * * * *

At last, the full Council convened, with the Four Eldest Elders in place. The sides of the tent were rolled high, to allow more to see, and the Singers were spread out to echo the words so that all may hear.

Keir stood before them. "The ways of the Plains have not changed in living memory," he said, standing tall and confident before them in gleaming black leathers and chain armor.

"Our old ways have kept us flourishing for that time. But now they fail us."

Keir went on, talking of the diminished rewards from raids, of the deaths of babes in the thea camps, of the pain of the life-bearers required to provide future warriors. "We can no longer continue, and expect to thrive," Keir said. "I stand here before you with a vision of the future that calls for the Tribes to unite under a WarKing. A WarKing to weave two peoples to the benefit of both. You have seen the wagons that I have brought from Xy. With things the thea camps need, and I offer it to all. My Warprize brings knowledge of healing, to aid all." Keir took a breath. "True healing, not the false promises of the warrior-priests who now wander the snows at their own hands.

"We bring a new strength to the Xyians, a will to fight that they had lost, a need to grow and expand. New blood to blend with their wisdom. New trade routes that we will find, and guard with our strong blades. New ways of considering truths." Keir paused, and glanced at Lara. "Weaving new patterns into both lands."

"And if we don't name you WarKing?" Ietha stood, her arms over her chest, her face tight.

"I will return to Xy, with Lara," Keir said simply. "I will see to it that Simus, as Warlord of the North, has the supplies he needs to support his army and thea camps." Keir lifted his chin. "And I will come again, next season, and the next and the next, as you diminish and we thrive."

Joden kept a straight face but exchanged a sideways glance with Simus. Truth, yes, but a harsh truth. Perhaps too harsh.

"Enough," Essa rose from his seat. "Let us exchange truths before we decide."

Debate they did, long and hard. Essa held them until the stars appeared, and recalled them to Council before the stars disappeared. "The snows come," he said to any that complained. "And we must make a decision."

Until, finally, the voices grew quiet and thoughtful, and all had a chance to express their truths. "Are there any others who wish to be heard?" Essa asked. When there was no response, he continued. "We will vote. Many have been permitted to speak in this session, but only Elders and Eldest Elders hold the right of decision. "Elders," Essa demanded, his voice loud and clear for all to hear. "How say you?"

* * * * *

Joden took his position behind the Warlord and Warprize. Simus stood next to him, as serious as he had ever seen the man.

Keir held out his hand to Lara, who stood beside him. "You started this, flame of my heart."

Lara took his hand, her smile bright. "But it took all of our lives and loves to bring us to this point, beloved. And this isn't the end, you know. It's just the beginning."

"Wind Winds told us that, once," Simus said. "That every ending is a beginning. And every beginning was an ending in itself."

Horns blew from the Heart.

Joden faced forward with them, to see the four Eldest Elders ranged on the Heart, waiting. A path lay before them, with warriors crowding around the Heart, waiting. Joden had never seen so many warriors in one place before, and he suspected he never would again.

"Stand forth, Keir of the Cat." Essa called, his words echoed by the Singers for all to hear.

Keir started walking, Lara at his side.

Joden and Simus followed, two steps behind.

As they passed, the warriors knelt. It was like a wave before them, as all the warriors, every warrior knelt. Joden's heart began to beat faster.

He and Simus stopped at the stone's edge, but Keir and Lara continued on.

"Keir of the Cat," the Eldest Elder Singer called again. "Kneel, and offer your sword."

Keir pulled one of his swords and knelt, offering his blade between his two hands.

Essa spoke loudly, his voice carrying over the crowd. "Keir of the Cat, Warrior of the Plains. You come before us as a candidate for WarKing. Do you wish to serve the Plains?"

"I do," Keir's voice was strong and clear.

"Keir of the Cat, we of the Council entrust you with the lives of the all of the People of the Plains. From the youngest babe to the oldest of the Elders. Will you take responsibility for these lives and hold them dear?"

"I will," Keir vowed. "I will be their WarKing in all things. Their flesh is my flesh, their blood is my blood."

"Keir of the Cat, the Council of the Elders names you WarKing," Essa drew a deep breath, and placed the tips of his fingers on Keir's blade. "May the very air of this land grant you breath."

Lightning Strike moved closer and placed his fingers on the blade. "Keir of the Cat, the Council of the Elders names you WarKing. May the very earth of this land support your feet."

Reness placed her fingers on his blade. "Keir of the Cat, the Council of the Elders names you WarKing. May the very fires of this land warm your skin."

Nires was next, and there was no hesitation in his actions or voice. He placed his fingers on the blade. "Keir of the Cat, the Council of Elders names you WarKing. May the very waters of this land quench your thirst."

"Rise, WarKing, and serve your people," Essa commanded.

Joden caught his breath as the warriors around him roared their approval. Drums, joined the chants of 'Heyla' and it seemed the very earth shook.

"The snows are upon us!" Essa declared. "The Council of Elders is closed, until the warmth and new grass appears. But for this night, let the celebration begin!"

This brought new shouts of approval, and the warriors surged forward to greet the WarKing, and begin the pattern dancing. No matter that he had no voice; he couldn't be heard in this crowd even if he had shouted to the winds.

A tug on his arm, and Joden looked to see Amyu standing next to him. Her brown eyes bright and confident, one of Golden's feathers woven into her hair. She tugged at his arm, and he lowered his ear to her lips.

"Joden of the Hawk, warrior of Xy, Seer and man that I love. I say this truth to you." Amyu was crying as she almost shouted the words in order to be heard. "I am sworn to you. Forever." She leaned in closer. "You can tell me your part later."

Joden roared his laughter and delight and swung her into his arms.

CHAPTER FORTY-ONE

The Tribes of the Plains were united under WarKing Keir of the Cat and his Warprize, Xylara, Queen of Xy. Xy grew and prospered under their reign, and the joint reign of their children, Xykeirson and Xykalya.

In time, as trade routes grew, the Plains and Xy became a great trading nation. Under the reign of Xyothur, son of Xykalya, a trading hub grew around the Heart of the Plains. As generations passed, a castle was built around the great circular stone, and the throne of the WarKing placed in its center.

In another few generations, a city grew around the castle. Schools of learning were established, of magic and healing.

In time, the Plains and Xy were merged in men's minds. Xy was a mighty kingdom, with trade routes on both land and sea. Farms and other towns grew on what had once been the Plains. The land was well ruled by the Sons and Daughter of the Blood. Peace and prosperity drew other kingdoms to pledge themselves to the Xyian Crown.

All hailed the Golden Age of Xy, and the stone beneath the throne rang with cheers of the people.

But in time the lessons of the past were forgotten.

The Sweat returned. All that had flourished was lost in a plague and death, war and chaos.

And with that ending, a new beginning. A new struggle.

For the restoration of the Blood of Xy.

ACKNOWLEDGMENTS

Many thanks to Amanda Modrowski and Nyssa Clark, both speech therapists, who put up with endless questions from their Auntie Bea. My pre-readers, Patricia Merritt, Kandace Klumper, Elizabeth Candler, Elizabeth Cogley, Denise Lynn and Stephanie Beebe, who put up with worried texts from a needy author. Special thanks to Anna Genoese, my editor and Sarah Chorn, my copy editor. All their time and efforts make me look like a star.

I would be remiss if I didn't mention my long suffering writer's group of Helen Kourous, Spencer Luster, and Marc Tassin, who each month give me the gift of their friendship and their truths about my first drafts.

To all my family and friends who fill my life with love, support and friendship. Many thanks and apologies for occasionally whipping out paper and pen and muttering to myself.

As usual, any and all mistakes found within are mine, and mine alone. My name is on the cover, and if I am claiming the glory, then I can own my mistakes!

ABOUT THE AUTHOR

Elizabeth Vaughan is the *USA Today* Bestselling author of *Warprize*, the first volume of The Chronicles of the Warlands. She's always loved fantasy and science fiction, and has been a fantasy role-player since 1981. By day, Beth's secret identity is that of a lawyer, practicing in the area of bankruptcy, a role she has maintained since 1985. More information can be found at her website, WriteandRepeat.com.

Beth is owned by incredibly spoiled cats, and lives in the Northwest Territory, on the outskirts of the Black Swamp, along Mad Anthony's Trail on the banks of the Maumee River.